HIS WAKE-UP CALL

BOOKS BY JAN THOMPSON

CITY/COASTAL/BEACH ROMANCE

Seaside Chapel (7 Books)

JanThompson.com/seaside

Savannah Sweethearts (12 Books)

JanThompson.com/savannah

Vacation Sweethearts (8 Books)

JanThompson.com/vacation

ROMANTIC SUSPENSE/THRILLERS

Protector Sweethearts (6 Books)

JanThompson.com/protector

Defender Sweethearts (6 Books)

JanThompson.com/defender

Binary Hackers (4 Books)

JanThompson.com/binary

JanThompson.com/books

HIS WAKE-UP CALL

SEASIDE CHAPEL
BOOK TWO

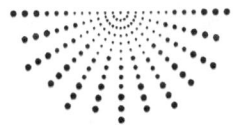

JAN THOMPSON

GEORGIA
PRESS

HIS WAKE-UP CALL (SEASIDE CHAPEL BOOK 2)

Published by Georgia Press LLC
Author Website: JanThompson.com
Book List: JanThompson.com/books
Book News: JanThompson.com/newsletter

Book Cover by Carpe Librum Book Design

Second Edition eBook ISBN: 978-1-944188-71-9
Second Edition Paperback ISBN: 978-1-944188-76-4

To my Lord and Savior, Jesus Christ, who died on the cross to save me from my sins and rose again from the grave to give me eternal life in heaven.

For God so loved the world that He gave His only begotten Son, that whoever believes in Him should not perish but have everlasting life.
—John 3:16

ABOUT THE SEASIDE CHAPEL SERIES

Welcome to *USA Today* bestselling author Jan Thompson's **Seaside Chapel** Christian beach romance series. These novels are set on real-life St. Simon's Island, Georgia—a beach town where history is all around and the future is a moment away—and the neighboring fictitious Seaside Island, where the rich and famous in Jan's story world live.

Savor the small-town atmosphere and the warm southern beaches of St. Simon's Island and the idyllic Golden Isles along the Atlantic Ocean. Enjoy the music of the orchestra and hymns of the church, and hang out with our Christian friends who attend Seaside Chapel, a little church by the sea known for its beach weddings and fair share of love and life.

As these Christians grow in their knowledge and understanding of God, they are tested in their spiritual maturity, their love lives, and their relationships with others. Share their heartaches and healing, and cheer them on as they celebrate faith, family, and friends.

JanThompson.com/seaside

- Book 1: His Longing Heart
- Book 2: His Wake-Up Call
- Book 3: His Morning Kiss
- Book 4: His Quiet Serenade
- Book 5: His Waiting Love
- Book 6: His Beach Retreat

While Seaside Chapel novels can be read as standalone stories, you can see a bigger picture of the Seaside Chapel community and get a glimpse of the futures of previous characters if you read Books 1-6 in order.

A FREE EBOOK FOR YOU!

A Christian beach romance novel, *Ask You Later* is the story of artist Leon Watts, who returns to Tybee Island and Savannah to jump-start his fledgling career. This novel is a part of the Savannah Sweethearts collection, and happens one year before the Seaside Chapel series begins.

Download this FREE novel now:
JanThompson.com/ask-seaside

YOU ARE READING HIS WAKE-UP CALL

SEASIDE CHAPEL BOOK 2

Single thirty-something Sebastian Langston hires his sister's best friend to be his fake girlfriend for the summer in order to win back his ex-fiancée whom he lost to a billionaire.

THE DESPERATE JILTED MAN...

Restaurateur Sebastian Langston cannot believe that his ex-fiancée, Talia, would leave him again. They've broken up so many times that he is sure she'll return to him...until he sees her with a billionaire. Now he has to fight to get her back. Sebastian cooks up an idea in which he hires a beautiful girl who can make Talia jealous. Poor starving harpist Emmeline O'Hanlon needs money and seems willing to help him reach his objectives.

THE DREAMY RENT-A-GIRLFRIEND...

When her best friend's older brother offers her an unusual proposition, Emmeline has no idea what she is getting into. However, her van is dead, her rent is due, and she is forced to take the job. The short-term business agreement would only last one summer, or so Emmeline thinks. More than money for graduate school, she needs Sebastian's funding to resume the search for her long-lost brother. Sebastian promises to enlist one of the top private investigators in the region to find Claude. In return, all she has to do is smile and make Talia jealous. How hard can it be?

THE DUET THAT CAN'T GO WRONG...

So begins this ill-advised scheme to drive Sebastian's ex-fiancée back to him. He thinks his plan-on-a-whim will succeed because it has to. He will turn thirty-four next September, and he wants to be a father by the following summer, preferably to the first of a passel of Talia's future children. As they keep up the ruse, Emmeline's ethereal harp starts to sound like a siren song that distracts Sebastian from his goals. Soon, he rows away from his lane and begins to forget his original purpose for hiring her...

His Wake-Up Call is the second novel in *USA Today* bestselling author Jan Thompson's Seaside Chapel

Christian small-town beach romance series. This book is the expanded second edition of the previously published *Step with Me.*

His Wake-Up Call (Seaside Chapel Book 2)
JanThompson.com/wakeup

Seaside Chapel
JanThompson.com/seaside

Sign up for Jan Thompson's mailing list:
JanThompson.com/newsletter

HIS WAKE-UP CALL

CHAPTER ONE

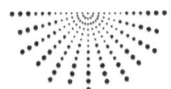

*S*ix months after his fiancée left him for a billionaire, Sebastian Langston still wanted to get her back. His goal spun in his head as he mindlessly drove through the streets of St. Simon's Island, heading to the Fire Pit Service at his church.

Even though his bank account was way smaller than Jared Urquhart's billions, Sebastian felt that he had a chance because he had a long history with Talia, who had dumped him several times and yet still returned to him after she was exhausted with her new boyfriends.

Sebastian represented someone dependable who was always there for her, offering her a shoulder to cry on whenever life was hard. Was life really hard for Talia? What could be easier than withdrawing money from a trust fund every month to spend it all on entertainment?

Still, he always took her back. Surely, she would return after she realized the errors of her ways.

Any day now, Talia. Come home!

After months of missing her, Sebastian had gotten worried. Talia hadn't called. She hadn't shown up at the business meetings at the restaurant they both co-owned on Jekyll Island next door.

His sister, Skye, had told him to let her go. If she was sleeping around, she was not the kind of woman he would want to marry and have kids with, was she?

Still, Sebastian held out hope that Talia would show up at his front door as she had done countless times before.

Talia would beg for forgiveness. Of course, he'd forgive her.

She would ask for a fresh start. Sure, no problem.

She would whisper in his ear about her undying love for him. He would lap it all up.

All those boyfriends of hers hadn't lasted as long as her relationship with Sebastian. Someday, Talia would stop running off and they could marry and start a family. Sebastian could imagine how beautiful their kids would be...

This time, it seemed different for Sebastian. It felt like he was going to lose Talia forever, that her wandering days had led her far away from him, that Jared had so much more to offer her. Free plane rides around the world on his private jet, for example. Or vacations in the many Urquhart summer homes in Europe.

Sebastian had none of the above—except for his stable love and dependability, both of which money could not buy.

Take that, Jared.

Maybe it was time to spice it up a little. But how?

Sebastian found himself in the Seaside Chapel parking lot. *How did I get here? Did I run any red lights?*

He parked his SUV as close as possible to the pavilion behind the church buildings. There were two buildings in all: the main Seaside Chapel sanctuary and the one-hundred-year-old wedding chapel.

Sebastian had been eyeing that wedding chapel for a long time. He had catered wedding receptions both in its basement and outside on the grounds. Someday, he would like to be married there.

Soon, he hoped. He wasn't getting any younger. He wanted a passel of kids with Talia. He'd talk to her about that after he got her back.

Sebastian grabbed his Bible and iPad from the backseat and made it halfway down the boardwalk toward the pavilion before he started wondering if he had locked his vehicle. He clicked his key fob a couple of times, but it was too far away to send a signal to his vehicle. Maybe the key fob battery was dying down.

He drew a deep breath and debated whether to walk back to manually check his SUV doors or leave them alone. After all, St. Simon's Island was a safe place with very low violent crime rates.

While he was trying to decide, he found himself already walking back to his SUV. Apparently, his legs had a mind of their own.

Seconds later, he confirmed that his SUV was actually already locked.

He stepped aside to let a familiar truck by. It parked a couple of vehicles away. Benicio Ketteridge and Matt Garnett stepped out of the truck.

Sebastian walked toward them as Matt opened his extended cab door to retrieve a guitar.

"You missed dinner with us and Tristan," Matt said.

"What dinner?"

"This evening. Ivan couldn't make it, so it was just the four of us," Matt reminded him.

Benicio ambled toward Sebastian. "You were supposed to pick up the tab for dessert."

"That's today?" Sebastian checked his phone. "It doesn't say."

"We moved it from Monday, remember?" Matt closed his doors and locked them.

Sebastian scrolled up. "Oh. Forgot to change the date. Sorry, guys. I'll pay for dinner next time."

"You'll pick up the tab for the entire dinner?" Benicio slapped Sebastian's shoulder. "You're the man."

Sebastian followed Matt and Benicio as more vehicles filed in. The church parking lot was almost full. It was the beginning of summer, the weather was warm, and the Wednesday night outdoor service was a hit this time of year, not only for regular church members but also for visitors to the Georgia coast.

Sebastian turned his head when he heard a noisy engine that sounded like it was about to fall out. It seemed to come from an old, decrepit van. When it passed by him, he noticed that his sister's close friend was at the wheel. Her hair was tied up in a knot on top of her head, but little curls dangled all around her face.

A harpist, Emmeline O'Hanlon was one of the three musicians in Treble Trio. The other two being Sebastian's sister, Skye—who organized the group and was the lead singer—and Avery Chung, who played the trumpet. Lately, Ivan's wife, Brinley, would play accompaniment for them at the piano, although she was not considered a permanent member of the group yet.

That was pretty much all he knew or cared about the trio. However, Skye had told him a lot about Emmeline and Avery, who were both still single—not that it mattered to Sebastian. In fact, he hadn't seen those two ladies much except when they sang at church or at a wedding his restaurant catered.

Emmeline climbed out of her van, wearing a loose-fitting empire-waist dress with a modest neckline and a delicate flower print on it.

She had indeed changed.

Sebastian recalled that a year before, all Emmeline had ever worn were form-fitting clothes that made her look like she had been at the gym all day long—and left nothing to the imagination. She had hung all over Ivan McMillan, who had no long-term interest in her. After Ivan's wedding to Brinley, Skye told Sebastian that Emmeline had spent some time with her parents in Atlanta. Perhaps she reformed then.

A ping from his phone made Sebastian check his notifications. Skye asked him to save her a seat because she was going to be late.

A personal chef, Skye would always be late to the Wednesday night service until she could find another chef to handle preparing dinner for her clients that evening.

Sebastian walked briskly toward the pavilion, and found almost all the back seats occupied. He ended up sitting in front of the podium, where Benicio was welcoming guests.

The former US Army chaplain was now an associate pastor at Seaside Chapel, working primarily with the teens in youth camps and mission projects. Sebastian wondered how a bachelor with no kids of his own would be able to handle other people's kids.

Kids.

Someday, Sebastian wanted to have kids with Talia.

Yeah. Talia.

Unfortunately, she was gone. How on earth could Sebastian get her back? What would make her leave that billionaire playboy and return to Sebastian?

Perhaps all was not lost. Talia was still Sebastian's

business partner at their thriving Saffron on Jekyll. He could still see her on a professional basis.

Granted, Sebastian worked hard to make the restaurant popular with both the locals and island visitors. For the most part, Talia was a hands-off partner who pretty much let Sebastian do whatever he wanted.

Hmm...

Sebastian wondered how he could make Talia jealous. That was one of her weaknesses. Could he use that to his advantage?

He looked to find Benicio staring right through his mischief. Did pastors have x-ray vision?

Worse yet—God would see it all. What if God looked inside Sebastian's heart and read his mind?

Still, he wanted Talia back. If he could get her back in his arms, he could worry about the rest of it later.

The rest of what?

Ramifications of dating an unbeliever, for example. Well, he had prayed for her salvation. Wasn't that enough?

When Sebastian looked up again, his sister was walking toward him. Skye plopped herself down on the seat next to him just as her phone rang. She sent it to voicemail and muted the phone.

"You made it out of the kitchen alive," Sebastian whispered in Skye's ear.

She shook her head and rested it on his shoulder for a split second before sitting up straight again.

"How about I send you a chef for a few weeks until you find a permanent one?" Sebastian asked.

"You would?" Skye looked surprised.

"I'm selling the catering business anyway, and I've already told my employees."

"Did they quit on the spot?"

"Some have started looking for a new job, but Chef Joseph is transitioning to Sage Café, though I don't know if he'll like it there. He might be a good fit for you —although I don't want to push him your way."

"I've worked with him before," Skye said. "Will you ask him? I just need an extra hand for the summer."

"I'll talk to him." Sebastian squeezed his sister's shoulder.

"Any prayer requests?" Benicio asked.

Sebastian sat through at least half a dozen serious prayer requests from those in attendance, ranging from life-threatening illnesses to deaths. Argo Perry's cancer had returned. Hayden Hartley's grandmother had fallen and broken her hips. Matt's brother needed a better-paying job.

Sebastian wondered if he should say, "My fiancée left me—again."

More hands went up. Benicio pointed to someone sitting somewhere in the back. "Emmeline."

Sebastian could not see her from where he was sitting, but he could hear the concern in her voice.

"Please continue to pray for my missing brother, Claude. My parents' wedding anniversary is coming

up, and it would be a miracle if Claude comes home."
Emmeline's voice cracked. "It has been five long years."

"We'll keep praying. God works miracles," Benicio
said. "Let's go to the Lord now."

Sebastian could hear Emmeline sniffle—or someone
did.

It tugged at his heart.

And he didn't know why.

CHAPTER TWO

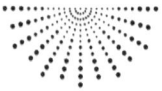

*A*fter the service, Skye hugged her brother.

"What was that for?" Sebastian asked.

"For sending Chef Joseph my way."

"Well, it's only for the summer—and I need him on some Saturdays for weddings."

"I'll take what I can get," Skye said.

Sebastian kissed her forehead. "You're the only family I have. I don't want to see you burned out."

"Oh. I like being your only family." Skye chuckled. "It's a good thing Talia left."

"She'll come back."

"That's not a good thing." Skye pulled away and frowned. "She's no good for you, and you know that, Seb."

"I don't want to hear it."

"Figured." Skye picked up her Bible and purse from the chair. "I'm going home and straight to bed."

"Talk with you later."

Sebastian stayed to chat with Matt and Benicio. Mainly, he wanted to apologize to them for forgetting their dinner. Matt stepped off the pavilion and down some steps that led to the beach, and Sebastian followed him. Benicio was starting the fire pit.

Dusk settled over the ocean, and stars lightly peppered the sky above them. Sebastian was walking toward the fire pit when he saw Emmeline standing near the shoreline. The wind picked up her hair and blew it about her shoulders. She had let loose her wavy butterscotch-blonde hair, and it was dancing around her face and shoulders, as her dress billowed in the wind.

When she turned around, she wiped her eyes.

Sebastian nearly lost his footing in the sand.

Throughout the next half an hour, all Sebastian wanted to do was watch Emmeline chat with her loud friend, Avery, who made Emmeline laugh. Her laughter carried in the wind and into Sebastian's ears, distracting him from understanding what Matt and Benicio were saying.

After a while, Emmeline's laughter subsided, and Sebastian turned to look for her. She was nowhere to be found. The night was dark, save for the pavilion lights.

"If anybody wants some more chicken nuggets, come get them!" Someone shouted from the pavilion.

Yes, usually some people brought food to the

Wednesday night service. It wasn't Sebastian's turn, and he wasn't hungry.

While other people milled around the fire pit, Sebastian took the opportunity to leave, following a few people who had the same idea.

He walked to his SUV and backed out of his parking space. A few vehicles were in his way, so he waited for them to leave the parking lot.

Under a street lamp, he saw a woman in a dress standing in front of a van. It was Emmeline.

Sebastian inched closer as she lifted the hood and peered inside. She tapped her phone. Looked at the engine. Tapped some more. Swiped here and there. Scrolled. Then looked at her engine again.

Sebastian stopped his SUV next to where Emmeline was standing. He parked it and got out.

Emmeline glanced his way. "Hi, Sebastian. How's Skye doing?"

"She's fine. Do you need any help?" Sebastian asked.

"I'm trying to match the photos here with the parts of my engine." Her voice was rising, and she seemed to be catching her breath.

"I can see that. What's wrong?"

"My van won't start. The lights won't come on."

"May I take a look?"

"Yes, you may." Emmeline smiled.

Sebastian didn't know too much about vehicle engines, but if the lights didn't come on and the car didn't start, he figured they could check the battery first. "Let's try to jump-start your van. See if that works."

"Okay. I don't have jumper cables."

"I do." Sebastian retrieved his jumper cables and connected the two batteries at the terminals with the giant alligator clips. "Go put your van on idle. I'm going to start my SUV and see if we can get some juice into your battery."

Sebastian left his SUV running as he walked over to Emmeline, who was standing by her van.

"How are you doing these days?" Sebastian asked as they waited for the batteries to do their thing.

"Same old, same old." Emmeline's voice seemed weary.

"Are you still working at the bookstore?"

Emmeline nodded. "And in the music library, plus SISO, plus playing at weddings."

"That's a lot of work."

Sebastian had catered for the Sea Islands Symphony Orchestra a few times in the past year alone. He had seen Emmeline by her harp at those events, but he hadn't paid much attention to her.

Why now?

He wasn't sure.

"I wanted to do just one full-time job, but I can't commit to staying long in town because I'm leaving for grad school in August," Emmeline explained.

Matt and Benicio came by to see what was going

on. When they saw that Sebastian had the matter under control, they left the two of them to resume their small talk.

Mostly they chatted about Skye and how busy she was running Skye's the Limit personal chef service.

"Let's see if you can turn on the headlights," Sebastian said after a while.

Emmeline climbed into her van. Sure enough, the lights came on.

"You should take your van to the shop tomorrow." Sebastian unhooked the jumper cables that linked the terminals of the two batteries.

Emmeline nodded. "Thank you for your help tonight."

"No problem. Let's make sure you can drive out of here before I leave." Sebastian coiled up his jumper cables and put them into a plastic carton at the back of his SUV.

"If there's anything I can do for you, please let me know," Emmeline said.

A thought popped into Sebastian's head. He wondered if it was a good idea. "Well..."

"Yes?" Emmeline waited.

Sebastian debated whether to broach the subject. Even though Emmeline had asked, he wasn't sure if he should take up her offer.

"Sebastian?"

"Yeah?" Sebastian drew a deep breath.

"Aren't we friends?"

"By way of my sister, Skye. So yes, we're friends."

Emmeline stared intently at him. "Let's hear it. How may I help you in return for charging up my van battery?"

Sebastian cleared his throat. "About your prayer request this evening..."

"Claude?" Her eyes widened under the street lamp.

Sebastian nodded. "I might be able to help."

"How?"

So he told her.

CHAPTER THREE

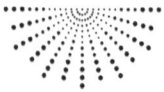

"I'm going to do it." Emmeline O'Hanlon made up her mind five days later while eating lunch with her best friend.

"Noooo!" Across the table, Skye put down her chicken sandwich. "You're just enabling my brother to mess up his life. Don't help him."

Emmeline laughed. She barely knew Skye's older brother, but from what she'd heard at church, in the Seaside Chapel women's Bible study group, and previous information from Skye herself, she doubted that Sebastian Langston was as problematic as his sister made him out to be.

If he were, the restaurateur wouldn't have been the youngest chef in the southeast to own an award-winning restaurant.

"I have to find my brother." Emmeline sipped more tea. It was a tad too sweet.

Around her, the lunch crowd was thinning. She had to get back to work soon, but she valued Skye's input on this matter, and had agreed to hear her out.

"It's been five years, Em. Who knows where your brother is now?"

"Exactly. I've used up all my savings to find Claude. Crowdfunding fizzled out three years ago. He's still lost out there somewhere." Emmeline's voice caught. "Heaven forbid he's dead."

"Don't say that."

"In any case, I'm out of money. I have to hold down four part-time jobs that don't give me healthcare."

"Doesn't SISO—"

"SISO?" Emmeline wondered why Skye had brought up the Sea Islands Symphony Orchestra. "We only get paid when we play, and you know how often harpists play."

"Well..."

"Speaking of harps..." Emmeline sighed. "My van— you know, the one that carries my harp for me—has passed its expiration date. Last Wednesday night after the Fire Pit Service, the battery gave out. Your brother happened to be there at the right time to charge up my battery."

"Glad you were able to get home safely."

"I have no money to replace the battery. In fact, I will start grad school this August with only half of the funds I need."

"We all have financial difficulties," Skye said.

"It costs money to find my brother is what I'm saying. Money I don't have." Emmeline chose her words carefully. "I don't think my parents can wait for me to get out of grad school, go on concert tours, earn more money, and then look for Claude after that."

That could take a while.

Emmeline anticipated being enrolled at the University of Georgia for a good two years. She'd have to work along the way to pay for her master's program in harp performance.

She sighed again, almost too deeply this time, giving away her concerns.

"What your brother says he'll do for me right now, this summer, is amazing. An answer to prayer."

"Em, my friend." Skye paused, as if searching for words herself. "I'm not sure he had God in mind when he made you the offer."

"But don't you see?" Emmeline protested. "No money exchanges hands."

"This is Sebastian we're talking about. Everything is a transaction to him."

"Bottomline is, he helps me find my brother, I help him get his ex-fiancée back. What could possibly go wrong?"

Skye shook her head vigorously. Her hair bounced around her ears. "This is not the way to get there, Em. What else did Sebastian offer you?"

"That's all. It's a one-for-one deal. He helps me to find Claude. I help him with his Talia problem."

"Talia is not just a problem. She's my brother's doom, Em."

"Two months. That's all. Come first week of August, I'll be at UGA. Be happy for me, Skye."

No response.

Emmeline watched Skye resume eating her sandwich.

Thinking, thinking.

As for Emmeline herself, she had finished her baby kale salad. Wished she had ordered more, but this offer from Sebastian had caused her stomach to knot up a bit.

It was too good to be true.

Then again...

"Come on. It can't be that bad. You've always had good things to say about your brother." Emmeline stirred her iced tea.

"He's not thinking straight at this time, Em."

Yeah?

Emmeline wondered whether there was any truth in what her best friend had just said.

Still...

"It'll be only for two months until Talia gives in or I pack up and leave for Athens. That's all. I view it like a summer job. I had many summer jobs when I was in college."

"That's just it." Skye threw up her hands. She leaned forward.

Emmeline could feel the tension in her voice.

"Emmeline Eleanor O'Hanlon, listen to me. A

rent-a-girlfriend position—eek, did I say that?—is not a job. It rates up there with call girls and women of the night. It looks really, really, really, really bad on your résumé."

"I trust your brother. He's a Christian. He goes to church at Seaside. If he tries to hurt me, I'll call up Pastor Gonzalez and have them excommunicate him."

"Seaside Chapel is not a Catholic church. It doesn't excommunicate anyone."

"Okay. Throw out, then."

"I'm about to throw *up*, Em."

"You were the one who told me about your brother's plight, Skye."

"To ask for prayer, not for you to sell yourself. What will your future husband think?"

"Not to worry. I'll be single the rest of my life."

Emmeline remembered the last time she held her last boyfriend's hands only the summer before. Yeah, when Ivan MacMillan had told her he was simply going out with her, nothing more. In his mind, he hadn't been Emmeline's boyfriend at all.

Four months later, Ivan met the love of his life. Happily married now, Ivan had it made with Brinley.

"Listen, girl." Skye wagged a finger. "This is my brother we're talking about. His on-again and off-again fiancée is messing with him. He's not thinking straight. He's reacting to her irrationally. That's why he's in this emotional wreck."

"He looks fine at church..."

"He's very needy. I won't let you ruin your life on account of him."

"It's business—"

"Aarrggh! Did you say *business*?"

"Calm down, Skye. Look, I'll make a deal with you. I'll set down rules. No touching. No hugging. No kissing. If he oversteps those boundaries, I'll call you and you can rip him apart. Deal?"

Skye seemed to calm down.

Emmeline's eyes grew wide at the clock on the wall behind the checkout counter some tables away. "Have to run. Rehearsal in half an hour, but I have to put together the wedding music folder for the ensemble."

Why, oh, why did I wait until the last minute?

They paid for their lunches and parted ways outside the café.

The June sun beat down on Emmeline. She didn't burn easily; it must be due to the genes from her mother's side of the family. She made the short trek to her van parked across the road by Neptune Park, where kids were playing and shrieking in their cute little voices.

No children for me in the foreseeable future.

She sniffled.

Beyond the playground, tourists milled about, taking photographs around the water's edge and the pier, oblivious to her plight.

She had to jiggle the key in her van door to get it to unlock. She yanked the door hard to open it.

Story of my life.

She had bought the van from another student at college. It had been on its last leg then. And now...

Thank You, God, that it has lasted me five years.

Emmeline climbed in.

The van wouldn't start.

Oh no.

Ten minutes to rehearsal.

Emmeline tried to breathe.

She had to drive all the way up the center of the island to the SISO studios for the string rehearsal. It would take more than ten minutes to get there.

Oh, she should've left sooner.

If she kept showing up late, she was going to get fired from SISO, even if they needed her as the music librarian. She had to keep her apartment.

No way was she going to live in her van again.

She tried to crank up the engine one more time.

No go.

Emmeline speed-dialed her friend. "Skye! Have you left? Good! I need a ride. My van has died again!"

CHAPTER FOUR

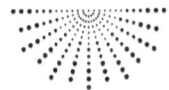

*E*mmeline sprinted out of the elevator door into the third-floor hallway and nearly tripped on the old carpet. She was late, late, late because she'd had to wait for the tow truck guy who had to be paid on the spot and in cash before he would tow her van to the shop.

Ninety-dollars-from-her-grocery-funds later, here she was.

Thank God, Skye had returned to the café to pick her up and drop her off here. What a friend.

"Whoa!" It was a male voice that Emmeline did not want to hear in a million years. "You tripped, Juliet."

Creepy hands and fingers were on her arms.

Emmeline shrieked and shrank back from Rafferty's grip. "Don't touch me!"

"Just trying to help you get back on your feet."

"Did you hear me, Rafferty Reid? Don't. Touch.

Me." Emmeline straightened her floral summer dress as she strutted away from Rafferty and toward the sound of strings.

They've started rehearsing without me.

Well, it wouldn't be for long before she was done with the Sea Islands Symphony Orchestra.

On the drive there, Emmeline had texted Sebastian to tell him she would take the summer job. He texted back almost immediately, asking to meet tonight for a planning dinner at his flagship restaurant on Jekyll Island.

Well, how in the world was she going to get there without her van? She'd have to borrow a car.

Or cancel.

"I'll always be your Romeo..." Rafferty was singing now behind her. Loudly and—

Well, that's some good tenor.

"She walks on the catwalk..."

"Quiet, Rafe!"

Still, she didn't care for the xylophone player digging up her past. Sure, she had modeled beachwear while in college, but she only did it to support her schooling. She couldn't help it if certain genes ran in her family. Her mother had been a sought-after model back in her day.

And Father, well, he was that harpist of harpists. During one of his concerts some forty years ago, he had met Mom backstage somewhere in Prague, the result of which had eventually produced two offspring, Claude and Emmeline.

Thanks to genetics, both of them had been child models, long before they picked up the harp. In other words, they had been earning income since they were little kids. Unfortunately, all that savings had dried up —every penny—in the last five years the O'Hanlon family had failed to find their long-lost Claude.

Today, playing the harp was all Emmeline wanted to do. She took a deep breath and prayed feverishly that she wouldn't lose her job two months before she went to grad school.

She opened the door to the practice room.

Conductor Bouvier Petrocelli's booming voice punched her eardrums.

"O'Hanlon! Late again!"

"Sorry, sorry, sorry…" Emmeline's jelly legs dragged her all the way to her harp. She slid onto her seat. "My van died."

"And I care because?"

"Sir—uh, I got here safely." Emmeline looked around the room to see if she could get some sympathy.

None.

Warren Yamaguchi looked at his violin. Misty Miller was frozen in play with her bow and cello. The rest of the string ensemble seemed to be pretending they didn't hear anything.

"As I was reminding everyone, the Brock-Flannagan wedding is next Saturday." Petrocelli waved his baton in the air.

Ah, the Senator's daughter.

Senator Brock, also known as Senator Broke, was marrying his youngest daughter off in July, right in the middle of a hot summer.

Emmeline hadn't voted for him in past elections. All he wanted was to reclaim the marshes for strip malls. But he had attended many fundraisers. Emmeline met him and his daughter at the Oglethorpe Charity Dinner on Jekyll back in December.

Yes, that one in which she had seen her ex-boyfriend, Ivan, and his then girlfriend getting cozy. She had felt jealousy then, because she wanted Ivan so badly, she couldn't sleep at night.

It's a sin to covet, I know.

Forgive me, God.

"We should be able to do this even though it's a last-minute addition to their program right after they switched out the groom," Petrocelli continued. "I don't understand young people these days, but as long as we get paid, we get to keep the studio."

And if we get to keep the studio, I get to keep my job.

Emmeline's feet inched toward the harp pedals as she listened.

Petrocelli lifted his copy of the program for the string ensemble to see. "We should be able to complete everything in two hours. On time!"

He glared at Emmeline.

In keeping with the series of unexpected circumstances in Emmeline's life, her cell phone pinged at that very second.

Emmeline reached for her pocket—

"No, O'Hanlon. No, no, no."

So we're all talking, talking, talking in triplets now?

"It could be the van service center," Emmeline said.

Petrocelli made some sort of gestures with his baton. "If I didn't know your father, I wouldn't have let you talk back to me like that. In fact, even though I do know your father, O'Hanlon, you shouldn't be talking to me like that. Do you understand?"

"Yes, sir." Emmeline always felt embarrassed when Petrocelli made it sound like she wasn't in SISO on her own merits but due to her connections, being Kipp O'Hanlon's daughter and all.

"The program is right in front of you. Mostly similar to the Jefferson-Yang wedding last summer. You remember?"

Everyone nodded.

"When the guests are taking their seats, we'll start playing. Nothing too complicated." Petrocelli shrugged. "O'Hanlon, since you were late, I had Rafferty put the folders together for us."

Only the worst assistant music librarian in the whole world.

Emmeline couldn't imagine the clean-up she would have to do when she got back to the music library after this rehearsal.

Her heart thumped. She hoped there'd be enough time for her to get the library back in order, walk home ten blocks, get ready, and borrow a car to get to the dinner meeting tonight.

"Miss O'Hanlon!"

Emmeline straightened her back. "Yes, sir?"

Petrocelli swept his arms in front of him. "Go on."

"Go on what, sir?"

"Go on and play the processional." Petrocelli strode toward her music stand and whacked it. "Read the program, which the rest of us have."

Gingerly, Emmeline opened the black folder and skimmed it. There were music sheets for about ten numbers. Some of the music sheets were upside down and dog-eared. Signature Rafferty mess.

She flicked the plastic pages to the first page.

Oh no.

The processional wasn't Johann Pachelbel's "Canon in D." It was Enrique Granados's "Oriental."

She must've read the wrong email. All week long she had brushed up her "Canon" from last year.

"Is this another last-minute change?" *I'm dead.*

"What have you been practicing, O'Hanlon?" Petrocelli seemed to have read her mind.

"I—well, Pachelbel?"

Petrocelli made some guttural noises that Emmeline couldn't decipher. They sounded like what her brother Claude's cat made when it was coughing up hairballs.

"Well, since I arranged this, I should be able to sight-read it." Granados had composed it for the piano, and though this piece was usually played on the guitar, Emmeline had arranged it for their string ensemble.

Petrocelli's face showed various shades of red and purple.

Emmeline gently pulled the Lyon & Healy concert pedal harp toward her, placed its neck on her right shoulder, and nodded to the rest of the ensemble. She felt the strings in her fingers as "Danzas Españolas Opus 37 Number 2, Oriental" came forth out of her harp.

She watched Petrocelli's reaction.

He seemed pleased.

Why wouldn't he be? She had played this wedding arrangement many times over, except not in the last six or seven months.

Still, it had always been at someone else's wedding.

Someday, maybe...

No. I'll never be married.

God, help me to be contented living single.

Emmeline willed herself to fade into her concert harp. This was her world now, probably for the rest of her lonely life.

In the middle of "Oriental," it all came back to her, the eighth notes, sixteenth notes, the trills, the acciaccaturas. She could see in her mind the *ritardando* measures, the *segno* symbol where she repeated the piece. She saw every page in her head, her heart, her being.

She let the notes wash over her, the strings an extension of her fingers. She plucked and strummed as if she were at a wedding.

Though not mine.

Two-thirds through, Emmeline couldn't see the notes on the music sheets nor the strings extending out of the spruce soundboard.

Sorrow trickled down her cheeks.

What in the world...?

She stopped abruptly, a plink calling attention to her lost focus. She quickly wiped her face with a flick of her fingers, hoping that no one had noticed.

The rest of the string section continued to play without her.

Petrocelli nearly threw the baton at her. He didn't look happy. He opened his mouth to speak, but a background applause stopped him.

Like everyone else in the room, Emmeline turned toward the solo clapping.

Sebastian Langston.

Standing tall and buff at the door wearing a blue tee shirt and indigo jeans was the guy who could help her find her brother—and thereby saving her money that she could now use to go back to music school.

How did he get in here?

Besides, our dinner meeting isn't until seven.

"I want *that* arrangement at my wedding," he said.

CHAPTER FIVE

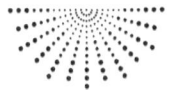

"**W**hy were you here so soon?" Emmeline asked Sebastian after the rehearsal was over.

Sebastian Langston had sat through the entire repertoire, the lone cheering section, watching Emmeline mostly, trying to immerse in her world.

If this ruse were to work, it required Sebastian to look like he was very interested in Emmeline.

He wasn't sure if they could pull it off, but Skye had told him that, in addition to being a harpist, Emmeline was also a principal cast member of the fledgling Theater by the Sea, the perfect no-name stage actress for his plan to win back Talia.

"I have a meeting with Mr. Petrocelli at three." Sebastian watched Emmeline tilt her harp onto the trolley, securing the neck and wider part of the harp with straps, like safety belts.

Around them string ensemble members were either putting away their instruments or talking with Conductor Petrocelli.

"What are you talking to him about?" Emmeline looked up.

"Curious one, aren't you?" Sebastian narrowed his eyes at her.

"As long as it has nothing to do with me, I don't care, really." Emmeline waltzed—at least Sebastian thought she waltzed—around her harp. There was something about her movement, fluid and graceful, like a ballerina onstage.

"It has everything to do with you. I'm hiring SISO Strings to play at Saffron on Friday nights starting in July." Sebastian pointed at her. "That includes you."

"All part of your plan?"

"Absolutely. Act one." Sebastian noticed that her eyes were hazel, and she didn't have any makeup on. No freckles anywhere. Not a scratch or a scar either. Her arms were like those of a porcelain doll.

Why hadn't he noticed her before?

He had passed by Emmeline at church many times over the past year, but hadn't paid her any attention, and hadn't talked to her much, even though they were in the same Sunday school class.

Emmeline and his sister Skye were also in the same Seaside Chapel women's Bible study group that met at the pastor's house. Thus, Skye had mentioned her before, but Skye had many friends.

Now that he was standing this close to Emmeline, he realized that she had perfect teeth and cute dimples.

Perhaps it was the lighting above their heads playing tricks on his vision.

Must be it.

It was odd that Emmeline was still single. A beauty like this...

Sebastian wondered how Talia would react if she saw him with Emmeline.

He reached for the trolley, and Emmeline didn't protest. She simply stepped back.

The way she stepped back was so graceful—

No.

Think of Talia.

All of this is to get Talia back.

That's all there is to it.

Sebastian wished Talia had made up her mind and be done with it. His thirty-fourth birthday was coming up. There was to be a bash at Saffron on Jekyll. He wanted to make an announcement, to tell the world that they were getting married.

But Talia had dumped him again for the fourth time.

This on-again, off-again relationship has got to stop.

This would show her. Nothing like a little bit of competition, especially from one so...so...

Sebastian cleared his throat. "How heavy is this harp, anyway?"

"About ninety-some pounds." Emmeline clicked on

the lever to release the wheel locks on the trolley. "My lap harp is only nine pounds."

"Which do you play more of?"

"It really depends on what's required. The concert harp has forty-seven strings and the lap harp only has twenty-two."

Emmeline stepped in front of him to lead the way, her long hair flowing behind her.

I could follow her anywhere—

No.

Sebastian shook his head. *Think of Talia!*

This plan had better work. Sebastian had a lot riding on it.

He was quite sure that Emmeline was the right candidate. She was single, unattached, and in need of help finding her brother, whatever his name was.

Well, his friend Matt Garnett would probably not approve. And when Ivan McMillan came home from his vacation in Vienna in a couple of weeks, he'd probably think less of Sebastian after he found out what he was doing.

Maybe he shouldn't have asked Ivan's ex-girlfriend to do this.

"Have you ever considered playing a lighter instrument?" Sebastian asked. "You know, like the triangle?"

Emmeline laughed.

That laugh. It's the sound of a bubbling brook...

No. Stop it.

Thank God it was a short trip past the water fountain and break room to the music library.

Emmeline suddenly stopped walking. Sebastian nearly plowed the trolley into her.

"What in the world?" Emmeline gasped.

Sebastian parked the harp that had blocked his view. He stepped around Em.

Em? I'm calling her Em now?

Folders, music sheets, boxes were all over the floor and bench and counters.

Sebastian watched Emmeline survey the damage. His eyes flicked to the clock on the wall.

There was only half an hour left before his meeting.

"Looks like someone is slightly disorganized," Sebastian said.

"Rafferty."

"Is that your assistant?"

Emmeline nodded. "The thorn in my side."

"It doesn't look too bad. Someone was looking for things."

"They were all classified and sorted. How hard would it be to read the labels on the shelves?" Emmeline asked.

"I gather this bothers you."

"You think?" She was near tears. "I'm not sure if I can make it to our dinner meeting."

"Sure you can. I'll help you. I have half an hour." Sebastian started to gather up the music sheets.

35

"Don't touch anything. I don't need any help from non-librarians." Emmeline reached into her skirt pocket and pulled out a hairband. She gathered her hair over one shoulder, and tied it up in a ponytail.

Sebastian couldn't get over Emmeline's hair. Tied to one side and hanging over her left shoulder, her hairstyle made Emmeline's face change yet again.

Standing there in front of him in her flats, she was perhaps six or seven inches shorter than he was. That made her quite tall, maybe five-nine or -ten. Never had he dated anyone this tall. It might be a nice change.

And that bluish-and-purplish floral summer dress looked nice on her.

He could stare at her all day.

Not good.

Focus, Seb. Think of Talia.

"What color are the flowers on your dress?" Sebastian asked, not knowing why he wanted to know. Had to know.

"Periwinkle."

"Really?"

"Is that your feeble attempt at small talk?" Emmeline asked.

"I'm trying to get to know you more."

"By staring at my skirt?"

Sebastian wasn't sure how to respond to the accusation. "I wasn't exactly staring at you, although you do have lovely hair."

"Should I say *thank you* at this point?"

"It's unscripted." Sebastian sighed. "Why don't you relax? I know this mess is making you uptight."

"Well, it was partly my fault. I was late to work."

"Look, I can help you put the music sheets back, if you like—though I now have only twenty minutes left to spare."

"That's not enough time, Sebastian." Her voice cracked.

Sebastian hushed her. "It'll be okay. It's just paperwork."

Emmeline chuckled.

"See? Feeling better already. Maybe you can tell me what you're doing and I'll assist." Sebastian kept his hands to himself, but he wanted to touch her smile.

Could smiles be touched?

"You'll assist?" Emmeline's eyebrows rose.

"Yes. I'd be happy to."

Sebastian felt drawn to Emmeline. He was standing close enough to her to catch the light floral perfume. It seemed to go with her summer dress.

She looked so feminine, so pretty, so...

So kissable.

CHAPTER SIX

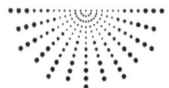

*H*alfway through her brief overview of classification numbers, collections, and sets, Emmeline realized that Sebastian's eyes had glazed over, and she had lost him among the pile of music sheets.

"Well, maybe I'll explain all this stuff some other day," she suggested. "Don't you have a meeting to attend?"

"In five minutes." Sebastian stretched. "You want some soda?"

"Sure. Anything with caffeine in it." Emmeline reached for her purse.

Sebastian lifted his palm. "I'm buying. What kind of soda?"

"Classic Coke. Thank you."

Emmeline watched him walk away, looking

relieved that he didn't have to do all this menial labor trying to get things in the right order.

He seemed to be an athletic guy with a straight back.

Mom always said to never date a guy who slouched. *Mom.*

She should Skype her parents sometime soon. They were going to celebrate their fortieth wedding anniversary this fall. The best anniversary gift she could give them would be the safe return of their only son, Claude, composer and Juilliard graduate.

Five years. It has been five. Please bring my brother home, dear Lord.

Claude had suffered an emotional breakdown at a concert in the metro Atlanta area, when he was filling in for the conductor that unexpected evening. He cussed out the entire audience and walked off the stage. Disappeared into the night and hadn't been seen since.

Emmeline sniffled. This was why she had to do this trade with Sebastian, regardless of what Skye had called it or what she had implied. Unsavory. Beneath her.

Whatever.

Besides, Sebastian was supposed to be in love with that Talia Cavanaugh-Perry. If Talia knew what was good for her, she wouldn't have dumped Sebastian.

From what Emmeline had gathered from her single female friends at church, Sebastian was one of the eligible bachelors on the sea islands, second only to Jared Urquhart, who was now dating Talia.

Must be a small world among the wealthy.

Talia, the younger daughter of Argo Perry, who had worked all his life to start and keep the Scrolls independent bookstore.

Talia, the spoiled trust fund baby who didn't have to work a single day of her life.

Talia, the biological daughter of the wealthy Blaise Cavanaugh-Perry, also known as old money.

Talia, the spoiled. Talia, the—

Uh-oh.

God, forgive my tongue.

Emmeline hung her head.

My tongue is a fire.

Like it says in James 3:6.

She tried to remember the other verses that Olivia Gonzalez had told them last Tuesday night at the Seaside Chapel women's Bible study group.

She'd have to look up those verses later. Whatever they were, she knew she was guilty of them all.

Meanwhile, here was a world of problem—

"Need any help?"

That voice.

Rafferty!

Emmeline spun around. "You did this!"

"Let's work together." Rafferty was reaching for her arm again.

Emmeline shrank back. "I told you. Don't. Touch. Me."

Rafferty kept walking toward her.

"You heard the lady."

Emmeline and Rafferty both turned their heads toward the voice.

There was Sebastian, a head and shoulder taller than Rafferty, two cans of soda in his hands.

"Who are you?" Rafferty puffed out his chest.

Emmeline rolled her eyes.

"I'm her knight in shining armor." Sebastian stepped into Emmeline's personal space, as if to protect her. "And who are you? The court jester?"

Emmeline saw Rafferty tighten his grip around his xylophone mallets. He looked like he was about to snap the rattan handles into pieces.

"Ah, a stage actor in our midst," Rafferty said. On his way out of the music library, he raised his voice. "This is not over yet, understudy!"

Emmeline waited until he was out of sight. When she turned toward Sebastian, he was staring at her.

"Thank you," she said quietly.

Sebastian shrugged. "I do that all the time."

"Sure you do."

"You have an admirer, I see."

"He was lead in our last *Romeo and Juliet*, and apparently it hasn't worn off." Emmeline explained the Theater by the Sea to Sebastian. "I joined a few months ago."

"I know. Skye told me. I'd like to see a play or two sometime."

"Well, we'll have a series of outdoor plays before summer is over. We're doing Jane Austen parodies this year."

"Sounds good." Sebastian pointed to the glass door. "If I close that door, will we have some privacy?"

Emmeline raised her eyebrows.

"To talk," Sebastian added.

"Oh yes. Of course." *Duh.* "Then again, don't you have a meeting to go to?"

"When I was at the vending machine, Petrocelli texted me saying he needs another thirty minutes before he can meet with me."

"I see."

"So I have time to spare, and I figured I'd have a chat with you, if you don't mind."

Emmeline shrugged. What could she say?

If Sebastian did anything she didn't want, all she had to do was call Pastor Gonzalez, and he'd be taken care of. Or she could file a harassment suit and the public would take down his signature restaurant, that Italian seafood place she had heard much about but had never been to.

She was sure Sebastian wouldn't try anything stupid. He had a reputation to keep.

Additionally, they were both Christians, and he would have to answer to God and to her parents—especially to her father.

My dad can beat up your dad.

She chuckled.

"What's the inside joke?" Sebastian sipped his soda.

"Nothing."

Why is he looking at me like that?

She glanced down at her dress to make sure her bra wasn't showing. And at her skirt to make sure it covered her knees. No point giving a single man any ideas.

Since Emmeline had started attending the women's Bible study a few months ago, she had felt a conviction to develop her inner character and work on modesty.

She had sold her low-cut blouses and short skirts through consignment sales. From the sale, she had bought some modest clothes from Matt's thrift shop. She felt freer wearing them. No danger of wardrobe malfunctions.

When Emmeline and Ivan McMillan briefly dated a year ago, she had been naïve about flaunting her assets. She had since learned by watching Ivan's then fiancée, Brinley, that God appreciated inner beauty more than her outer, decaying self.

Decaying? Yeah, decaying because she was getting older, after all.

Twenty-five years old and nothing to show for it but an undergraduate degree in music and four part-time jobs. It was her minor in music librarianship, not her major in harp performance, that had gotten her this job at SISO.

When the principal—and only—harpist had left for an out-of-state big city orchestra, Emmeline auditioned for the job, and earned it.

"How old are you, Sebastian?" Emmeline put away the music sheets as fast as she could.

"Thirty-four this September."

Emmeline studied his face. His mousey brown hair was kind of cute hanging over his forehead. "Thirty-four? You don't look a day over thirty."

"Thanks! Skye said you just turned twenty-five. Happy belated birthday."

"We're nine years apart in age."

"Not that it matters. Hey, I appreciate your doing this for me."

"I think I get the better end of the deal," Emmeline said. "Two months might not be enough to get Talia's attention."

"We'll keep up the charade even after you go back to UGA—if we have to."

The charade.

"Oh, I almost forgot about the house rules," Emmeline said.

"House rules?"

Emmeline nodded. "No touching. No hugging. No kissing."

"I get the no kissing. But holding hands? Hugging? They all make our stage play."

"Stage play? Is that how you look at this?"

"We have to make this realistic enough for Talia to believe I've moved on."

Emmeline sighed. "You know, I'm not entirely sure this is going to work."

"Sure it will." Sebastian crushed his soda can. Tossed it into a trash can nearby. "Talia is the jealous sort. She sees me moving on, she'll want me back. Just you wait and see."

Emmeline didn't know Talia at all, except that she was the daughter of her employer at Scrolls, the independent bookstore whose doors stayed open only because the owner had other income sources.

"Could we at least hold hands?" Sebastian asked.

"Let me think about that."

Something buzzed. Emmeline reached for her purse.

The text message came from the van service center. She called them back.

"That sounds bad." She walked about near the windows.

The afternoon sunlight shone in, warming her up. She stood in the sun for a while listening to the bad news. "I don't know, Joey. Sounds over the top."

Emmeline looked in Sebastian's direction. He was staring back at her, eyebrows wiggling.

"Look, Joey. I'm not putting three thousand dollars for a refurbished engine into a van that's worth half as much." Emmeline drew a deep breath. "What do you mean *I don't know?* I saw my van's value on Kelly Blue Book."

She paused. "Fifty dollars? What? You want me to give you my van for fifty dollars? Listen here—no, you listen—"

She turned around, and smacked into Sebastian's chest.

Oomph.

Emmeline staggered back, barely able to keep the phone in her hand.

Sebastian motioned for her to hand him her phone.

"Now?" she mouthed.

He nodded.

"Hold on a sec, Joey." She gave the phone to Sebastian.

Emmeline stood there, waiting, watching. She could hear the mechanic still chattering on the phone, unaware that someone else was now listening.

Emmeline went back to filing the scattered music sheets.

Things have got to get better for me, God. Please?

She was stacking up music folders as she listened to Sebastian.

"Joey, right? Good. This is Sebastian, Em's boyfriend. Tell me what's wrong with her van."

Em? He's calling me Em?

CHAPTER SEVEN

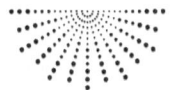

By the time five o'clock rolled around, Emmeline was lying prone on the pine floor of the music library, the last stack of folders next to her.

All done.

Whatever Rafferty had flung at her had been corrected.

Well, it wasn't really his fault. Emmeline had been late to work. Ironically, if not for Rafferty—as disorganized as he might be—the rehearsal wouldn't have happened.

Great. Now I have to thank Rafferty.

Emmeline's gaze went to the window. The sky had turned overcast. It was supposed to rain this evening.

If she hurried up and walked fast, she might make it home before it rained. Sometimes there were abandoned umbrellas in the lost-and-found closet. Or maybe a poncho of some sort.

Every bone in her body ached. She had never hurt like this. It might be stress. Or overwork. Or a lack of sleep. Or all of the above.

Once she walked home, she would have to call a cab to take her to dinner with Sebastian. She had the money now from the sale of her van to the mechanic at a good price that Sebastian had negotiated for her.

Well, maybe she could cancel or reschedule the meeting. After all, he had given her the check. He could email her Talia's schedule. There was no need to meet in person—

The door flung open.

"Dinner's served!"

What?

With Sebastian's long strides taking him to her faster than she could sit up, Emmeline found herself looking up at an imposing man.

He stretched his arms to give her a hand. He gently pulled her to her feet.

"I thought you left," Emmeline said.

"You have no transportation. How were you planning on making it to our dinner meeting?"

"I was going to borrow a car, call a cab, or reschedule."

Sebastian nodded. "Uh-huh. I knew that could be an issue, so I brought dinner to you."

"How do you know what I like to...? Ah, Skye told you." *Again.*

Emmeline straightened her skirt.

"You two have enough lunches together for her to know your favorite dishes."

"So you're now thinking for me." Emmeline put away the last folders.

"I wouldn't put it that way. Getting Talia back is the most important project I have right now." Sebastian ushered her to the door. "I want to go over her schedule for the next two months."

"Seriously, you could email it to me."

"You and I barely know each other. To pull this off, we need to spend time together, every day, or at least more than I see Talia at work."

Emmeline knew that Talia co-owned Saffron on Jekyll with Sebastian. It was because of that restaurant that Talia had quit her occasional gig in SISO. Emmeline had no opinion on Talia at the timpani because they often didn't rehearse together.

"Too bad she doesn't play the timpani anymore," Emmeline said.

"Yep. Making her jealous would've been easier if you two were at the same events more." Sebastian invited her to go ahead of him to the break room.

What awaited Emmeline wasn't what she had expected. One of the folding tables where SISO members ate lunches and snacks had been converted into a proper dinner table complete with a white table-cloth and two place settings.

"A bit much for a takeout." Emmeline stared at the covered dishes.

"Our business meeting. You didn't expect us to talk about the most important project of my life over greasy hamburgers, did you?" He pulled back a folding chair.

"I'd better wash my hands. Dust from the music sheets." She walked nervously to the sink. She couldn't find any hand soap. She used the dish liquid instead. Now her hands smelled like lemon zest.

After she sat down, Sebastian placed a cloth napkin over her lap. He lifted the lid on her dish.

It was salmon. Her favorite!

"Wild Alaskan Salmon," Sebastian said. "Grilled with thyme and butter."

The way I like it.

"I'm going to have a chat with Skye about telling people things about me," Emmeline said.

"I'm not one of the people. I'm her brother and your boyfriend for the next two months."

Boyfriend.

That word rubbed Emmeline the wrong way.

"Don't blame Skye. She's a reluctant witness. She thinks this whole ruse is a stupid idea."

"She tried to warn me." Emmeline glanced at the door.

"No one can hear us. Everyone has left the building," Sebastian announced. "It's just you and me."

"Should I be scared?"

"You can trust me. I don't want you. I want Talia back."

Somehow Sebastian's words stung Emmeline.

I don't want you.

Neither does anyone else.

CHAPTER EIGHT

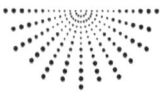

"**Y**ou and I are actors on a stage, and Talia is our audience," Sebastian explained to Emmeline as they ate.

He could tell she was a bit wary about this play. But she needed his help to find her brother, and if he could convince her that this was nothing more than a theatrical production, she might buy it, and the whole project would work.

Still, seeing her looking doubtful made Sebastian wonder whether his plan—wrought in the pit of lies and deception—might have been better off abandoned.

He watched Emmeline chew another small piece of salmon.

Why isn't she eating much? What happened to this being her favorite dish?

"Have you tried reasoning with Talia? Talk to her?

Tell her how you feel about your non-relationship? Have a meeting like this one?"

Sebastian smiled. "Talk doesn't work with Talia. She's visual."

"You hope that she sees the error of her ways and decides to marry you."

"Something like that."

"You can't make people decide, Sebastian. You're not God."

"Of course."

"What if instead of an object lesson for Talia, it's one for you?" Emmeline asked.

"What do you mean?" *It's all my fault now?*

"What if her dumping you is God's way of telling you to move on?"

"Move on?" Sebastian couldn't believe what he was hearing. "Talia is the only one for me. We've known each other since we were both seventeen. She was my first—uh..."

Emmeline's eyes got bigger. "So you've dealt with premature intimacy."

Whoa.

Sebastian cleared his throat. Skye hadn't said anything about Emmeline being this brusque, this unvarnished.

She had been a thing of beauty until she opened her mouth.

"God's timing is everything," Emmeline continued.

"If she was the one for you, you wouldn't have taken advantage of her."

"Me? Not me. It was her who made me... How dare you!" Sebastian held his breath and counted to ten. "Okay. Are you always this blunt, Emmeline?"

She gasped.

Then her shoulders sagged.

"I do have a problem with my tongue," she bleated.

"I'd say. Look, it's not cheap paying a PI to find your brother, okay? All you have to do is to hang out with me and make Talia see what she's missing."

"Then you get her back."

"Right."

"Whether or not it's God's will for you."

Wow. This is a mistake. This woman is the wrong actress. Is it too late to fire her? She could tell the world. Then what?

"This game of pretense could backfire," Emmeline said.

"If it does, I'll blame you. You're the actress here."

"I'm not a very good one, you know. I was fired from the last local production of *Les Misérables* because I couldn't remember my lines."

Sebastian wondered now. "Play along and you'll be fine. It's not like we're going to do anything serious. Most of the time, we'll just be going everywhere Talia goes so she'll see us."

"Business partners. This could get complicated."

"Well, I've arranged for her to do more publicity

the next two months. Various ensembles from SISO are going to play every Friday at Saffron. We'll also be more involved in some charitable work around town, like feeding the homeless—if we have time."

Emmeline's fork dropped with a loud clink on her plate. "Sorry, sorry."

Sebastian thought Emmeline looked shaken. Why? He decided to ignore it.

"Anyway, I'm thinking about four events in two months." He stared at her.

Those eyes...

That hair...

He cleared his throat again. "Do you have anything going on the next two months?"

"We have SISO concerts and the Theater by the Sea to keep me busy. I work in the SISO music library year-round. I'm also preparing to go back to UGA. The rest of the time I work at Scrolls—"

"Scrolls? Perfect. You've interacted with Talia then?"

"She doesn't talk to us. She's the boss's daughter and all that."

"Sounds like Talia." Sebastian picked up his phone sitting on the table next to his plate. Swiped and tapped. "What's your email? I'll send you Talia's schedule. I want you to send me yours. For each event, I want the date, time, venue, and all that fun stuff."

Emmeline gave him the information he wanted.

Then said, "What if it's not God's will for you to get Talia back?"

"Are you rephrasing your earlier concern in a different way?"

"I asked you the same question and you didn't seem to know."

"What are you now, Em?" He pocketed his phone. "My conscience?"

"Oh, that's above my pay grade. I'm concerned. You're my friend's brother. If you're hurt, Skye could be hurt too. I don't want to see her hurt. She's like a sister to me."

"She's not going to get hurt. This doesn't concern her. And you're not the director of this play. I am. You're only an actress I've hired to play a small part. Remember that. And besides, what do you know about love?"

That came out all wrong but there was no retracting it now. Sebastian felt bad seeing Emmeline's lips quiver.

Then her eyes turned steely.

"You're right. I know nothing." She placed the napkin on the table. "I suppose Skye has told you all about my sorry life."

"She hasn't said much. Finish your salmon, please. I have it flown fresh every morning from Ketchikan."

"I didn't ask for it." Emmeline stood up. "Thank you for dinner. I don't think this arrangement is going to work out. Find yourself another actress. I can look for my brother on my own. I've been doing that for five years."

"Yet you haven't found him," Sebastian snapped.

Those eyes.

Something in her eyes? They're watery.

Oops.

Sebastian wondered what he had said that might have pushed a button.

He watched Emmeline purse her lips and walk away from him, her dress swishing around her as she held her head up. The cascade of her hair was so pretty he wanted to run his fingers through it.

No.

Think of Talia.

Sebastian pondered whether to go after Emmeline. He decided to give her a few minutes.

How was she going to get home without a vehicle? The least he could do was offer her a ride.

He counted the minutes as he ate his apricot tart dessert. Then he packed the rest of Emmeline's unfinished dinner into the picnic basket. He'd let her take it home. She could reheat it. He hated to let that salmon go to waste.

As he was cleaning up, he could hear rain starting to fall on the rooftop. There was a bit of distant thunder, probably over the Atlantic.

Sebastian went down the hallway calling out Emmeline's name. No answer. She wasn't in the music library. Or the practice room.

He knocked on the door to the ladies' restroom. "You in there?"

"What do you care?" The muffled answer came.

He waited.

And waited.

And waited some more. She was in there a long time.

"Emmeline, are you okay?"

No response.

"Hey, listen. It's raining outside. How are you getting home?"

No response.

"I'm not leaving until you tell me you're okay."

Silence.

Sebastian knocked on the door again.

"Go away, Seb!"

She called me Seb.

"Okay. See you later, Em."

It was still raining when Sebastian hauled the picnic basket to his car. He started his silver hybrid BMW i8, turned it around, and backed it into a parking spot facing the front entrance of the building.

He sat in his car and waited, hoping that was the door Emmeline would come out of. At least five minutes later, she did, a small umbrella in her hand. She set the alarm, exited the door, and had a hard time opening the umbrella.

Sebastian shook his head as he watched Emmeline put the flimsy umbrella, one side tilted, over her head.

Wind and rain came at an angle, making the umbrella practically useless.

On the sidewalk, she held down her skirt with one hand as she battled the wind with her other hand holding the umbrella. She lost the fight, and the wind blew the umbrella clear out of her hand. She went chasing after it.

By now she was soaking wet as she attempted to walk against the wind.

Great.

Sebastian started the engine. Pulled up his car by Emmeline, and opened the passenger side door, which raised up like a bird wing into the air.

He honked.

Emmeline jumped up at least a foot high.

"Em! Get in!" Sebastian shouted.

"Get lost!" Emmeline kept walking.

Sebastian's car rolled forward. "Please?"

"No! Go away!"

The wind pushed Emmeline back. The same wind also pushed the driving rain into Sebastian's car. He honked again. "Please! Get in!"

This time Emmeline gave in. She climbed into the passenger side. Her face was pink and her eyes were red.

It tugged at Sebastian's heart. He felt bad all over again.

He no longer cared that his brand-new leather seat

in his hundred-and-fifty-thousand-dollar car was covered with rainwater from Emmeline's clothes.

And oddly enough, neither did he care that his plan to win back Talia had failed before it began.

All he could think of right now was that he had to get Emmeline home so she could change into some dry clothes and not catch a cold.

And that he wanted to hold her hand.

CHAPTER NINE

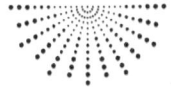

ou can't possibly be serious." Matt Garnett didn't look up.

The de facto lay counselor to the single men in the Seaside Chapel men's Bible study group was tagging another heirloom earring and placing it in the glass cabinet next to all the other old earrings that no one seemed to be buying these days at Garnett Antiques.

"I can't be more serious! I'm talking about my future children here, Matt." On the glass surface, Sebastian saw his own reflection, but he couldn't read his own frown.

Perhaps something at the back of his mind bothered him still. Perhaps it was the animated voice of his younger sister, Skye, still ringing in his ear, warning him that this was a bad idea.

Then again, last evening in the rain, he had

managed to convince Emmeline to help him with his scheme.

Sebastian knew that Matt was a rational man. Maybe he was right. Maybe this was a mistake. A whim he should box and shelve away like what Matt was doing now to the rest of the old costume jewelry from his last picking.

"You mean, what would Pastor Gonzalez say?" Sebastian asked.

"No, Seb. What would *God* say?"

"That's the thing. I don't know what God says about this. I thought He wanted me to marry Talia and have kids. Now Talia has dumped me for that...that..."

"That filthy rich but handsome dude who happens to own Jekyll Island Resort."

"I don't know what Talia sees in his yacht."

"Jared Urquhart has a yacht?" Matt stopped in his tracks. Turned his head. "Sold!"

"Don't mock me, Matt." Sebastian's shoulders slumped. "I didn't poke fun at you when you gave me that sob story about your ex-wife."

"I'm sorry. I shouldn't have. But your story is funnier than mine."

"More tragic, you mean?"

Matt came back with a small box. It was ornate and it looked like a music box. He placed it on the glass surface right in front of Sebastian. On the box were carvings of two lovers under a spreading willow tree.

"A piece of advice, Sebastian. Not everything is

either a tragedy or triumph. A lot of times things are in the steady middle, not opposite extremes of our emotional range."

"But the Bible says we should be either hot or cold, not lukewarm."

"I think you're misinterpreting scripture there." Matt wiped the box with a soft chamois cloth. "You should be on fire for God, but here you are, on fire for Talia. If you put her above God, then she becomes your idol, and you're no longer hot for God. Get it?"

"You know, I think you're misinterpreting the verse too. Maybe we should ask Pastor Gonzalez what it means."

"We can't keep asking the pastor when we don't understand a verse. Isn't he always telling us to search God's Word first and not take his word—man's word—for it?" Matt said.

"We could ask Ivan. He'll be back."

"He's still on vacation."

"Who's teaching this Friday then?" Whoever the Bible study teacher was, Sebastian would ask him.

Maybe he'd say something Sebastian wanted to hear rather than what God might chide him for.

He was certain God wasn't happy with him. If He were, why did he lose Talia in the first place? They'd been happy together for years—

Well, all right. On and off happy.

But happy nonetheless—that was, when they were together. About half the time. No. A third of the time...

What am I doing wrong, Lord?

"You."

"What?" Sebastian's eyes grew big.

"You're teaching Friday. You agreed, remember? We told Ivan he could stay an extra week in Vienna if he wanted to. Benicio's out of town this week. You said you'd step in."

"I did? No way."

"That's what I said." Matt shook his head. "From that look on your face, I'm gathering you haven't prepared. The Bible study is three days away, Seb."

"We're reading Jude." Sebastian shrugged. "It's a short book. How hard can it be?"

"You can't take God's Word lightly, friend."

Sebastian shook his head. "I know exactly what you're up to, Matt."

"What did I say?"

"You're trying to stop me, aren't you? You tell me to read the Bible to prepare for this Friday's Bible study, when in reality you think that, if I opened God's Word, then He's going to talk to me about Talia."

"You said that. I didn't."

"You know—for a fact—that God is going to tell me no."

"Don't put God in a box, Sebastian. God doesn't always say no."

Sebastian furrowed his eyebrows. "Hmm... Have you been talking to Skye? She says the very same thing."

"There. Take it as a confirmation."

"You don't get it. I'm not losing Talia again."

"Reality check, Seb. You've already lost her. She dumped you months ago."

When Sebastian didn't reply, Matt continued. "Friend, all I'm saying is that you'd better be sure you're doing the right thing *before* you do it. Otherwise, you're going to break three women's hearts: Talia, your sister Skye, and her friend Emmeline, whose heart has already been broken multiple times over."

CHAPTER TEN

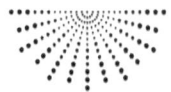

After finishing her afternoon shift at Scrolls, Emmeline cycled ten minutes from the Village to Olivia Gonzalez's house with her small nine-pound Celtic lap harp strapped to her back.

Her old, rickety bicycle held up, and she made it just in time for food. Her tummy rumbled as the pungent aromas from multiple slow cookers on the kitchen counter wafted toward her when she stepped into the sunroom next to the kitchen.

The year before, they would have their Bible study first before they had dinner, but some of the ladies had to work late, and by the time they showed up, the Bible study was pretty much over.

So this year, the Seaside Chapel women's Bible study group decided that they'd start the Bible study at seven to let everyone have some dinner first. Late-comers would not miss much. After the Bible study, those who wanted seconds or thirds were free to stay, eat, and chat.

In the fall, Olivia had made this an indoor-outdoor room but in the summer, she would shut the door and turn on the fan and air conditioner. Emmeline was glad because she needed to cool off from the sweaty bike ride.

Emmeline walked to the corner of the sunroom where they usually set up their instruments. She placed her lap harp next to her friend Avery Chung's trumpet case. The shiny case told her that Avery had a solo tonight at the Seaside Chapel women's Bible study group.

Skye Langston walked into the room as Emmeline was about to go get something to eat.

"I don't know if I'm going to remember all the words to the new song," Skye said, going along with Emmeline to the kitchen.

Well, to be fair to Skye, they hadn't rehearsed much since telling the pastor's wife that Skye would be more than happy to sing tonight, accompanied by Emmeline's harp.

"Don't worry about it," Emmeline assured her friend. "Put the lyrics in front of you."

"I feel like if we're going to do this for a while—and maybe even form a group—I need to have the words memorized."

"You'll have them memorized soon enough, but we only started rehearsing together last Sunday." Emmeline picked up a paper plate and put what looked like samosa on it. "Don't be too hard on yourself."

"Bad news is I'm going to Miami all next week for the food festival. I'm not going to have enough time to practice."

"As we sing the same hymns over and over, you'll get it. It's like all the wedding songs I play on my harp. I play almost the same songs all the time."

"Oh, like singing in the shower. Except I'll sing in the kitchen."

"Just don't burn yourself." Emmeline laughed.

She dished out some salad that had dressing in it. Reminded herself that she could bring a salad the next time it was her turn. There were so many women in the Bible study group that they rotated the potluck list every Tuesday night. As she recalled, her turn wouldn't come for another couple of weeks. That saved her money too.

When Emmeline looked for a place to sit down, she realized that Skye was sticking to her like glue. It amused her. "Something you want to talk about?"

"Yeah. How is it going?"

Cryptic-like.

"Going well," Emmeline replied.

"No one's a pain?"

Emmeline didn't know how to answer that. It had only been one day, though she felt that she knew Sebastian more now.

"That bad?"

"Don't read too much into it, Skye. I was just thinking about how to answer your question in the fairest and most objective way."

"I see. Really bad, then."

"No." Emmeline was surprised at Skye's premature assessment.

More and more women came in and scattered about them on folding chairs and sofas, making it hard for her to speak her mind.

"It's... It's...uh..." She wasn't sure what to say, really.

"I knew it!" Skye hung her head. "Look, I'll talk to him and put an end to this."

"No. Wait. Please."

"Huh? I thought you said—"

"I said nothing, Skye. You took my hesitation as doom."

"It's not?"

"Not at the moment."

Skye looked relieved. "Okay. Whew. I tell you what. Any slightest stupid trick, you call me, and I'll give him what's what."

"I appreciate your concern. Now let's finish our appetizers because it looks like we're about to start."

The samosa dipped in mango chutney hit the spot. Emmeline rushed to the bathroom to wash and dry her hands.

Then it was back at the music corner where Avery was already standing in position with her trumpet. She was going first with her trumpet solo.

Nothing like a trumpet to keep everyone awake at dinnertime.

"Hey, Avery. How's your day?" Emmeline asked.

"Pretty good. Got a promotion."

"Woo-hoo!" Emmeline high-fived her friend from the Sea Islands Symphony Orchestra. "We've been praying for that, haven't we?"

"Sure have. Either a promotion or that I find a new job."

"What are they going to have you do now?" Emmeline unzipped her harp bag. She'd bought the Celtic harp used, but it worked fine. She liked it a lot because it was light, portable, and its twenty-two strings were sufficient for most songs she played on the go.

Emmeline looked up at Avery, waiting for her friend to explain her good fortune.

"I'm now the assistant to the editor-in-chief," Avery announced cheerfully. She stood about half a head shorter than Emmeline.

Emmeline liked Avery, though all she ever talked about was either her work as an editor at a small press or her trumpet studio.

Avery had spoken very little about her family, still overseas. All Emmeline knew was that her brothers and sisters were scattered everywhere, from Australia to Asia to Europe to North America. She wondered how they had family reunions.

For Emmeline, all she had to do was drive to Atlanta.

Well, without her brother Claude, there wasn't much hope of a proper family reunion.

Lord, please bring Claude home. Please!

Olivia Gonzalez welcomed everyone and opened their meeting with a quick prayer, before Emmeline began to play accompaniment for the hymn singing. Skye was leading, but she also played her guitar.

Emmeline was glad they sang before they did their Bible studies. Some people said that it would take up too much time, but with only one hymn, it would hardly take any time. The hymn prepared their hearts after a long day at work or, for some, at home with little children. This Bible study was their break from the humdrum of daily routine and monotony.

As for Emmeline, she could play the harp all day, all week, all year, all her life. As she plucked and strummed the nylon strings, she knew that she had found her calling. Not as a music librarian or a stand-in girlfriend or a stage actress, but as a harpist playing hymns to encourage the people of God, to bring cold water to a parched throat, rain shower to a dry land, to remind everyone that God loved them and had not forgotten them.

Skye's voice was clear and sure as she led the women in singing the new hymn, written by one of Olivia's daughters. The lyrics ministered to Emmeline's heart, and she prayed that it would minister to the other women in the room as well.

When they finished singing, Emmeline put away her harp, and Skye, her guitar.

Emmeline was proud of her friend for not forgetting the words. Skye didn't just have a singing voice, but she could also play the classical guitar fairly well.

Emmeline wondered if Sebastian could play the guitar too, and if he had a singing voice as well. She had never heard the siblings sing a duet at church or anywhere else...

Wow. Stop right there.

Why am I thinking of Sebastian?

Olivia Gonzalez asked everyone to turn their Bibles to Psalm 37:4.

Emmeline settled into the corner of a sofa and flipped the pages of her worn Bible as quickly as she could to get to the verse.

"Let's read. 'Delight yourself also in the Lord, and He shall give you the desires of your heart.' That's Psalm 37:4." Olivia's fingers were still on her Braille Bible. "This is our memory verse for this month, and let me warn you, there will be a test when you least expect it. At least that's according to my own experience."

So true.

Emmeline wondered how she was going to be tested.

"The more time you spend with God, the more God will help you have the right desires that are best for you, your skill set, your talents, your life." Olivia did not turn her head this way or that.

Emmeline had underlined the verse before, but this time she wanted to memorize it for sure. Not because of the pop quiz that Olivia had mentioned, but because she wanted to spend the rest of her life serving God through harp music.

She'd travel everywhere and play her harp in churches and at retreats.

That's what I want to do.

CHAPTER ELEVEN

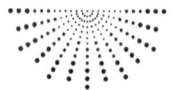

"*D*on't you have anything better to do?" Emmeline pushed the cart of books towards the fiction shelves at the Scrolls bookstore the next day.

Following her, Sebastian's Polo aftershave lingered in her nose but she tried to keep her cool.

"What's this?" she asked again. "Follow Someone to Work Week?"

"Yesterday, you asked me why I was there, and today you asked me if I had anything better to do. You must think I'm unemployed."

"I can't remember what I said to you yesterday, Sebastian." Emmeline stopped at a bookcase and started shelving.

"I told you that immersion in your world is how I'm going to get to know you more."

"Yes, but just because you know where I work and

when doesn't mean you have to be in my face all the time. Maybe that's how you lost your ex."

Sebastian seemed to brush her off. "They say if you want to know a language you've got to immerse yourself in it."

Emmeline didn't look at him. "And what language are we learning?"

"Love."

The book Emmeline was holding slipped out of her hand and hit the carpeted floor with a thunk.

Sebastian picked it up. As he handed it back to her, he whispered in her ear. "Talia is stopping by in an hour to see her dad. Come see me in the café in forty-five minutes."

He was too close for comfort.

Emmeline's mind went blank.

When she said nothing, he continued, "I'll buy you a cup of coffee."

"I'm not on break in an hour," Emmeline managed to say.

"Okay. No coffee for you. Just walk by or something. Say hello. Make it look like something's happening between us."

Something's happening all right.

Mr. Glue here was stuck to her, and she couldn't shake him off. It might pay dividends only if he helped her find her brother. "About my brother, when do we get to that?"

"No worries. I've called Helen Hu. You remember

Helen? She found the Stradivarius violin for the Brooks family."

"Right." She knew all about it and then some.

Yes, that old episode had resulted in her loss. Then again, her short relationship with Ivan—prior to Brinley's arrival—had been one-sided. Emmeline had desired him, but he hadn't reciprocated beyond their platonic lunches.

Never again would she open up her heart to anyone.

It had almost always been one-sided.

"Helen is busy this week, but she's going to carve out a bit of time next week and drive down from Savannah on Thursday evening to talk with us," Sebastian said. "We'll meet at my house and go from there. I've already sent her a retainer."

"I don't know what to say."

"You want your brother back, don't you? Helen's a hunter, and if anyone can find your brother, she will. After all, you did give her a very small area to search in."

"Metro Atlanta is not small." When Claude had gone missing five years before, Emmeline had mobilized a Facebook group to search for him.

Over the next two to three years, all the sightings had been in the southeastern area. She felt those were strong sightings, especially the ones in Georgia, because she knew her brother well.

In spite of his emotional issues, Claude had always

loved their parents. He wouldn't want to be too far away from them.

Hence, her belief that Claude would hang around the metro Atlanta area.

"To her, it's a small area. She searched the world over on every continent for Brinley's violins, remember?"

"I bet that cost a lot to fund."

"Untold millions over decades. Helen's father began the search before he passed away." Sebastian handed her another book from the cart. "The good news is that I don't think it'll cost that much to find your brother."

"I hope not." Emmeline wrinkled her nose and tried to hold it all in. No point showing Sebastian her vulnerability when it came to her lost brother.

As a performer, she had learned to put on an air that conveyed whatever she wanted the audience to see. Whether playing the harp or playing a role onstage, her true feelings had never been an issue.

And yet...

Somehow in front of Sebastian, she was unable to maintain the shell that had kept her safe for years.

Sebastian squeezed her shoulder. "We'll find Claude."

"You remember his name."

"Sure."

Somehow Sebastian ended up pushing the cart for

Emmeline as she put new books on the various fiction shelves.

Then it was on to the non-fiction section of the bookstore. Emmeline couldn't shake Sebastian from her side. He kept tagging along, hoisting big hardcover photography books and heavy cookbooks for her.

When she paused a moment too long at a large coffee table book about the history of harps, Sebastian picked it up and carried it around with him.

"What are you doing?" Emmeline asked.

"I'm going to buy this book for you."

"That's not necessary."

"I know. But it's on sale. Only nineteen ninety-nine."

Emmeline shook her head. "Have you considered that maybe you're taking this too far?"

"It's just a book."

"Not just this book. Everything. This bubble you put us in."

"It'll be a happy bubble when your brother comes home."

Slowly, Emmeline nodded. "Yes. It'll be worth it."

"Worth all your time and trouble. You'll see. I do appreciate what you're doing for me. Kind of selfish of me, I know, but it also benefits you."

"To be sure. Now go sit in the café, and let me finish my work."

CHAPTER TWELVE

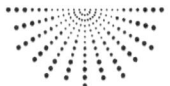

*A*t a bistro table by the window of the bookstore café, Sebastian settled down with a cup of coffee and a cinnamon roll.

The roll didn't taste as bad as it looked, and while he could've done better, he couldn't remember the last time he made them himself. He wondered if he could even remember the recipe and ingredients.

The bistro chair, albeit cushioned, was uncomfortable under him. It was too low for his long legs. The table was too small for his long arms. He felt like a giant Alice in that house.

Ah, what a man does for love.

At least he had Talia and his sister Skye.

Sebastian felt sorry for Emmeline. And possibly for hundreds of thousands of families of missing persons.

Claude O'Hanlon was Emmeline's only brother and her parents' only son. He couldn't imagine what it must feel like to lose a family member for five years, not knowing where he had gone or whether he was dead or alive.

Would Emmeline be devastated if Helen Hu discovered that Claude was dead?

Sebastian texted Helen to confirm that she was still coming to town on Thursday. She texted back an affirmative.

He tried not to get any sticky sugar on the pages of the harp history book as he turned the pages. Constantly glancing at his watch, he barely read the words.

He was fascinated, though, by how pretty the harps looked. Music appreciation was the extent of his musicality. If he were anyone, he would be the cheering section.

Yes, he would cheer on Emmeline. Hearing her play "Oriental" the day before had touched his heart in more ways than one.

He hoped that Talia would be okay with his choosing that piece for their wedding day. Well, it would be during the family processional, so she wouldn't even hear it if she were still in the bridal room at Seaside Chapel.

Would Talia agree to marry at that church?

Lately, she had been complaining about how long Pastor Gonzalez's sermons were, and how he seemed to be looking in her direction when he preached about sins and such.

Sebastian had noticed that Talia had been falling away from church activities, first skipping the Wednesday night Bible studies, and then saying she had a headache at precisely five o'clock every Sunday afternoon, when he was supposed to pick her up for the evening service.

It had gone downhill from there as she started missing Sunday school at nine o'clock, and going into the sanctuary late for the morning service. She had been so late one Sunday morning that not only had the choir finished singing and vacated the loft, but Pastor Gonzalez was well into his eighth of ten points when Talia walked in and sat in the back.

They had always sat in the back. Sebastian wanted to move up front to be closer to the singing and music and choir.

But Talia wanted to sit in the back row. Always the last row. That way she could be the first to leave church. Sometimes she left before the service was over, before they sang the last hymn, the last prayer, before the greeters went to the door to open it for the congregation to file out.

Then in recent months, Talia had stopped attending Seaside Chapel altogether. It had happened the week after she had broken up with him.

Sebastian kept telling himself that Talia had found a new church. There wasn't a shortage of churches on St. Simon's Island, Brunswick, and the surrounding area.

It's my fault, isn't it, Lord?

Sebastian knew that it would take time for Talia to return to church. He hoped she would return. Why wouldn't she? She had grown up at Seaside Chapel. She had been there longer than Sebastian and Skye had lived on St. Simon's Island.

Talia's dad, Argo Perry, was no longer a deacon at Seaside Chapel, but he still attended. Sebastian wondered if he should talk to Argo about his daughter's spiritual condition.

But I'm not her Holy Spirit.

Through the bookstore windows, the afternoon looked warm. If this were another day, Sebastian would've wanted to walk around and get some sun and maybe catch some surf. But not today. Not now.

Not in the next couple of months of his stratagem to get Talia back.

Bushes, small trees, and potted plants by the sidewalk outside Scrolls were in bright hues and reminded Sebastian of those hanging flower pots in Victoria, British Columbia.

That was exactly it. Talia had suggested to her dad about those plants, and somehow Argo Perry had worked with the city to let his bookstore sponsor flowers and container gardens on the city sidewalks. He'd paid quite a bit for that, but for Talia, the now eighty-year-old man would do anything.

Did Jared know that bit? That Victoria was Talia's favorite place in the whole world?

Did he also know that Talia disliked shellfish and had never cooked in her life? It was ironic that it had been Talia's idea to turn Saffron on Jekyll into a steak-and-seafood restaurant.

Sure, Jared could hire a personal chef for her the rest of her life, but Sebastian knew how to cook. Did Jared know how to cook?

Clearly, Sebastian would win hands-down.

Outside the windows, vehicles and tourists and locals came and went. Sebastian glanced at his watch. Talia was late.

Then from the corner of his eye, he spotted her red Porsche. When she came out of the passenger side, Sebastian's heart sank. He couldn't see who was in the driver's seat, but he could guess. The car left the scene.

Sebastian hoped he couldn't find a parking spot.

Talia clicked and clacked her way through the bookstore lobby and practically ignored Sebastian as she went to the counter to get her usual cappuccino on the house.

He watched her sit there, waiting for her dad to come out of the storeroom or wherever he was this time of day.

Sebastian looked around, wondering whether Emmeline remembered it was time for her to make a casual appearance. He texted her. No reply. He texted her again, about five more times. And then one more time for good measure.

No reply.

Sebastian watched Argo Perry amble to the café. He kissed his daughter on the cheek, and led her to an empty table to talk.

Argo saw Sebastian and waved. Talia simply frowned as she sat down. She seemed to have either gained some weight or her clothes were one size too small. She could barely hold her curves together sitting on those little bistro chairs.

Funny what went on in Sebastian's mind. Only weeks before, he would have found Talia in that pose appealing.

Today, he felt nothing.

Nothing!

It was as if Talia no longer turned him on.

What in the world? What was happening to him? What happened to true love?

While he was contemplating the vagaries of life, the front door opened again and his nemesis walked in.

Jared, oh Jared.

Sebastian tried to get back to his harp history book but couldn't. He found himself staring at Jared Urquhart invading the life of the one person whom Sebastian was supposed to care for the most—other than his own sister, Skye.

Jared's hands and palms and fingers were all over Talia's thighs. Why didn't Argo stop that lusty show of affection inflicted on his supposedly church-going daughter? He just sat there, oblivious to the obvious.

The bookstore manager came up to Argo to tell him

something. Sebastian couldn't hear it but Argo left with the manager.

While he was gone, Talia reached for Jared.

And Sebastian's world ended at that point, when the two lovebirds smooched in front of everyone in ways that little children shouldn't be seeing.

Disgusted with their shameless public show of affection, Sebastian slammed shut his harp history book, left his half-eaten cinnamon bun and empty coffee cup on the table, and walked out of the bookstore.

Standing there under a leafy tree, catching his breath, he heard the rustling of leaves and looked up.

A mockingbird flew away from a branch above his head as he felt a splat of something warm and runny on his left tee shirt sleeve.

CHAPTER THIRTEEN

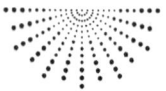

*E*mmeline thought about the Christmas concert announcement at the Wednesday night service, and felt bad that she would no longer be able to participate in her favorite events once she went back to music school.

Well, at least for the next two years.

After that, if she were to travel with a music group or something, she probably would not come back to Seaside Chapel—except occasionally, if at all.

The possibilities saddened her, and she hung her head as she walked down the hallway after the evening service to retrieve her harp from the music room for the orchestra rehearsal. When she returned to the sanctuary minutes later, she saw Sebastian coming around the hallway.

"I would offer to help you but you're almost there." He came alongside Emmeline.

"Well, I still have to roll it back after the rehearsal, but I can handle it."

"I'll do it for you."

"No need. It'll be at least an hour from now. You don't have to stay until the end of the rehearsal."

"I have time."

Emmeline set up her harp. "Funny, isn't it? You have all that time. I guess your restaurant runs itself."

"Pretty much." Sebastian folded the trolley, and put it where Emmeline pointed, off to the side.

"Glad to see you in church," Emmeline said.

"I don't work Wednesday nights so I can. Did you see me back there?" Sebastian asked.

"Sorry. No. I was looking straight ahead at the pastor teaching." Emmeline waved to other Seaside Chapel orchestra members, some of whom were in the Sea Islands Symphony Orchestra. The only difference was that no one got paid when they played at church. This was a free ministry.

"I'll be sitting over there."

"Feel free." Emmeline watched Sebastian walk to the pews. He settled down on the front row directly in front of her.

Now she felt self-conscious. Thank God she had on a pair of jeans. Some lady orchestra members didn't realize how much church members could see up their skirts at eye level.

Since she had broken up with Ivan last fall, and spent more time focusing on God's Word, Emmeline had begun to dress modestly not because she was turning into a conservative spinster but so that she didn't cause any men—married or unmarried—to stumble.

For that bit of insight, she'd have to thank Olivia's Bible studies.

The orchestra director went through several hymns for their choir accompaniment. Usually, they didn't practice the congregational songs ahead of time. They would sight-read those.

Unfortunately for Emmeline, not every hymn required the harp. She wanted to play it all the time.

All the time!

Alas, she must console herself with the fact that every time she was privileged to play at all, it was a gift from God.

Yes, and that her audience was God alone.

May You be glorified, Lord.

Otherwise, the two hymns that had harp arrangements in them were a wash because by the time they played those pieces in August, Emmeline would be long gone to Athens, back in graduate school.

In some ways, she felt sad thinking about leaving this place. She hadn't been here long, no more than a year, but the people had been kind to her, and helpful in so many ways whenever she had van trouble.

Speaking of which...

At least three people knew of possible used vans

she could buy. She might yet find one or wait until she arrived at the University of Georgia.

Meanwhile, on St. Simon's Island, her friends, especially Skye, had offered to give her a ride whenever it rained. Everything was going well.

Everything but one matter.

CHAPTER FOURTEEN

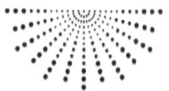

"**M**ay I see it again?" Emmeline asked Matt Garnett. She was standing at the jewelry counter at Garnett Antiques, having skipped lunch to come here this hot Thursday.

Now she was salivating over something she used to not be able to afford—and now she didn't want to afford.

There it was in a corner beneath the glass counter. The periwinkle agate bead necklace she had wanted for a couple of months.

A hundred and fifty dollars.

Matt Garnett had said he'd save it for her for a few more days.

Matt unlocked the cabinet and lifted the cardboard tray with the necklace on it. "Would you also like to see a matching bracelet? Only an additional forty dollars."

Emmeline knew she couldn't afford another forty

dollars for this. It would be close to two hundred dollars. She needed the money for rent and food.

She stared at the pretty stones that Matt showed her.

And shook her head.

The necklace and bracelet would have to wait.

"I don't think I want the necklace anymore, Matt. Thank you for holding it for me."

"I can put it on layaway, if that'll help you."

"I don't want to owe you anything. Besides, I would want to wear them tomorrow night, so the timing won't work out."

"Friday night? You have a date?" A slight smile.

Or was that a sly smile?

"Just dinner at a restaurant. It's fancier than I'm used to—so I kinda have to dress up."

"That kind of dinner. With someone I know?"

Emmeline hesitated.

"He better treat you right."

Emmeline didn't want to say anything more.

"Tell you what, sister." Matt pushed the tray toward Emmeline. "I'll let you wear these on Friday night if you bring them back Saturday morning."

"Seriously?"

"I trust you."

"I don't trust myself. What if I break them?"

"Just for one night. My offer ends in ten seconds."

Emmeline closed her eyes. "Wow. Thank You, God."

When she opened her eyes, the bracelet and neck-lace were still there. "I'll take care of them."

"You'd better. Don't forget. I want them back first thing Saturday morning. We open at ten."

"I promise."

Matt wrapped up the bracelet and the necklace in bubble wrap. Handed them over to Emmeline's shaking hands. "Want an apple? Fuji this time."

"Love Fuji."

"Go on to the back and get yourself one from the fridge."

"You sure? Don't want to put you out."

"Apples are us." He laughed.

Emmeline went to the small kitchenette. On the refrigerator door was a photo of Matt and his friends.

Emmeline was about to open the refrigerator door when she spotted Sebastian and Ivan in the photo. They were all on a boat of some sort. She didn't recog-nize the others, except for Benicio and Tristan from church.

Emmeline picked a Fuji apple from the refrigera-tor. She rinsed it off under the faucet, dried it, and began to eat it. It was juicy and cold.

Walking back through the store, she saw some more things she wished she could afford.

Oh well. Truly, I don't need much.

Thank You, God, for this apple and the necklace and the bracelet.

"Thanks, Matt!" She waved on her way out.

"Anytime!" Matt was busy with a customer.

Outside, the bright sunshine made Emmeline cover her eyes. She checked to make sure her bike was still parked at the bike rack. Yep.

She sat on a bench to finish her apple before she entered Matt's thrift shop next door, where she made a beeline for the formals. She had to find a black dress for the dinner date.

Her first pretend date with Sebastian.

She wondered what he was trying to accomplish with the double date. It could all backfire on both of them.

Additionally, she'd be out nine dollars and ninety-nine cents plus sales tax for the black dress unless she found one that she could wear to SISO performances here and at UGA. Then it wouldn't be a total loss.

When she came out of the thrift shop, Rafferty was leaning against the wall next to her bicycle.

"Are you stalking me?" Emmeline snapped at him.

"You were in there awhile. Long line at the changing rooms?" Rafferty sidled up to her.

"What do you want?"

"That's a loaded question."

"Don't get any ideas. I'm not available." Emmeline strapped the bungee cord around the plastic bag from the thrift shop, and prayed that the wrinkle-free dress was really wrinkle-free. Then again, she only had to ride it four blocks back to Scrolls.

"Why? You found yourself a rich boyfriend, and now you think I'm trash?"

"Leave me alone, Rafferty."

"We work together."

"But we're not together. Get me?"

"Oh yes, I want to get you."

"If you keep harassing me, I'm going to talk to Nigel." Emmeline regretted it the moment the words came out of her mouth. She couldn't talk to Nigel Miller. She needed that theater job too.

"Speaking of Nigel, Heaven is smiling upon us, Emmeline."

"There is no *us*. Never was, never is, never will be."

Rafferty didn't seem to hear her. "Ryan has the flu. So I'm Mr. Wickham now."

"No!"

"No, what? No, it's too bad Ryan has the flu? Or too bad someone else has to play Mr. Collins?"

It's too bad you're Wickham.

In Jane Austen's original *Pride and Prejudice* novel, Wickham and Lydia ended up marrying each other. In the Theater by the Sea parody, the playwrights decided to keep that bit.

Why, oh why?

Emmeline wished they had changed it.

How could she play Lydia Bennet with Rafferty all over her?

"You think I can't handle it?" Rafferty's face contorted. "I have two weeks to learn my lines, and I'm pretty good at memorizing. For instance, I memorized your face."

Emmeline began pushing her bike away from him.

"You need a ride somewhere?" Rafferty asked.

"Can't you see? I have transportation."

"We'll just put that old bike on my flatbed."

"No need. I have to go back to work. Now get out of the way before I run over you."

Rafferty threw up his arms. "Suit yourself. See you Monday night at the rehearsal."

As Emmeline rode away, she tried to think of how she could be sick on Monday night. Or switch roles.

It was too late, really. She had been happy that Nigel had picked her to play Lydia instead of Elizabeth. Now she felt that her involvement in the Theater by the Sea was a mistake altogether. Sure, it was only for the summer. But she had thought she could fend off Rafferty.

Ah, she wished she had more foresight.

Foresight.

She seemed to need foresight in everything, including what could be one of the biggest mistakes of her life, playing a stand-in girlfriend in what amounted to a reality show for Talia Cavanaugh-Perry.

This was real life. Not a stage play.

Sebastian was delusional to think that lies could bring Talia back to him.

Love has to be based on truth, right?

CHAPTER FIFTEEN

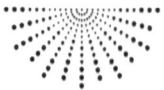

*B*y the time Emmeline cycled five miles in the warm Friday afternoon, from the SISO studios to her basement apartment, she was all sweaty and grungy and worn out.

She wished she didn't have to work four jobs to pay for rent and food. Even when she moved to campus housing in Athens, Georgia, in early August, she'd still have to work at least two jobs to supplement her partial scholarships to UGA.

If she sent another harp demo CD to a few more organizations, she could get more scholarships that might take care of the rest of her schooling. If she could get out of grad school without any student loans, she'd be better off.

Somehow, she had to support herself for the rest of her life. No double-income family situations for her in sight.

Sometimes God calls us to live alone.

She unlocked the door to her apartment, and pushed her bicycle into her one-room hovel. She took off her helmet to air out her matted hair.

The old used bicycle was her only transportation at the moment. She had to rely on friends to transport her harp.

Sooner or later, she would have to buy a vehicle even though Skye and several other church friends had volunteered to help her move to Athens. Matt Garnett had offered one of his cargo vans to carry her small amount of furniture, and he didn't want money for gas.

It's nice to have friends.

She locked the door, turned around, and saw the vase of flowers on her small folding card table that doubled up as everything, from her dining table to her writing desk. She picked up the card at the base of the vase.

It was from Sebastian.

How does it feel to get flowers from a fake boyfriend?

Emmeline sighed. If she felt anything at all for Sebastian, it was pity.

And here he was sending her flowers.

For what? The card didn't say. That was a good thing because the landlady's son had undoubtedly read it.

Aarrgghh.

It made her mad that he had the keys to her apartment. She made her rounds around the studio apartment to make sure Bart wasn't hiding behind the curtains, before she undressed to take a quick shower.

To be sure, she locked her bathroom door.

The phone call came while she was still in the shower. She sort of heard her cell phone ring, but ignored it.

Next thing she knew there was a knock on the door.

It startled Emmeline and put her into a frenzy because she had barely gotten out of the bathroom and was still wrapped in a towel.

She threw on her black dress—thank God it was really wrinkle-free, as advertised on the faded label— and ran to the door, damp towel around her hair. She peeked out the peephole.

And had to let him in.

"Sorry I'm early." Sebastian stepped into Emmeline's space.

He was wearing a dress shirt that looked like it was made of silk. His pants were charcoal, and hung over polished shoes. He was too rich for her hole in the ground.

He stared at her bare feet. Emmeline felt self-conscious, especially since she knew her nail polish wasn't as shiny as it had been on the first day she painted her toenails.

"I wanted to sit in the car and wait, but some guy was staring at me from the balcony upstairs," he said.

"Bart, the landlady's son."

"He lives above you?"

"Directly." Emmeline wished she could afford a better apartment, but the landlady had given her a great deal.

A bad deal, perhaps.

"Let's hope he's not a peeping Tom." Sebastian folded his arms.

Emmeline shuddered. "I think he's harmless."

"What you think and what he is are two different things."

"Like the play we're putting on for Talia?"

Sebastian dipped both hands into his trouser pockets.

Emmeline wondered if he was nervous. He had folded his arms, and now he hid his hands.

Okay, I'm just reading too much into this. "Have a seat somewhere. I'll be ready in a minute. Have to dry my hair."

Sebastian stepped toward her card table. "I see you received my flowers."

"They're lovely. Thank you."

"You don't like roses?"

In the bathroom—its door left open so she could hear him—Emmeline unwrapped the towel from her hair and shook out her curls. "Must you read meaning into everything? I said the flowers are lovely."

"But you prefer something else."

"How did you figure that?" *Really!* "What I prefer is my own business."

"I'm thinking there is a wall between us," Sebastian said.

Emmeline stepped out of the bathroom. "There will always be a wall between us. We're not exactly friends. Our only connection is your sister, Skye."

Sebastian looked hurt. "We could be friends."

"It's best that we aren't." Emmeline slid into her favorite pair of strapped sandals. She wished she had bought two pairs of those when they had been on sale at Walmart. *Oh well.*

Emmeline felt she had gotten a good deal. Ten dollars for her black dress that modestly covered her calves so she didn't have to wear knee highs. And the borrowed stone necklace to make her look pretty and all.

Sebastian pointed to her necklace and bracelet. "You like lavender."

"Periwinkle."

"It goes well with your dress."

"Thank you. I'm ready to go."

Emmeline locked the front door, wondering what that was for since Bart could enter it anytime he wanted. She wouldn't be surprised if he'd gone through her things.

Someday she'd own her own house, and no one else could get in.

She was aware that Sebastian was standing next to her, watching her lock the door. She tried not to be self-conscious. Years of having been in stage productions had taught her to allay those butterflies in her stomach.

This was only a play. Nothing more, yes?

She followed Sebastian to his car.

"Have a nice evening, Miss Emmeline!" The rough voice came from above their heads.

There was Bart, leaning over the rusty railings upstairs in his house robe. His hairy legs were sticking out as if the robe was all he had on.

"Thank you, Bart," Emmeline said.

"Nice car there. I've always wanted a Beemer."

Sebastian didn't respond to Bart. He unlocked the car door for Emmeline. After the door lowered and clicked shut again, he hurried to the driver's side as if he couldn't wait to get out of there. He backed out the car over the cracked and uneven driveway.

Emmeline watched him, wondering what he was thinking.

"How could you live there?" Sebastian finally asked as they turned onto Frederica Road.

"The rent is dirt cheap," Emmeline said.

"The company is dirt."

"Not your worry, is it?" Emmeline thought of her borrowed necklace and bracelet, the thrift shop dress, the Walmart sandals that looked like fake leather, and the hand-me-down purse that had a torn inner lining.

"I have a bad feeling about Bart."

"He's pretty helpful, really. Carries my harp to the van. He even fixed my van."

Sebastian chuckled. "The one that died?"

"He seemed to know what he was doing."

"How do you know he didn't break it?"

"Ha-ha."

"I'm worried for you, Em."

"Don't worry about me. It's not your concern. I help you with Talia, you help me with my brother. And we're done."

"Speaking of Talia, I was trying to merge your schedule with mine, and I tell you, you're everywhere."

"What do you mean?"

Sebastian turned toward Emmeline as they stopped at a red light. "Your schedule is like a pile of laundry."

"What? Are you running my life now?" Emmeline asked.

"Let's see. You have four part-time jobs, no health-care, no guarantees."

"Four? I have four jobs?"

"Em, I'm serious here."

Emmeline knew he was, but this was her life. She had come to St. Simon's Island for the music librarian job. It had begun as an hourly job until the budget cuts over Christmas.

So she had picked up the shelving job at Scrolls and roles at the Theater by the Sea to pick up the slack. It filled in her gaps in pay, but someday, this multiple-job life had to stop.

As for wedding music, she wanted to do it, though

it didn't pay much. It paid more than her infrequent participation in the Seaside Chapel orchestra, which didn't pay anything.

So, yes, four part-time jobs.

But what does it matter to Sebastian?

"I do what I can. I'm a harpist. I can't get a full-time job as a musician on St. Simon's. If I were playing some other instruments, and at the upcoming SISO Hall, then maybe I might get a small salary. But the concert hall has been delayed yet again."

"Couldn't you teach harp? Maybe you'll get a more stable income that way?"

"I'm leaving in August. There's no time to set up a studio."

Sebastian didn't say anything as he drove on Seaside Island Road to get to the F. J. Torras Causeway.

"When does the semester start?" he finally asked.

"August seventeenth, but I'll get there a couple of weeks early to find a roommate and rent an apartment. I'll probably skip orientation since this is not my first time at UGA."

"What if I still need you after you're out of here?"

"What do you mean?"

"If Talia and I...you know."

"I suppose we could keep up appearances. As soon as you're back in her good graces, the project is over, right?"

"It could take a while."

"We'll need a deadline. How about by the end of the year?"

"Fair enough. And your brother?"

"We'll be all right. God will help us find him if he wants to be found. Considering how long I've been looking for him, the trails have all gone cold."

They drove in silence over rivers and tributaries. Ocean Highway took them to Jekyll Island.

Emmeline had nothing to say to Sebastian.

She thought that he didn't wish to talk. He seemed to be deep in thought about something.

Then: "You seem to be accepting of things, Emmeline."

"Accepting of things? What does that even mean?" Emmeline sat very still in the plush leather seat.

All those years of acting classes had taught her to keep a part of herself closed to the world, and here was Sebastian probing. What was he doing?

"Such is life. It is the way it is," Sebastian explained. "That sort of acceptance."

"You read me wrong, Sebastian. More than anything in this world, I want to find my brother. I am determined to find him. He might not know the Lord, and I want him to see that God loves him, that he doesn't have to be alone in this world, foraging here and there. I want him to come home. Come home to our parents and to me and to family. So, do I question if things could be better? All the time."

"What about being married and having kids?"

Emmeline laughed. "I'm pretty confident that God wants me to be single the rest of my life."

"Such is life?"

"Such is life."

"I rest my case, Em."

CHAPTER SIXTEEN

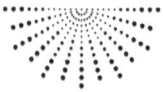

Sebastian did not like the way Jared Urquhart ogled Emmeline at all. He didn't know why he felt protective of her, but he did.

It was the same feeling he had when Rafferty accosted Emmeline in the SISO music library on Monday and earlier this evening, when her landlady's son paraded himself in his bathrobe above her apartment.

What was it about Emmeline that attracted losers?

Losers?

Am I a loser too?

The evening wind on Jekyll Island was balmy and salty, and the sounds of the ocean were calming. If not for that, Sebastian would've lost his focus on the reason for the double date tonight on the rooftop deck of his restaurant.

It seemed he wasn't the only one.

On the other side of the table, Talia had hardly touched her food. He thought he could see icicles hanging about her, and he knew why.

Sitting next to Talia, her date for the evening—and the man who had yanked her away from Sebastian—was another one of those trust fund brats with Mediterranean islands to inherit from their parents.

Well, this man whom Talia had spoken highly of had talked to no one but Emmeline since they had all been seated at their open-air table.

"You must come to my house," Jared said to Emmeline.

His voice was smooth.

Talia gasped.

Jared turned to her. "We'll all be there, of course, sweetie. I'm talking about that harp in the family room. The one the decorator thought would add to the charm?"

"Yeah, yeah." Talia wasn't amused.

"She could play it." Jared pointed to Emmeline. "Next Friday night. Let's have another double date. This time at my house."

Sebastian noticed that Emmeline wasn't sure how to respond. Reflexively, he reached for her hand. Held it. It was cool and trembling.

He felt bad that he had put her in this unscripted situation. He rubbed her hand with his thumb. Slowly, he felt warmth return to her fingers.

Emmeline took a small sip of water. "Next Friday? I'm sorry I can't make it. Rehearsal night."

"Rehearsal?" Jared's eyebrows rose.

"I'm in the Theater by the Sea," Emmeline said calmly. "We're doing some plays this summer starting next weekend. Have you bought your tickets?"

"I should." Jared turned to Talia. "We should buy season tickets."

"I'm not into plays." Talia's reply sounded condescending.

Sebastian wondered whether she was jealous of Emmeline's interaction with Jared.

Jared seemed to be ignoring Talia's remarks.

"May I—we—watch you rehearse?" Jared asked Emmeline.

"Well..." Emmeline said slowly. "To be sure, we don't always rehearse at the same time. Nigel sets the schedule, but it gets moved around. I say Friday, but he could move it to any day of the week, really. He has to find low-cost places for us to rehearse."

"Who is this Nigel?" Jared asked. "Give me his number."

Talia sprung out of her seat. "Excuse me. I'm going to the ladies' room."

Sebastian watched her go.

He felt pressure on his hand.

What?

Emmeline was squeezing his hand. He looked at her. She was making some sort of eye gesture to him that was so subtle he couldn't figure out what in the world she was trying to say.

Then she wrote with her finger on his palm.

Two letters: 'g' and 'o.'

Oh. "Excuse me," Sebastian said. "I'll be right back."

"Take your time, man." Jared waved him off.

Somehow Jared's voice grated on Sebastian.

As he stepped down the stairs to the restrooms below, he glanced back to find Jared staring at Emmeline, who was leaning back in her chair.

Sebastian didn't know why, but every fiber in him wanted to punch that smile off Jared's face.

Yet, he had to go after Talia.

After all these years, he'd been trained to go after Talia.

CHAPTER SEVENTEEN

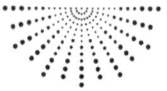

By the time Sebastian reached the bottom of the stairs, Talia was nowhere to be found. The good news about being a co-owner of Saffron was that everyone knew who Talia was. The maître d' pointed this way and that and Sebastian found Talia at the bar.

"Why did you do it, Seb?" she asked as Sebastian sat down beside her.

"Do what?"

"Bring Emmeline to take Jared away from me. Do you think that might drive me back to you?"

"Huh?" Sebastian hoped his surprise appeared genuine.

The bartender came, but Sebastian waved him away. He didn't drink anymore. He wasn't against it, as evidenced by his own restaurant, but it was a personal decision. It was another rift between him and Talia that might never be reconciled.

She was looking for a drinking partner these days, and he didn't play the game any longer, not since he found out that alcoholism ran on both sides of his family.

Sadly, it was too late for his parents, who perished when their vehicle wrapped around a train locomotive in the middle of the night, leaving him and his sister Skye orphaned and destitute in their early teen years.

A compassionate uncle had taken the two siblings in, and put both of them to work in his restaurant in Jacksonville. In that kitchen, at fourteen years old, Sebastian had known he wanted to be a chef for the rest of his life.

Unfortunately, he hadn't been cooking much the last several years since he opened Saffron on Jekyll. Talia had talked him into it. Saffron had propelled his—his and Talia's—reputation to international status. Soon they had hired a new chef de cuisine so that Sebastian could spend more time managing the restaurant. The restaurant had thrived.

But it had taken a toll on their relationship.

And had removed that which he had enjoyed doing the most: cooking.

"You moved on. I moved on." It was all Sebastian could think of saying.

"You had to date a siren."

"Em?"

"Oh, so we're calling her Em now?"

Sebastian bristled. "You have Jared. I have Em. Yes, Em. What's your beef, Talia?"

"Nothing, I guess."

"You broke up with me. Almost every time we've had this conversation it was because you left me for someone else."

Then it dawned on Sebastian. Why hadn't he seen it before?

He had been a prop for Talia all along. A fallback. A backup boyfriend.

After a bad relationship, Talia would crawl back to Sebastian as if he'd take her back, as if nothing had happened, as if they were meant to be together all their lives.

And he'd fallen for it every time. Always waiting in the wings, never going anywhere, just hanging around until she called him back into her arms.

Always.

"Jared's just a fling, Seb."

"Do I want to hear that?"

"Is Emmeline a fling? She goes from boyfriend to boyfriend."

"I don't think she does."

"Now she's snagged you."

"Snag? That's a fighting word, Talia."

"Call it what you may. She's still a siren, and you're heading for a shipwreck."

"And you're not?" Sebastian blurted.

Talia looked stunned.

Putting down her drink, she picked up her purse, and walked away toward the front entrance of the restaurant that they had worked together for the last five years to build and establish.

She walked past the wall whose colors they had picked together back in the days when they had been an item, back in the days when they had a reason to hang out and make Saffron a successful restaurant.

Had their relationship been more business than personal? Talia had poured money into the restaurant, and Sebastian had put his chef skills to the test in the Saffron kitchen. Between the two of them, they had made Saffron an award-winning restaurant. Perhaps that business partnership had caused them to spend more time together than they should have.

Somehow, Sebastian found himself standing in the kitchen watching the hustle and bustle and clangs of stainless-steel pots and chefs yelling and hurrying. He felt surreal, as if he was watching an old film reel of happy memories.

How did I get here?

Wasn't he sitting at the bar a minute ago?

"Hey, boss! Is everything okay?" Chef Onada stopped in front of Sebastian. He was holding a container of vanilla beans.

Sebastian nodded. "Fine. Stopping by to see how everything is going."

"Perfect. Best job in the world."

"I agree. Carry on." Sebastian stepped back as servers passed by him, carrying trays of beautifully plated dishes of scallops and shrimp and fish.

I miss all these.

Sebastian wondered what it all meant. He had lost the kitchen and lost Talia. What else would he lose?

Did these things mean that much to him?

Losing the kitchen was one thing. He could always rebuild. But losing Talia might be more painful. Or was it?

He couldn't feel her anymore.

Funny.

It was as though what they had together had never been theirs in the first place. He had known Talia for seventeen years. They had grown into each other. Now they had grown up and grown away from each other.

Good or bad?

Sebastian couldn't remember when he left the kitchen but he found himself in a slow walk up the stairs to the top deck, where he had left Emmeline with Prince Charming.

Light music—a waltz—floated down toward his ears. He could hear applause amidst the undertones of the nearby ocean waves.

What's going on up there?

At the top of the stairs, Sebastian froze.

There, right in front of him and everyone else, Emmeline was in the arms of Jared Urquhart, whose thighs were lost in Emmeline's flowing black dress. She looked like an ethereal beauty floating on a dance floor as they twirled around the deck, the June breeze fingering her wavy hair. Above the dancing duo, the moon shone.

Sebastian had a good mind to walk up to them and tap Jared on the shoulder. But he knew better.

Emmeline is not mine.

No one is mine.

I'm all alone, God.

CHAPTER EIGHTEEN

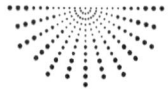

"*D*id you leave the lights on?" Sebastian asked as he parked his car in front of Emmeline's apartment after that long evening.

The dinner in his stomach had settled after his shock of having seen Emmeline dancing with Jared on the rooftop a couple of hours before.

The drive from Jekyll Island to St. Simon's Island had been quiet, and Sebastian had tried to make small talk until he realized that Emmeline was asleep.

The poor girl, working herself to death all week long.

Sebastian wondered if she ever had enough rest.

He had to wake her up. There was no choice. They had reached her dinky apartment.

"Huh?" Emmeline rubbed her eyes.

"Lights, Em. Did you leave your lights on?" Sebastian asked again.

"I don't remember. Why?" Emmeline gathered her purse.

Sebastian pointed his nose toward the second-floor balcony. There was that loser again in his bathrobe. He had on headphones, and he was picking his nose.

"Hope Barf—I mean Bart—up there didn't enter your apartment while you were gone."

Emmeline shrugged. "Sometimes he does. The flowers you sent me? They were on my table when I got home this afternoon."

"That's bad." *I knew it.*

"Don't worry about me. Take care of yourself and Talia." Emmeline opened the car door to get out.

A voice came from above. "Hello, Emmeline."

Sebastian could hear it with his windows halfway down. Bart's voice sounded floaty and icky-like.

"Hi, Bart. Staying up late?" Emmeline's voice was sweet and unassuming.

"Just making sure you got home safely. We take care of our tenants."

"Thank you. I'm fine."

Sebastian was about to put his car in reverse when he heard Bart speak again. "Is that your new boyfriend?"

"Uh-huh." Emmeline sounded noncommittal.

"If he is, why didn't he kiss you goodnight?"

Through the windshield, Sebastian saw Emmeline open her purse.

Her keys jingled in her fingers. "It's our first date. Don't worry, Bart."

"If this were *our* first date, Miss Emmeline, I would've kissed you good. So good you'd pass out."

Pass what?

Sebastian turned off the ignition, left the lights on, and stepped out of his car.

Emmeline's eyes looked startled in the headlights as he walked toward her, pulled her toward him, glided his fingers past her soft chin and neck, and wove them into her hair.

Sebastian wanted to say something to her, but he couldn't find the words to describe the way she looked in the light. Her hair was fine, her skin was soft...

Everything about her compelled him to pull her closer against his chest.

Oddly, everything seemed right, as if this were meant to be between them. He felt Emmeline relax into his chest as if she were supposed to be there all along.

Or is she playing the part?

Sebastian dipped his lips toward hers. *Gently does it.*

She gasped. It was very good acting indeed.

Bravo, Emmeline.

Their kiss was so real that Sebastian felt it all the way home to his house by the marshes, and then all the way to the morning hours when he woke up to the sound of his alarm clock.

Had it been a dream?

On his bed, he closed his eyes to remember the kiss.

It hurt because he couldn't have more of it. He wanted to drive back to Emmeline's apartment to draw her into his arms again.

And again.

It was a terrible thing to be thinking about for a moral Christian man who was supposed to be in love with someone else.

In love? With whom?

With a shadow from the past.

Somehow Sebastian couldn't bring himself to imagine kissing Talia anymore now that he had tasted what a heartfelt kiss felt like.

Then again, what if Talia was right?

Was Emmeline a siren, and was he heading for a shipwreck?

After all, Sebastian had made a deal with Emmeline to put on a show.

This is not real.

This is a stage play.

Sebastian should call off the whole ruse, and confess to Talia that he had done it to get back at her and to get her back.

Yet it wasn't Talia he wanted to talk to.

It was Emmeline he wanted to see and be with.

What is happening to me?

CHAPTER NINETEEN

*S*ebastian had broken all of Emmeline's ground rules. No touching. No hugging. No kissing.

They had both agreed on one exception: hand-holding. But they had gone beyond that.

He had kissed her last night, and now Emmeline wondered how long it would take before they broke the fourth wall, and exposed the entire charade to Talia.

If that happened, would Sebastian blame her for failing her end of the bargain? Would he still help her to find Claude?

Emmeline decided that it would be in their best interests if they stuck to the script.

Well, first she had to know what Sebastian's script was. He seemed to be playing it by ear. He was most affected by Talia's new boyfriend—for instance, in the Scrolls bookstore that Wednesday afternoon.

Emmeline recalled that awkward afternoon in the bookstore, when she had agreed to step into the café, where Sebastian was supposed to be waiting for her. Unfortunately, she had to help several customers along the way. Between going here and there to find books and gifts, she had tried to see what was going on.

She had seen Sebastian's face when Jared and Talia made out in front of him.

Perhaps they had been putting on a scene for him too.

And then there was that dinner on Friday night. Sebastian had been positively frowning when Emmeline had danced with Jared. No idea why, really.

Why would he be upset? Wasn't the whole idea to get Talia back?

For all practical purposes, the double date had backfired. Instead of Talia getting back together with Sebastian, Jared and Talia had left the restaurant separately, and Sebastian was still with Emmeline.

Oddly, Sebastian seemed happy to be with her.

And what was that about when Bart had taunted Sebastian and he took the bait outside her apartment? He should've left her alone and gone home.

Now Bart might think she was easy.

What's done is done.

Squeaking wheels broke her muse, and Emmeline blinked. Oh yes, she was pushing a cart of music folders to a rehearsal room at the SISO building.

The long hallway, stark and tunnel-like, made

Emmeline's mind wander into something else more interesting.

On Saturday and Sunday, she had been browsing through online advertisements, searching for a van to transport her harp. She couldn't ride her bicycle all the time. It rained in Georgia and the roads would be treacherous for cyclists, rain gear notwithstanding.

The last thing she wanted was offers from willing Bart and Rafferty to carry her harp for her when it rained. She might accept rides from Jared, maybe, but just because he looked nice and clean didn't mean he was a winner.

There isn't any good man around!

Good? She remembered what the Bible said. There was no one good but God.

Emmeline suddenly realized she was standing in the middle of the rehearsal room, holding a stack of music folders in her hands, facing all those music stands and seats, and daydreaming.

She scolded herself and got moving.

Quickly, without tripping over anything in the tight space, she finished putting the music folders on the stands. Then she went back to her cart, picked up more folders, and filled the rest of the music stands. This was for tomorrow evening's rehearsal—which didn't include harp music, unfortunately.

If SISO used more harps in their repertoires, she'd be paid more.

Oh well.

The clock on the wall said it was five. She hadn't had dinner, but there was no time to walk home and eat. She was behind by an hour because she had been practicing her harp for the Brock-Flannagan wedding that coming Saturday.

Without a car, she had to depend on someone else's benevolence to pick her up and take her to the Theater by the Sea rehearsal tonight at Rafferty's house. Emmeline wished she could avoid Rafferty altogether, but he had an empty basement that led out to a patio with plenty of outdoor space for seventeen people to rehearse.

Nigel and Misty Miller had started Theater by the Sea with their own funds, and anything anyone could contribute or donate always helped the fledgling theatrical troupe.

Later in the fall, after Emmeline had gone back to school, Theater by the Sea would tour the southeastern United States with members who could afford to take time off from work.

Either way, she'd be done with Rafferty's unwelcome attention.

Meanwhile, there's tonight.

Rafferty would probably be overprepared with his rendition of Mr. Wickham. Well, Emmeline wasn't going to give him any leeway about it. She could be · professional and as long as Nigel was satisfied with her performance, she could pull off a don't-touch-me Regency evening.

In fact, she decided she would cosplay Elizabeth Bennet the entire evening and treat Rafferty like the Mr. Collins he should be. That should throw him off.

Then again, her role in the play was Lydia Bennet, and that character ended up with Wickham, also known as Rafferty.

Story of my life.

She rolled the cart back to the music library, turned off the lights, and locked the door. She checked the doorknob again. Just in case.

Of course, it's locked.

At the vending machine, she bought a ham sandwich and a bottle of Coke. She had about twenty minutes before Nigel and Misty Miller would pick her up from the SISO studio.

Emmeline liked the Millers. Nigel was like an older brother to her. Misty was soft-spoken except when she was onstage. Then she was a veritable Mrs. Bennet, fit for film. Emmeline often thought that Misty could go far, even to the Alliance Theater in Atlanta and beyond.

Emmeline reminded herself to invite Misty to the Seaside Chapel women's Bible study on Tuesday nights at Olivia Gonzalez's house. She wasn't sure if Misty would go, but if she didn't ask, Misty might not go at all. Misty didn't know anyone else at Seaside Chapel. Still, the Bible study was open to all women, not just members of that little church by the sea.

Emmeline's cell phone rang as she was finishing up the stale ham sandwich. She let it ring.

It stopped and rang again. She picked it up without looking.

"I'm at the door. Let's go."

Sebastian!

"Sorry. Go where? I have a rehearsal tonight," Emmeline said.

"Exactly. I'm your chauffeur." Over the phone, Sebastian seemed overly enthusiastic.

"What's going on? Where's Misty?"

"Who?"

"Why are you picking me up?"

"I called Nigel and asked him when and where the rehearsal is." Sebastian's voice calmed.

Emmeline tried to find the words to respond to that. "Why call him? You could've asked me."

"After last night, you might want some space."

"Yes. And this is space? You're going out of your way to pick me up to take me to a rehearsal?"

"We have to stick to the script." Sebastian sounded serious. "You know there's a last-minute change of rehearsal venue?"

"What? Hang on." Emmeline checked her text messages.

For some reason, maybe a dead cell zone or something, she hadn't seen the messages. She scrolled.

There it was, the message she had missed.

Two hours ago, the location of the rehearsal tonight had been moved to an address she wasn't familiar with.

"Hello?" Sebastian asked.

"Looks like I missed a message. The rehearsal has been moved to a new location," Emmeline said. "So what's going on?"

"Jared's going on."

"Jared...?" *Oh no.*

"Yep, Jared. He is now underwriting quite a large chunk of Theater by the Sea productions, and the rehearsal tonight is at his house."

"So this is his address."

"Yes. And guess what? Talia will probably be there. Or not. But you and I are going. That's all. So lock up and come downstairs. Have you eaten?"

"Yes."

"Well, you shouldn't have. Dinner's on Jared. We'll go and find out what he's up to."

"So we're sleuthing now? On top of our pretenses?"

Sebastian laughed. "Don't turn philosophical on me. It's all pretty straightforward. Oh yes, and Nigel said to tell you not to forget to bring your script. He said you do that a lot. Do you, Em?"

"Do I what?"

"Forget things."

Emmeline didn't respond.

"Like last night. Do you still remember?" Sebastian asked.

"What about it?"

"Outside your apartment?"

Emmeline didn't need the reminder. "That."

"Yes, that. I meant it."

"Afterwards?" Emmeline wasn't sure what Sebastian was really asking.

"No, when we you-know-what, I meant it."

The kiss?

He meant it?

Emmeline didn't care for all of this confusing juxtaposition that Sebastian had dragged her into. But it had been her fault for agreeing to the trade, and now she must live with it if she wanted to have any hope of seeing her brother again.

It was ridiculous that her family's future depended on Sebastian Langston's winging it.

"You do remember," Sebastian added.

"Yes."

"Me too," Sebastian said. "But have no fear. If it bothers you too much, know that it'll be over soon, and we can both move on."

CHAPTER TWENTY

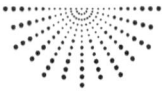

*E*mmeline settled onto an ottoman by the accordion doors that separated the Urquhart entertainment room from the outdoor room and pool with the fountain. It was quite a luxurious rehearsal space that Jared Urquhart had generously offered to Theater by the Sea.

The cast members scattered around Emmeline in the terrace room, sitting on expensive chairs and antique sofas. The rest of the cast hadn't arrived. Some would get off work later, and some had other obligations.

Eventually, they'd start rehearsing at seven o'clock, so there was plenty of time for Emmeline to mill around and eat a second dinner.

Only she didn't want to mill around.

Emmeline wanted to get out of here badly, but she was stuck. She needed the money from the summer play. Juggling all these part-time jobs was a strain, but it would only be for a while. After that, she'd be at UGA.

Well, she'd have to get more jobs to make up for what her scholarships wouldn't pay for, but at least she'd be closer to her Master of Music degree—unless, of course, she could always try to win more scholarships.

For now, she was going through the motions of working in the SISO music library on Mondays and Fridays, shelving books at Scrolls on Tuesdays through Thursdays, repeating lines on stage on Friday nights and Saturdays, and playing at weddings or SISO concerts whenever they needed a harpist.

No rest for the weary.

Across from her, Nigel Miller and his wife sat down on a love seat next to a grand piano. Right next to the Steinway grand was a gilded Salvi Apollonia concert grand harp that Emmeline had been itching to touch.

Nigel had a mound on his plate, while Misty's plate only had vegetables on it. They sat shoulder to shoulder and looked cute together. They complemented each other well, Emmeline thought. Someday...

Not for me.

"Ingrid has a migraine," the Theater by the Sea director announced, as if to Emmeline.

"Not again. I'll be praying for her."

"Pray for yourself too, Em. You're standing in for her as Elizabeth Bennet tonight."

Standing in.

A metaphor of my life.

Always the second best.

"Ingrid felt bad that she couldn't make it tonight," Nigel added.

Ingrid? Oh, Ingrid.

Emmeline asked God to forgive her for being self-centered. Tonight wasn't about her standing in. Ingrid had a medical problem, and that was worse than Emmeline's feeling sorry for herself that she was second best.

Then again, she wasn't going to be playing the part of Lydia tonight.

That amounted for something.

While Emmeline was sorry that Ingrid couldn't make it to rehearsal, she was not sorry she didn't have to play Lydia opposite Rafferty's Wickham tonight. Anything to avoid him was most welcomed.

Thank You, Lord. And please heal Ingrid.

Thank You, Jesus. Amen.

Her mind went quickly to the script she had brought. It was on the marble floor next to her purse at her feet. She was trying to figure out how to balance her dinner plate on her lap while reaching down to get the script, when a hand appeared and picked up the folder for her.

"Thanks," Emmeline said.

"No problem." Sebastian gave her that affable smile she'd been getting to know all week.

He sat down next to her on the floor, but he was tall enough and the ottoman was low enough, that he only needed to tip his head up slightly to talk to her face to face.

That smile he gave Emmeline wiped away the discomfiture that had hung over her from the moment she stepped into the Urquhart cottage on Seaside Island, and saw Talia's scowl as Jared greeted Emmeline with a kiss on each of her cheeks.

The first thing Emmeline had done after that was to run to the powder room to wash off Jared's saliva, much to Sebastian's amusement.

Talia had continued to scowl as a stream of fetching men and women filed into Jared's house for the free dinner and rehearsal.

Emmeline wondered how long Nigel was going to keep them tonight. Sometimes they had rehearsed until midnight because he wasn't satisfied with their performance. Could Talia stay glowered that many hours? Or would she leave?

Emmeline was finishing up her almond chicken, and scanning Elizabeth Bennet's lines in the script, when Jared walked into the room, Talia right behind him. He seemed to be searching for something. Or someone.

"There you are." Jared made a beeline for Emmeline, but Talia stopped in her tracks.

Emmeline tensed as Jared spoke.

"Miss O'Hanlon, when you finish your dinner,

would you do us the honor and play something on my harp?"

"Well, I don't have anything prepared for this evening."

"Don't you have events coming up?"

"Just a couple of weddings. All I have are wedding songs." Emmeline laughed.

"I like wedding songs."

As Jared spoke, Emmeline saw Talia walk out of the room. Emmeline glanced at Sebastian to see what he was going to do.

He was oblivious to Talia. It seemed that his attention was on Jared.

"Give us a preview of the wedding songs," Jared said. "Play a few. Two, three, whatever."

"Let me think about it."

"Thank you. Much appreciated." Jared was off, perhaps to look for Talia, perhaps not.

Emmeline ate the rest of her dinner in silence.

"You don't have to do it," Sebastian said quietly. "Don't let him pressure you."

Pressure.

Emmeline looked around the room. She loved working with Nigel and Misty Miller, but she had a bad feeling about Theater by the Sea now being underwritten by Jared in this complicated situation she was in.

Would they always rehearse here at his house every week for the next two months?

Would she have to play the harp at his beck and call every time she came here? Could she stand it?

She shouldn't have danced with him on Friday night.

"What would you like to hear?" Emmeline asked Sebastian.

He seemed visibly moved that she had asked him. "Maybe what you played on Monday at the SISO studio?"

Soon, Emmeline did.

"Oriental" came through on the harp, which had been long unused. She played it slowly and somehow it quietened the chatter in the room.

Sometime after she had begun strumming and plucking, Jared came back to the room, and sat down somewhere near his pool table. He didn't make any attempt to get near her, and for that, Emmeline was grateful.

Emmeline added arpeggios here and there wher-ever she felt she could fit them into the time signature.

When she was done, Sebastian asked her to play it again, all six minutes or so of it. And as she did, he crossed the floor to sit on the piano bench next to the harp.

Jared didn't leave his barstool.

From the corner of her eye, Emmeline saw that Jared was watching Sebastian.

In the middle of the piece, Emmeline couldn't help noticing that Sebastian was staring at her. There was a heartbreak there, but she couldn't see past the wall of pain.

Obviously, he was a romantic as he had wanted his ex-fiancée back, but here in this big and crowded room, he was alone in his quest.

Emmeline felt sorry for him, and wanted to help him.

Even if Talia didn't deserve this man.

CHAPTER TWENTY-ONE

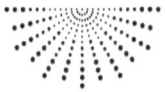

"*I* knew I'd find you in here." The voice was shrill, the tone hostile.

Sebastian didn't have to see Talia's face to know that she had been fuming. She had found him, she wanted a few words with him, and she wouldn't take no for an answer. So there. That was classic Talia.

In retrospect, Sebastian shouldn't have hidden in the kitchen. But the kitchen was where he found comfort, even though this was not his type of kitchen. He was still in Jared's house, and he wasn't going to leave without Emmeline.

Talia parked her five-inch Michael Kors espadrilles on the Spanish terra cotta tile floor, going toe to toe with Sebastian's Crocs, and still came up to only his shoulders.

He was leaning against the central island and had been looking out the panoramic window to the backyard pool, where the Theater by the Sea cast members were rehearsing their Jane Austen mishmash under a pergola.

Over Talia's head, he could see Jared standing around holding a script, as if he were going to be in the play too. Above the backyard, the coastal Georgia sun was setting, casting a vermillion dome over the rehearsal theater.

"Look at me, Sebastian Langston."

Sebastian rolled his eyes down.

"Why her?" Talia snipped.

"Her who?" Sebastian knew to whom Talia was referring, but he wanted her to say it for the record. That way, she couldn't backpedal later on, and say that she had been thinking of someone else.

Really, he was sick and tired of her equivocation these five or six years they had tried to be serious with each other in their often fragile non-relationship.

He hadn't seen it then, but he saw it now.

There was nowhere to go but out.

"Emmeline O'Hanlon. Why her?" Talia poked her sharp fingernails at Sebastian's plaid shirt.

"Why not? She's single. I'm single."

"No nefarious motives?" *Poke. Poke.*

"Like what?" Sebastian tried to fold his arms in front of himself, but Talia was too close.

Her petite frame was all tight and rigid, and she didn't move an inch back.

"Like trying to lure Jared away from me?"

Jared?

So this is about Jared.

"You couldn't be more wrong, Talia." Sebastian stood his ground. "We broke up six months ago, remember?"

"I thought you wanted me back. I can show you all the emails you sent me up to a week ago. I'm guessing you brought in Emmeline to break up my relationship with Jared so that you could have me back, and he could have her."

"That's a crazy plot."

"Crazy? It's unfolding before our very eyes." Talia pointed to the window.

Yes, indeed. Jared was out there, inching his way toward Emmeline.

Until Sebastian had met Emmeline, he'd truly believed that Talia was the one God had in store for him. Now he realized that Talia wasn't the only eligible woman in the world. And he didn't even want her family fortune. Only love.

He wanted only love.

It was the truth. Amidst all the make-believe, this was the truth that Sebastian felt in his heart.

"We've both moved on," Sebastian reminded her again, willing himself to believe it too.

"I have. Have you?" Talia lifted her chin. "Yet, you think that by running off Jared, you could get me back."

"Run him off?"

"You're pushing Emmeline at my Jared." Talia

shook her head. "You and I, Seb. We can't work out. I can't make the commitment you want of me."

"We don't have to worry about that anymore, do we?" Sebastian knew Talia's pattern. She was prone to wander, but then inevitably, she would come back into his arms.

Only this time he wasn't sure if he wanted her anymore. They had broken up for the last time.

This entire ruse was a bad idea. He should have moved on. Gone out with Emmeline like a proper gentleman, not coerced her into playing this game. He'd taken advantage of her emotions and her sorrow over her missing brother.

Now the only way to end this was to stop going out with Emmeline because they weren't really a couple.

Lord, why didn't You stop me from doing something this stupid?

"So you think Emmeline will marry you? Give you the gobs of kids you want?"

Sebastian chuckled. "We're just going out."

"So were we. On and off since we were seventeen, Seb. Should I ask what went wrong with us?"

Many things. Sebastian didn't know where to begin. "Kids, for one. We fought over whether we should have kids or not. It seemed premature and silly."

"I told you how I feel about us. Marriage, no. Kids, maybe."

Sebastian bristled. "You know my beliefs. Marriage comes before kids."

Talia stepped back. "I'm not sure if I buy all that anymore, Seb. It's too traditional for me. I think I'm going to stop attending Seaside Chapel. I think they conduct too many weddings."

"That's a lame excuse, Talia. You used to like weddings."

"They're overrated, Seb. Look what happened to my parents. Separated and heading toward divorce. Dad was even a deacon at church. There's something wrong with that picture."

"You can't say that's the way it goes for everyone. And you can't project all these human sins on a holy God."

"Whatever, Seb." Talia started to walk away. "I'll see you at the Saffron meeting tomorrow."

Sebastian realized how difficult this was going to be. Talia was no longer in a relationship with him, but she was still his business partner and majority shareholder of Saffron on Jekyll. The restaurant had to continue.

"Is Onada really going to quit on us?" Talia asked, switching focus.

"Who said he was?"

"I'm hearing he's now asking for a pay raise."

"He's worth it." Sebastian knew that several other prominent restaurants had oohed and aahed over Onada's signature dishes.

Until Sebastian got back into the kitchen, their restaurant's success rested on Chef Onada's shoulders.

Sebastian didn't want to deal with interviewing chefs for a replacement at this time of his life.

"Let's give him a raise," he concluded.

"We'll talk about it," Talia said. "I'm open to suggestions."

And she also had veto power.

Why Sebastian had agreed to let Talia have the majority of the shares of Saffron on Jekyll, he couldn't remember. It had been his moment of weakness. Now she had the final say on everything, including chefs' and cooks' salaries.

At the doorway, Talia stopped. "How did you end up with Emmeline, anyway?"

"Well, we were talking one day, and here we are." Sebastian had rarely left out details from Talia, but this time he would.

The whole inception would implicate him, and cause much strife between him and Talia in their business partnership, not to mention drag Emmeline through the mud.

It was only recently that this ill-advised idea had born fruit in Sebastian. There he had been, sitting in Sunday school listening to the long list of prayer requests when, across the room, Emmeline had burst into tears.

It had been the fifth anniversary of her brother Claude's disappearance from a concert he'd been conducting in metro Atlanta. They'd looked everywhere for him. Her parents had been growing weary and in poor health. Their wedding anniversary was coming up, and Emmeline had wished that her brother could be home for Christmas.

And here they were.

"This conversation is not over," Talia hissed from the arched door. "You keep her away from my Jared, or I'll never forgive you, ever."

Her Jared?

When Talia left the kitchen, Sebastian turned back to the window above the farmhouse sink. The sky outside was dark now. Overhanging string lights on the pergola enabled Sebastian to see the stage actors crackling with mirth.

Sebastian's eyes zigzagged from face to face looking for Emmeline.

She wasn't there.

CHAPTER TWENTY-TWO

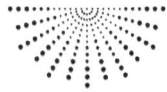

"*I* would like to hear your demo CD. Might get you some sponsorship."

Jared was standing a bit too close to Emmeline for comfort but if she stepped back, she'd topple over the topiary plants by the accordion glass doors.

She had just finished a scene rehearsal, and Nigel had given her a break while he worked on poor Rafferty flubbing his Wickham lines.

Emmeline was on her way to go indoors for a drink of water before her next scene, when Jared stopped her at the door to tell her how much he liked her playing his harp.

She tried not to read too much into what Jared was saying. She didn't want to have anything to do with him, if possible, since she had an obligation to Sebastian.

Speaking of whom, where is he?

"I'm serious," Jared said, as if Emmeline hadn't heard him. "Everybody needs sponsorship."

Emmeline felt a hand on her shoulder. She knew whose it was.

"Sponsorship of what?" Sebastian asked, standing closer to Emmeline.

"I want to hear more of her music," Jared said.

"In that case, you're welcome to attend SISO concerts whenever I play," Emmeline said. "We have several outdoor concerts next month, though I'll be in only one. I'll get you the date later. The rest of the time, I'll be at private weddings."

Emmeline was also playing gigs at Saffron, but that was not her information to share. She glanced at Sebastian and he didn't say anything about it. Maybe it slipped his mind.

Or maybe he didn't want Jared there, when she did play at Saffron.

"In a couple of weeks my church is having another outdoor service on the beach. We call it the Fire Pit Service. I'll be playing a Celtic lap harp. Would you like to come to that?" Emmeline glanced at Sebastian again.

He didn't look happy at all that she had invited Jared.

"A lap harp?" Jared asked.

His emphasis on *lap* seemed to cause Sebastian to react visibly.

From the corner of Emmeline's eye, she spotted Nigel waving to her.

"Gentlemen, I have to go." She swallowed. "I really need to get some water for my throat. Seb, could you please get me a glass of water?"

"I'll get it." Jared started going.

"No, I'll get it." Sebastian.

"I'll—"

"Boys? Children?" Emmeline said. "I'll get it. Just show me where the kitchen is."

"I'll show you," Jared said.

"I'll go," Sebastian said, and he was gone.

Emmeline laughed all the way back to their makeshift "stage" by the pool. *Juveniles.*

Jared was right behind her. "What's wrong with him, huh?"

Emmeline didn't respond. She was looking at her script. Reading Elizabeth's lines meant she wasn't practicing her own lines. Still, she was paid either way, and that was enough for her.

Someday, she'd just have one job and it'd be playing the harp.

"If I get a lap harp, would you teach me to play it?"

Emmeline stopped walking. "I'm not sure if Talia would appreciate that request."

"Talia? What about her?"

What does Talia see in this guy, anyway?

"Or would you prefer to teach me on the harp I already have?"

Oh boy. Jared is persistent.

"I understand that our theater will be rehearsing here every week," Emmeline said. "I would rather not feel pressured into playing your harp or teaching you to play. My dad is the harp teacher. Not me. I don't have enough patience to teach."

"Emmeline!" Nigel's voice was loud and carried through the evening air.

Everyone else yelled her name as if echoing him.

"Coming!"

Just as Mr. Darcy and Lady Catherine were taking up their positions beside Emmeline's Elizabeth, Sebastian came out with a tray of cold bottled water for everyone.

How thoughtful.

Sebastian winked at her for whatever reason. She didn't have time to figure it out as she began that banter with Lady Catherine in a scene at Rosings. Emmeline couldn't imagine how big the Lady's residence might be, but the script called for Elizabeth to appear intimidated.

Intimidated?

That's easy.

Emmeline didn't have to pretend. She'd been intimidated all evening.

CHAPTER TWENTY-THREE

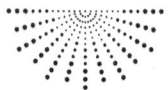

*E*mmeline adjusted her backpack over her shoulders, grabbed her bicycle helmet, opened the front door of her apartment, and came face to face with Bart.

She shrieked.

How long had he been standing outside her door?

Bart made a show of stepping back, his flabby triceps jiggling out of his muscle tee shirt. He was wearing a pair of faded pajama bottoms.

"What do you want?" Emmeline pushed her bicycle out of her apartment, slammed her door shut, and locked it.

What's the point? Bart still has the key.

"What do I want?" Bart stepped closer to Emmeline. "Many things."

His cigarette breath made Emmeline cough.

"But I digress. This morning, however, it's about what you want, Miss Emmeline."

"Make it quick. I have to get to work." Emmeline pushed past him.

Bart grabbed the bike and stopped her. He pointed to a black van parked in the courtyard. "Behold, your new van, Miss Emmeline."

"You're giving me a van?" Emmeline laughed.

"You can have it for five hundred dollars."

I knew it.

"Does it even run?" Emmeline leaned her bicycle against the wall outside her apartment.

She followed Bart to the cargo van. The vehicle might drain her gas bill, but it looked like it was big enough to transport her harp or even for her to live in— if she had nowhere to go.

Yet, the closer she walked toward the van, the more it seemed too good to be true. There were little round holes pockmarking the side of the van, holes scattered all over in random patterns looking like constellations, holes that hadn't disappeared in the black spray paint.

To begin with, rain could seep in through those holes and ruin her harp inside.

"If you don't like black, we could have it painted over with your favorite color." Bart rumbled his way to the back of the van.

Periwinkle color all over? I think not.

Emmeline stepped forward after Bart opened the cargo door. The entire interior had been stripped down to the frame. There were dark stains of some sort here and there on the floor.

"What are those splotches?" Emmeline asked.

"Grease."

"Red grease?" Emmeline raised her eyebrows.

"Grease comes in many shades and hues."

"It doesn't look like grease, though."

"Nothing some bleach won't take out." Bart waved his arms about. "See all that space, huh? You can put two or three harps in here. What do you think?"

"I don't know."

"Look. This is a work van. Normally you'd pay at least forty thousand dollars for a brand new one. But this one is special."

"I can see that."

"Special, Miss Emmeline. Just for you. Five hundred dollars."

"Doesn't look like it's worth that much." Emmeline backed away.

"Trust me. It's worth more than that. I'm doing this as a favor for a friend. He wants to get rid of it quick."

"Quickly."

"What?"

"Get rid of it quickly."

"What I said." Bart shut the back van doors. He pointed to the roof of the van. "You can put two fifty-foot ladders on there."

"Why would I need even one fifty-foot ladder?"

"You never know." Bart went to the front. He lifted the hood. "Come see this engine. It's a beauty."

"I've seen enough, Bart. I have to run."

"Two seconds."

Two seconds?

Beep. Beep. That's two seconds.

Emmeline sighed and humored him. She peeked into the engine. She had no idea what she was looking at. It looked clean, and somewhat shiny in parts. It looked like someone had packed extra stuff under the hood, but which part was added on? She had no clue.

Bart lost her in his ramblings about pistons and crankshafts and superchargers and whatnots.

Emmeline felt dizzy. "Stop."

"You're impressed." Bart smiled.

"No. I have no idea what you're talking about."

"Okay. Let's just say the engine has been souped up."

"Is this a getaway vehicle?"

Bart seemed hurt by her question.

"Let me think about it and let you know, okay? I'm going to be late if I don't leave now." Emmeline walked back to her bicycle for her own getaway.

"I'll leave the van here only until tomorrow. Is that enough time for you to call your mechanic?"

"I didn't say I want it, Bart."

"You need transportation. Maybe this van is from God."

"You told me you don't believe in God." Emmeline put on her helmet and strapped it in.

"Make me, then, Sweet Emmeline."

Emmeline laughed. "You can't make someone believe in God. I can tell you about Him, but you have to decide for yourself."

"You call yourself a Christian, and yet you never invited me to your Bible study." Bart curled his lips. "You know, the one you go to every Tuesday night from seven to nine?"

"It's for women only, Bart."

"All the better. I can handle women."

"There's a Friday morning Bible study for men. They meet at the Scrolls bookstore. You could attend that."

"Why should I? I'm not interested in men."

"A Bible study is not a social club. It's for—"

"Don't shove your religion down my throat. So what's it gonna be, Miss Emmeline? If you don't buy this van, don't expect me to give you a ride when it rains."

"Don't worry about me. I'll be fine."

"This is a good van. Zero to sixty in seconds."

Seriously?

"Thanks, Bart. I'll let you know, okay? If someone else wants it, that's the way it goes." Emmeline climbed on her bicycle. She looked around for her helmet, when she realized it was already on her head.

"You can tell me the truth." Bart looked dejected. "You don't have the money."

"I don't have the money, and I don't want the van," Emmeline said.

"Four hundred?"

Emmeline shook her head.

"Three hundred?"

"Sorry."

"How about I buy it for you? We can share the title."

In your dreams.

Emmeline laughed, and peddled quickly out of the driveway.

CHAPTER TWENTY-FOUR

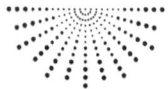

*T*wenty minutes!

Emmeline lost twenty minutes chatting with Bart, and she was late clocking in at Scrolls. There was no time to change into the clean clothes she had brought in her backpack. There was hardly any time to wipe off her sweaty face as she made a mad dash to the customer service desk.

No one was working behind the desk, and there were two people waiting to be served.

Whatever happened to Wednesday being a slow day, the day when nobody showed up at customer service for help?

Someone help me get organized!

By the time Emmeline assisted the second customer to order the children's books she wanted, there was a third person at customer service, and she was bad news.

Still, Talia Cavanaugh-Perry looked amazing in her jogging outfit—except for that pinched face.

"May I help you, Talia?" Emmeline asked as calmly as she could.

"Yes, Emmeline. Stay away from him."

Which one?

"I'm working at the moment. My break isn't until eleven o'clock."

"I suppose you don't know that I own half this store. If I want to talk to you right now, you drop everything and talk to me."

Oh. I had no idea.

Emmeline had thought Talia only came and went in her father's bookstore. "Yes, ma'am."

Talia rapped the table. Spoke through clenched teeth. Her voice was low. "Stay away from my Jared."

Jared.

Obviously, Sebastian's scheme to win back Talia hadn't moved an inch.

"Are we still in high school?" Emmeline had no idea how that came out of her mouth.

Forgive me, Lord Jesus.

I thought I was over my sharp tongue.

"I can fire you on the spot," Talia snapped.

"For what?"

"For being late for work. This is the third time this month."

So she checked my schedule? Looked for ways to get rid of me?

"I'm sorry. I'll stay late to make up for it." It meant being late for church tonight or skipping it altogether. But she needed this job.

"It doesn't work that way. You can't just come and go. This is a business."

It dawned on her that she'd better check if Talia had the power to fire her. As far as Emmeline was concerned, that role rested on Argo Perry, Talia's dad, with advisement from the manager of the store.

Talia was neither her dad nor the manager.

"I'm sorry, ma'am." Emmeline kept her voice down.

"Sorry doesn't cut it," Talia said. "But I'll give you another chance if you stay away from him."

"Jared or Sebastian?"

"Jared, woman. Why do I care about Seb? We broke up."

"It seems he still cares for you."

"He does?" Talia frowned. "Whatever for?"

Emmeline shrugged. "Talks about you all the time."

"Really? Well, tell him I've moved on." She pointed fingers—daggers—at Emmeline. "Get between Jared and me, and I'll see to it you don't work here anymore."

"If I lose this job, I'll have to take more roles in Theater by the Sea. As you know, we now rehearse our plays in Jared's backyard. I'm going to be at all the rehearsals at his house, which could be several times a week."

Talia's lips moved but Emmeline couldn't hear anything.

"All summer," Emmeline added for good measure. "I'm not complaining, since I need the income. Story of my life, Talia. Have you ever had to work four part-time jobs to make ends meet?"

"Aren't you going back to school?"

"Yep. First week of August." For the longest time, it couldn't come soon enough.

Now, Emmeline wasn't sure. She was starting to get to know Sebastian—never mind.

"Then you're gone by August?" Talia asked.

"Gone. Out of your sight."

"What about Seb? I thought you two are going out?"

"Yes, we are. Whatever God wants for us is where we'll go."

Forgive me, Lord.

I shouldn't have played the God card.

Then again, in her heart, Emmeline genuinely believed it.

Whatever God wants is what I want.

Talia stood there in some sort of thought. There were no other customers behind her now. If she wanted a standoff, Emmeline could give it to her all day. Sitting at customer service on Wednesdays was usually uneventful.

"Maybe I can help you, girl," Talia finally said.

"Help me how?"

"If you work more hours here, you wouldn't need to be in the theater."

Emmeline nodded. "Or work in the music library at SISO or play harp at weddings, though I enjoy both."

"I'll keep all that in mind." Talia strutted away.

"Thank you, ma'am." Emmeline wasn't sure if Talia heard her.

Having ameliorated Talia's concerns, Emmeline couldn't help feeling better about her day. It had started poorly with Bart trying to pawn off the getaway van on her. It was improving now with potentially more hours and pay at Scrolls.

It would be sad for her to leave Theater by the Sea, but truth be told, she'd rather work at Scrolls. No lines to memorize, less of Rafferty to fend off. And her work life would be simplified down to three part-time jobs instead of four.

By the time her break came, Emmeline was on top of the world. Sebastian had texted her and confirmed that Helen Hu would be coming to town Thursday evening and could meet them after Emmeline got off work at Scrolls.

Dinner would be at Sebastian's house. He was cooking.

Emmeline had never been to Sebastian's house. She didn't even know where he lived, whether it was on Seaside Island, St. Simon's, or Jekyll. She knew that Skye lived in the Village near the grocery stores where she shopped for her clients, but Emmeline hadn't asked about her brother.

Why should she? If not for trying to find her own brother for their parents' sake, Emmeline would not have crossed paths with Sebastian Langston.

Then a thought sprung into her head.

God knows who to bring into my life.

CHAPTER TWENTY-FIVE

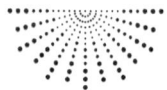

$\mathcal{B}$y the time Emmeline cycled home from church on Wednesday night, she was exhausted. She had been working all day starting at ten in the morning at Scrolls and ending at ten o'clock at night at Seaside Chapel, rehearsing with the sanctuary orchestra for the upcoming Sunday morning church service, and then with Skye for their duet in next Wednesday night's Fire Pit Service.

Twenty minutes of cycling home in the summer air gave her time to pray and thank God for a fruitful day. She couldn't wait for Thursday evening when she could talk to Helen Hu about finding Claude.

Thank You, Lord Jesus. Thank You. Thank You.

Emmeline showered to soap off all the gunk she had probably picked up on her skin and hair while cycling on the streets.

She brushed her teeth as quickly as she could. Drank a glass of water. And crashed onto her bed, shutting out the world.

Until she heard her door rattle.

Something crashed.

She sprung out of her bed, cell phone in hand. She peeked out of her bedroom door. There were shadows in her living room. She shut her door and locked it.

She punched in 911 on her cell phone.

"Someone's inside my house," she gasped, giving the dispatcher details.

She couldn't stay in this closet bedroom. There were no windows, no exit. The only way to get out of here was through the front door or the windows there.

She slid into her sneakers, put her cell phone into her pajama shorts pocket, and prayed like crazy.

Help me, Lord.

"Emmeline, oh Emmeline...!" Slurry voice—unmistakably Bart's—ricocheted in her ears.

Oh. It's just Bart.

Maybe she should cancel the 911 call for help.

Emmeline unlocked her bedroom door.

There he was, standing in her living room, Bart the intruder. At the end of an outstretched arm was a keychain with a key dangling on it.

"Your new van!" he wailed.

"Did you just enter my apartment without my permission?"

"I own this p-place." Bart swayed. "You're j-just a renter, Em-Emmeline."

Emmeline skirted Bart and made her way to the front door. "You're invading my privacy, Bart. Please leave now."

"I'm d-dropping off the key—is all, Em-Em-Emmeline." He began to sing.

"You're drunk." Emmeline swung the front door open.

Bart lunged and grabbed her.

She screamed. And ran. And screamed.

She pounded on the nearest door.

Nobody responded.

She dashed to the next door.

No one there.

She glanced back.

There was Bart, coming after her, pointing to the van and singing something off-key.

Suddenly he sprinted toward her.

Emmeline freaked out, ran down the driveway, tripped, and fell forward on the slope. She stretched out her palms to break her fall and slid chest down on the grimy, dirty driveway.

She scrambled to her feet and kept running, quite aware that she had lost her right shoe. Not going back.

She sprinted into the night down the street as Bart's voice faded into the distance.

The next subdivision was up ahead. The roads

were dark and empty. A dog barked from behind a chain-link fence.

That one.

Instinctively, she headed for the house with the barking dog. She rang the doorbell, pounded on the door. Glanced behind her. Nobody was around her but herself out here on the porch.

She reached into her pocket. Her cell phone was still there. She hit 911 again.

Her palms and knees burned.

The door cracked. A chain in her way.

"Help me!" Two words spurted out of Emmeline's mouth.

"Do you have an ID?" The man asked.

"What?" Emmeline breathed in and out, and tried to calm down. "I live in the apartments next door. Someone invaded my home. I escaped and ran here for help. I've called 911 twice. I need someplace safe to stay until the police arrive. Help me."

"I don't see anyone chasing you."

"He could be coming down the road right now. I don't know. Help me!"

"Let me ask my wife." The door slammed in her face.

Emmeline's eyes darted back and forth. The dog was still barking. Maybe this was a bad idea. The dog could give away her location.

The door opened again. This time a woman in a housecoat greeted her with a shotgun pointed at her.

"I just called the police. They'll be here in minutes. You can sit inside and wait."

"Thank you, ma'am."

"Would you like some water?"

"Yes, please," Emmeline answered into the double barrel inches from her face.

CHAPTER TWENTY-SIX

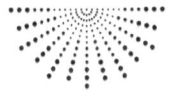

"*C*-consensual!" Bart repeated himself ad nauseam after he looked like he had failed the breathalyzer test.

He staggered his way toward the Glynn County police officer taking his statement. "It w-was consensual."

Sebastian clenched his fists in his cargo shorts pockets as he watched the scene before his eyes.

Behind Bart and the officer, Emmeline's apartment door was wide open, revealing the small folding table and worn thrift-shop couch, where they had found Bart. He had apparently returned to the apartment and fallen asleep on the couch, leaving the door open for the police to enter when they arrived shortly thereafter.

Emmeline had called 911 twice, the first time from her own apartment and the second time from the house she had found shelter in. The neighbor with the shotgun had also called the police, for good measure.

The police had picked her up at that house, and brought her back to the apartment. The paramedics arrived shortly afterwards. They'd probably thought something huge was happening.

No one had died, but this was big enough for Sebastian.

And he didn't know how to deal with it.

He turned toward Emmeline sitting at the back of the open ambulance. The paramedics were putting a giant Band-Aid on her bleeding knee. She was staring at her skinned palms. Sebastian was sure they'd hurt in the morning.

He'd only been with Emmeline a week and a half, but he'd come to care for her. This kind of situation made it harder for him to let her go.

It bothered Sebastian that someone as sweet as Emmeline could be in such a predicament. It broke his heart.

Emmeline stood up and limped. "Do you want the blanket back?"

"No, you keep it." The paramedic disposed of the gauze and iodine swabs.

"Thank you so much, Phil." Emmeline's voice was soft. "Say, next Wednesday night, my church is having an outdoor Fire Pit Service. Might it be something you'd like to come to? I'll play my harp, we're going to sing and eat, and talk about life and such."

"Life and such?" The paramedic smiled.

"Life and such." Emmeline nodded. "Seaside Chapel. Right next to Massengale Park."

"I know where Seaside Chapel is."

"You do?"

"Yes. I know some people who go there."

"Well, I hope you can make it next Wednesday night. Come for the potluck dinner—you don't have to bring anything—and leave early if you have to get back to work."

The paramedic shut the door. "Thanks for the invite, Miss O'Hanlon."

"Emmeline."

"Emmeline O'Hanlon. See you around." The paramedic nodded to Sebastian, who tried to be civil.

Sebastian shook his head. He didn't understand Emmeline. At a time like this, how could she be thinking about inviting people to church?

Before Sebastian could say anything, the police officer—who had been talking with Bart—came toward them. He took a statement from Emmeline.

The whole time, Sebastian rubbed her shoulders as she shook.

"He said you let him in." The officer swiped his iPad.

"No, sir. I did not. I was sleeping in my bed. I heard the front door open. He has the key. As you know, he's the landlady's son."

Sebastian could feel Emmeline's shoulders tense under his fingers.

"He has been entering my apartment without my permission," Emmeline said. "This is the first time he's been drunk in my apartment in the middle of the night."

"So it makes a difference if it's day or night?" Sebastian bristled.

The officer glanced at him, and Sebastian decided not to say anything more.

But Sebastian knew then and there that he was going to get Emmeline out of this apartment complex.

As he listened to the rest of Emmeline's statement, her description of the entire situation made him angrier and angrier.

He tried to shut up, but he couldn't. "You cannot defend Bart, Em."

"He's drunk. He wasn't aware of what he did."

"He entered your apartment under the influence, and scared you half to death. Then he slept on your couch until you came back." Sebastian looked at the police officer for support. The officer didn't respond.

"She's a single woman living alone," Sebastian emphasized. "He's been harassing her ever since she lived here."

"Right now it's just he said, she said," the officer said. "There are no witnesses."

"Because nobody came out of their apartments to help me." Emmeline sniffled.

"I'll file this, and we'll see if there's enough evidence to press charges," the officer said.

That satisfied Sebastian. Not entirely, but enough to wear the night.

He had been sleeping soundly when his sister Skye called him. Apparently, in her panic, Emmeline had called Skye, forgetting that she was in Miami all week. Sebastian had sent her to fill in for him at the Southern Florida Food Festival.

Skye called Sebastian, and he sped out of Seaside Island at a hundred miles an hour.

When all was done, Sebastian led Emmeline back to her apartment. "Get your clothes and stuff. You're not staying here tonight."

"I have nowhere to go."

"We'll figure that out tomorrow. For now, how does a hotel sound?"

"I can't—"

"Hush, Em." They went inside her apartment.

The first thing Sebastian saw Emmeline pick up was her Celtic lap harp. She put it by the door. Then she went to her bedroom and closed it.

He sat on the couch and used his phone to find a hotel between Scrolls—where Emmeline worked three days a week—and his cottage on Seaside Island. He heard the shower running, and then drawers opening and closing.

Emmeline came out of her bedroom, changed into

jeans and a tee shirt, and rolled an old suitcase with a pair of sandals tied to the handle.

Sebastian lifted the harp by the door. It was super light. He took the suitcase from Emmeline instead. "You get the harp."

When Emmeline decided to lock the front door, Sebastian found it amusing.

"Not funny." Emmeline nudged him.

"Oh, not funny at all." They filed into the car, luggage and shoes and lap harp and all.

In the car, Emmeline began to weep softly. She tried to hide it among the sniffles.

"I think I'm catching a cold," she said.

Sure.

"I'm sorry I woke you up."

"No, Em. You didn't wake me up. Skye did. I'm glad, truly. You should've called me right away instead of her."

"She's the closest friend I have on the island. I forgot she's in Miami until Saturday."

"You were under duress."

She looked away.

Sebastian reached for her hand and held it. It was shaking again. "I'm going to pray for you now, Em. God has protected you and will continue to do so."

She nodded.

"Remind me not to close my eyes since I'm driving."

Emmeline chuckled.

There. It's coming back.

He could hear it. That bubbling brook coming up to the surface. He wanted to see that joy again.

Slowly, Sebastian began to pray. "Father God, what a night we've had. Thank You for keeping Em safe from that piece of garbage—forgive me, Lord, for calling that piece of garbage a piece of garbage."

Sigh. "Let me start over."

He glanced at Emmeline as they passed some street lights. She didn't look happy.

"You need to be serious when you pray, Seb. It's very bad when you don't respect God. Even Bart needs Jesus, you know? I feel sorry for him."

"Did I hear that right?" Sebastian asked. "Seriously, Em?"

"I want him to know God and have a new life in Christ. He doesn't have to live the way he has been. It's not me he wants. It's Jesus he needs."

"I can't believe you said that, Em. How can you be so forgiving of Bart? Who knows what he could've done had you not left the apartment? He was drunk!"

"Exactly. He had no idea what he was doing."

"He could have done anything then."

"We see things differently."

"I don't want you to get hurt." Sebastian gunned the gas pedal. "I've seen it before. Alcoholics and their angst. You never know what's going to happen day to day."

"I'm not sure if Bart is an alcoholic. He's not drunk

all the time. I don't think we should assume things we don't have proof of."

"He could be a functional alcoholic. My parents—"

Oops.

Emmeline waited. Then: "Your parents? It's not about Bart, is it? The situation tonight triggered some memories, didn't it?"

Sebastian nodded. How much should he tell her? How much not to tell her?

He shouldn't have said anything at all. He had told Talia about his parents and their untimely deaths. One alcoholic in the house was bad enough but he and Skye had had the misfortune of having two alcoholics for parents.

Talia had reacted with indifference. No pity. No sympathy.

He hadn't told anyone else about his family save for his close friends, Matt Garnett and Ivan McMillan.

But Emmeline? He hardly knew her.

"Now I am really sorry I called Skye, and that she called you," Emmeline said. "I should've called someone else."

"Rafferty, the court jester?" Sebastian wasn't sure why that guy was the first person who came to his mind.

"Funny, Seb." Emmeline's bubbling laughter returned.

Sebastian liked to hear it. Over and over.

She could do that the rest of his life...

What am I saying?

"I have friends from church, Seb. I could have called anyone from the women's group from Olivia Gonzalez down the line of at least ten women who would have helped me. I don't need Rafferty."

"Or me."

"No offense, but that's right. I don't need you. Truth be told, you don't need me either, Seb. You only need Jesus. Don't forget God."

Don't forget God.

"Got it. Here goes." Sebastian paused. "Father God, we come to You with grateful hearts. You have protected Em tonight from danger and harm. I pray that You will heal her scrapes and bruises, and let this episode tonight not linger in her beautiful life. Forgive us of our sins, and lead us in Your everlasting way. In Jesus' name, I pray. Amen."

He thought that was pretty good until Emmeline started praying.

"And dear Lord Jesus, I pray for Bart. Please work in his life and show Your grace and mercy to him. Whatever is going on in his life, lead him to You. For such a time as this, You have placed me there in that apartment so I could maybe pray for Bart. And I pray for his mother too, dear Betty in the nursing home. It must be difficult for Bart not to have anyone but a dying mother. She's frail, Lord. Give her strength and comfort in her last days."

Such is Emmeline.

Sebastian's heart filled with guilt when she said her *amen*. He felt properly chastised for being selfish.

His mind went to their stage play for Talia. He had to stop this charade to free Emmeline from participating in something that she probably shouldn't be in.

He knew why she had agreed to his crazy proposal. It was his fault for having manipulated her into it. He had played into her desperation, her anguish over her lost brother.

Sebastian had taken advantage of her.

Forgive me, Lord. This has to end.

How?

Sebastian pulled into the valet parking at Blue Ocean Beach Villas.

"No way, Seb. I can't afford this place." Emmeline looked panicky in the entrance light shining through the windshield.

Sebastian felt her hand tense in his.

She retracted it from his grasp.

"It's on me," Sebastian said. "After what you've gone through, you deserve to be pampered."

"I'll only be here for what?" Emmeline's eyes were on the clock on the dashboard. "Four hours? Then I have to go to work."

"After work, I'll take you back here and you can rest. Tomorrow you can decide where you can stay for the summer."

"Only until the end of July."

So soon.

Sebastian felt a tug in his heart he hadn't felt in —huh?

Forever.

Something bothered him that he couldn't pin down.

CHAPTER TWENTY-SEVEN

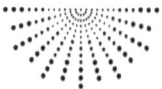

*E*mmeline wasn't sure what to think of Sebastian sticking to her like chewing gum on tennis shoes on a hot summer day.

On Thursday, he had insisted on picking her up from the Blue Ocean Beach Villas, and dropping her off at Scrolls. She wasn't sure how she was going to get to work at the SISO studio on Friday, but she knew she didn't want Sebastian following her everywhere.

"Just call me whenever you need to get somewhere." His voice seemed insistent.

He kept his eyes on the road as he drove his i8—which seemed to be his favorite ride—but Emmeline could see that he was concerned.

"Don't worry about me, Seb. I'm planning to get my bike from my apartment—"

"I don't want you going back there."

"Not alone. Avery's giving me a ride." Emmeline

was happy she had worked out her living arrangements. "She said I could stay with her. Is that a great friend or what?"

"God provides."

"Yep. God provides." Still, she knew that Avery was busy. Staying with her meant living with the sounds of trumpet from morning until night. Avery's trumpet studio was in her basement, and it wasn't soundproof at this time.

When Emmeline emailed several friends from the Seaside Chapel women's Bible study group, asking if she could stay with them, taking turns, until it was time for her to move to Athens, she hadn't expected many to respond.

Surprisingly, every single woman she emailed had asked her to stay at their house rent-free.

Perhaps she could stay one night at each place. However, they didn't live near the Village. It meant she had to cycle a lot. She wished she could stay downtown, but beggars could not be choosers.

Still, it was nice of everyone to let her stay with them.

Even the pastor's wife had offered her a guest bedroom.

However, if at all possible, Emmeline didn't want to stay at the pastor's house. She might have to explain to Olivia Gonzalez why she was going out with Sebastian when they were not in love with each other.

What's this behavior from Sebastian?

"I want to make sure you stay as far away from Bart as much as possible, and for that matter, Rafferty. And maybe even Jared."

That behavior.

"I'll be fine, Seb. God will protect me. I'll get my bike today and you won't need to be my chauffeur."

Sebastian looked insulted. "Is that all you think of me?"

"Be serious." Emmeline moved her legs and flinched. "Ow."

"Your knees hurt, don't they?"

Emmeline nodded. She didn't want to pull her skirt up to look at her knees in front of Sebastian. The skinned knees, bruised and bloody last night, weren't feeling much better this morning.

"I'll keep praying that God will heal you."

"Thank you." Emmeline's fingers went to her skirt, trying to straighten out the creases.

It was no use. She had pulled the floral summer dress out of the dryer a day late. It was all wrinkled—and to make it worse, in her haste last night vacating her apartment, she had stuffed it into her suitcase, which put even more creases into it.

"You know you could borrow an iron from the hotel." Sebastian slowed down his BMW.

"I wasn't sure if it costs any money to do that. Didn't want to put you out." Emmeline reached for her tote bag at her feet as they approached the front entrance of Scrolls.

"Don't worry about it, okay?"

It was time to tell him. "Why don't I see you tonight at seven o'clock when we meet Helen?"

"You're going to cycle to my house? What if it rains?"

"I'll be okay. I'll bring a change of clothes."

"Cycling at night... I don't like the sound of it."

"I've done it before. I have reflector strips on the bike and my backpack."

"It's dangerous for you to cycle at night." His voice was sincere.

"It's dusk, not night."

"It'll be totally dark after dinner, Em. I don't want you to get run over."

Emmeline didn't want to tell Sebastian that she couldn't afford to rent a car even for one day, let alone for six weeks.

"Look, Seb. Don't worry about me. You take care of your Talia situation. I'll be fine."

Honks blared at them from behind Sebastian's car as he slowed down near Scrolls. Traffic crawled.

For some reason that Emmeline couldn't read, he reached for her arm as he pulled to a stop near the Scrolls front entrance.

He didn't let go of her arm.

"If I don't get out of your car now, Seb, you're going to get a ticket." Emmeline narrowed her eyes at him. "Then you'll be sorry you chauffeured me around."

"I'm not sorry about anything." He let go of her arm

and raised the passenger side door for her. "That lavender dress looks good on you."

"Periwinkle," Emmeline said as she exited the car.

"Whatever. I like it."

"Thank you, I guess. See you at seven."

"No, Emmeline. I'm picking you up after work today."

Emmeline didn't respond. She spun around on the sidewalk and headed for the Scrolls front door. That was when she realized that someone was looking out of the window on the café side.

A familiar face.

She pretended not to notice.

She held the door open for a mother pushing a toddler in a stroller. When she reached the foyer where the new fiction titles were propped up on a round table, she glanced toward the café.

Sure enough.

She waved to Talia Cavanaugh-Perry, who was having coffee and donuts with Jared Urquhart, his biceps pushing through his shirt sleeves.

Emmeline had started working at Scrolls just a few weeks before the school year ended and teen workers had found better paying summer jobs at the hotels and in the tourism industry.

For all practical purposes, Scrolls was a fledgling bookstore, but its owner, Argo Perry, had worked hard to try to keep the doors open. Being estranged from his wife seemed to be affecting the pensioner. Hushed words among the Scrolls employees indicated that he lacked the funds to stay in business beyond Christmas.

Most readers now shopped online. Independent bookstores weren't the only ones suffering; chain bookstores didn't fare any better these days. The good news with Scrolls was that the employees still had a paycheck.

For now.

Talia motioned for Emmeline to come toward her.

Emmeline glanced at her watch. She lifted a finger to indicate to Talia that she would be right back. She went to the back of the store, clocked in, and put on her Scrolls name tag.

When she returned to the café, Talia was sitting on Jared's lap, just like she had done last Tuesday. Prior to that, she hadn't paid attention to the lovebirds.

It was funny how things that mattered came into focus, but then Emmeline didn't have any recollections from the past. According to Sebastian, Talia had been on vacation in May and early June, around the time Emmeline started working at Scrolls.

"What happened to your hands?" Jared was the first to notice.

Emmeline turned her palms up. A large Band-Aid was taped over the base of each palm. "I fell."

"Clumsy girl," Talia said.

"I guess I was."

"How's Sebastian doing?" Talia moved on.

Jared was kissing Talia's neck, but his eyes were on Emmeline.

Emmeline felt sorry for Sebastian. *Is that the kind of woman he wants back in his life?*

"He's fine," Emmeline said. "I have to get to work."

"Or I'll fire you." Talia laughed.

"I'm in the store working, Talia. Would you like me to help you with something?"

"More coffee."

"Will do." Emmeline picked up Talia's coffee cup. She returned with a new cup and fresh coffee.

Jared's eyes were still on Emmeline. By now, Talia had started to notice.

"Let's get out of here," Talia said.

"Would you like the coffee to go?" Emmeline asked.

"No. I've had enough coffee." Talia headed for the door.

Jared took his time to get going. As he passed by Emmeline, he squeezed her arm. "I'll see you at the rehearsal tomorrow night."

Emmeline said nothing, but a thousand thoughts fought around in her mind. This situation had the potential of becoming a huge mess. There were once three people in the ring, and now Emmeline was the fourth.

She didn't want to be in any part of it. This was other people's problem, not hers. She had enough problems of her own, as it was.

Have mercy on me, God.
And have mercy on Sebastian too.

CHAPTER TWENTY-EIGHT

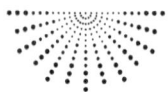

That afternoon, Sebastian found Emmeline tidying up the children's play area at Scrolls. She seemed pretty efficient and quick as she put away the stuffed animals and board books, in spite of her bandaged hands.

"You again," Emmeline teased as she bent over to arrange the board books on a low shelf.

"Can't get rid of me."

"Don't you think you'll wear out your welcome after a while?" Emmeline stood and placed two hands on her waist.

"What do you mean? We've only been going out for two weeks."

"Why are you here?" Emmeline asked.

"Good news and bad news." Sebastian tried not to look worried, but he knew he had to break the news to her one way or another.

Emmeline drew a deep breath. "Give me the bad news first."

"Remember how I made such a big fuss about Helen Hu coming to town tonight?" Sebastian asked.

Emmeline nodded. "Today being Thursday..."

"Well, she can't make it. She just called me, saying that something came up, and she's on her way out of state."

"Oh." Her voice was quiet.

"She said she's going to try to fly in Saturday and have dinner with us." Sebastian tried to sound upbeat.

"Okay."

Sebastian couldn't read that face. Was she sad? Upset? He couldn't tell.

Emmeline arranged little wooden chairs around a little round table. "Maybe we can invite her to church on Sunday."

"She might go."

Emmeline nodded. "So what's the good news?"

"I need to show you something," Sebastian said.

"I'm working."

"We don't have to leave the store. Just need to go up front to the café area." Sebastian started walking.

Emmeline followed. "Speaking of the café, guess who I saw this morning."

"Talia." While not surprised, Sebastian was curious about Emmeline's interaction with his ex-fiancée. "Before or after the gym?"

"I guess after. Jared was with her."

Sebastian didn't want to know whether Talia was sitting on Jared's lap. Sometimes he wanted to believe that Talia was simply making him jealous, but he had been beginning to wonder if that was even true.

"Anything else I need to know?" Sebastian asked.

"No. But it's uphill for you, if you know what I mean."

Sebastian led Emmeline to the window. The afternoon sun brought gold sparkles out of Emmeline's hazel eyes that matched her hair, now tied up in knot. A chignon or something.

"Yes?" Emmeline asked.

"Uh, oh yes. Look outside. See the blue Chevy Suburban LTZ parked near the bird tree?" Sebastian pointed.

"Bird tree?"

"Right outside the front door."

"Bird tree?"

Sebastian nodded. "A word of advice. Do not stand under the bird tree."

Emmeline's hand went to her mouth, and Sebastian could hear a muffled guffaw.

"Not funny, Em."

"We're standing here looking at a tree," Emmeline said between chuckles. "What's the reason?"

"It's not the tree. The blue Chevy's mine."

"Okay. Wonderful." Emmeline stepped back.

Sebastian lifted Emmeline's hand nearest him. It was soft and supple and he wanted to hold it forever.

He placed the remote clicker in her palm. "Drive it as long as you want."

"Oh."

Sebastian leaned toward her. "Don't like it? How about you drive my i8 then?"

"Your little putt-putt car?" Emmeline sniffed. "The one with jump seats for backseats and a tiny basket for a trunk?"

"It's not that small."

"It's no bigger than my concert pedal harp."

"Well, that Chevy has enough cargo space to transport your harp."

Something made Emmeline smile.

"What?" Sebastian asked.

"Nothing." Her hand was shaking again. Sebastian held it, stroked it. "How are your scrapes and bruises?"

"Uh, b-better. Thank you for asking."

He folded her fingers over the key fob. "There's only one condition."

"What?"

Sebastian reached for her face, wiped the single tear off with an index finger. "Promise me you won't go back to that apartment alone."

She nodded. "I'll give the SUV back before I leave town."

Leave? Don't leave.

Emmeline peered out the window. "It does look like it has enough room to carry my pedal harp."

"I think so, though I had to eyeball the space and

remember how big your harp is in its case, with wheels and all."

"How are you going to get home?"

"I'm going to see Matt Garnett in his shop. He'll give me a ride." A few blocks of walking would do him a world of good.

Get this knot off my chest.

Emmeline shook her head.

"What?"

"I can't believe all that you've done for me." She reached up, kissed him on the cheek and hugged his neck.

Sebastian didn't want to let her go.

He didn't know why.

CHAPTER TWENTY-NINE

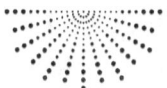

$\mathcal{M}$att Garnett's office was a storeroom stacked from floor to ceiling with steel racks of boxes and vases and antiques—or junk, depending on how one looked at it.

As he waited for Matt to send off a customer, Sebastian tried to get comfortable on a barstool by a cluttered desk with scratched solid wood legs—oak or hickory, he couldn't tell—that disappeared among more boxes of stuff on the floor.

On the table, something caught his eye: periwinkle stones protruding out of a cardboard box. The box was unlabeled.

He reached for it. It was a necklace. He picked it up. A bracelet fell out of the cluster.

They looked like what Emmeline had worn to the double date last Friday.

What are they doing here?

"Pretty, aren't they?" Matt shut the door and sat down in his office chair. "Periwinkle agate."

"Saving them for someone?" Sebastian thumbed the stones.

"You've seen these before." Matt pointed with fingernails covered with oil and grease stains. Probably working on another antique vehicle, Sebastian thought.

Must be nice for Matt to have a job he liked.

As for Sebastian, he wished he could get back to the kitchen. Maybe someday he could hire someone he could trust to run the business end of his restaurants to free him up to be a chef again. Sometimes he wished he hadn't given Talia fifty-one percent of the company shares.

Matt went on. "She wore it last Friday night."

She?

Emmeline.

"Why are they here?" Sebastian put the necklace back into the box.

"Three twenty for the set but I'll settle for two hundred dollars if you want them."

Either way that's a lot of money for Em. No wonder they're still here.

"One eighty and I'll take them."

"Can't be cheap about love, Seb."

"Love? Who said anything about love?" Sebastian shifted on the barstool.

"Your eyes, dude. The look of love."

Sebastian pointed to the single lamp above them.

"You can tell that in this dimly lit room? Nah. You're just jesting, man."

"I'm not."

"Stop looking into my eyes."

Matt rocked in his swiveling office chair. "Seb, you can't love two people at the same time. You'll always love one more than the other, and it'll be unfair to the other one. Ask me how I know."

Sebastian remained very still.

"In the end, I lost both of them, Seb. Three years and I'm still alone. My penance for a divided heart."

"That was before you were saved."

"Right." Matt stopped rocking. "And you led me to Christ, Seb. Now I'm seeing that you yourself are backsliding in your Christian walk."

"I'm not backsliding."

"No? Then tell me why there are two women in your life?" Matt asked.

Sebastian cringed.

He hadn't planned on there being two.

"You've got to make up your mind," Matt continued. "Talia or Emmeline."

"You can tell that by my response to jewelry?"

"Nope. You're leading Emmeline on. She's in love with you."

"No, she's not. She's leaving town at the end of July. She told me over and over."

"Her heart will always be here on St. Simon's Island. I'll blame you for that."

"I'm meant to be with Talia." Even as he spoke it, Sebastian wasn't sure if he believed it anymore. Since Emmeline showed up, a lot of things had changed.

His desires now ran counter to his obligations or what he had perceived to be his obligations. "Talia was..."

"There you go," Matt said. "You said she *was*."

Have I moved on?

"You don't have to marry the first one you you-know-what with," Matt said.

"It's not that."

"You two were young and made mistakes. Besides, you weren't even saved. And from the prayer requests we've had at the men's group, seems like Talia may not know the Lord even now. We're talking unequal yoke here."

"You're preaching."

"Bottomline is that you weren't married to each other, and there was no baby."

"You mean teens can sleep around and it'll be fine?"

"Seb, you know I'm not saying that. The Bible says such physical intimacy is a special thing reserved for a husband and his wife. Premarital intimacy and adultery are both sins in the eyes of God. The repercussions are tremendous and life-altering. Ask me how I know."

"That's why I'm trying to do the right thing, Matt."

"By marrying Talia even if you two go together like hot oil on cold water?"

"What's that supposed to mean?"

"You don't love Talia."

Sebastian stared at his friend. "How'd you figure that?"

"You'd be married by now."

"Well, two people in love don't necessarily have to be married."

"But you're the marrying kind."

Marrying kind?

"That's why you and Talia were engaged twice—or more—and you were dumped several more times. You're not meant for each other." Matt rocked in his chair again. "Have you prayed about this?"

"Will you stop that rocking? It's annoying." The chair going back and forth was making Sebastian dizzy.

Matt leaned forward. "My advice for you is to ask God whom you should be with the rest of your life. There's only one woman for you."

"I know." Sebastian wondered if it could be that easy.

"Then again, old friend, you've already chosen, haven't you?"

CHAPTER THIRTY

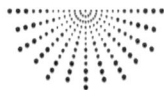

*E*nrique Granados's "Oriental" sounded through his mind with such clarity that Sebastian thought he was dreaming awake. Pity the tune kept repeating only several measures, dancing in his ears like a broken record.

He could see Emmeline, plucking at the strings of her pedal harp, her fingers and arms an extension of the soundboard, her butterscotch-blonde hair floating in the wind. They were outside, on the top deck of Saffron on Jekyll, but no one else was there at the restaurant. He was the only audience.

She kept playing the same measures over and over.

And over.

Sebastian opened his eyes.

The music was still all around him. Then it intensified and seemed to come only in one direction. He turned his head.

There on the side table, his phone on its charger echoed the "Oriental" in his dream.

Sebastian stretched across the king-sized bed until he reached his phone. On the vertical screen was his sister's face. Above her face was the time.

It was 2:07 a.m.

Sebastian tapped the screen to talk to Skye. He activated the speaker phone. "It's two in the morning, Skye. If this is an emergency, call 911. Don't call me."

"What's wrong with you?" Skye was feisty when she was tired. There was no messing with her when she was in a bad mood.

"What?" Feign ignorance. That would make Skye hit the ceiling.

But Sebastian truly didn't know what she was talking about.

"Someone in my women's group forwarded me an email from Emmeline."

"Is she okay?" Sebastian put his head back on the feather pillow.

The last time Skye called him had been Wednesday night—had it only been a couple of days?—when Emmeline had been trying to get away from Bart.

"She has been sending out emails on Thursday asking around for a place to stay through July."

"I thought she'll be staying with Avery from next week onward." Sebastian rolled to his side, the comforter mangled in his legs. He was wearing an undershirt and boxers, feeling comfortable, and wanting to go back to sleep if he could get Skye off the phone.

"For one night. She's going to rotate through a bunch of homes. In exchange, Em offered to clean their houses," Skye continued. "Mow their lawns, walk their dogs, babysit their kids."

"Sounds fair."

"Sebastian Reginald Langston! You are her boyfriend. You should be taking care of her."

"Technically, Skye, I'm only pretending to be her boyfriend. Besides, she's independent, and I want to respect that."

"She's like the sister I never had, Seb. I don't want to see her out in the street."

"She's not going to be. Don't worry."

"I want you to take care of her, Seb."

"I already did. She's staying at the Blue Ocean Beach Villas all weekend. Who's paying for that? Me. And she's driving my Chevy. You're welcome, Skye. How nice of you to acknowledge my generosity."

"One weekend at the hotel, and then what?"

"I was going to figure out something."

"She's ahead of you, Seb."

"No worries. It'll only be for about a month and a week or so. After that she'll be at UGA." Sebastian tried to keep his voice even and calm.

"You don't sound happy for her."

For us.

Sebastian knew Skye would pick up on his

emotions, even over the phone. The siblings might be four years apart, but they had been taking care of each other since they had been teenagers.

"I told you I don't like this plot of yours to get Talia back," Skye said.

"How does that have anything to do with Emmeline's housing situation?" Sebastian rolled on his back. *I really need to get some sleep. Long Friday coming up.*

"Don't you see, Seb? You got Em involved in your life, and inevitably you're in her life. Like it or not, you're both a part of each other's lives now, and in the future, you'll look back and realize this was your timeline that shaped whatever is to come."

"What are you saying?"

"I don't want to see Em hurt."

"Skye—sister, buddy—listen. Em is tougher than you think."

"I don't care how tough she looks to you. I've known her for a year now. I know she is vulnerable, and I don't want you taking advantage of her. I don't want her moving from house to house cleaning bathrooms and changing diapers for the next six weeks."

"I don't either. But I'm spending a ton paying Helen Hu to find Em's brother. I'm not spending money renting a house for her to live in for only a month. Renting a house is not part of our deal."

"The deal to get Talia back and mow over Emmeline in the process?"

"No. I care for her."

"Who? Emmeline? Talia? Which one, Seb? You need to stop leading both women on."

"I'm not—"

"Want to know the truth, big brother? Talia is history, Seb. History. Your relationship is over. Dead and gone. If you don't move on, you will never have a chance at happiness with someone who might be truly God's choice for you."

"Skye, you can't even get a boyfriend, so don't tell me about God's choice." Sebastian could hear his sister exhale loudly. "My relationship with Talia might be complicated—"

"As in nonexistent complicated?" Skye sounded tired. "Seb, I've been on my feet all evening at the cooking competition. I got back to my hotel room forty-five minutes ago to this mess. I'm asking you to do some-thing about it because I'm quite sure if you hadn't inter-fered with Em's life, everything would've been fine."

"So it's my fault now?"

"I'm not totally blaming you. That Bart fellow is icky, but we have all told her to move out. Who knows if your being there affected him, made him feel compet-itive. He's never entered Em's house at night before."

"That we know of."

"Em's a light sleeper, and she had a new lock put in for her bedroom door a few months ago."

"Good for her."

"So you're going to fix the situation?"

"Already did. The hotel bill is on me. I told you."

"Until Sunday."

"Em has four jobs and she can pay for a place to stay in July without our help."

"Four part-time jobs," Skye reminded him.

"Those extra hours that Talia promised her should come soon."

"Talia?" Skye sounded surprised. "Oh, I see. Talia offered her extra work at Scrolls?"

"So she could quit the theater."

"Interesting."

"Yes, but if it worked out, it'll be only through July. She'll go back to music school"—Sebastian's voice caught and he didn't know why—"and it'll all be over."

"So Talia ruined your life, and now you're ruining Em's."

"It's not like that—Skye? Hello?"

What is wrong with her!

Sebastian turned off his phone, returned it to its charger on the side table. He adjusted the pillow under his head, and rearranged the light blanket to tuck himself in.

But sleep wouldn't come.

All he could think of was Emmeline Eleanor O'Hanlon.

Emmeline, the siren harpist.

Emmeline, the beautiful Christian.

Emmeline, who had told him, "Don't forget God."

Whose plan is this to bring Talia back to me?

Do I even want Talia back?

She's Jared's girl now.

Even man's plan could work, right? Talia had talked to him more in the last two weeks than in the last two months since she had dumped him for Jared Urquhart.

To make Talia jealous, Sebastian knew he had to go further with Emmeline.

And ironically, he wasn't prepared to do that with impunity.

The closer he had been to Emmeline, the stronger his feelings were for her, and the less he had thought of Talia, though Emmeline kept bringing her up.

He was confident that Emmeline had no idea that he hadn't been playacting when he kissed her that night outside her apartment. He had wanted Bart to stay away from her.

He hadn't been playacting either when he stood between Emmeline and Rafferty. Or Jared.

And on Wednesday night, after Emmeline's ordeal, he had wanted to put his arms around her and protect her forever.

Some things are never meant to be.

CHAPTER THIRTY-ONE

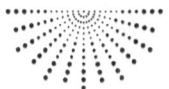

*S*uch a luxurious hotel stay couldn't possibly last.

Emmeline felt like it was someone else's vacation, not hers, as she stepped into her tower room at the Blue Ocean Beach Villas. Still, she felt pampered after a long day of music library work and the final rehearsal for the Brock-Flannagan wedding coming up on Saturday.

She almost didn't see the blinker on her hotel room phone as she waltzed about the open space. The concierge had left a message ten minutes prior that she had a visitor waiting for her, poolside.

At the name, Emmeline jumped into her flip-flops and dashed out of her tower room. She took the elevator down to the outdoors toward the oceanside pool.

"Skye! What are you doing here?" Emmeline

waved to her friend, who was sitting on a deck chair facing the ocean.

"I'm offended." Skye Langston didn't get up. That pout.

Sigh. "You are? Why?"

"Your emails."

"Which ones?" Emmeline sat down on the empty deck chair next to Skye's.

"About a place to stay?"

"I didn't send you one," Emmeline confessed.

"Exactly!" Skye sat up. "And why not?"

"You were out of town. You're busy. And you're Seb's sister. Conflict of interest."

Skye was silent.

"Who forwarded you my email?" Emmeline asked. "Avery?"

Skye refused to say.

"Aren't you supposed to be at some food festival?"

"I didn't win the cook-off last night."

"I'm sorry. Next time then. When did you return?"

"I took the first flight out of Miami this morning. But Saffron's chef is there for the next two days. They won't miss me."

"We'll always miss you, Skye."

Skye took off her sunglasses. "Em."

"Yes?" Emmeline kicked off her flip-flops and stretched on the lounger.

The wind kept kicking up her skirt. She finally put

her flip-flops on top of her skirt to keep it down. Otherwise, the lounger was quite comfortable and she felt like she was falling asleep.

"I have two guest rooms, Em," Skye said. "Sometimes when chefs come to town, they stay with me, but hardly anyone else. I could use a roommate through July if you promise—promise!—not to clean my house. I have a housekeeper who does that, and I have someone else clean up my kitchen and do the dishes for me. So you are not allowed to do any work in my house."

Emmeline thought for a good long minute. "I'll pay you for the rent."

"No. My stupid brother has troubled you enough. This is the least I can do."

"I could offer to cook, but compared to your chef skills, I'm like PBJ, you know."

"Didn't I say you're not to work in my house?" Skye shook her head.

"What can I do in return?"

"Maybe between the two of us we can drive some sense into my brother."

Emmeline laughed. "I've been praying for God's will for his life."

And mine too.

"Good prayer, Em."

"Want to see my tower room—I mean, suite?" Emmeline perked up.

"Sure."

As they walked, Emmeline pointed up. "You can see it from here. That corner space there on the top floor. I woke up to the ocean this morning."

They got in and out of the elevator. Emmeline unlocked the door to her suite.

Skye waltzed in. "This is really nice."

"I know. I called reservations just to find out how much each night costs." Emmeline pointed to the balcony. "Nearly fell out of my cushy chair."

They laughed.

"You see why I need to get out of here, Skye. I can't impose on Seb like this. And he's letting me use his SUV to haul my harp around."

"I know. I spoke with him last night."

Emmeline stood at the balcony, letting the wind blow her hair about. The June air was warm but she liked it. She'd never been one for cold weather and snow.

Give me sunshine and ocean anytime.

Sadly, she'd be landlocked at UGA soon.

"How's the situation with Talia?" Skye asked. "Seb said it's slow going."

"Talia told me to stay away from *Jared*."

"Uh-oh. That doesn't sound good."

"We're rehearsing plays at Jared's house because he's underwriting Theater by the Sea. Sebastian goes to watch us. Talia shows up to hover over Jared. I just want to go back to music school."

Skye hugged her. "I hear you. I'm sorry Seb dragged you into his messy life."

"I agreed to it. I know, I know. You told me so."

"My brother is blind."

"Like I said, I'm praying for him, for God to show him His will." Emmeline squinted "Hey, lookie there. Porpoises in the water."

"Where—oh, I see. Nice!"

They stood there for the longest time until Emmeline remembered she had to get ready, eat dinner, and go pick up Sebastian for the Friday night rehearsal.

"Would you like to come?" Emmeline asked.

"To what?"

"Watch our rehearsal."

"No, thanks. I don't have the patience. But I want you to pack up, and give me your luggage. I'll take it back to my house. You're coming over to stay with me until you go back to Athens."

"Seb said you were bossy."

"Is that a yes?"

"Well, okay. Thank you for the offer, Skye. I packed light, so it shouldn't be too hard to get my stuff together if you give me about five minutes."

"Sure. I'll just sit here and fry." Skye settled on a bistro seat by the balustrades facing the ocean on the little balcony. "Want to get some dinner?"

"Sure. Let's ask Seb if he wants to join us."

Skye paused for a moment.

"What?" Emmeline said.

"You are developing feelings for my brother."

"How did you come to that conclusion?"

"You're thinking of his well-being."

"Because I thought he might want to join us for dinner? Anyone can care. That doesn't mean I feel anything."

"Has he kissed you?"

Emmeline continued stuffing her suitcase. That was all the luggage she had brought with her. Sebastian had kindly delivered her harp to the SISO building.

"He has, hasn't he?"

Emmeline looked up. "Feel free to have a conversation all by yourself."

"I'm going to kill him."

"If you must know, Seb was protecting me from Bart."

"And how did he do that?" Skye was in her face now.

Emmeline packed her toiletries as quickly as she could. "Well..."

Skye put her hand on her forehead. "Uh-oh. My brother kissed you."

"It was the only way to tell Bart to back off."

Skye rolled her eyes. "I cannot believe you're on his side."

"It's how I saw it." Emmeline zipped up her duffle bag. "It's like the rest of what Seb has done for me. He puts me here to protect me from Bart, who has the key to my apartment, as you know. He lets me use his SUV so that I don't have to cycle in the rain. Oh, and he stood up to Rafferty."

"You believe what you just said?"

"Pretty much."

"Then your love life is doomed, Em. Doomed."

CHAPTER THIRTY-TWO

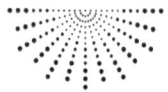

A long day didn't prevent Sebastian from insisting on accompanying her to Jared's house and sitting by the outdoor pool to watch Emmeline and her friends in the Theater by the Sea rehearse for their upcoming Jane Austen parody series.

There would be four outdoor weekends in July, if Sebastian could endure it all.

His eyes were on Nigel Miller directing the rehearsal, but his mind was constantly thinking of how he could approach Talia about their non-relationship. More than anything, he wanted to know if they were done with each other.

If they were, he could move on.

Sure, Talia had kept saying she had moved on, and Sebastian had told her what she wanted to hear.

Yet, somewhere tugging at his conscience was a past he couldn't let go of, an obligation to that woman whose innocence he had taken when they had both been seventeen, attending Frederica High School.

God, do You forgive me for that?

Should I marry Talia because of what we did seventeen years ago?

They had been young and stupid and rebellious. Well, Sebastian's parents had been rarely home. They paid the rent, left food in the refrigerator, and then they were gone to who knew where.

Sebastian and Skye had been left on their own. And on their own, Sebastian didn't know any better. Talia had come over every afternoon, and she had made the first move...

Not an excuse.

Fortunately, for both of them, Talia hadn't become pregnant. Was that the mercy of God?

But now she hung over Sebastian like a dark cloud, reminding him of the sins of his youth. Should he succumb to his own way of fixing it by marrying her—a woman who still had no problem sleeping around?

Am I a hero or a coward?

Sounds coming from the house caused Sebastian to turn his head.

Talia.

The stage actors were oblivious to Sebastian's mental battles. They were laughing and cutting it up as they strutted about the flagstone floor next to the shimmering blue pool and noisy fountain.

Emmeline was in the middle of the crowd, enjoying herself.

Apparently, the actress playing the role of Elizabeth had quit altogether, and Emmeline had now taken over the role of Elizabeth. Rafferty was stuck alternating between being Wickham and Mr. Collins.

As far as Sebastian was concerned, it was a much ado about love. He should google this Jane Austen, or whatever her name was, and try to be more interested in the Regency era, but if not for Emmeline's sake, he had no use for it. The only literature he ever wanted to see were the updated menus for his two restaurants.

Sebastian left his deck chair and ambled back into the entertainment room, where he found Talia behind the bar.

Talia didn't look up. She was pouring something.

As Sebastian reached her, he saw that it was her favorite sangria, something he couldn't have.

"Talia, we need to talk." He slid onto a barstool.

"Jared's expecting me in a few minutes. This is a bad time." She drank that concoction deeply from the tall crystal tumbler.

"It won't take long." The last time they had talked was last Friday night in the kitchen in this cottage. The rest of the week, Talia had canceled their business meetings and lunches, and avoided him.

"Out with it, then, Seb." She didn't offer him any of her drink.

"What went wrong with us, Talia?" Sebastian placed both elbows on the counter.

"I don't think anything did. We just grew up."

"But you kept coming back to me."

"Old habits."

"Meaning what?"

Talia shook her new curls. "Meaning nothing, Seb. You're safe."

"I'm safe?"

"Always. You're like my best friend, Seb. We're business partners, besides, and we see each other at Saffron."

"I'm confused."

"Take my word for it. We'll never be more than friends, but I like your company." Talia poured extra Bacardi into her sangria.

The pungent smell of it reminded Sebastian of his parents' binge drinking before they had left the house to party with their friends. Sebastian had dreaded the morning after when their house smelled of vomit. It had been too much to ask a fourteen-year-old boy to deal with. He and his sister had to grow up fast.

"What do you want from me, Seb?" Talia asked.

"We should marry." His own words sounded hollow.

Sebastian regretted even saying it now.

No, I don't want to marry Talia, but it would make everything right, right?

"Marry each other?" Talia laughed. "Whatever for?"

"Pastor Gonzalez said that when two people are married they become one physically. The fact that we'd done—you know—meant that we had done what God meant for two married people to do."

"This is the twenty-first century, Seb. If I were to marry everyone I slept with..."

Sebastian clenched his fists on the granite bar counter. "I didn't want to believe that."

Even though I know it's true.

Talia laughed. "Don't tell me not to have fun, Seb. Come on."

"Among other things, you could pick up all sorts of incurable diseases."

"Don't worry, Seb. I won't be able to give them to you since we don't do anything together anymore—since you had your Jesus moment."

That was a long time ago.

There's truly nothing left between Talia and me.

Why am I hanging on to her?

Since Sebastian had rededicated his life back to God some years ago, he had told Talia that he was determined to wait until marriage before they resumed their physical relationship.

Talia had taken it badly—or so he had thought—and moved to London, and she had stayed there until several years ago when she came home after declaring she had been bored out of her mind.

When Talia had come home to St. Simon's Island, Sebastian talked to her about Christ, but he wasn't sure now whether it had meant anything to her, even though they had attended Seaside Chapel as a couple and remained celibate whenever they were together.

Still, when Talia was with someone else, she didn't go to church on Sundays, and Sebastian didn't ask what she did on Sunday mornings. Not his business.

He wondered now if she had been playing along only to keep his company—in between her conquests.

Am I simply a filler?

Somewhere at the back of his mind, something had bothered him. What would happen if Talia became bored with him after they married?

Right now, Sebastian wondered if her conversion was genuine. Who was he to judge? He had told her that if she believed in the Lord Jesus Christ, she would be saved. She had said *yes* multiple times over. Wasn't that enough?

Everything after that was between her and God, though Sebastian wondered if Talia truly knew what it meant to believe in Jesus.

I'm not the Holy Spirit.

"I want God's love for us," Sebastian said.

"God's love?" Talia looked at him, as if with pity. "Look, I have to run. He's waiting for me upstairs. Good night, Seb."

"Tell me you don't live here."

"I don't live here."

"Sleepovers?"

"None of your business." Talia walked away.

Why is she doing this to herself?

The pain in his chest now moved to his shoulders. He knew why.

This was how Talia was. There was no way he could ever change her. Only God could change this woman's heart.

Until then, her pattern was the same. She would get tired of her boyfriend, they'd break up, she'd go see who else was out there, they'd break up, and she'd be back with Sebastian again.

Why did he let her do that to him?

This isn't love.

Not God's love, anyway.

There in front of him was Talia's empty tumbler and the pitcher of leftover sangria, which she had forgotten to put back into the refrigerator. Next to the pitcher was the half-empty Bacardi bottle.

How could an ex have such a hold on me?

Sebastian reached for the pitcher and started pouring the red liquid into Talia's tumbler. He studied the mix of liquid and pieces of berries floating in it.

As he was looking at it, he felt someone touch his arm.

Warm fingers.

CHAPTER THIRTY-THREE

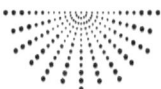

*E*mmeline leaned toward Sebastian's ear as he sat stock still at the counter, one almost-guilty hand on that tumbler that could have done him in.

He dared not move.

Her lips were so close to his ear that he could feel her warm breath.

"You're worth more than this, Sebastian Langston," Emmeline whispered.

Her words were so soft that Sebastian wanted to cry.

"You don't need this." Emmeline rubbed his arm. "Let me take you home."

"It's not what it seems." Sebastian didn't meet her gaze.

"I saw you pour it."

"I didn't drink it. It was Talia's."

"I don't see her."

"She just walked out. Went upstairs to be with Jared."

"Oh. What did she say to you?"

That made me go this far? "Many things."

"Let's go," Emmeline said.

"What about your rehearsal?"

"My scenes are done."

Sebastian's watch said it was not even nine o'clock. "I can't go home and sit there. I'm mad at Talia."

Or maybe I'm mad at myself.

"Want to talk about it?"

"No." Sebastian wasn't sure how much he wanted to tell Emmeline.

If he revealed his foolishness, what would she think of him? Would she use it against him later? He hardly knew her.

"Then let's go do something." Emmeline reached for Sebastian's hand.

"Like what?"

"I don't know. Watch a movie, maybe. Safer than getting drunk?"

Sebastian let her lead him toward the front door. "I haven't set foot in a movie theater in years."

"You missed all that movie popcorn?" Emmeline chuckled.

"Too much partially hydrogenated oil."

"What about the soda?"

"Too much high fructose corn syrup."

"Well, more for me. You don't get any, Seb."

They reached Sebastian's SUV.

"Hand me the keys," Sebastian said.

"No. I'm driving." Emmeline reached the driver's side first before she unlocked the doors.

"You don't believe me. I didn't have a drop. I'm telling you the truth." Sebastian climbed into the passenger side.

"Use your phone and find us a movie that starts ASAP. I don't want to stay up all night."

Sebastian was surprised that Emmeline had ordered him around. "May I remind you that it's Saturday tomorrow?"

"May I remind you to look at my calendar? The Brock-Flannagan wedding is at two. You saw us practice last week. All those last-minute changes?"

Sebastian remembered now. "That's seriously weird. Changed out the groom and changed the program."

He began to hum the Granados song as he looked up possible movie options on his phone, and remembered that first Monday of their charade. He had heard "Oriental" coming from a harp as he walked down the corridor on the third floor at SISO studio two Mondays ago. He had stood at the doorway watching Emmeline weep at her harp.

"You like that music," Emmeline said.

"Yes. Very much. I kept hearing it in my head, especially when I need it."

"God provides music as therapy sometimes. You

remember the Old Testament when David played the harp to soothe Saul's soul?"

"I'm Saul? Is that how little you think of me?"

"Silly pickle." Emmeline laughed.

Her laughter, crystal chimes by the sea, mollified the stab wounds in his heart.

"Silly pickle? A new term of endearment?"

Emmeline ignored him. "If you want, I'll play the harp for you. Both my harps are back there."

Sebastian looked where she pointed. "I know you're playing the pedal harp tomorrow. When do you play the lap harp?"

Emmeline nodded. "Next Wednesday night's Fire Pit Service, remember? Your sister is singing."

"The one you invited Jared, and by default, Talia to." At his own mention of Talia, Sebastian sank into the leather seat.

"Are we going to sit here all night or are you going to pick a movie?" Emmeline started the SUV. "See what's showing at Midland 10."

Sebastian tapped his phone, and read the listing of movies showing between then and ten o'clock. In the end they picked one that started at 9:45 p.m.

"I didn't know you like suspense," Sebastian said.

"Doesn't everybody?"

"Talia only likes to watch chick flicks... I take that back. She watches whatever her current boyfriend does —I'm sorry. I don't want to talk about Talia."

"Sometimes when someone has been a part of your life for a long time, it's hard not to bring them up."

Sebastian nodded. "I'm sorry I brought you into all this."

Emmeline pulled into Midland 10. "You've done so much for me, Seb. Helen Hu is a big step forward toward finding my brother. I don't think helping you out with Talia is enough to make up for what you're doing for my family."

Sebastian wasn't sure what to say, so he didn't say anything. Somewhere in his heart, he wanted to get to know Emmeline more. But until he was really over Talia, he couldn't do much to explore where his heart wanted to go.

As far as Talia was concerned, there was nothing between them, but Sebastian felt he hadn't let her go.

Until he let Talia go, he couldn't be free with Emmeline.

For all practical purposes, Talia was history.

But the memories of her...

How do I erase all these memories of Talia?

"How often do you come here?" Sebastian asked as Emmeline parked the vehicle.

"Not since Ivan and I—uh... Well, I've been busy."

Sebastian didn't want to intrude but maybe talking about Emmeline would take his mind off Talia. "Ivan and you? When you dated that summer?"

Emmeline nodded. "Funny how it went. I thought

there was something between us, but there wasn't. God shut the door."

"The door was never meant for you, Em. I knew that because I know Ivan. He and Brinley are made for each other. Someday, your prince will come."

Emmeline set the brake. "Sure. Until then, I'll always be second best."

"Me too! I'm not Talia's first choice." Sebastian didn't know what else to tell her.

Here he was proving her words. Talia was his first choice, not Emmeline. Then again, Talia had disqualified herself with her sleeping around.

Well, they were not married. She could do whatever she wanted, though ultimately, she had to answer to God, not to Sebastian, for her actions.

Why can't I let her go?

"You're still carrying a past guilt," Emmeline said. "Have you asked God to forgive you?"

Sebastian nodded.

"Then this is false guilt, yes? Are you greater than God, who has forgiven you the moment you asked Him to?"

"No."

"You think this is your penance—a punishment you sentenced yourself to as a way to atone for your past. The past is over, but the memories are in your head, and you're unable to deal with them."

Whoa. "What did you say?"

"You still want Talia back, even if she has moved

on." Emmeline got out of the SUV. Sebastian realized too late that he was slow to open her door for her. She was standing outside the vehicle waiting for him.

"We're meant to be together." As Sebastian said those words, they felt bitter on his tongue.

"Are you sure?" Emmeline asked.

Sebastian had no answer.

"My dad had a saying when Claude and I couldn't decide what to do about something," Emmeline added. "He said sometimes we need to retreat, spend time with God before we can move forward. You need to meet with God, Seb. Don't forget God."

Sebastian didn't know what to say.

They were in a public place—well, an almost empty parking lot—and he didn't want to talk about life-changing events on their way to watch a movie.

He opened the movie theater door for her, and followed her to the ticket counter. He cut in front of her. "Tickets are on me, but I'm not paying for food coloring and artificial flavoring."

"I can get my own ticket. This is not a date."

Sebastian smiled. "That's why you're paying for popcorn and soda. We'll call it even."

"Fair enough."

After Sebastian paid for the tickets, they headed to the concessions. There was a line. It was Friday night, after all.

"You-know-who was at Scrolls on Wednesday, and she had a talk with me about us."

"Now you tell me?" Sebastian wondered why Talia had confronted Emmeline at all.

"I forgot. It was on a Wednesday, remember? I had a lot on my mind."

"Oh. Yes. Sorry. I'm glad you're okay. I didn't mean to be insensitive."

"It's all right. The conversation with her was brief, if you must know. She told me to stay away."

"From me?" Sebastian perked up.

"No. From Jared."

CHAPTER THIRTY-FOUR

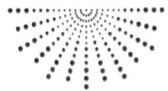

Saturday couldn't come fast enough for Sebastian. He arrived early for lunch with his sister Skye but it was intentional. He had shaven carefully, nicking nothing this morning, and put on clean clothes right out of the dryer. He had to stay up half the night to wash his favorite pair of shorts that he generally wore for at least two weeks before laundering.

Everything on him smelled like Bounce this morning as he sat on the barstool at the granite island, chatting with Skye and staring at the white box with lavender ribbon on top that he'd brought with him.

"Something on your mind?" Skye asked.

Someone. "Why do you ask?"

"You seem antsy."

"Antsy? Me? Nah. Do you have more coffee?"

Skye poured Sebastian another cup. "It's Emmeline, isn't it?"

"Who?"

"Seb. Stop. I can see right through you. She's still getting ready, if you must know. She should be here any minute now, but she has that wedding to go to. Did you sleep last night?"

"What?"

"Maybe you should go home. We can do lunch another time." Skye got off her barstool.

"No. We've been trying to have this lunch for weeks. Let's not postpone again." Sebastian's eyes were on the living room, on the other side of which were the bedrooms.

He thought he had heard a door close in the distance.

He downed his coffee.

Next thing he knew, Emmeline was standing in the kitchen with them.

"What are you doing here, Seb?" she asked.

"You look lovely, Em." He held out the box. "For you."

"What's the occasion?" Emmeline asked.

Sebastian shrugged. Too much, too soon for her, perhaps. His mind was going in a thousand different directions and he was surprised that none of those led to Talia.

Only Emmeline.

"Open it." Sebastian waited.

Emmeline placed the box on the island. Her eyebrows rose as she lifted the periwinkle agate necklace and bracelet out of the lined box. "Where did you get this?"

"I fought the store battle and slew the price dragon all for you, milady."

Emmeline laughed.

Oh, how he loved to hear her laugh.

"You knight in shining armor, you." Emmeline didn't look at Sebastian.

Next to her, Skye rolled her eyes. "Are you guys kidding me?"

"We're onstage," Emmeline said.

I wish we weren't.

Sebastian's heart sank. Slowly, he got off the barstool. "Let me help you put it on."

"You want me to wear it now?" Emmeline asked.

"Not if you don't want to."

"I'm just playing at a wedding." Emmeline lifted her long hair and turned around for Sebastian to fasten the clasp at the back of the necklace.

He didn't want to touch her but there was no choice, really, as his fingers brushed against the nape of her neck.

Flooding into his mind were the bright lights in front of Emmeline's old apartment that evening when he had shown Bart that Emmeline was taken.

It had begun as something extraneous, but he hadn't felt quite the same since that night he had kissed her.

At the back of his mind, Sebastian was fully aware

that he was beginning to transfer his attention from Talia to Emmeline. It wasn't fair to either person.

Maybe what Emmeline had said to him last night was true.

My dad had a saying when Claude and I couldn't decide what to do about something. He said sometimes we need to retreat, spend time with God, before we can move forward. You need to meet with God, Seb. Don't forget God.

"It'll look lovely with your black dress." Sebastian reached for the bracelet.

As he placed it on Emmeline's wrist, he wanted to kiss her wrist, but it would be inappropriate.

Inappropriate? How?

They were both unattached at the moment. Talia had dumped him months ago—he just had to get over it.

Emmeline glanced at her watch. "I have to run. I'm always late. We have lunch first, do a bit of warm-up, then start playing at one o'clock. Don't want to miss lunch or the warm-up."

"Let me help you with your harp." Sebastian followed her to the front door.

He watched her play with the agate stones around her neck and wrist as he loaded the harp into the back of the SUV.

"Thank you, Seb." Emmeline pecked him on the cheek.

He wanted more, but it might be too soon for her.

"Off I go to another wedding." Emmeline walked toward the driver's side. "Always someone else's."

"Someday it'll be our—I mean, we'll have our turn."

Emmeline smiled and patted him on his arm. "You, maybe. Not me, Seb. I'm going to be single the rest of my life."

"How did you figure that?" What did she mean?

"It's better this way."

"Safer, you mean?" Sebastian stepped closer to Emmeline.

"Safer to be alone. Less trouble. Less heartache."

Sebastian reached for Emmeline's hand. It was soft in his. "The Bible says it's not good for man to be alone."

"There's a time for everything." Emmeline sat down in the driver's seat and buckled in. "Thank you again for the lovely jewelry. That's more than generous of you. Tell Matt I'm glad he kept them."

"I'm glad too." He stood at the open vehicle door, not wanting her to leave.

"Did he try to sell them to you?"

"No. We were talking, and he had the box sitting on his table in his office."

"He didn't put them back in his jewelry case?"

"Maybe he didn't get around to it. Maybe they were meant to be yours."

"I love these, Seb. I really do. I've wanted them for a long time."

"Okay. I better let you go." He closed the vehicle door for her.

She smiled and started the ignition.

As the SUV pulled out of the driveway, Sebastian waved, with a heart so bereft he wanted to run after Emmeline and stop the vehicle and make her promises...

Promises that he might not be able to keep.

Her parting words lingered in his heart.

There's a time for everything, Seb.

CHAPTER THIRTY-FIVE

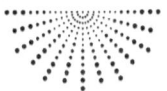

$\mathcal{W}$atching Emmeline drive his SUV away from Skye's house was difficult for Sebastian. He turned around and stopped at the front door to catch his breath.

He tried to get the front door to close properly.

This old house was quite a find for Skye. It was five minutes away from the Village grocery stores, and in the center of everything. From here, Skye could dart up and down the island to her clients' kitchens.

He trudged back to the kitchen, where Skye was plating two bowls of she-crab soup. He helped her carry the tray through the hallway to the deck out back, where they were eating lunch.

Sebastian sat down on the other side of the teak table on the porch overlooking a small garden. This was where Skye preferred to eat. The table was long, seated at least twelve, and it always reminded him of the days of yore when he and Skye had made a pretty good team cooking up a storm for their friends and neighbors.

Those were the days before Saffron on Jekyll, when Sage Café was a tiny hole in the wall that tourists walked past on their way to the pier, and Choosy Chef Channel hadn't discovered them yet.

How Sebastian longed to return to those days!

"What's going on between you and Em, Seb?" Skye asked.

He wondered sometimes if he should sell his forty-nine percent to Talia and walk away from Saffron. He wanted to get back to the kitchen to cook again. He really did. He had watched how happy his sister was singing in the kitchen.

"You didn't answer my question." Skye placed both hands on the table on both sides of the bowl of soup.

"What?" Sebastian studied the Band-Aid on Skye's thumb. "Cut yourself again? Please be careful, little sister."

"Okay. Let me try this one more time. Talia or Emmeline?"

Emmeline. "Let's say grace first and we'll talk. You say it, Skye."

Skye said the shortest prayer she had ever prayed over their meal at the table, and Sebastian wished he had prayed so he could delay the inevitable.

Forgive me, Lord.

"You're in trouble, aren't you?" Skye asked.

"This soup is very good."

"Thank you. Picked up a new recipe at the Miami Festival—don't change the subject, Seb."

"What subject?"

"Emmeline. Or Talia. Take your pick."

"I'm thinking of selling my shares of Saffron to Talia and starting over," Sebastian said.

Skye's spoon froze in midair. "First, you gave her the majority shares, and now you give her your livelihood? What does she know about the restaurant business?"

"Funding."

"Beyond that?"

"I'm not sure I want to work with her anymore. I need to step back and get some clarity. I'm no longer sure I want to spend the rest of my life with her."

"It's Jared, isn't it?"

"I'm getting the idea that she's sleeping with him."

"So you go after Emmeline."

"No. It's not—"

"I'm sorry, Seb. But you can't use Em as a backup plan. She's too precious for you to fool around with."

"I'm not..."

"You hate being alone, and she's available because of this stupid charade."

"I don't..."

"You know I consider Em my younger sister. You mess with her, and I'm never speaking to you again."

"Those are fighting words."

"You bet they are."

They ate their soup in silence until Skye spoke again.

"It's like you're afraid to let Talia go because you think she's the best there is, but I tell you, big brother, she's one of the worst there is."

"Don't say that about her."

"You know I'm telling you the truth. Other than your buddies, I'm probably the only woman outside your circle of friends who would tell you that awful truth."

Sebastian had to agree with his sister.

"Talia is—how shall I put it? She's all things to all men." Before Sebastian could defend Talia again, Skye raised her palm. "When she's with you, she's a proper Southern belle, wearing white, going to church. When she's with Jared, she's a party animal. When she's with her other boyfriends, she's whatever they want her to be."

"Not all at the same time."

"Listen to yourself, Seb. You can't defend her. She's an adult, doing whatever she wants, and she will pay for her actions. You can't bail her out anymore. You need to start thinking about your own life and what God wants for you."

Sebastian said nothing.

"Maybe God wants you to have someone who is..."

"Perfect?" Sebastian snapped.

"Let me finish, Seb. Maybe God wants you to have

someone who is growing in her relationship with Him, who desires to please God."

"A good Christian girl?"

"Only God is good. You know that. But what if He has someone in mind for you, someone who will grow with you through the ups and downs of life?"

"A life partner."

"Someone you don't have to manipulate circumstances for. Someone who doesn't have a circus you have to participate in."

"Circus?"

"And if God wants you to be alone for a while, you need to have patience. If you're meant to marry, that special someone will come along."

Sebastian studied his sister.

"What?" Skye asked.

"Are you talking to yourself or to me?"

"What do you mean?"

"You've been alone for a while, Skye. Are you waiting for someone?"

"I only want the right man that God brings to my doorstep."

Sebastian laughed. "Be careful what you wish for!"

"Therein is your problem, big brother," Skye said.

"My wish?"

"No. Your impatience." Skye sat back in her chair. "It's totally okay to be alone, to live alone, you know."

"That's because you're super picky and you hate anyone messing with your life, especially your kitchen."

"No one touches my kitchen."

"See?"

"Besides, I'm too busy. Oh, speaking of busy, I got a call from Choosy Chef Channel."

"No way!" Sebastian groaned. "I've been waiting for them to call me about showcasing Saffron on their restaurant shows."

"Well, maybe we could get Saffron some publicity."

"What did they call you for?" Sebastian asked, trying to contain himself.

"They put me on the shortlist for the regional cooking show, but they decided that since I'm a personal chef, they wanted to see if they could follow me around as I cook for people."

"Wow. I'm happy for you, Skye."

"I could prep my meals in the Saffron kitchen."

"That will be terrific. Anything you need, little sister."

"But if I'm going to be using Saffron's kitchen..."

"Yes?"

"I'm thinking..."

"Uh-oh."

"Sell me your Saffron shares," Skye said.

Sebastian's spoon fell out of his hand and splashed into his bowl of soup.

CHAPTER THIRTY-SIX

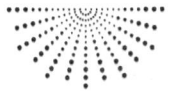

"Oriental" was strumming in Emmeline's mind when she returned to Skye's house later that afternoon just before dinner, and sneaked into her guest bedroom without alerting anyone in the backyard. She was quite sure someone had heard the front door chime, but no one came looking for her when she tiptoed barefoot down the hallway.

She heard music in the backyard, and figured that might have masked the SUV coming down the driveway and the door opening and closing.

A little tired from all those wedding festivities, Emmeline had been distracted throughout the entire Brock-Flannagan wedding by the periwinkle agate jewelry that Sebastian didn't have to buy for her.

She kept telling herself that Sebastian was only trying to be nice in return for her helping him with his relationship issues.

But he might be taking it too far now with the hotel stay, SUV, and now the jewelry.

Lord Jesus, give me wisdom.

Well, the wisest thing for her to do was to get offstage. Pronto. Yet, here she was, waiting to meet the private investigator whom Sebastian had hired to find Claude.

They were getting closer to finding him. She was sure of it.

She couldn't back out now.

Couldn't afford to.

There was no other way to find Claude.

Emmeline heard laughter and merry voices coming from the direction of the outdoor kitchen near the back porch. She quietly changed out of her black dress, her only one for SISO concerts.

She carefully took off the periwinkle necklace and bracelet and placed them in a tray on a side table.

She had wanted these for months.

Couldn't afford them.

God had provided for her. Or was it Sebastian pushing buttons he shouldn't be pushing?

Emmeline drew a deep breath as she threw on a T-shirt and a pair of shorts. She slid on her sandals and made her way out.

Keep my heart safe, Lord. Thank You, Jesus.

The smell of steak drew her toward the giant Weber grill.

"Hi." Sebastian was wearing a Sage Café apron. He

had a long pair of stainless-steel tongs in one hand and a thick mitten in the other. "How was the wedding?"

"Lovely." Emmeline felt worn out. Wondered how long all this running around would last.

"You played 'Oriental' on your harp?"

Emmeline nodded.

"That's my current favorite."

Emmeline didn't want to go any further there. *Nip everything in the bud.* "Need any help?"

"Nope. Skye and I have it under control. Helen should be here any time now. Want something to drink? Cooler's over there."

Emmeline grabbed a bottle of cranberry juice. "Where's Skye?"

"She forgot the rolls. She's gone down the road to get some. She'll be back."

"We don't need rolls."

"What I said." Sebastian opened the lid of the charcoal grill. "How do you like your steak?"

"I want it done. Nothing pink inside, but not overdone. Thank you."

"Okay."

"Very few people can get it right."

Sebastian looked offended. "Are you testing me?"

"I was trying to tell you not to worry about it. I'll eat whatever."

"Whatever? Is that a challenge?"

"No..."

"I'm going to get it right," Sebastian said. "I know

how to grill filet mignon, you know. That's how Saffron got started. All that seafood came later when Talia invested in the restaurant."

He cleared his throat.

Emmeline sensed a hesitation as if he didn't want to talk about Talia. She decided they should talk about something else, but what was there to talk about?

The aroma of steak was heavenly.

"You do like to cook, it seems." Emmeline wanted to leave but Sebastian was alone, doing all the grilling. She felt sorry for him, and decided to make small talk.

"I love to cook," Sebastian said. "I could do this all day long. Not grilling, I mean, but cooking."

"Why don't you?"

"I don't get much of a chance these days."

"Why not?"

"Talia—I mean, our restaurant already has a chef de cuisine. I hired him to free me up."

"Free you up to do what?"

"Exactly, Em." Sebastian eyed her.

"Do you find it hard to balance your relationship if your ex is also your business partner?"

"It used to be fun."

"Sometimes the best ideas don't work out." Emmeline glanced back at the house. "Hope Skye and Helen make it to dinner."

"Or it'll just be us. I don't mind that at all."

Emmeline walked with Sebastian toward the outdoor dining table, the smell of steak in her nose.

She wasn't sure if she deserved to eat filet mignon. She was the hamburger sort of girl only because steak was expensive on her side of the railroad tracks.

Still, Sebastian hadn't made her feel that way—that she was beneath him or anything. He was what normal people were, nothing too fancy like Jared and his opulence, and not too bottom-feeding icky like Bart, the landlord's son.

"If you could do anything in the world, you would still choose to play the harp, right?" Sebastian threw the question at her as they stepped up to the porch.

"Yes, of course." Emmeline followed him. "And you want to be a chef. You don't want to run just the business end of a restaurant."

"You know me well."

Hardly. "All we can do is pray for God to show you what to do."

Even as she said it, Emmeline felt like a hypocrite. Part of her truly wanted God's best for Sebastian. The other part of her was hiding behind mentions of prayers and God, as if He were a shield from her own foolishness to have agreed to go along with Sebastian on this wild scheme in the first place.

How do we unravel this Gordian knot, Lord?

"Where do I sit?" Emmeline shouldn't have asked.

"Next to me."

Yep. I shouldn't have asked. "Seriously."

"We need to keep up appearances."

Emmeline hesitated but she had to ask. "Or is there more, Sebastian?"

"I want more."

"But we can't have more."

"Maybe we—I—got it all wrong."

"We began our relationship on a pretense. Until we get right with God, we can never be right with—or for—each other."

Sebastian stared at her.

Something still hung in the air between them, unresolved and unsaid as Skye walked in with her precious rolls, and Helen Hu in tow.

They must've arrived at the front door at the same time.

Helen Hu of Hu Knows, Inc., was a hoot.

She had them all laughing throughout dinner with tales of how she trekked all over Europe for five months looking for Brinley's family heirloom. The 1692 Damaris Brooks Stradivarius that had been lost for over seventy years finally appeared in an obscure little museum storage outside Vienna.

Emmeline couldn't imagine the amount of money that the Brooks family had dished out to get the violin back in time for Ivan to practice on it for his wedding to Brinley.

Emmeline would've played in that wedding. However, she had another wedding on the same day.

Yes, she could be objective, step back, and let Ivan

go. It hurt a bit, but she could tell that Ivan and Brinley were made for each other.

Could she tell if her own turn came?

Oh, but I could be single the rest of my life.

And I'll have to be content with that.

Then again, was that what God wanted for her life?

"So." Across the table, Helen Hu dried her eyes. "Emmeline, tell me about your brother Claude."

The time has come!

Maybe, just maybe, Claude might be home for Thanksgiving or Christmas. She could only wish and pray. "Much to tell. Where do I begin?"

"The day Claude ran away."

Emmeline bristled. "You mean when he walked out of the concert hall?"

"Part of tracking where one might disappear to is to find out the psychology of their decisions and actions. So yes, I meant it when I said Claude ran away. My job is to find him."

Emmeline's lips quivered. She blinked a few times.

Under the table, she felt Sebastian's hand over hers. It was warm, felt a bit greasy, possibly from all the grilling, but she didn't care. It was nice to be comforted.

"Maybe we should wait until we finish dinner," Sebastian said quietly.

"That's fine too. I'm taking the morning flight out, so I have all night."

Emmeline wasn't sure if she had all night. She wanted to go to church in the morning not only because she had a sanctuary orchestra rehearsal at eight o'clock, but because God had been her only anchor and hope that Claude might be found again and returned to the O'Hanlon family intact, and she felt she was honoring God by serving in His house of worship.

Emmeline took a deep breath. "Give me a minute to gather my thoughts."

"Didn't I tell you to write everything down before I got here?" Helen asked.

"I forgot to forward her the memo," Sebastian admitted. "I'm sorry, Em. Slipped my mind."

"That's okay." Emmeline knew that when God gave her opportunities, she had to seize them or they would vanish.

She figured she could—in a very short time—tell Helen all she could about Claude and how he had an emotional breakdown. There wasn't a whole lot to tell after he had disappeared and then the rest of it now was Helen's job, wasn't it?

She did it in an hour flat. Not always organized like this, Emmeline felt that she had lived with this so long that it was just a matter of listing all the highlights for Helen. And that was all she had.

"Claude was last spotted at missions in Five Points and Marietta," Emmeline added. She had since released Sebastian's hand from under the table.

I'm a big girl. I can take care of myself.

"He gets around." Helen Hu closed her iPad.

"Probably walked or hitchhiked." Emmeline folded her arms. What else was there to tell?

Skye was crying when she brought desserts. "I will be praying so hard that Claude comes home, Em. So sad."

"Thank you, Skye." Emmeline felt strong, felt the Lord's strength with her. "God is going to take care of everything."

Helen laughed. "I'm not God."

"Yeah, but He's working through you to bring Em's brother back." Sebastian's voice was heavy.

"I hate to put a pall over this dinner," Emmeline said.

"No, you're not. It's a good thing. We're getting closer to finding Claude just by having Helen here."

He spoke with such confidence that Emmeline began to believe it was going to happen.

CHAPTER THIRTY-SEVEN

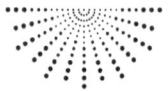

"You haven't heard her play 'Oriental,' have you?" Sebastian asked Skye when they were eating their desserts.

Emmeline was still elated, recollecting the last hour in her head, and remembering how happy she had been that Helen Hu had started the search for her brother even before they finished their main course.

The PI had made a call to her Savannah office, and just like that, the hunt had begun.

Thank You, Jesus!

"Haven't had the chance," Skye said. "Whenever we rehearse, we're singing hymns."

"I prefer hymns, actually." While Emmeline appreciated that Sebastian liked that Enrique Granados dance song, it wasn't the only one Granados had composed, and it wasn't the only thing she could play.

She continued nibbling on the delicious pastries

that went with the peach cobbler that Skye had made for their dinner meeting.

"I'm sorry," Sebastian said to Emmeline. "Didn't mean to put you on the spot. I bet you're exhausted. How long did you play this afternoon?"

"Two to three hours in total, but the various strings took turns, so it wasn't like I played straight through." Emmeline finished the peach cobbler.

Adjacent to Emmeline, Skye was still working on her dessert. "I want to hear it sometime, Em. Not tonight, if you're too tired."

"But tonight, if I'm not too tired?" Emmeline felt she could roll her harp out here and do it. She could play harp all day long.

She felt Sebastian's hand rub her shoulder. She didn't move. She remembered three nights ago when Bart had caused her so much trouble. Sebastian had rubbed her shoulders then too, and she hadn't said anything.

He reached for her hand. He was gentle with the scabs forming at the base of her palm. Emmeline appreciated the care.

But it can't last.

"Hey Helen, could you look into this guy named Bart Whatever?" Sebastian asked Helen, who was on her iPad across the table. "Give her his last name, Em."

"No." Emmeline touched his arm.

Sebastian ignored her. "Em won't press charges, but surely you can find something to hang him on."

Emmeline retracted her hand from Sebastian.

"What did he do to her?" Helen's dark eyes were blazing like it was time to pick a fight, and she was going to win again.

"I don't want to hear this." Emmeline got up and left the porch.

Skye followed her into the kitchen. "It's time someone stood up to Bart."

"I don't want any trouble."

"Trouble is my brother's nickname. When he puts his mind to it, watch out."

"What does he want from me, Skye?"

Skye shrugged. "I really don't know, and I think neither does he. God will sort it out."

"Meanwhile, what do I do? I'm stuck." Emmeline sighed. "I should've listened to you. I'm sorry. I'm such an idiot."

"My brother is a bigger idiot."

"Did you just call me an idiot?" Sebastian crossed the floor in a jiffy and was standing like an umpire, his chest all puffed up.

It reminded Emmeline of Rafferty trying to be taller in the music library the week before.

Emmeline began to laugh.

"Made you laugh." He was staring at her. "Skye, give us a moment, will you?"

"We don't need a moment," Emmeline protested.

"Yes, we do."

"For what?" From the corner of her eye, Emmeline saw that Skye was gone.

"For this." Sebastian lowered his lips toward hers.

Emmeline stepped back. "What are you doing?"

"I don't want Talia back, Em. I want you."

"Have you prayed about this?"

"No."

"Go talk to God first, and then come back to talk to me." Emmeline folded her arms.

"Okay. I will. I guess I'll go now. How about if I pick you and Skye up in the morning for church?"

Church?

Emmeline couldn't believe he sounded nonchalant.

"This is so wrong, Seb. We can't go to the house of the Lord in pretense."

"I'm not sure if I want to pretend anymore either. I'm done with Talia. I want to move on. I want us to move on together."

"Then what happens when Talia returns?"

"She won't."

"You can't *promise* me that."

"I guess I can't."

"Skye was right. This entire thing is a mistake. You may never get Talia back and I may never see Claude again."

"I don't want Talia back."

"The deal is that you're helping me with Claude and I'm helping you get Talia back. If you cancel the deal, what about Claude?"

"I don't care. I'll still help you with Claude."

"For nothing?"

"I want you."

"See? Think about what you just said." Emmeline blinked away her tears. "We can't continue this ruse. It's going too far. I'm not for sale."

Sebastian looked hurt. "For sale? What are you talking about?"

"You can't love two people at the same time."

"I don't—have you been talking to Matt Garnett?"

"Nope. Anyone with common sense can see that. This is not a polygamist society."

Sebastian laughed. "I promise you I'm serious."

"Don't promise what you don't understand."

"Look, Em. I'm trying to say that I'm done with Talia."

"You weren't last week," Emmeline reminded him. "What's going to happen next week? What will go through your mind next week?"

"I don't want to be alone."

Emmeline nodded. "I think that's the root of your entire problem, Sebastian."

CHAPTER THIRTY-EIGHT

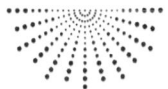

*a*fter a rehearsed exchange of soul-piercing words, Darcy escorted Elizabeth off the makeshift outdoor stage. The play ended at Neptune Park under a full moon and balmy June breeze coming off the St. Simon's Sound as the whole Theater by the Sea cast went back onstage for an encore.

Principal cast members were named, and Emmeline had the brightest smile that Sebastian had seen all week.

Could it be because Helen was on the hunt for Emmeline's missing brother?

Could it be that she really liked being onstage in this theater?

Could it be none of the above? Something like, maybe she'd seen Sebastian from the stage, how he'd paid attention to every scene she had been in throughout the one-hour play?

Sebastian waited patiently in his folding camp chair by the picnic blanket under the living oak. On said picnic blanket, Jared and Talia had been groping each other all evening, a sight that left Sebastian feeling absolutely nothing.

Does this mean I'm free?

Still, he hadn't moved from his chair because this was the spot he had told Emmeline he'd be, and he didn't want her to think he skipped the play, though Jane Austen hadn't been exactly his cup of tea. He tolerated the genre now that he was going out with Emmeline, but his fare had always been more action-adventure stuff.

A clink made him look. Jared was dumping bottles into the recycling bins and trash into the right bins. Talia wasn't doing anything, not even packing the picnic basket they'd brought.

Jared had insisted that they all came to the play together to support the theatrical group he was now underwriting. Talia had no choice but to attend, though Sebastian wondered how much of the play she had paid any attention to.

Sebastian hadn't spent his entire evening watching the play either. He had checked his emails here and there—whenever Emmeline wasn't onstage. Now that the play was over, he folded his camp chair and stuffed it into its carrying bag. He tossed soda cans and sandwich wrappers into the trash.

"You were great, Emmeline!"

Jared's voice scratched Sebastian's eardrums like a cat's claws.

Sebastian turned his attention to Emmeline, who had arrived at their little picnic spot.

"Flubbed a few lines. Ad-libbed a couple more." She stood closer to Sebastian than to Jared. "Not Alliance Theater material, I'm afraid."

Sebastian slung the strap of his camp chair carrier over his shoulder and reached for Emmeline.

Emmeline glanced in Talia's direction. Sebastian followed her gaze.

Talia was standing behind Jared, her face shriveled. If she kept at it, only Botox could straighten out all those wrinkles.

"Jared, help me with this blanket." Talia bent over —her assets bulging out of her low-cut summer blouse— as she tugged at a corner of the picnic blanket.

Once upon a time, such disregard for modesty had turned Sebastian on, but no longer. Tonight was proof of it.

Here he was, with his ex, and he felt nothing for her.

Have I let Talia go?

His new problem was Emmeline.

She didn't believe he was genuinely interested in her.

Sebastian leaned down toward her ear. She smelled like summer, the cool of night, the bright of day, time off, and respite from work.

He knew he would henceforth associate summers with Emmeline. Forever.

"You were great," he whispered softly. He didn't touch her, didn't put his hand on her shoulder, didn't weave his fingers into hers.

When he looked up, Jared was staring at Emmeline.

"Let's go, Jared." Talia was already walking away.

"See you next week, right?" Jared waved. "Rehearsal at my house."

Neither Sebastian nor Emmeline responded. When they were far enough away, Sebastian stole a kiss off Emmeline's cheek.

"Was that scripted?" Emmeline asked.

"Backstage pass?"

"There's no backstage pass, Seb."

Sebastian looked hurt. "I wanted to."

"What are we doing?" Emmeline asked. "Talia's gone with Jared. You said you no longer want her. Are we still staging a play for her? Whatever for?"

"I don't know what I'm doing."

"Exactly. We had a plan to win her back for you. Now you've changed your mind about your goal. I still need my brother found. You're paying a lot of money for nothing."

"Not for nothing."

"For charity then?"

"I don't want you to pay me back."

"You're confusing not only yourself, but me, Seb. You asked for a backstage pass a minute ago."

"Well..."

"Something is totally off with us here."

In the distance, Jared looked back. Waved.

Neither Emmeline nor Sebastian returned his wave.

"Let's get you home," Sebastian said to Emmeline.

"Home? I don't have my own. You mean to Skye's house?"

"Yeah." Somewhere in Sebastian's heart, he wanted to give Emmeline a place to stay.

A house.

A home.

Anything she wanted.

CHAPTER THIRTY-NINE

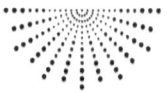

The call came just after midnight on Sunday, and all Emmeline could do was scream.

Part of her was upset that she hadn't worked fast enough and made it happen soon enough for Mom and Dad, and part of her was upset that God hadn't held back the deadline.

What if Dad died tonight?

Skye came running down the hallway and banged on her bedroom door.

Emmeline wiped the tears off her cheeks and climbed out of bed, her phone still in one hand. She could barely unlock the door.

"Em! What's going on?" Skye pushed her way in.

"Dad had another heart attack. He's at the ER." Emmeline was in the walk-in closet now, hauling out her suitcase. She barely made it out of the closet when she pushed it over and unzipped it. "I have to go home, Skye."

"I'm coming with you."

"No need. It's a five-hour drive."

"Let's see if we can get two plane tickets. I have miles."

"No." Emmeline dumped a few clothes into her suitcase. Then she was in the bathroom squeezing toothpaste on her toothbrush.

"Oh, I forgot. You can't fly." Skye was right behind her.

Emmeline shook her head as she vigorously brushed her teeth. All her life, she had had a fear of flying. How she was going to tour the world playing harp was anybody's guess.

Last summer, when Ivan had regaled her with old stories of his crossover concerts across Europe and Asia, they had all sounded exotic and vacation-like, but truth be told, it would be a nightmare for her to get on the plane.

Such a confining space. No grass beneath her feet. No fresh air. He had said sometimes they'd flown fourteen to eighteen hours non-stop.

Never mind. She was going to tour only in North, Central, and South America.

Now Dad may never see me play on the world stage.

Emmeline couldn't hold it in.

She shook the water off her toothbrush, careful not

to hit the beautifully painted washbowl that Skye had said she'd bought from Sandpiper Galleries at the pier.

"Don't leave without me." Skye's face was in the mirror. "I'll drive."

"No need, Skye. You've done enough for me."

"I'm your friend. Don't shut me out. I can help. I'll drive you."

Emmeline relented. "All right. I guess two sets of eyes on the road in the middle of the night are better than one. Maybe we can take turns driving."

"Give me five minutes, and I'll be ready to go."

"I need ten. I'm going to take a shower. I want us to go straight to the hospital."

"Okay. I guess I will too." Skye was almost out of the bathroom when she turned around. "Don't you think we should pray first?"

"Why didn't God stop this?"

Skye hugged her. "Em, let's not question God."

"It's my dad's third heart attack in five years."

"This world is messed up, Em. Let's get you to Atlanta and then we'll talk. Want me to pray for safety?"

Emmeline nodded.

Skye's prayer was swift and sure, things that Emmeline should have been able to pray about, but at this moment, she was so emotionally saturated that she was glad Skye could pick up the slack.

"You're a keeper," Emmeline said after Skye finished asking God to heal Kipp O'Hanlon.

"What are friends for?"

"I have very few friends like you." She thought for a femtosecond. "In fact, none but you."

"Well, I'll ask for favors later." Skye sailed out of the bathroom. "Don't leave without me!"

~

*E*mmeline drove up Interstate 75-85 just as the Atlanta dawn broke in the sky over Stone Mountain to the east.

Skye was asleep in the passenger seat. She had driven the first half of the way while Emmeline had tried—tried!—to sleep. She finally dozed off one hour into Macon.

Emmeline's adrenaline was going, and her anxious heart kept her awake, like little doses of coffee percolating through her system.

It did help that there was a full moon tonight, and in the cloudless sky, everything looked gray and defined all the way from Macon, up Interstate 75 to where it merged with Interstate 85.

In the bleak night, somewhere between Grady Hospital, which she'd passed to her left, and Midtown, she found the humility to pray and seek God's forgiveness for getting upset at everything.

But this is Dad.

"I don't want him to die, Lord." Emmeline barely whispered.

Her knuckles were getting less tense.

It was silly not to use the cruise control, but whatever.

"Don't let Dad die, Lord. Make him well so he can enjoy Claude when we find him."

It was even more urgent now that they find Claude.

"Please find Claude, Lord," Emmeline prayed. "You know where he is. Show Helen pronto, and bring him home."

"Amen." Skye barely opened her eyes. Her head rolled to one side. She looked rather cute asleep.

Emmeline wondered if Sebastian looked that cute asleep...

Banish the thought!

Emmeline hit the gas pedal, went over the speed limit by at least five miles, and then slowed down again. The last thing she needed now was to get a speeding ticket. She had to get to Emory Hospital fast, but safely.

She had turned off the GPS earlier. Not needed. She knew how to get to Atlanta. She'd grown up in Atlanta, even though Dad had been from Dublin—Ireland, not the Dublin in Georgia—and Mom had been born in Baltimore.

Now, she turned on the GPS again to find the Emory Hospital parking lot she had to pull into shortly. Emory was not only a teaching hospital, but also a university and medical school. Mom had told her which building she had to find.

"Breakfast." Skye stretched. "Feed me."

"What?" Emmeline realized that Skye was now truly awake. "I'm sure they have a cafeteria."

"Okay. Are we there yet?"

"Almost." Emmeline's voice cracked.

She remembered all those childhood days when Mom and Dad would take the two kids on road trips.

Claude and Emmeline would take turns asking, "Are we there yet?" just to hear Dad put on his Irish accent and scold them.

Please, Lord, heal my dad. I love him so much.

As the GPS directed Emmeline to the right street turns, one of the passages that Dad had read to her—when she had been a child—flooded into her mind.

Psalm 103:1-5.

Little did she know it would come in handy today. A reminder that God is the Great Physician. The Healer of all healers.

Bless the Lord, O my soul;
    And all that is within me, bless His holy name!
    Bless the Lord, O my soul,
    And forget not all His benefits:
    Who forgives all your iniquities,
    Who heals all your diseases,
    Who redeems your life from destruction,
    Who crowns you with lovingkindness and
tender mercies,
    Who satisfies your mouth with good things,
    So that your youth is renewed like the eagle's.

CHAPTER FORTY

Sebastian took it upon himself to be the deliverer of bad news in Sunday school, but it had come with a price. The entire class had believed that he was Emmeline's boyfriend, for real.

While it hadn't begun that way, the last two weeks of choreographed dates had caused him to develop strong feelings for Emmeline, something he hadn't felt for Talia. Not ever.

He wanted something more meaningful with Emmeline.

He didn't want to pretend anymore.

"So they're there now?" Benicio Ketteridge asked.

As per usual, he asked for prayer requests before he taught. In some other Sunday school classes, they had someone else do it, but this class was small enough that Benicio seemed to be able to do it all.

The only thing the former Navy chaplain didn't do was...

Sebastian couldn't think of a thing.

"Yes, they drove through the night," Sebastian explained. "They're waiting for Em's dad to come out of his quadruple bypass surgery."

Sebastian wished he could be with Emmeline now to hold her hand.

Silly me.

She can take care of herself.

"We'll keep praying," Benicio said.

Everyone concurred.

Benicio asked for more prayer requests, and then picked a few people to pray for all the requests this morning.

Brinley Brooks-McMillan prayed for Emmeline and Skye. She still looked jet-lagged, as did Ivan. They'd flown home from their European vacation only a few days prior.

God had brought the couple home safely. It was an answer to prayer.

"God's mercy should never be underestimated." Benicio opened his Bible. "He protects us even when we don't realize it."

Are you protecting me, Lord, by sending Em away?

Sebastian wasn't sure how that popped into his head.

Or are you protecting me from Talia by giving me Em?

He caught himself.

Beautiful Em is not mine.

She might never be.

Sebastian straightened his sagging shoulders. How could it be this hard? He had gone through a grueling six months in a chef school in Paris. He thought that had been hard.

This is harder.

"Have you all memorized Psalm 37:4?" Benicio looked around the room, and his eyes seemed to stop at Sebastian. "You know Pastor Gonzalez has encouraged everyone to think of God more. I know your men's and women's Bible study groups are studying this verse all month. Be sure to make some personal applications."

Personal applications?

Sebastian was sure Matt Garnett had kept his secret. Well, if he had broken up with Emmeline and started over, there would be no stage play, no charade, no ruse, no pretense.

Right?

I don't want to let her go, Lord.

Across the room, Matt was flipping through his old Bible. Sebastian remembered their conversation on Thursday.

Seb, you can't love two people at the same time. You'll always love one more than the other, and it'll be unfair to the other one.

"Delight in the Lord!" Benicio's voice boomed.

"Delighting in the Lord comes first before getting the desires of your heart."

What is the desire of my heart?

~

"*W*hat? She's not coming back to St. Simon's? Why?" Standing inside Seaside Chapel, by a bay of windows, Sebastian stared into his phone.

Skye's tired face was on FaceTime.

Down the hallway, Matt, Ivan, Brinley, and a few others were waiting for him at another side door. They had all planned on going to lunch together after church.

He waved to them, motioning them to go ahead without him.

He'd join them soon enough. Or not. Right now, he had lost his appetite.

"Her parents have no one else, Seb. No other relatives in town. Her mom's going to need her to help with her dad. Long recovery ahead. And she only has a short time before she goes back to UGA."

"I guess that makes sense. You look like the pits, Skye. How much sleep did you get?"

"A bit here and there. I'll sleep more later. I'm coming home this evening. I have to get back to work tomorrow. Em has your SUV, and I'm assuming you're letting her keep it."

"Indefinitely."

"Good. Nice of you, Seb."

"I want to be more than nice. I want her, Skye. Oops. Did I say that aloud?"

Silence.

Sebastian tried to read Skye's expression on his phone screen, but he didn't have to.

"Seb. Brother—big brother. Lost-in-the-woods brother. I'm talking to you. Yes, you. Sebastian *Trouble* Langston."

Uh-oh.

He knew what was coming every time his sister began her speech like that. Fortunately, he had earbuds on so no one could hear Skye. He started walking toward the church exit leading to the parking lot.

"If you want Em, you need to lose Talia. You will not give my friend partial love. It doesn't work."

"I've lost Talia. Months ago, when we broke up."

"Your emotions are still hanging on to memories of her."

Memories.

"The way it seems to me, you haven't completely let go of Talia. Until then, you won't be able to love anyone freely."

"You don't—"

"Every time Talia calls you, you go running back to her. Until you no longer have any feelings for her, until you can tell her no, you're not free to love."

"She hasn't called me lately."

"Just you wait. It's a cycle, and at some point, she's

going to get bored of Jared, and just you wait. She's going to call you."

"I won't answer."

"You say that, but I've seen you let her come back to you before, as if you're a parking place."

"I don't need to listen to this."

"So you made a mistake in high school. Forgive yourself and move on, especially if you have asked God to forgive you."

Sebastian knew his sister was right.

"I'm tired. I'm exhausted. I'm telling you that you can't fool around with Em. She's too precious for this. Your stupid scheme could ruin her for her future husband. Don't you see?"

"Husband? Ruin her? I don't want to ruin her. I want to—"

"I'm not done. Let her be with her family, okay? It's just as well that she doesn't return to St. Simon's. You're messing with her heart. Meanwhile, you need to settle your problems with Talia. Without Emmeline."

"Without Em? I can't—"

"Leave her alone, Seb. She's already lost her brother. Now she might lose her father too. Leave her alone."

Her brother.

Claude.

Sebastian climbed into his car. "I get the message, little sister. I appreciate your concern and care."

"Good." Skye looked relieved. "Will you pick me up at the airport at eleven fifty or so?"

"Sure. Anytime, Sis."

Skye looked away then back at her phone camera. "Gotta run. I'm in the cafeteria having lunch and I need to get back to Em. See what she needs."

"Tell her I'm praying for her. The entire Sunday school class is also praying for her."

"I'm sure she appreciates all your prayers."

"Keep me posted."

"Will do." Skye hung up.

Sebastian sat there staring at the steering wheel. He'd trade in his BMW i8 if it could speed up the search for Claude. That would make Emmeline happy.

I want to make her happy.

I don't want to ruin her. What is Skye talking about?

There was nothing he could do about Emmeline's dad. That was up to God, the doctors, and his therapists.

Long recovery ahead, Skye had told him.

But Claude...

Sebastian knew that he could do something about Claude.

He speed-dialed Helen Hu.

CHAPTER FORTY-ONE

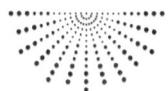

ednesday's forecast called for rain that hadn't come. Sebastian drove alone to the Fire Pit Service at Seaside Chapel, giving him time to think and pray in his rental car.

Funny thing, he didn't miss his BMW i8 at all. He wondered what had gone through his own mind when he had bought that fast car. He couldn't think of any road on St. Simon's Island where going from zero to sixty in seconds took him further than his compact two-door rental.

All week long, Sebastian had eaten his meals alone, walked alone, slept alone, and woken up alone. If not for the Seaside Chapel men's Bible study group meetings, Sunday school classes, church services, and the Sage Café kitchen crew, he'd be totally isolated from the world.

There was no Talia.

No Emmeline.

No one.

As Sebastian had suspected, Talia had moved in with Jared. However, they didn't live on Urquhart Island. They relocated to Savannah, where Jared had a business office. Sebastian was sure Jared had told Talia about the Urquhart family history dating all the way back to the early days of Georgia's founding. Knowing Talia, Sebastian doubted she was interested in the history of coastal Georgia at all.

All Talia was interested in was herself.

Why had Sebastian been attracted to Talia then, if there was nothing in the relationship for him?

Arriving at the church parking lot, Sebastian found a spot as close as possible to the Seaside Chapel pavilion. He decided against taking his umbrella with him, even though the sky was cloudy and it looked like rain would come.

If the rain came, he'd run back to his vehicle and take off.

If the rain came...

Rain would henceforth always remind Sebastian of that moment he had seen Emmeline walking on the sidewalk outside the SISO building some fifteen minutes from church. Her flowery periwinkle dress all askew, her hair wet and stuck to her face, the cheap umbrella twisted up. Yet she had refused to get in his car.

How could they have gotten into a fight the first day they had officially connected?

It had begun with a pretty face and a pretty walk. It had moved beyond that to something more heartfelt between him and Emmeline.

She had fought it.

Or, at least, she had tried to fight it—fight them.

For good reasons.

And it's all my fault.

Sebastian didn't remember how he ended up sitting next to Benicio Ketteridge on the pavilion, but there he was, a distance away from the Seaside Chapel back parking lot.

It had been two weeks since Emmeline had moved home to Atlanta.

Since then, Sebastian had been incommunicado with her, save for her curt and brief messages. He'd been the one to send more words per day than she had per week. He had been praying for her as she cared for her dad in recovery and her mother in distress.

Since the day Emmeline had left St. Simon's, Sebastian had stopped paying any attention to Theater by the Sea or any happenings in the Sea Islands Symphony Orchestra.

Every time he heard harp music, he thought of Emmeline.

And only Emmeline.

It might be why he couldn't have her. If all he thought about was her, where was God in the picture?

Don't forget God.

"You okay?" Benicio asked, putting his waterproof Bible underneath his folding chair on the pine floor of the pavilion.

Trust Benicio to hone right into his problems.

"Life is good," Sebastian replied.

"God is good," Benicio said. "Life on earth can be so-so."

"That's what I meant. God is good."

"He's always good. No matter what."

"Don't forget God." It came out of Sebastian's mouth just like that.

"Sounds like something Emmeline O'Hanlon would say." Benicio raised his eyebrows at him.

Sebastian averted that glint in Benicio's eyes. "Good reminder for believers, for sure."

"She's *gone* gone?"

"Looks like it." Sebastian didn't want to talk much in public about his personal angst. But the crowd was thin tonight. Only regulars were there.

Perhaps the rest stayed home due to the potential rain. That was why they'd met at the pavilion instead of on the still-damp beach. And no fire pit tonight for the Fire Pit Service.

"So why don't you take a vacation and go see how she's doing?" Benicio asked.

Why don't I? "She's moved on."

"You've only started going out with each other."

"A month ago next week."

"Been counting days, huh?" When Sebastian said nothing, Benicio continued, "Look, I'm not one who can give you relationship advice. In fact, I'll need some myself, but I can see you're in the dumps. Not the silly Seb I know."

"Me? Silly?"

Uh, what about that stupid charade he'd dragged Emmeline into?

Okay. Busted.

"All I know is this: when I was a chaplain, I had to deal with lots of Marines who didn't talk about what bothered them. You need to get it out before it takes you out."

"Meaning I'll implode or explode?" Sebastian chuckled.

"Meaning you'd self-destruct. Need I spell it out?"

"When do you stop teaching, Ben?"

"It's a gift, man. What's your gift?"

Sebastian had to think for a good minute. "Don't know. Cooking?"

"Cooking's not a gift, Seb. But it might be a manifestation of a gift that God has given you."

"I want to cook for people. I haven't done that in a while."

"Hmmm. Maybe your gift is helping others. But it's been suppressed. Backtrack, Seb. Go back to where you belong."

I belong with Em.

What did I just say?

"I'm stuck, Ben." *I've lost Talia and I can't reach Em.*

Benicio picked up his Bible. "Well, that's what we're going to talk about this evening. How to get out of stagnancy in your spiritual walk with the Lord."

"Pastor Gonzalez shared his sermon notes with you?" Sebastian knew that Benicio was on the shortlist for assistant pastorship at Seaside Chapel, but he hadn't kept up with the goings on inside the church beyond what he had heard here and there.

The men's group didn't talk much about third party information like that. Church business remained inside the church.

"Nope. Didn't you get the memo this afternoon? Pastor Gonzalez's flu has taken a downturn, and he's lost his voice. I'm teaching tonight."

Sebastian hadn't checked his email all day. "That's why most people didn't show up. That's really bad, Ben."

"Hey, the old silly Seb is back." Benicio pointed a finger at him as he walked away to get set up for the cordless microphone.

It was then that Sebastian noticed Benicio's new right leg. Sebastian had been so full of his own misery the last two weeks that he hadn't been paying attention to anyone else outside his little coconut shell.

Did Benicio have the new stars-and-stripes prosthetic on Friday at the Bible study? Sebastian couldn't remember.

Now Benicio's patriotic leg reminded Sebastian that he'd had plans to celebrate the Fourth of July weekend with Emmeline, plans now dashed because she wasn't there.

He had it all scheduled on his calendar. A drive up to Savannah to watch the fireworks by the Savannah River. A stay—in separate rooms—at one of the historic inns. Dining with her in five-star restaurants.

Holding her hand all the way there and back.

Now she was five hours away, taking care of her parents.

What was that like?

Sebastian and Skye had been orphaned early enough he didn't quite have to go through taking care of elderly or sickly parents.

Yet, he imagined it was a full-time job. Possibly draining on the caregivers.

He wondered if Emmeline had time to keep up with her harp. If she still played that Granados piece. If she remembered those moments when she had played that piece in his presence.

Nah.

CHAPTER FORTY-TWO

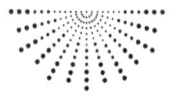

"*I* was talking to a friend recently, and he told me he's stuck," Benicio told the small crowd after he prayed.

Sebastian wondered what Benicio was up to.

Note to self: Be careful what I say to Benicio. It will be used in a sermon.

"It's one thing to be stuck in a rut," Benicio said. "Maybe you have a business or family issue. You can almost always find a solution for those things, right? What if you're stuck spiritually? As far as I know, spiritual stagnancy is harder to resolve."

Am I stuck spiritually?

Sebastian stared straight ahead, trying not to make any eye contact with Ben, knowing that his Sunday school teacher and friend was probably looking his way.

"You know what the first step is to fixing spiritual stagnancy?" Benicio asked. "Sebastian has the answer."

Sebastian's eyes flicked toward Benicio's. The latter nodded. Gestured for him to answer.

"Uh... Don't forget God?"

"Absolutely, Seb. That's the key. If you're stagnant in your walk with the Lord, the first thing you'd want to do is go to God. Right away. Seek His face. His counsel. His solution."

Go to God. Right away.

I failed, then.

Sebastian recalled that night after dinner with Helen, that evening he had found Skye and Emmeline chatting in the kitchen as they cleared the dishes and put away the leftovers.

After Skye left them alone, Sebastian had felt the urge to kiss Emmeline, but she had refused him. Shortly after that, she had said something profound to him.

Go talk to God and then come back to talk to me.

Had Sebastian forgotten God?

It seemed he had.

"Turn with me to Matthew 6:33." Benicio flipped the pages of his Bible with such efficiency that he was on the verse sooner than Sebastian could type the reference in his tablet Bible software.

When everyone was ready to go, Benicio asked someone to read it aloud.

Skye did.

Skye.

Sebastian felt bad that he hadn't even noticed his

sister's arrival at the Fire Pit Service. He hadn't said hello to her for days now.

Skye read in her clear, crisp voice that cut through the wind and sounds of the surf in the backdrop.

The surf.

Have I been so full of myself tonight I didn't even hear the surf?

The sounds of the ocean waves ebbing and flowing all around the group reminded Sebastian that God's world and days continued, and that He, the Maker and Creator of it all, continued as well.

Don't forget God.

"Beautiful, Skye." Benicio stepped forward. "Would you read that again for us?"

"Sure thing." Skye still had her finger on the verse.

But seek first the kingdom of God and His right-eousness, and all these things shall be added to you.

That was all the sermon Sebastian needed to hear tonight. So far, he had placed himself—not Emmeline or Talia—above God.

It was time to refocus his priorities.

Henceforth, God came first.

Help me follow through, God.

In his heart, Sebastian prayed. If God wanted him to have Emmeline, then they'd see each other again in God's time.

If not, then God would bring to him the right girl-friend. Someday.

If not, he'd learn to wait for God.

Wow. Did I say all that?

Sounds pretty good, but...

Sebastian tapped on his iPad and typed all that in because he knew he'd forget what he'd resolved. He knew himself, that when troubles came, he'd do that one thing Emmeline had warned him about.

He'd forget God.

"What now?" Benicio continued. "What is your action plan to get out of that spiritual quicksand you're in? You can't save yourself. Call out to God and He will reach in and pull you out."

Spiritual quicksand? I'm in one now.

It was all Sebastian thought about the rest of the time.

When Skye stood up to sing a few more hymns, Sebastian could see the spot where Emmeline would have been sitting down with her lap harp. Instead, Matt Garnett with his guitar had taken her place.

He liked Matt and all, but he was no Emmeline.

By the end of the third hymn, Sebastian knew what he had to do.

It was as clear as Skye's voice and as confident as the ocean's dance.

It was as calm as God's Word and as certain as God's will for his life.

Time to get up.

JAN THOMPSON

And cook something.

CHAPTER FORTY-THREE

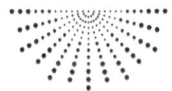

*C*alming Mom in the surgery aftermath had been more difficult than Emmeline had expected, possibly because it was the third bypass surgery that Dad had gone through in the last five years. Every time they had ended up in the hospital, Mom had been more distraught than before.

In the few weeks since Emmeline had arrived at her parents' home, she had taken care of everything for them, from paying the bills to watering their plants to feeding the cat to fielding phone calls from their friends and family.

Every now and then she had thought of Sebastian and wondered how he was doing, but more important things had delayed her from emailing him.

By the end of each day, Emmeline was exhausted and all she could do was crawl into bed to catch some sleep before the next day started all over again.

One piece of good news was that her parents' church had been bringing a steady stream of meals for them. No one needed to taste either Mom's cooking or hers.

What would Sebastian say if he found out she could barely scramble an egg?

Sebastian?

Does it matter what he thinks of me anymore?

Still, Sebastian was on her mind. Was he closer to getting Talia back?

Emmeline felt bad for leaving him high and dry with that news she had sent him by way of his sister Skye two weeks ago.

She wasn't returning to St. Simon's Island.

Emmeline glanced at her watch. Five o'clock.

Her parents weren't home yet from Emory. Traffic must've been bad. Friends from church had played chauffeur this afternoon and taken her parents to see Dad's cardiologist. When they had offered to take care of the doctor's appointment, Emmeline had to say yes.

Why not? It was a big to-do taking Dad to the doctor, even with the free lunch thrown in. Dad was, at best, a difficult patient. He'd rather suffer at home than wait at the doctor's office.

Emmeline had considered the opportunity to catch her breath as a blessing from God. She sat on a rattan chair and watched the world go by as the sun moved in and out of the rustling trees in the front yard.

One more month, and it would be the first day of the fall semester at the University of Georgia.

If all went well with her parents, Emmeline would be driving to Athens from Roswell in two weeks, to the day.

If they still needed her help, she'd postpone her enrollment at UGA to the spring semester.

So far, things were going well.

Thank You, Lord.

She sighed.

Not all things.

She owed Sebastian an apology for not being able to keep her end of the bargain. She needed to make sure that he hadn't kept paying Helen Hu to search for Claude. Of course, she wanted her brother found, but not at Sebastian's unrewarded expense.

Next thing she knew, she was inside the house looking for her cell phone.

Sebastian picked up at the first ring, as if he'd been expecting her to call.

"No apologies needed, Em. I understand."

"It's not fair to you," Emmeline said.

"No worries. Besides, Talia moved to Savannah."

"She did? Why?"

"She moved in with Jared."

"Oh."

"It's over. I'm officially single." A pause. "I've been single for months. I just didn't see it for what it was —is."

"We all find our way forward."

"With God's help, we won't be wandering around."

"Exactly. Look, I'll find a way to pay you back for Helen Hu."

"No."

"I can't put you out like that, Seb."

"Then have dinner with me."

"One dinner?"

Another pause. "One is better than no dinner at all. I'll cook."

"It'd better be good."

"Are you questioning my ability to cook?"

Emmeline laughed. "I'll find a way to get your SUV back to you."

"You can keep it until we have dinner together."

Emmeline walked about in the family room. "I'm not even driving it anymore. Mom wants me to use their old car to keep the engine going."

"I can get around. Don't worry about it."

"In your little putt-putt car."

Sebastian chuckled. "Well, how are you, Em?"

"Me? I'm fine. Well, truth is…I'm exhausted."

"I bet. Must be hard to take care of one parent, let alone two."

"They're not invalids, but still… Yes, I'm thankful that we have church friends who are helping out. In fact, I have a few hours off this afternoon since I don't have to take Dad to the cardiologist."

"Good. Well, we miss you. I miss you."

Emmeline didn't respond to that.

"Everyone's praying for you over here, from Pastor Gonzalez to our men's group. Keep me—or Skye —posted."

"Sure. Please tell them thanks. We appreciate all prayers."

"Will do."

"What are you doing these days to keep busy?" Emmeline stood by the window.

There, with the bits of sun rays reflected off the window panes, she remembered the first time Sebastian had gone to the SISO building—where he had talked to her mechanic, fended off Rafferty, and told her he wanted a certain piece of harp music played at his wedding.

It seemed so long ago now...

"Me? I'm getting back to the kitchen." There were hints of joy in Sebastian's voice.

"Isn't cooking what you love?"

"Yep. Probably as much as you love your harp."

"I do love my harp."

"I miss hearing you play."

Emmeline turned back toward Dad's harp in a prominent corner of the family room, away from the fireplace and windows.

"Hold on a sec, Seb." She placed the cell phone on the music stand to one side of the harp, and turned on the speakerphone.

She adjusted the bench behind the harp, and sat

down. "So. What do you want to hear?"

"Anything. 'Oriental,' maybe?"

"Aren't you tired of that?" No reason for her to revive his interest.

Her phone call to Sebastian wasn't to keep their connections alive, but it was for apologies and closing out an ill-conceived chapter.

"Not when you play it. You can play that piece for me every day for the rest of my—uh..."

Emmeline felt awkward.

This is exactly what I had feared.

Then again, she had felt something for Sebastian too, hadn't she? Still, no need to fan it.

There was silence between them. Emmeline figured they were both pondering their end of the bargain.

Bargain?

Well, it had begun as a deal.

Now, Emmeline didn't know anymore.

"How about something else?" she asked, giving Sebastian a way out.

"Surprise me."

Emmeline pulled the harp toward herself. She strummed. "Can you hear that?"

"Loud and clear."

"I'll play you one of Dad's favorite hymns. Do you want to hear 'Wayfaring Stranger' or the one I arranged myself?"

"Yours."

"Fanny Crosby wrote the lyrics for 'For You and Me.' Are you familiar with that?"

"No."

"You might be more familiar with 'O Love Divine,' another arrangement from the nineties." Emmeline strummed.

"Yes, I've heard that at church before," Sebastian said on the phone.

"This is a new arrangement of my own. I did this for Dad's birthday ten years ago."

"What did you title it?"

"I called it 'Divine Love.' Ready?"

"Yeah."

Harp music filled the room as Emmeline played and sang.

> *O Love divine, amazing Love,*
> *Was brought to earth from Heaven*
>   *above;*
> *The Son of God, for us to die,*
> *That we might dwell with Him on*
>   *high...*

When Emmeline finished playing the hymn, there was silence on the cell phone. She thought she'd lost Sebastian and that she would have to play it all over again.

Then she heard some sort of sniffle. "Are you coming down with something?"

"Allergies. Just allergies."

CHAPTER FORTY-FOUR

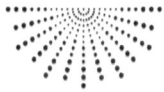

"*S*top calling and texting me repeatedly at all hours of the day and night." Helen Hu's voice was terse. "Let me call you when I have news."

Sebastian mumbled into his phone. "I just want Em's brother found."

"So do I. Have to use up your retainer, you know."

"Appreciate your honesty there." Sebastian slid onto the chaise lounge on his deck overlooking the marshes.

He wished he'd bought a house facing the ocean, but those cottages were expensive. If he had to sell this house to help find Claude, he might do it. A place to stay was nothing for him. He'd bought this house for his future together with Talia.

Except Talia had taken her future somewhere else.

In a way, Sebastian felt that he, too, had moved on.

"Since you're calling me now, Helen, does that

mean you have news?" Sebastian swatted a couple of mosquitoes from his thighs and arms.

The citronella candles weren't working too great this late morning. Those buzzers came around the clock. Used to be they'd come out early mornings and late evenings. These days the entire southeastern United States seemed to be infested with them —*Smack!*

"As a matter of fact, I do."

Sebastian sat straight up. "Why didn't you say so?"

"I'm still miffed that for the last three weeks you've called me incessantly and texted me until my phone memory runneth over."

"I'll never understand you, Helen."

"Don't get personal with me, Sebastian."

"What's the news?"

"How soon can you pack?" Helen asked.

"You found Claude!" Sebastian sprang up and bounced on his deck.

He felt a bit silly, but no one else was around. He had paid a goodly sum for this deck, and as the owner of said overpriced deck, he could do whatever he wanted.

"We've had many sightings, but this one is pretty good. I sent photos to the O'Hanlons, and they pretty much confirmed it's Claude. I'm going to see them this afternoon before they serve dinner at the soup kitchen, and I thought you might want to tag along, considering that it's your reward money that has accelerated our search."

That.

"I still can't believe you're doing this for some girl you just had a few dates with."

"It's more serious than that, Helen."

"In that case, if you want us to do a background check on this lady friend of yours, just call my office."

"I'm not sure if that's necessary."

"We can do the entire thing on her, including blood work. You don't want to marry someone only to mess up your babies due to blood type incompatibility."

Huh?

"Helen, focus. You were talking about Claude, remember? Claude O'Hanlon."

"What? Oh yes. Sorry about that. I've been up all night on another case."

"Maybe you need a break. Come to St. Simon's. Take a sabbatical."

"I just might, if I can fit it into my calendar." Helen sighed loudly. "Okay. Claude O'Hanlon. I'm meeting the family at four o'clock this afternoon. Can you be there?"

"I don't want them to know I put up the reward money."

"They don't know. But the whole family was having a cry-fest and I thought maybe you'd want to comfort your lady friend."

"Em? She's tougher than you think."

"Fine. Forget I suggested it. I'll let you know what we find."

"Wait, Helen. I didn't mean I'm not going. Are you kidding?" Sebastian checked the time on his phone. Almost eleven. "Let me see if I can get a flight out in the next couple of hours. Hold on a sec."

"I don't have a sec. Text me."

"You just said stop texting you."

"I'll make one exception. Gotta run, Seb. Have another case to open."

"Thank you, Helen. I appreciate all your hard work."

"Don't thank me. Thank God. It's a miracle we found Claude. Do you know how many thirty-something mentally ill men are wandering about these homeless shelters all across the Southeast?"

CHAPTER FORTY-FIVE

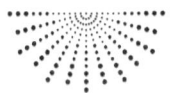

"She's here! She's here!" Mom flitted from throw pillows on the couch to armchair and then back at throw pillows, rearranging them as she went.

"Did you hear that?" she practically screeched. "She's pulling up the driveway."

Emmeline straightened up some coffee table books, praying quietly for her parents that they'd stay calm.

She also prayed that Claude would really come home soon. It sounded too good to be true, but then if she walked by faith, she shouldn't doubt God's provisions.

She had to trust that God would answer their prayers one way or another.

Even if the answer is: You'll never see your brother again until you go to Heaven.

Emmeline picked up some scattered travel magazines. Mom had been at it again, dog-earing cruise pages she wanted to show Dad when he felt better. Not that it was any surprise to Dad. Both her parents had been thinking of taking an Alaskan cruise for the longest time, but they'd never gone.

Now with Dad's heart attack, Emmeline wondered if she should suggest they go on their vacation before it was too late.

Dad stayed in his favorite recliner on the other side of the coffee table, stroking the cat on his lap.

Claude's cat—who sometimes answered to "Dinner" when he didn't feel like responding when called by his real name, Chase—was pushing ten years old. The ginger cat's facial fur had turned whitish.

He preferred nothing better than to nap on Dad's lap. Often they'd sit together for hours with either Mom or Emmeline having to turn off the television after Dad had dozed off.

Dad tried to appear calm, but Emmeline knew he had been as excited as Mom when Helen Hu called this morning to say they had spotted Claude at the DeKalb Soup Kitchen off Memorial Drive.

Two days prior, someone had seen him in the Marietta area. How he managed to get from Cobb County to DeKalb was anyone's guess. He'd have to walk or hitch a ride around Interstate 285 either through Dunwoody or in the Chamblee area.

Emmeline couldn't imagine what life was like on the streets.

She held back a tear as the doorbell rang.

"Get the door, Em." Mom plopped down on the couch, all ladylike.

Barefoot, Emmeline padded toward the front door. On both sides of the door were stained-glass panels preventing her from seeing who was outside.

It had to be Helen Hu, but one couldn't be too sure. This was neighbor-friendly Roswell, but this was also metro Atlanta, where they locked their doors two ways and set their house alarms every night.

She peeked through the peephole. Saw no one.

The doorbell rang again.

"Open the door, dear!" Mom's voice became impatient. "It's Helen."

Emmeline unbolted the door.

And stared over Helen's head. "What are you doing here?"

"To talk about Claude, of course," Helen said.

Emmeline pointed at Sebastian. He had some sun on him and a fresh haircut. "Him. Why is he here?"

Helen Hu, on five-inch stiletto heels, came up to about Emmeline's shoulders. "He's why we found Claude this soon."

Mom was right behind Emmeline. "Please come in, Helen."

Emmeline let Helen through.

Sebastian remained where he was standing.

Emmeline was suddenly embarrassed. She stepped outside and closed the door behind her for a private word with Sebastian.

"I'm so very sorry." She sighed. "I don't know why I was rude."

"You were shocked to see me." Sebastian lifted her chin. "I missed you too."

He missed me?

Emmeline didn't respond to that. Neither did she step away from Sebastian's touch.

"Let's go inside," she said.

"You mean it?"

To show that she did, Emmeline gave him a quick hug.

"Next time, I want a longer hug." Sebastian grinned.

"Dream on." Emmeline opened the door.

Helen Hu's animated staccato voice drew them both into the family room to join the conversation.

Mom began to cry a little. The cat perked up when Mom began to sniffle loudly. He leapt off Dad's lap and rubbed against Mom's legs.

When Dad looked her way, Emmeline had no choice.

"Mom, Dad, this is Sebastian Langston." Emmeline watched Dad's expression as Sebastian walked to the recliner and shook Dad's hand.

"He's a—a—uh, friend." It was all she wanted

to say.

"You work for Helen?" Dad asked him.

"No, I have my own business." Sebastian glanced at Emmeline.

Emmeline didn't say a word. In fact, she hadn't said anything about Sebastian to her parents since she had arrived in town several weeks ago.

Mom simply waved to Sebastian. She was busy swiping Helen's tablet to look at the slideshow.

Emmeline sat down next to Mom. Leaned over to look at the footage of a soup kitchen. "Is that Claude in the line?"

"It is Claude. He looks older. My baby looks terrible." Mom started to weep again.

Somewhere in the room, Emmeline knew there was a box of tissues, but she suddenly couldn't remember where. Her eyes were looking for it, when the box magically appeared in front of her.

Sebastian was one step ahead of her.

"Thanks." Emmeline handed it to Mom.

Sebastian crossed over to the other side of the coffee table, and sat down on a chair next to Dad.

Dad was eyeing him. "So you're a friend of Em's. On St. Simon's or at UGA?"

"St. Simon's. We attend the same church."

Dad nodded as if it explained everything. "And what do you do?"

"I own a restaurant."

Emmeline looked up. "Two?"

"Sold my share of Saffron to Skye," Sebastian explained. "We signed the papers a few days ago."

"Oh. I haven't talked to Skye since last week." Emmeline couldn't get over the idea that Sebastian and Talia were no longer business partners.

What did that mean?

CHAPTER FORTY-SIX

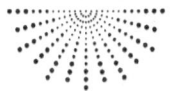

"Two hundred thousand dollars?" Emmeline gasped.

If she weren't sitting down in the RV parked outside a soup kitchen in Marietta, she'd be wobbling on her knees and tripping in that small compartment.

Two hundred big ones.

Reward money for finding Claude.

Emmeline glanced over at Sebastian, who was on his phone. He seemed unaware of how shocked she was to hear the staggering amount that Helen Hu offered to any homeless shelter or soup kitchen that could help them find Claude, and bring him home to his family.

Suddenly the back of Helen Hu's RV felt stuffy, stifling, steamy. Emmeline closed her eyes. Leaned back against the vinyl seat.

"Money can open mouths," Helen Hu said nonchalantly, as if she had used money before to buy information.

The RV door opened, and two men climbed in. They looked like oversized linemen in grungy clothes. Dressed to blend in to the soup kitchen crowd, Emmeline supposed.

"Might not happen today, Helen," one of them said. Emmeline thought his name could be Hugo, but she forgot. "We tried."

"I know."

"I'm surprised they don't have a bigger crowd for lunch."

"And they canceled dinner tonight for some reason." The other man sat down next to Helen. "The volunteers told us that tomorrow evening, after church services, they might get a crowd. Extra bowl of soup for everyone if they attend church—morning or evening— and bring the program from the service."

"Until then?" Helen asked.

"We just have to call it a day," the first man said. "Come back tomorrow after church."

"Well, today is the second day of nothing." Sebastian stretched.

"Patience," Helen replied.

Patience.

Emmeline needed more of that, even after five years of waiting for her brother to come home.

The night before, they had been at a homeless shelter in Newnan, in south Atlanta, having received tips from some volunteers that a man fitting the description had been spotted.

That hadn't panned out.

Emmeline closed her eyes, prayed for calm and peace and God's perfect will for her brother.

You know where Claude is, Lord. Show us where he is. Bring him home. We love him so much. We've missed him so much.

"The family is sure that was him in the photo," Helen said. "Earl, your thoughts?"

"Transients." Earl shrugged. "They move around."

Emmeline stayed quiet, but she appreciated the fact that Earl hadn't called her brother homeless.

Then again, that was what Claude was: homeless.

She wondered what really happened in his mind five years ago when he had snapped.

Helen Hu had recommended that their family physician and a mental health expert to be on standby because Claude would need all the help he could get.

Emmeline knew that her brother needed God, most of all.

She felt a hand on her shoulder. It was warm and assuring.

She looked up.

Sebastian said nothing. In fact, he had said very little since they had boarded the RV some two hours ago after Hugo had called, announcing they had arrived at this soup kitchen near the city square.

Saturday was a busy time in Marietta, but today's soup kitchen crowd was thinner than usual.

"So why don't ya'll go home, and we'll text you when we have something?" Earl asked.

It sounded like a good idea.

Helen looked at Sebastian and Emmeline. "Hugo and Earl will handle the situation, all right? I have to go to a meeting with my cousin. I'll be staying overnight at his house, going to church with him and my other cousin, and then he's taking me to the airport. I'm flying out to San Antonio again. Duty calls."

Emmeline nodded. "You've done so much, Helen. Thank you."

"Don't thank me." Helen pointed to Sebastian. "Thank him over there."

"Thank God," Sebastian replied. "He never fails us."

Don't forget God.

Emmeline's own advice to Sebastian about the other matter now came back to her own heart.

"I've got to go. Devon's waiting for me." Helen peeled herself off her seat, and patted Sebastian's arm on her way out of the RV. "Love my new car."

Emmeline heard her. "What's that about?"

"Nothing," Sebastian said.

❧

They made it home in time to find Emmeline's parents taking an afternoon nap in the living room. Only Claude's cat greeted them.

"No, Chase, he's not home yet." Emmeline picked him up.

Sebastian stood by the closed front door, near the coat tree in the hallway, watching Emmeline coo to the cat, and him purring back at her.

In the living room, Emmeline's mom stirred in her rocker. She suddenly announced it was time to cook dinner.

When Emmeline's mom disappeared into the kitchen, Emmeline let the cat go and stepped close to Sebastian. She reached for his face.

He wondered what she was up to.

A kiss was too much to ask.

"She only makes one kind of meatloaf," Emmeline whispered.

Ah, no kiss.

Sebastian chuckled. "Is that a warning?"

"Just a caution. I hope you have a strong stomach for questionable ingredients."

Sebastian burst out laughing.

Emmeline's palm flew to cup his mouth. "Shhh!"

She was standing so close to him that he thought her eyeballs looked as huge as those giant gulab jamun sweet dessert balls in Indian restaurants.

Slowly, Sebastian reached for her hand. He lifted it away from his mouth and gently kissed her palm.

Emmeline's eyes remained wide, and then she began to smile.

"Are we sneaking around?" she asked.

"Yes, you are!" Mom's voice came up behind them.

Startled, Sebastian dropped Emmeline's hand.

Her mom laughed.

And now Sebastian knew where Emmeline got her laughter from. He wondered if Mrs. O'Hanlon was how Emmeline was going to look like at sixty-something. Tall and beautiful, with smiling eyes...

And trailing a smoky smell of something—

"Burning?" Sebastian marched past the two women, straight into the old kitchen.

Smoke wasn't coming out the oven, but the intense smell of something charred was. Sebastian wondered whether to open the oven door to find out. He glanced at the old dial, and it was set to five hundred degrees.

Five hundred!

What is this woman cooking?

Eleanor O'Hanlon waved her hands and laughed again. "Oh, don't worry about it. It'll thaw, and then it'll cook."

"Thaw?" Sebastian asked.

"It's leftover meatloaf, but I forgot to take it out of the freezer."

"You can't thaw frozen meatloaf in an oven at five hundred degrees," Sebastian said as calmly as he could.

"Well, I might have forgotten to clean the oven from the last time I burnt the lasagna. The cheese sort of overflowed out of the pan."

"Sort of? So, the high heat is now charring the bits of once-cheese at the bottom of the oven, you're saying?"

"Why are you asking me all these questions?" Emmeline's mom placed her fists on her hips. "This is not your restaurant!"

CHAPTER FORTY-SEVEN

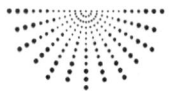

*S*unday came and went without any sign of Emmeline's brother in any of the metro Atlanta soup kitchens that Helen Hu's men had been monitoring.

As far as Emmeline knew, they had sent out more email blasts to the area missions, homeless shelters, ministries, and churches in the hope that the two-hundred-thousand-dollar reward money would invoke alertness and trigger memories.

All they needed was a sighting.

A verifiable sighting.

Claude had weaved in and out of visibility, and that was frustrating to Emmeline. Yet, in front of her parents, the last thing she needed to do was show her impatience.

Besides, the fact that Claude had been spotted on

Thursday meant he was still lurking in the Atlanta area.

But it was Sunday now. In three days, he could have walked out of Atlanta—or walked all over the city. The weather was hot, yes, but if he walked in the cool of night...

Emmeline shut another drawer in the kitchen. She was sure she had put Sebastian's SUV key in one of these drawers, but it wasn't there now.

A small panic rose in her chest.

She went back to the first drawer—

There it is.

Thank You, God.

She must've been thinking too much and not paying attention. She spun around to return to the living room, but didn't go far.

Sebastian was standing there, hands in his jeans pockets, his green collared shirt nicely buttoned. It was the same shirt he had worn to church that morning.

"I was going to bring the key to you." Emmeline held the key in the air. "Are you packed and ready to go?"

Sebastian nodded. He took the SUV key from her.

"I still think you should wait until morning," Emmeline said.

"You want me to stay."

"To stay alive. Are you sure you'll be able to stay awake, driving through the night?"

"Caffeine will keep me awake."

Emmeline tried not to be overly concerned.

"I checked the weather forecast. Clear night all the way to the coast." Sebastian pointed to the clock on the wall. "I should be home around six in the morning—if I start driving in half an hour."

He was taking the SUV back to St. Simon's Island, back to his work, back to his life.

Emmeline held back a tear.

I have to let him go.

Sebastian reached for Emmeline's elbow. "I want us to be together, but this seems like the wrong time."

"You want us to be together?" Emmeline felt a bit confused.

Had their ruse morphed into something more now?

Sebastian nodded. He stepped closer.

"We need time to think through this," Emmeline said. "I'm sorry our plan failed, Seb. Talia moved on with Jared."

"Moved *in* with Jared." Sebastian expelled a breath, as if in relief. "I did find out she wasn't mine to begin with. She was never mine."

And he wasn't ever mine to begin with either.

"Let God work it out, right?" Emmeline suggested.

Sebastian nodded again.

"Neither of us got what we wanted. You don't have your ex back. I don't have my brother. But we still have God."

"God is all we need," Sebastian added softly. His thumb rubbed Emmeline's elbow.

"Maybe what we wanted isn't what God has planned for us. I want my brother back." Emmeline blinked a couple of times. "What if... What if he's dead?"

"Hush." Sebastian wrapped his arms around her.

Emmeline wanted to rest her head on his shoulder forever, but she could not.

She peeled back. "You'd better get going. It's a five-hour drive, remember?"

"I could use some coffee to go, if you have any."

"I'll make some." Emmeline stepped toward the stove to check if the kettle had water in it. She filled it with filtered water, saying nothing to Sebastian.

She was fully aware that he was standing there, waiting for her to speak. She had nothing to say to him. This was goodbye.

She found Dad's French press in the dish rack nearby.

"Tell me where the coffee is," Sebastian finally said.

Coffee.

Ah, the simple things in life.

"The coffee beans are in the freezer." Emmeline pointed. "I think there's a grinder on the bottom shelf in the cabinet next to the fridge...unless Dad moved it."

It was still there.

"Glad we don't have to go looking for it this late at night," Sebastian said.

Would it have made Sebastian stay longer?

Emmeline shrugged.

Such is life.

Minutes later, the smell of freshly ground arabica filled the kitchen.

CHAPTER FORTY-EIGHT

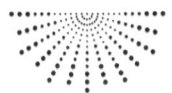

*H*e couldn't let Emmeline go.
He simply couldn't.

Lord, please don't make me let her go.

A travel mug in one hand, and his shoulder bag in the other hand, Sebastian found his feet stuck to the polished oak floor of the O'Hanlon family home in Roswell, Georgia, unable to take another step toward the front door that led to the driveway, where his SUV waited to whisk him back to a faraway coast.

Away from the siren song...

Emmeline was at the door, unlocking it, looking outside.

"Isn't it kind of late to see who's around once you have the door opened?" Sebastian asked.

"I forgot to look through the peephole, not that I could see anything much through it, anyway." Emmeline stepped aside to let Sebastian through.

The night air, a mix of warm and cool, floated into the dim hallway.

Sebastian still stood there.

"Are we letting mosquitoes in?" Emmeline waved for him to move. "Need any help with your luggage?"

"No." Sebastian hung the shoulder strap over his left shoulder, and forced himself to walk.

The coffee in the stainless-steel travel mug sloshed around.

"Oops. Sorry." Sebastian righted the mug, as drops of coffee splashed out and fell on the floor.

"Don't worry about it. I'll clean it up later. It's the West Nile virus I'm afraid of right now."

Sebastian nodded. His heavy feet moved past Emmeline. As soon as he was outside the threshold, Emmeline shut the door.

There they were, standing in the illumination of the porch light. The trees rustled a little bit, and the night sky was partly cloudy.

"Looks like you'll have a nice drive back to St. Simon's," Emmeline said as she walked with Sebastian to his SUV.

He remotely unlocked his doors and put his coffee mug into the cup holder between the two front seats.

"I'll mail the travel mug back to you," Sebastian said.

"No need. The next time I see Skye, she can give it to me."

"Skye? What about me?" Sebastian went around the back of the SUV to put his bag in the cargo compartment.

"Well, you too, if we ever see each other again." Emmeline folded her arms across her chest. "We're still friends, after all."

"Only friends?" Sebastian closed the cargo door. "If circumstances had been different... If I had accepted the fact that Talia had left me for good, would you have gone out with me?"

"I don't know." Emmeline's voice gave away nothing.

Sebastian waited.

"We saw each other all the time at church, but nothing happened until this project of ours," Emmeline explained. "Otherwise, we both have very busy and different lives."

"You don't think Skye would've set us up?"

"No." Her voice was curt.

Sebastian's shoulders sagged. "I don't think so either. I'm not your type."

"It's not that. I wasn't thinking of dating anyone. I wanted to go back to grad school. Get my master's degree. Maybe get into a better financial state so that I wasn't juggling multiple jobs, you know."

"I hear you."

"And I want to help Dad keep his harp quintet going—quartet at the moment because he can't play for a while. I'll have to fill in now, sooner than I'd expected."

"You have plans." Sebastian understood what Emmeline was trying to tell him. Or at least, he thought he understood. Thing was, he had his own plans too. They had backfired.

"We both have our own plans," Emmeline said.

"As opposed to God's plans?"

"Opposed? I don't think our plans are necessarily in opposition to God's plans, particularly if we're in His will or on the right path with God." Emmeline dropped her arms to her sides. "Speaking for myself, I'm always evaluating my plans, knowing I have to be flexible enough to adjust my plans to match God's best for my life."

"Your life and mine."

"If God hadn't brought you into my life, Seb, my family wouldn't be closer to finding Claude."

"God does work out all things for our good." It was all Sebastian could think of to say.

"If not for you and Helen, we wouldn't have known that Claude is still alive."

"That's all God's doing, Em. I credit Him."

"He worked in my life through you, Seb."

Sebastian played with his SUV key. "I like your parents, so I'm sure I'll like Claude when I meet him. But I like you most of all."

"When you meet Claude? You're very optimistic."

"Yeah. I'm confident Helen and her merry men will find him. He was in the area Thursday, and very much alive." Sebastian realized then that Emmeline hadn't responded to the other thing he had said.

I like you most of all.

"Any day now," Sebastian reminded her. "You call me, okay? Let me know when Claude comes home."

Emmeline nodded, tears in her eyes.

"No, no. Come here. It's going to be all right." Sebastian moved quickly, but gently. He wiped streaming tears from her cheeks with his thumbs.

He was close enough to kiss her.

But he didn't.

It was the wrong time.

"We've waited so long for Claude to come home," Emmeline barely whispered.

"Just a little longer." Sebastian wrapped her in his arms.

She was soft and huggable, even as she was heaving and weeping.

Sebastian held her for a while, as she let it all out.

"Let's pray, Em." And so he did.

Sebastian prayed for Emmeline, Claude, their parents, Helen and her search team, the halfway houses, the homeless shelters, the soup kitchens, the entire city of Atlanta, and beyond...

"And help us not to forget You, Lord," he concluded. "In Jesus' Name, I pray. Amen."

"Amen," Emmeline whispered into his shoulder.

Quietly, Sebastian let her go.

He did not kiss her forehead. Did not hug her any further.

It was still the wrong time.

And they both knew it.

CHAPTER FORTY-NINE

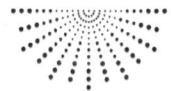

*S*easide Island insects chirped around his head, and coastal Georgia ocean waves pounded his ears, as Sebastian stood outside his SUV at this early morning hour, staring at the fluorescent green BMW i8 parked in his garage.

The last time he checked, his i8 was silver.

And he had sold it to Helen Hu to turn into cash as part of the reward money for the safe return of Claude O'Hanlon.

The Atlantic sun was slowly rising, casting more daylight on that green sports car taking up space where it didn't belong.

He glanced at his watch. It was 7:10 a.m.

He had left Emmeline's house around one o'clock in the morning. They had chatted a bit more sitting on the front steps of the house, Sebastian drinking coffee and listening to Emmeline talk about her brother.

When he had reached St. Simon's Island, he stopped at a twenty-four-hour diner to have some breakfast. He hadn't planned on sitting there for more than half an hour, but checking his email, he had lost track of time.

He had been thinking about sleeping all day until he opened the automatic garage door and saw the car.

Maybe he should have driven away, but something made him get out of the vehicle.

The front door of his house swung open.

"Hi, handsome!" Talia waltzed out in a sheer night-gown, with nothing underneath.

Help me, God.

She floated to the garage, glided on and off the hood of the green i8. "You like? Matches yours."

For the first time in Sebastian's life, he felt uncom-fortable with Talia, as if he were betraying Emmeline.

Wait a minute.

This is my house.

"How did you get into my house?" Sebastian asked.

"Celeste let me in."

"Celeste?" Sebastian's part-time housekeeper only worked on Fridays. Today was Monday. "She came here to let you in?"

"I've been here since Friday." Talia pouted. "I waited for you all weekend. Where have you been?"

"Out of town. Why are you here, Talia?" Sebastian didn't move from his SUV, but Talia was coming closer. "Stop right there."

Her nightgown fluttered in the morning breeze, and threatened to slide off her suntanned body.

"What are you doing here, Talia? You haven't been invited."

"Invited? I've been coming and going whenever I wanted for years." Talia looked hurt. "I was shocked—so shocked!—on Friday when I found that my keys didn't work. Why did you change the locks? How could you?"

"We broke up six or seven months ago now. You moved on with Jared. You're no longer welcome here."

"I'm back, Seb." She moved. "I slept in your bed for the last three nights."

What does that mean?

"What about Jared?" Sebastian asked.

"I dumped him. Or he dumped me. Whatever. It's over between us." Talia started to look sad. "He didn't want the liability."

"Liability?" *Uh-oh.*

"Our baby." Talia waved her long, manicured nails in the air. "But we won't think about the past. We're moving on."

"You're on your own, Talia." *For once.*

"I can abort, and it'll be back to old times—"

"You answer to God for your actions." Sebastian held up a palm to prevent her from getting any closer to him.

He felt sad that Talia had to throw herself at any man to get some attention.

"At least let me stay here, Seb. This is my safe place." Talia began to sob.

"Your safe place needs to be in Jesus, not my house." Sebastian felt sorry for her, but also regretted that he had mistaken lust for love all these years.

Lust? Yes, lust.

That was what he had for Talia, wasn't it?

It was clear to him now.

Now that he had found love—perhaps, even true love—he could see things as clearly as the sun was rising in the sky.

Whoa.

Startled by his own realization, Sebastian leaned back against his SUV for support.

"Are you kicking me out?" Talia suddenly raised her voice.

"You don't live here. Go home, Talia."

"I have nowhere to go, Seb, my love."

I will not pity her anymore.

"Go to your new flat in London, then," Sebastian said. "Start over with your baby. That's a lot of responsibility in itself. Does Jared know?"

Silence.

"You need to tell him."

Talia bristled. "He's seeing someone else."

Oh boy. "You still need to tell him that he's a father. It might change things."

"It might not."

"Whatever, Talia. We all grow up. I can't fill your

empty spaces. I can't be your backup boyfriend. I can't clean up your messes for you anymore."

"I thought we had something beautiful."

"We never did." It had all been pale in comparison to even a brief moment Sebastian had with Emmeline. "Many years ago, we had something. There's nothing between us now."

"You loved me."

"We were infatuated with each other." Yes, he had worshipped Talia like she was a movie star. An idol. "I've gotten right with God, and I need to stay pure."

"You mean you joined a monastery?" Talia's laugh was one of derision.

"No. I am turning to God to meet my needs, direct my life, show me what's best for me. Blessings upon blessings, Talia. You can have them too."

"With you, Seb. We can have blessings together." She paused, as if she had to forge words she could believe in. "And children. You wanted children. I can give you as many as you want. I'm proving I can."

"You still don't get it." Sebastian's heart was calm when he said it.

He knew he had to leave now, or Talia would lure him back into a past he'd rather forget. She had her ways, and Sebastian feared he might still be susceptible, in spite of all his spiritual talk.

He felt peace, though.

God's peace.

He hadn't forgotten God.

When he needed to be strong in the Lord, God had given him strength to say no to a woman who had been a negative influence for him.

He realized that Talia was still talking, this time about splitting restaurant shares in Saffron on Jekyll, and something about going back to church so she could raise her child right.

Anything to engage Sebastian in more entanglements.

Never again.

Quickly, Sebastian climbed back into his SUV and started the ignition. The driver's side window was still down.

"I'll pray for you, Talia, to find God's will for your life—and your baby's life. And Jared's too, for that matter."

He locked his vehicle doors. "In the meantime, get out of my house."

CHAPTER FIFTY

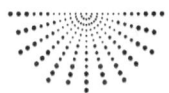

The next day, Sebastian called his real estate agent to list his six-bedroom Seaside Island house for two-point-nine million dollars, give or take. It was a fair price for the half-an-acre property. He couldn't list it for any more than three because it wasn't oceanfront.

He had hung on to certain memories long enough, but they were memories not worth clinging to. He had bought the house with Talia in mind, in the hopes of marrying her and raising their kids there.

How had he not seen her for who she was?

Perhaps he had, but had denied the truth of it.

No wonder he'd had no peace, only regrets, every time he had prayed about his life together with Talia Cavanaugh-Perry.

So.

Marrying Talia had been Sebastian's own idea, not God's.

Once upon a time, I did forget God.

How could Sebastian ever be Talia's only man? While he had remained celibate all these years since he had been saved, Talia hadn't done the same.

Seriously, he could not have expected Talia to have the same convictions as he did, especially if she wasn't truly a believer to begin with.

Then again, that's between Talia and God.

It was obvious to Sebastian now that Talia had used him as a prop only, a backup plan when no other more interesting guy had come along.

Strangely enough, Sebastian had wanted to be Hosea. While he wouldn't dare compare Talia to Gomer, Talia herself had said that she couldn't be a one-man woman.

If Sebastian had married Talia, what then? What would have happened after their wedding if—or when —Talia grew tired of him?

Talia seemed to be a wanderer.

And Emmeline?

Who was she, then, who dared to take up his offer for her to be his rent-a-girlfriend?

Only a year before, when Emmeline and Sebastian's friend from church—Ivan—had dated, Emmeline had been known to be flashy.

Those photographs Sebastian had seen in the newspapers when the Sea Islands Symphony Orchestra had been on tour were telling of Emmeline's skin-tight outfits.

That was then.

What a difference a year had made. Months after Emmeline had started attending the Seaside Chapel women's Bible study group and taking God's Word seriously, Sebastian's sister and the other women in the group had influenced Emmeline to focus on modesty and inner beauty.

Ah, so maybe that's where her favorite phrase came from.

Don't forget God.

By the time Sebastian had worked out an agreement with her to be his rent-a-girlfriend, Emmeline's flashy past was gone. She had experienced an epiphany, repented of her immodesty, and was now focused on more important things—like finding her brother, finishing school, getting a job, taking care of her family...

All the things Sebastian considered important.

In many ways, Emmeline was more in line with Sebastian's goals, hopes, dreams, and worldview than Talia ever was.

With his left hand unaware of what his right hand was doing, Sebastian found himself picking up his phone and calling Emmeline.

"*Y*ou don't have to explain to me," Emmeline spoke into her phone.

She was sitting on her bed, leaning against the headrest, a pillow on her lap. The ceiling fan whirred above her, easing off the late July heat that rose into her second-floor bedroom this time of year.

This bedroom in her parents' house was hers whenever she came to see them. Her childhood home in Dunwoody was no more, demolished to raise up some high-rise condominiums.

On her phone, Sebastian's face showed on the Skype window.

"I must," Sebastian said. He wasn't smiling. "She came to my house without my permission. She'd been staying there all weekend."

"Yeah?"

"I would have you know that I didn't go inside the house. I talked to her outside the garage, and then I went to Skye's house and I've been there ever since."

"You don't need to—"

"I put the house on the market this morning."

"Oh. Just tell Talia to go. It's not her house. Why sell it?"

"Too many bad memories."

"It takes a while to sell any house these days. Are you going to stay at Skye's the entire time?"

"Probably not. We'll start arguing after a bit.

There's not enough room for the two of us in her kitchen," Sebastian explained.

"I guess that's what you get with two chefs in the family."

"I'll rent or buy something closer to Sage near the pier." Sebastian shook his head. "I can't believe Talia came back."

"How did she get in?" Emmeline wasn't curious or anything.

Maybe just a tad.

"She knew the housekeeper would tidy and dust on Friday. She arrived when the doors were unlocked."

"So you didn't let her in."

"She told the housekeeper that we're back together. We're not, Em." Sebastian looked into the camera. "I told her to leave."

"And I need to know because?"

"She's pregnant."

"Oh. Wow. You said earlier—before I came up to my room—that she broke up with Jared."

"That's what she said. And now she thinks we should get back together. She expected me to take her back."

"Ironically, that's what you wanted."

"I'm glad God protected me from her." Sebastian hung his head. "I realized after being with you that... she wasn't for me. She's not the woman I love."

When Emmeline didn't reply, Sebastian continued speaking. "I'm in love with you, Em."

Emmeline sat up. This can't be happening. Not now. "No, Seb."

"Why not?"

"Your emotions are pretty strong right now. You feel with passion, and it might cloud your judgment."

"How do I... How am I supposed to know...?"

"Pray for clarity. Wait for God's timing." Emmeline sighed. "I should tell myself that."

"We both need God's direction."

"One of my dad's favorite verses is Psalm 119:105. 'Your word is a lamp to my feet and a light to my path.' I think we should spend time studying God's Word before we make any move."

"What are you suggesting, Em?" His voice sounded unsure, as if he didn't mean to ask it, but had done so involuntarily.

"That we need time and space."

"No... Please?" Sebastian sounded and looked quite desperate.

"Let's regroup next summer. If we still have feelings for each other, we'll go from there." As soon as Emmeline said it, she knew it was the right thing to do.

Next summer would be the midpoint of her graduate school.

By then, she should know where she would be heading: touring as a performer, or teaching harp somewhere. By then, she prayed that they would have found Claude. Or not.

"A year from now? Seriously?" Sebastian's jaw dropped. "Did you really say one year?"

"Today next July. I have to get back to school, and you have a restaurant to run. We need time and much prayer to see if we're meant for each other."

"I think I can figure that out in a few months—even a few weeks. Why do we need to stay away from each other for one year?" Sebastian asked.

Then again...

"I'm grateful that you've helped me to look for my brother. Whether he is found or not, I think you've done plenty. I don't want you to spend any more money looking for Claude."

"I'll do anything—"

"You've done so much. You've encouraged my parents, given us hope—God's hope—that Claude has been spotted. We'll figure out a low-cost way to mobilize the community to find him. I think my family can take it from here."

"There's more to be done."

"Maybe, but I don't want to owe you more than I already do, Seb. I think I kept my end of the bargain—I was your girlfriend for two months—almost, anyway."

"What am I going to do for one year?" Sebastian groaned.

"Lots of things. Pray and ask God to show you. Study the Bible. Be more involved at church. Do something you know how to do."

"Like what?"

JAN THOMPSON

"Cook, Chef Langston. Cook."

CHAPTER FIFTY-ONE

*A*utumn lingered deeper into November that year, the warmer months stretching out the season. Emmeline suspected that the upcoming winter would be a short one.

Meanwhile, the hemlock, oak, and tulip trees surrounding her parents' house played along with the autumn winds, shedding multi-colored leaves all over the yard.

Dad had regained his strength after that heart surgery in June, but he had found an excuse not to help rake the leaves this sunny Saturday afternoon. Claude's cat—only Claude would name a cat Chase—was napping on Dad's lap again, and until Claude came home, no one dared to stir a sleeping cat.

Mom pushed the empty wheelbarrow toward the pile of leaves that she and Emmeline had gathered. They filled the wheelbarrow with pretty leaves.

Shortly afterwards, when Emmeline returned from the composter in their backyard with the empty-again wheelbarrow, Mom was sitting on the front porch steps, taking a break.

"Is everything all right?" Emmeline asked.

"Yeah. Just a bit tired."

"I know the feeling," Emmeline said. "Had a long week of pedagogy and theory classes... You know how I love those."

"You've never enjoyed music theory as much as your dad and Claude..."

Mom's voice trailing off alarmed Emmeline.

"We'll find him—God will find him for us," she said softly.

Mom nodded. "So nice of Helen and that friend of yours to come all the way to Atlanta for Claude."

That friend of yours. "That was back in July, Mom."

"Has it been that long ago? Are you going to see him again anytime soon?" Mom asked.

"No."

It was all Emmeline could say.

Perhaps asking Sebastian to stay away from her for a whole year had been a terribly bad idea.

What was done was done!

He had agreed to it.

Emmeline wondered how Sebastian was doing these days. He probably didn't miss her. Apparently, he was busy with his restaurant.

Skye had kept Emmeline updated on the happenings at Seaside Chapel. Who was having a baby, who got married, who died, who survived cancer, and so forth.

Skye had also told Emmeline that Sebastian's house had a new owner who had added a second floor to the ranch—not that Emmeline cared. Talia had moved out of the country. Jared was pursuing her all over Europe because his mother wanted that grandson.

And most importantly, Sebastian was still single.

So was Emmeline.

"You don't have to drive back and forth every weekend." Mom leaned against the rake. "It's not like your dad and I need a caregiver."

Emmeline snapped back to her conversation with Mom. The leaves on the ground had piled up. She had been raking without thinking about it.

"When I was on St. Simon's, I couldn't come back as often. Now I'm closer."

"All that gas money."

"I split that with anyone who needs a ride back to Atlanta, Mom."

"Ah yes. I forgot."

"It's only ninety minutes of driving each way. A straight shot." Emmeline meant it. "I want to go to church with you and Dad on Sundays."

"We do love having you around." Mom got up and picked up her rake. "All right. But if you get too busy and have exams, we understand, okay?"

"I know." After raking for a while, Emmeline asked

Mom a question she had been meaning to ask for the last three or four months. "If Claude never comes back, will we be fine?"

"Fine?" Mom stopped raking. "We will never be fine. He's so much a part of us, that we will never be the same again. However, we will go on. God will give us the strength."

Emmeline sniffed. "I know He will."

"In the same way, Em, when your dad and I are gone, you will go on. Live your life, have a family, raise your children, and tell them funny stories about us."

"Mom, don't talk like that..." Emmeline dropped her rake, and hugged Mom tightly. "I'm going to transfer to Emory or Georgia State. I'll stay at home and take care of you and Dad, so you'll live a long, long time."

"Oh dear, dear." Mom clutched Emmeline's shoulders. "We're not going to drop dead tomorrow—well, we could, if that's God's will—but what I'm saying is that we must live every day to the glory of God."

Emmeline nodded.

"There's no need to transfer here and there. Too much trouble. Stay at UGA. Finish your master's, and then if you want to come back to Atlanta, you can." Mom looked at Emmeline. "Or if you want to go back to St. Simon's..."

Emmeline didn't know what to say about that.

Then she smiled. "I can't think about graduation

right now. If I can finish this semester without flunking, I'd be happy and eternally grateful to God."

"One day at a time. That's all we can do."

"Yep." Emmeline sighed.

"I know something's bothering you."

"Nothing, Mom."

"There you go. So tell me the truth, Em. What's really bothering you?"

CHAPTER FIFTY-TWO

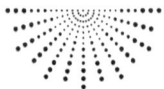

*O*n the day before Thanksgiving, Hugo called.

Emmeline did not want her parents to go to the mission in midtown Atlanta with her and Hugo, for fear of what they would find.

Claude was probably in worse shape than what they had seen on camera, and that could cause Dad to have another heart attack. Mom, for all her portrayal of strength, had just recovered from a bout with a cold.

Emmeline would prefer to have a bigger rescue team than Hugo, but the private investigator was the only person whom Helen Hu had sent from Hu Knows, Inc.

Earl had another assignment, and Emmeline did not expect Helen herself to show up on such a prolonged search like this.

She was grateful that Hugo was still working on the

case, and that Helen hadn't pushed it off to a less experienced private investigator.

Hugo had kept busy on the drive to midtown Atlanta. He was talking on the phone all the time with various people. Now he was chatting with the O'Hanlon's family physician about handling a mentally ill person.

Emmeline tried to block it all out, but at the back of her mind, she feared too. She had been praying on the entire drive. She still wondered how they were going to somehow persuade Claude to leave with them.

Sitting in the backseat, surrounded by tinted windows, Emmeline pulled her wool cap over her hair, preparing for the meeting with Claude. She had tied it up and stuffed it under the cap. Still, one way or another, she knew that Claude would recognize her.

That is, if he still remembers his family.

"What if he doesn't want to come with us?" Hugo asked on his headset.

Emmeline could not hear the answer.

She began to sweat.

Maybe it was warm in the van, but it was in the fifties outdoors this day before Thanksgiving. It wasn't too bad for this time of the year.

She prayed that Claude would have a warm place to stay when it was cold, decent food to eat when he was hungry, and people to love him when he was lonely.

He can get all three things at home.

Hugo pulled into a church parking lot where a large tent had been set up in an empty field adjacent to it. Emmeline could see numerous vans of varying sizes, each with markings of a different area church or ministry. They had come together to provide a Thanksgiving meal for the homeless and the city's poor, and to offer services and support for the needy.

"Keep your head down," Hugo ordered. "We don't want to spook your brother."

"How are we going to do this?" Emmeline asked.

When Hugo had called her that morning on behalf of Helen Hu, Emmeline and her mom were at the grocery store doing last-minute shopping for their family Thanksgiving meal the next day.

The university was closed for the entire week, and Emmeline had been home since Friday night.

In the two and a half weeks since Emmeline and Mom had raked the yard, Hugo had called several times. Most of them had been false leads, except one about a week prior.

Unfortunately, that afternoon, due to rush hour traffic heading the same way he had been going, Hugo had arrived late at the soup kitchen in Conyers.

Claude was gone.

But everyone had been given a flyer to the Thanksgiving lunch in midtown Atlanta.

And here they were.

"Stay in the van. I'm going in first." Hugo handed Emmeline what looked like a phone. Told her the PIN.

"I'll go live, and you can see me. If you spot your brother, let me know."

"Aren't there supposed to be hundreds, if not thousands, of people here?"

"Yeah."

"And only the two of us?"

"Not two. I've got twenty people mobilized on the ground. They all want a piece of that reward money. They're fanned out throughout the tent, looking for Claude."

"Okay. That makes me feel better." Emmeline realized he could not have told her earlier because he had been on the phone the entire time since he had picked her up.

"Stay in the van," Hugo repeated.

Then he was gone.

All Emmeline saw on the screen were shaky video images of what was in front of Hugo as he made his way into the tent. He moved in and out of the crowd of people, his attire blending in with the workers. Someone stopped him and handed him an apron.

"Claude, wherever you are, do you know that Jesus loves you so much?" Emmeline whispered.

Emmeline fished out a folded piece of paper from her fleece jacket pocket. She unfolded the staff paper. Hummed the tune on the first line—the rest of the page was empty—and returned it to her pocket.

He died for you, He died for me,

And shed His blood to make us free;
Upon the cross of Calvary,
The Saviour died for you and me.

She hummed more lines of the new partial arrangement of "Divine Love" as she returned to the phone that Hugo had given her.

When her eyes found focus, she froze.

Next thing she knew, she had jumped out of the van, and was rushing for the big tent.

CHAPTER FIFTY-THREE

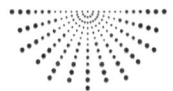

*E*mmeline made a beeline for the tables at the edges of the tent, surrounded by the open field and open roads on three sides. A fear lodged in her heart that her brother would walk away before she could reach him.

Still, she knew that he would only sit at the far end of a table, where he had more elbow room, where he could get up and leave if he wanted to.

Claude had always been claustrophobic.

This was a bigger crowd than Emmeline had expected. She prayed for divine assistance to help her spot Claude in the blur of people.

She walked here and there along the tables, trying to match her memory of Claude's face with the men sitting at rows of folding tables covered with Thanksgiving tablecloths.

Not a single table was empty. That made Emmeline's search all the harder.

She glanced at the phone that Hugo had given her to see where Hugo was, and quickly put the phone away. She had dressed to blend in, and it would make no sense for someone like her to be carrying an expensive phone.

She looked around.

Every table looked the same.

Everyone looked the same.

Everything looked the same.

She felt herself spinning in the tent—

Someone touched her arm.

"Wandering around, are we?" Hugo whispered in her ear.

"I saw him," Emmeline whispered.

When she turned toward Hugo, she saw that he was carrying a tray of food.

"We did too. He's back there." Hugo made an about turn, taking Emmeline along with him.

When they were three tables away, Emmeline stopped.

That...that looks like Claude!

He was wearing some sort of jacket with a thick and dirty scarf around his neck. He was hunched over his Thanksgiving meal of turkey, cranberry sauce, gravy, and cornbread.

He didn't have to look up. Emmeline knew it was Claude. The gobs of cranberry sauce and gravy slathered on those turkey slices gave him away.

That's how Claude likes his turkey.

And that scraggly beard. He had never been able to grow a proper beard, as much as he had tried since his college days.

Emmeline wanted to run to him and grab him and drag him home to their parents.

But.

Lord Jesus, we have no idea what he has been through. Help me to remain calm and do the right thing.

Hugo kept walking.

Emmeline stepped ahead of him, and took the tray from him. "Let me."

Hugo looked like he was going to say something in the negative, but then he gave up his meal. "I'll be around. Leave your phone on. I'm listening. If anything goes wrong, we are all here."

Claude is surrounded.

~

*Y*ears of stage plays had prepared Emmeline for this. She wandered around Claude's table, as if looking for a place to sit. She made big sighing noises to get his attention, and even brushed past his table at least once.

His table was not full, but she had to find a way to sit across from him, to talk to him face to face, so that he could see what she was going to do in front of him. Otherwise, her plan wouldn't work.

Finally, the man sitting across the table from Claude got up and left.

Emmeline stood by the table and waited.

"If you don't eat your food, it will get cold," Claude said to her.

Emmeline tried not to gag. He was missing a couple of teeth, and the rest of his teeth were all blackened.

His scraggly beard looked like it had been unevenly trimmed. There was a blob of cranberry sauce clinging to dear life in that tangled mess of unwashed beard.

She swallowed. "I have nowhere to sit."

Claude pointed to the seat across from him.

Invited.

Thank You, Lord Jesus.

Please bring him home to Mom and Dad.

Emmeline sat down. "Do you mind if I thank God for my food?"

"We already prayed. You're late."

Emmeline prayed quickly because she was afraid that when she opened her eyes, Claude would be gone.

When she realized how foolish that fear was, she felt chided.

The God of the universe who had made Claude, had kept him alive all this time he'd been wandering around, lost in the world.

Why wouldn't Emmeline trust God now to bring Claude all the way home to their family?

Emmeline ate one slice of turkey, and couldn't eat anymore. She watched Claude eat. He ate fast, as if he had run out of time.

Whenever he looked up, she looked down at her food.

"Better eat." Claude reached across the table and pressed a dirty finger right on top of Emmeline's turkey slices. "It's cold! Told ya."

His sleeves smelled like a portable toilet.

There was no way that Emmeline was going to eat the rest of her food now.

No way.

Even if that was her own brother who'd just touched her food.

What was she going to do?

Right now, all she wanted to do was run to the restroom and throw up.

But if she left the table, Claude could disappear. Or Hugo could jump on him, and who knew what was going to happen.

He's super stinky, but he's my brother.

He will always be my brother.

Emmeline sat there, unmoving.

Claude pushed his tray aside. "You want, I eat it for you."

"Th-thanks." Emmeline pushed her tray toward Claude.

"You're going to starve," he said. "The next hot meal is not until Sunday."

Emmeline started to sob. How could her brother—or anyone—go without food for three or four days?

Claude leaned her way. "Don't worry. I know where you can find food between now and then."

"Wh-where?"

"All those food places—restaurants and coffee shops—throw out food every single day."

"Every day?"

Claude nodded.

Emmeline began to realize that Claude still didn't know who she was. Had he forgotten his family? Had he lost his memory?

As Claude ate his seconds, Emmeline dug into her pockets and produced a pencil and her staff paper.

She unfolded it and put it flat on the table.

She hummed as she added more notes to the rest of the empty staff, drawing those quarter notes slowly, making a show of how arduous the task was.

It aroused Claude's curiosity. "What's that?"

Perhaps he hadn't forgotten everything.

"Music," Emmeline said.

"I know it's music. I can see. I can hear."

Emmeline kept composing. At the end of the line, she tapped the table with her fingers and hummed.

Then she erased what she had written. Wrote more bars of music notes. Once again, she deliberately went off key as she hummed. She erased again, and repeated the process, knowing the whole time that the real Claude would be annoyed.

Sure enough, across the table, Claude made some sort of grunting noise.

"Your humming doesn't sound right," he snapped.

Ah. He remembers the hymn.

Claude dug into his pumpkin pie. "What instrument?"

"Two harps."

"Harps...?" Claude stared at Emmeline.

She wasn't sure if that was a blank stare or if her humming of "Divine Love" had triggered more memories. She had arranged that piece a long time ago, back when Claude was still sane, and at home.

Before that awful night.

Emmeline kept going, pretending to mangle the melody. Tears pooled in her eyes.

"It sounds jarring. Your transition is off." The composer in Claude had returned.

Emmeline blinked. Teardrops fell onto the staff paper. She could not see what she was doing.

"Gimme." He sounded confident.

Emmeline looked up.

Those dirty fingers wiggled, asking for her paper and pencil.

She handed them over.

And as she sat there, Claude fixed her melody, the transition, time signature, and key.

"Whoa." Emmeline stared at the complex composition.

Only Claude.

"Two harps, huh?" Claude asked.

Emmeline nodded. "But we can't play the hymn."

"Why not?"

"This is a duet for my brother and me." Emmeline wondered if that was too much information, and too soon.

Well, she had spoken.

"Tell him I helped you..." Claude knotted his eyebrows. "Hmm...I know you."

"You do?"

He nodded. "You're Little M."

Emmeline gasped.

Claude hadn't called her Little M since they were in elementary school. What in the world was happening in that mind of his?

"And who's Big M?" Emmeline asked.

"Mommy, of course!"

So he remembered some things. Music. Little M. Big M. Mommy.

"Save your music." Claude shifted in his chair. "I have to go."

"Wait. What do you mean by *save your music*?"

"Record it. Or you will forget." He was standing up now. His hands were shaking. "No one will remember that you could ever play, that you were once a musician."

"God knows." Emmeline got up slowly. "God remembers."

"He'll be the only one." Claude looked sad.

"God gave us the gift of music. He keeps it safe for us."

"Safe?"

"Yes. We're safe in God's hands." Emmeline stepped toward Claude. "Will you play this composition with me?"

"A duet?"

Emmeline tried to speak calmly. "We will record it. Put it on MP3, CD, and streaming. No one will forget."

"No one?"

"Not even us."

"Little M?"

"Yes?" Emmeline stood there, wondering what was going to happen next.

"You have a big heart."

"No, I don't. I am so scared right now."

"Why?" Claude tipped his head toward Emmeline. "There's no thunderstorm outside."

That was twenty years ago.

"What's your name?" Emmeline asked.

"Turlough O'Carolan." He announced the name with pomp.

He must have forgotten his own name. However, of all the people in the world, he had to pick the name of an Irish harpist.

"Turlough, how about that duet?" Emmeline felt brave enough to ask.

"I don't have a harp."

"You can use my brother's."

"He has one?"

"He has at least five. You can try them all. I'm sure he won't mind."

"When?"

"Today, if you like."

"Right now?" His eyebrows met.

Meanwhile, that blob of cranberry sauce dislodged from his beard and fell to the grass at their feet. Claude squatted down, picked it up, and put the mess of sauce into his mouth.

He ate it with grass.

It broke Emmeline's heart. "Th-there's more sauce and turkey tomorrow."

At a table, not from a trash can.

"With cranberry sauce and gravy?" Claude leaned toward Emmeline.

"All you can eat." Suddenly his pungent smell didn't bother her anymore. "You'll never be hungry again."

"Then let's go," Claude said. "Is it a long way to walk?"

"Yes, but we can take the bus."

"The bus? Sometimes they won't let you in."

"They'll let us. This is a church bus."

Emmeline emphasized *church bus*, but she knew Hugo had heard everything.

CHAPTER FIFTY-FOUR

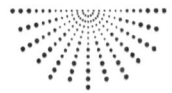

"Go on. Taste it." Sebastian waited.

At the kitchen counter where he was standing, his sister hesitantly lifted a fork.

His new baked salmon dish was nicely plated—if he did say so himself—but Skye had a critical palette. It helped—or didn't help—that they were both chefs in their own right, with very strong opinions.

Sage Café was closed on New Year's Day. The restaurant kitchen was quiet, save for the hum of the walk-in refrigerator. On normal days, the kitchen would be buzzing with people prepping for the day, but today nobody was there at nine o'clock in the morning.

"I don't know about eating a dinner dish for breakfast," Skye said. "Tell me you didn't stay up all night after the fireworks."

Sebastian didn't reply.

"You can't do this every night," his sister added.

"I want to get it right."

"It's a dish, Seb, not life. Life is more than bread, remember?" Skye swiped her phone and read a verse. "Luke 4:4. 'And Jesus answered him, saying, It is written, That man shall not live by bread alone, but by every word of God.' But you knew that."

Sebastian nodded.

"I know." She put her phone down on the table. "You have to get this dish the way you want it."

"Right."

"All right. I'll bite." Skye dug in.

Sebastian watched. He held his breath.

"Mmm... Very good. Not too much sage." Skye ate more. "What's this dish called?"

"The Wayfarer."

"Why?"

"Because it reminds me of..." Sebastian cleared his throat.

"Emmeline." Skye put down her fork. "I'm going to visit her soon. We're going to have lunch. Wanna come?"

"I'd better not. I promised to wait one year before I contact her."

"That's a long time." Skye drank some water. "You know what I think? You both have real feelings for each other."

"I admit we do."

"I pray that it will all work out. Don't make me regret buying those Saffron shares from you. It's costly."

Sebastian drew a deep breath. "About that, I'm sorry."

"I wasn't, but I will be if it comes to naught. You know that I really want to focus on my personal chef business. I'm not really good at managing a restaurant. It's stressful for me."

"I know." Sebastian leaned back against the stainless-steel countertop. "I can't buy them back from you."

"I don't want you to."

"I think you should sell it."

Skye looked up. "You worked for years to get Saffron on the map. I can't sell it."

"Then you'll be left holding on to something I don't want anymore."

"Because now you want to go where Emmeline is." Skye pointed a fork at him. "You better be sure she wants you there."

If only God would bring Emmeline back to him.

Then again, she had never been his in the first place.

Yet, he couldn't imagine being with anyone else.

"She's the one for me," Sebastian said. "For the rest of my life, she's still the one."

"That, you have to leave in God's hands."

"I know."

"Look at me. I've dated a few guys from church because they felt safe, you know?" Skye ate more salmon. "Yet, I don't feel that Hayden is the one. Or Matt."

"Matt's too old for you."

"Does it matter?" Skye laughed. "He's not the one for me. I think his heart is still with his ex-wife."

"Who has since moved on." Sebastian wondered whether his feelings for Emmeline were one-sided like Matt's.

Skye sighed. "It's impossible to find the right person to marry."

"Nothing is impossible with God. You need to wait for Him to prepare the person for you. He's not ready."

"Who is?"

"I don't know, to be honest. Someone God wants you to marry is being groomed for you," Sebastian said. "In the meantime, God is working in you too. He's fixing a few things here and there to make you ready for the man of your dreams."

"My Mr. Right." Skye smiled. "It's hard to tell who he might be. Scary."

"Not scary, but exciting," Sebastian said. "And it might not be who you expect or how you think it's going to turn out. Just wait on God. His timing is perfect, and so are His ways."

Skye nodded. "You're so right. We should prefer God's perfect plans over our own imperfect plans."

"And yet we live in a sinful, flawed world. God has to work hard on our unholiness." Sebastian recalled his crazy plan to win back Talia, only to discover that she wasn't the one for him.

"And God can wash away all our sins because Jesus

paid for it all so that we can have a right relationship with God."

"Amen, sister. Bottom line: don't forget God." Even as he said it, he wanted to cry. It had been what Emmeline had said to him the summer before when they had been together in their ruse.

Don't forget God.

Skye touched her brother's arm. "Likewise for you too, right? If Emmeline is God's chosen bride for you, He is preparing her as He is preparing you."

Sebastian sniffled a bit. "Are we talking about you or me?"

Skye chuckled. "Look at us. Preaching to ourselves. We've come a long way, haven't we?"

"We sure have."

"We have been looking out for each other since high school. Everyone is now gone but us." Skye's voice caught.

Sebastian figured she must be thinking of their aunt and uncle, who had provided them with jobs and a sense of stability their own parents could not provide.

"Ha. If we don't marry and have kids, this could be the end of the Langston line," Sebastian said with all seriousness.

It made Skye laugh. "You're silly."

Sebastian hugged his sister and then asked if she wanted more salmon.

Skye said yes and then turned serious. "We know that everything is in God's hands."

"Indeed." Sebastian dished out more salmon and sauce on her plate and his as well. "We just need to be careful not to miss what God gives us, leads us, shows us..."

He stopped talking.

Had God led him to Emmeline? And her to him?

He drew a deep breath. "It's Emmeline."

"What about her?" Skye dug into the salmon. "Mmm. This dish grows on you."

"It's her. I'm meant to be with her." Sebastian had never been surer of it than now, when he was away from Emmeline. He'd had more than five months to miss her.

She had stayed in Atlanta with her parents for Christmas. Neither had sent a greeting card to the other.

"Unfortunately, I made her a promise that we would not communicate for one year," Sebastian said.

"I made no such promise, so I can be the go-between for you."

"No."

"No?"

Sebastian shook his head. "A promise is a promise."

"It's all for good. Em is leaving next week for a semester in Vienna," Skye said.

"She is?" More surprises. Maybe knowing what Emmeline was doing or where she was going could help him pray for her—or at least not miss her that much.

"She'll be back in May," Skye added. "So she's not going to be around even if you break your promise."

"I'm not breaking my promise."

"Then turn your eyes on God for the next seven months. Focus on God and let Him prepare you to be the man whom Em needs."

The husband she needs.

"Then go to Em—if she's God's will for your life."

I know she is.

Now, more than ever, I know she is.

CHAPTER FIFTY-FIVE

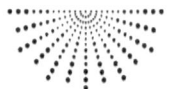

*I*t wasn't exactly the Vienna Philharmonic, but it was close enough and that was suffi-cient for Emmeline. As she entered the concert hall to the sound of her classmates warming up, she reminded herself that she never wanted to be as ambitious as the other musicians in her class, but that was because she preferred to stay close to home.

And yet, here she was, in Austria.

It had taken her friends three months to coax her into flying. She had been willing to forego the extra course credits just so she didn't have to fly. However, as a harp major, there was no avoiding the trip. Besides, nobody else in her class had a fear of flying.

In the end, she prayed through it, and God gave her enough strength to get on board the Boeing 777. Fortu-nately, in a plane that big, she could hardly feel the turbulence.

And now, she had a stamp on her passport as proof that she could venture outside her comfort zone.

Still, home was Atlanta, and Austria was the farthest away from home she had ever been. She used to think that St. Simon's Island had been far away from her parents in Roswell, but that was only five hours of driving between the two cities.

To get home from Vienna, Emmeline had to first fly for two hours to Paris. Then she'd change planes and fly for another eight-plus hours before she reached Atlanta.

It wasn't going to happen before summer unless she wanted to break her promise to Sebastian.

Who would make such a promise?

Well, the whole idea was to be sure that they were meant for each other. If they were, then when the one year was up, they'd still want each other.

If not, then they would go their separate ways.

Emmeline prayed for patience.

But first, her harp beckoned.

Still, the whole rehearsal was a blur. Playing the harp was routine for her. The strings were almost an extension of her fingers.

What wasn't routine was the thought of falling in love with a man so far away and whom she could not talk to for five more months. At this moment, they were literally on different continents.

By the time she reached her apartment—or flat, as they called it in Vienna—that she shared with three other string majors from UGA, she was exhausted and weary from all that thought ebbing back and forth in her mind.

Is this what longing feels like?

It was past ten o'clock at night in Vienna.

"Friday night, Emmeline," someone said to her.

She looked up. "Huh?"

Stacy, the violinist, snapped her fingers and chuckled. "Is he married?"

"What?" Emmeline had no idea what she was talking about.

"This man you're pining for?"

Emmeline shook her head.

"So what's the problem?"

"No problem." She didn't want to talk about it.

"Anyway, we're going out. Come with?" Stacy asked.

The other two music students surrounded them, nodding.

"No, thanks. I'll stay in," Emmeline said.

"You always stay in."

"I'm tired. Rehearsal and all." Emmeline kicked off her shoes. "Go, girls. I'd love to have the apartment all to myself."

"What will you do? Watch TV?"

"Probably. Read my Bible, and then go to bed," Emmeline said. "I want to get up early and take a walk."

"It's Valentine's Day tomorrow. Don't you want a date?" one of her friends asked.

"Don't need one." Emmeline smiled.

"I think her heart's taken." Stacy ushered the other two ladies out of the apartment.

Emmeline locked the door after they left. She took a warm shower and changed into her pajamas. She tried to read a book, but ended up feeling too sleepy to do so.

She brushed her teeth, climbed into bed, and fell asleep reading her Bible.

She didn't hear her roommates return to the apartment that night. In fact, she was dead to the world until the sun rose in the sky.

After getting into a tee shirt and a pair of shorts, she laced up her walking shoes. She threw her swimsuit and a pair of flip-flops into a tote bag, and left the apartment for the gym down the block. After walking on the treadmill for forty-five minutes, she changed into her swimsuit and swam a few laps.

Sitting alone in the hot tub afterwards, she closed her eyes and prayed for wisdom about her career. She wanted God's directions. Needed God to show her whether she should stay at UGA past her master's program.

She wondered if she could go for a doctorate in musical arts. She knew that once she left the university, it could be hard for her to return to academia. Her parents were getting old, and performing harp with Dad would be memorable for her while it lasted.

And for her brother, Claude, too.

Could they wait for another couple of years?

She could still perform with them during holidays and the summer break.

By the time she walked back to the apartment, she was famished for breakfast.

The front desk clerk flagged her down. "Miss O'Hanlon?"

"Yes?" Emmeline walked toward the desk.

The man pointed to a vase of flowers on the counter. "These flowers arrived for you."

Emmeline's eyes brightened. She smiled. "So sweet of my parents to remember me on Valentine's Day."

As she picked up the envelope attached to a long plastic stick in the vase, she felt bad that she hadn't sent her parents a card.

When she opened the envelope and pulled out the card, she was surprised. The flowers were not from her parents.

Dear Emmeline,
    Happy Valentine's Day!
    Five more months...
    Sebastian's Florist

Emmeline smiled. Sebastian had found a way to get

around their agreement not to communicate for a year. He had sent her flowers...from his florist.

His thoughtfulness warmed her heart and carried her through the entire semester.

CHAPTER FIFTY-SIX

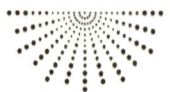

*S*ebastian's third-floor test kitchen faced the blue April skies over the Atlantic Ocean, but it wasn't the view that made him rent this three-level oceanfront resort property instead of buying it.

He was waiting for Emmeline. One way or another, he would find out soon—in three months when they met each other again—whether there was a future for both of them. If there was, then he would suggest they go house hunting together. If Emmeline had moved on, then Sebastian would make an offer to the landlord for this house.

He loved this place. The fact that he could open all the windows in the wraparound kitchen brought the springtime outdoors into his lofty abode, and gave him a much-needed change of scenery from his previous one-floor Seaside Island cottage, a sprawling ground-hugging ranch built in the 1920s.

That wasn't the only reason. When he had first seen the list price of this house, he knew he could pay cash for it, and still have a million dollars left over from the sale of Saffron to save up for a new restaurant somewhere in the metro Atlanta area or wherever he and Emmeline went—if they were meant to be together. In other words, setting aside the cash was easy because renting made him location independent.

Yes, waiting for Emmeline.

Standing at the panoramic window, its white plantation shutters quiet and waiting for a breeze, Sebastian Langston felt...

Like I'm missing something.

Someone.

The doorbell rang, strangely reminding him to turn off the burner in the open kitchen. The quinoa was done, basically. He covered the pot with its lid.

Then he went to get the door.

Benicio and Matt filed in, and then Ivan—by himself.

"Where's Brinley?" Sebastian asked. He had cooked enough shrimp stir fry for everyone.

Ivan handed him a bag of rolls that looked like they came straight off the supermarket shelf. "She's not sure if she wants to be one of *the guys.*"

"She can be one of us," Matt said. "I don't mind."

"I don't either," Benicio said.

"She's having lunch with her sister-in-law, and then they're going shopping," Ivan added. "I'm sorry, but she didn't tell you one way or another whether she was coming."

"No worries." If they had leftovers—a big *if*—Sebastian would eat it for lunch the next day.

The other two guys went outside to the balcony to take in the scenery. Matt and Benicio. Sebastian wondered who would be next in line to find a wife.

Certainly, Sebastian had once thought he would be the first from the men's group to be married, but had he gone forth with it, it would have been a tragic error.

Instead, God's mercy and grace had prevailed.

And now, eight months and one week after he had parted ways with Emmeline, Sebastian had drawn closer to God and His word.

Don't forget God.

Emmeline had said that the first day they had met in early June of last year.

Sebastian nodded, as if to her.

Only she wasn't here.

In fact, they had only talked on the phone once since that day he and Emmeline had agreed to wait a year. That was the night before Thanksgiving when Emmeline had called to tell him that Claude had come home.

Sebastian was glad that Emmeline had called him in person, rather for him to hear the news from Helen or Hugo, or Skye, for that matter.

He locked the front door and went back to his

kitchen, where his friends were walking about, lifting lids and sniffing at what he had prepared for them.

"What in the world is this concoction?" Matt asked —attempting to look bewildered—as he stood over a side dish.

"That's a facial." It was tamarind paste, but Sebastian figured Matt wouldn't care, since he hadn't been one to try new and exotic dishes.

"Nah. I can see right through your straight face." Matt shook his head. "You want me to taste it. Not going to do it."

"You read my face now? Have you been talking to my sister about my new dishes?"

"No, but I've talked to..." Matt hesitated.

Sebastian stopped in his tracks, a wooden spatula in the air. His heart skipped a beat. However, he wasn't jealous of Matt. He knew that Matt had no design on Emmeline.

And Sebastian was starving for information about Emmeline. "Ah... How is she?"

"Your sister's fine."

"I know my sister's fine, Matt. I just saw her in church an hour ago. I meant someone else...Emmeline."

"She's fine."

"Is she homesick?" Sebastian asked.

"Very. She said she couldn't talk to you but she wished she could."

Sebastian held on to the countertop for support. "She said that?"

Matt nodded. "But you two made a promise to each other to wait a year."

"I don't know why I agreed to it, to be frank." Sebastian sighed.

"She's almost halfway through her master's," Matt said. "Her dad wants her to be the principal harpist for his O'Hanlon Harps or something like that. They're touring this summer."

"Touring?" As in going somewhere far away and never coming back?

"The hired harpists are. As for Emmeline, she may stay in town in the metro Atlanta area. She wants to be available if her parents need her help with her brother."

"Claude." Sebastian leaned back against the counter and wiped his hands on a dishcloth. "How's Claude doing?"

"In treatment for his mental breakdown. He has memory loss, and is still incoherent sometimes," Matt said. "However, he's improving every day. He's under a doctor's care. He recommended music therapy."

"At least he's finally home."

Matt pointed a finger at Sebastian. "That's what she said. You should call her."

Sebastian shook his head. "We agreed not to communicate, but we talked then because of Claude."

Benicio picked up a dinner plate. "When did she say you can call her again?"

Yeah, so everybody in their men's group knew

about this moratorium. "One year. July, to be precise. But you knew that."

Ivan—who was washing his hands at the kitchen sink—laughed. "What's another three months if God gives you a lifetime together?"

Sebastian studied his friend. At a long lunch over the Christmas holidays, the two of them had discussed their lives. Sebastian had felt comfortable enough to tell Ivan about his woes. Perhaps it had been because Ivan had dated Emmeline. And Jared had pursued Brinley, who had since then married Ivan.

For all those possible reasons, Sebastian had wanted to get Ivan's reaction to his situation.

"So you made a mistake in high school," Ivan had responded at that lunch four months ago. "My grandma used to say that it takes two hands to clap. It was as much Talia's fault as yours. You both went overboard. Both of you were unsaved back in high school, so you were clueless. Thank God that there was no baby then."

Baby.

There's one now.

Jared's baby.

Not mine.

Matt waved a hand in front of Sebastian. "Are we going to eat or not?"

Sebastian cleared his throat. "Let's thank God for the food, shall we?"

No words came out of his mouth.

For some reason, all Sebastian wanted to do was weep.

Eight months and one week, all bottled up.

I have to see Emmeline again.

However, he had to keep his promise to wait for another three months and three weeks.

Almost four more miserable months.

CHAPTER FIFTY-SEVEN

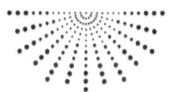

*O*n the very day of their one-year-apart anniversary, Sebastian googled and found out that the O'Hanlon Harps quintet would be performing at a cathedral in Buckhead, inside the Atlanta perimeter. The free concert would include a duet by Emmeline and Claude, playing several new compositions from their upcoming album.

Sebastian also knew that within a week of this harp performance, Emmeline would go back to the University of Georgia for her second year in the master's program.

His sister, Skye, had disclosed the fact that while Emmeline had been keeping busy, she was also still single. Skye didn't think that was going to be for long, with Emmeline's widening circles of musician friends and fans.

In other words, Sebastian had a small window to

see Emmeline again—to tell her what was on his mind —before she moved on.

One year had been a long time for him to think about his life and where he wanted to be. It had also been a time of emotional cleansing for him, as God washed away all his feelings that had been caught up with Talia's hold on his heart for many years.

God had given Sebastian mercy—he was sure of it —as he spent more time studying the Bible and getting his perspectives straightened out in the last twelve months, than he had ever before in his entire life.

He understood it now.

Don't forget God.

On the five-plus hour drive from St. Simon's Island to Georgia's capital city of Atlanta, Sebastian listened to the Bible from his phone plugged into his SUV.

Every now and then, he worried that Emmeline wouldn't be there when he arrived at the concert hall.

She might not even want to see me.

To allay his own fears, he prayed, and raptly listened to Galatians and Ephesians as he drove west on Interstate 16 past Macon. Driving north on Interstate 75 toward Buckhead, he listened to the entire books of Psalms and Proverbs, praying along the way.

The long drive became more bearable as God's Word stilled and silenced his heart.

Downtown Atlanta was in sight, and lo and behold, a traffic jam hemmed him in.

By the time Sebastian arrived at the church, the

parking lot was full, and he had to park three blocks down the road. The six o'clock heat would've been less severe if he didn't have to walk. Fortunately, his light summer jacket breathed, and his silk shirt underneath kept him somewhat cool.

He made a beeline for the sanctuary, took a program from an usher, sat down, and was thumbing through it before he realized that he had forgotten to eat dinner.

Too late now.

He scanned the pages for Emmeline's name, his fingers getting more tremulous by the minute.

It didn't matter. The entire concert was a blur the moment Emmeline, her brother, and the other three harpists stepped onto the stage.

For some reason, they played some of Sebastian's favorite pieces, including Enrique Granados's "Oriental," and what sounded like an updated arrangement of "Divine Love." He dared not think that Emmeline had a hand in their choice of repertoire for the evening because of him, but today was exactly the date they were supposed to evaluate where they were in their non-relationship.

Sebastian still hummed the hymn as he stood in line at the concession stand during the intermission. The soda and cookies carried him through the second half of the concert, when Kipp O'Hanlon came out to introduce his son and daughter, and to conduct a couple of jazzy string numbers.

At the end of the evening, Sebastian thought the encore lasted way too long. He wanted to run backstage to talk to Emmeline, but he didn't have to. In glittering gowns and black tuxedos, the members of O'Hanlon Harps stood in the rotunda to meet their sponsors, audience, and fans.

But Emmeline was nowhere to be found.

Sebastian didn't see her at all.

He was beginning to worry.

Kipp saw him. Waved.

"Do you know where Emmeline is?" Sebastian asked after their handshake.

"She's here somewhere." Kipp turned to tap his wife's shoulder. "Eleanor, have you seen Em?"

"She was talking to her professor from UGA. Probably still inside." Emmeline's mom saw Sebastian. "Oh! So nice of you to come. How have you been?"

Heartbroken. "I'm well, ma'am."

"Well, I'm glad. Em's been miserable for months."

"She has? Was she sick?"

"Lovesick, I think." Kipp laughed, and then went on to shake someone else's hand.

Before Eleanor O'Hanlon could say another word, Sebastian heard a chuckle.

He would be able to recognize *that* anywhere.

It was the sound of a bubbling brook.

There, coming through the tall doors of the sanctuary, was Emmeline, arm in arm with her brother, laughing at some joke.

She looked his way.

And stopped walking.

~

*H*e's here.

Stunned that Sebastian had remem-
bered the date, Emmeline waited as he walked toward
her and her brother.

His strides were brisk, and he seemed to be in a
hurry to get to her.

"Emmeline." Her name rolled off his tongue easily,
as if he had been saying it a lot to himself.

They stared at each other for a while.

Someone coughed and cleared his throat.

"Oh." Emmeline snapped into the realization that
Sebastian hadn't met her brother. "Seb, this is my
brother, Claude. Claude, Sebastian Langston."

Claude extended his hand. "Ah, the dude Mom
talked about."

Startled, Emmeline tilted her head. "Mom talked to
you about him?"

"Well, Mom and Dad talked. I was in the vicinity,"
Claude said.

"What did they say?" Emmeline glared at her
brother.

"Well, it was a strange conversation. Something
about meatloaf recipes. What is that about?"

Emmeline and Sebastian grinned at each other.

"Don't worry," Claude added. "It was all good, Little M. Mom thinks you're sad, and we need to be supportive."

Okay, there's that.

Emmeline was moved. "Thank you for caring."

"What are brothers for?" Claude turned toward Sebastian. "So. Has it been one year since you last saw Em?"

Sebastian nodded.

"What's one year? I haven't seen my sister in five years. Top that."

"Five years is a long time," Sebastian said.

Claude gave Emmeline's shoulder a light squeeze. "It feels like only five days sometimes."

"That's because you don't remember most of the last five years." Emmeline grinned.

"Yeah, that too. Time flies when you're under a bridge."

Emmeline wrapped her arms around her brother. "I'm so glad you're home. I love you so much, Claude."

"Let's not get mushy in public, Little M." But his voice cracked.

My brother loves me.

Thank You, Jesus, for bringing my brother home.

"Well, I'll leave you two alone to catch up—not that you can be too alone in this crowd," Claude said. "I'll go see if Mom and Dad need anything."

"Glad to meet you, Claude," Sebastian said.

Claude waved. "Take good care of my sister, all right?"

"Will do." He paused briefly. "I promise."

Emmeline watched the exchange with happiness in her heart. She loved it that her brother and Sebastian seemed to get along at their first meeting.

But what did he just say?

I promise.

"A promise is a very serious thing," Emmeline reminded him.

Instead of answering her right away, Sebastian stepped toward her, a grin on his face, right in the middle of the rotunda, among the crowd of people chattering and bantering and laughing, right under the chandeliers casting a warm light on them.

CHAPTER FIFTY-EIGHT

Sebastian rested his face against Emmeline's hair, its fresh fragrance of lavender shampoo floating into his nose. "I missed you so much. I was sure I was dying."

He could hear her chuckling softly against his neck.

Then she lifted her face. "I didn't think I'd see you today,"

"I waited all year for this." Sebastian tried to keep his voice normal, but he couldn't hide his agony. "I kept my word."

Emmeline smiled. "Thank you for the flowers on Valentine's Day."

Sebastian remembered ordering those. He had to do it since he missed her, but he had to also keep his word not to contact her.

"You signed it 'Sebastian's Florist.' Very clever."

Sebastian didn't reply.

"I wish..." Emmeline stroked Sebastian's arm. "I mean, a year—what was I thinking?"

"We, Em. We agreed to do this together, for our sake."

Emmeline sighed.

"It was a good idea. I spent the last twelve months in God's Word," Sebastian explained. "Yeah, I cooked— and Sage Café is doing very well—but my primary focus has been on God's Word. Like you said, 'Don't forget God.' Remember?"

Emmeline nodded. "I camped out on Psalm 119:105 for a while this year."

Your word is a lamp to my feet
And a light to my path.

"Good one, Em. Want to know what I studied, among other scripture passages?"

Emmeline nodded.

"That *delight* verse. Do you remember?" Sebastian asked.

"Yes, we memorized it in the women's group last year." Emmeline turned pensive. "I do miss the coast, our church, our friends."

In more ways than one, Sebastian was happy to hear that. "But first, we focus on God. 'Delight yourself also in the Lord, and He shall give you the desires of your heart.' I believe it."

"Psalm 37:4."

"My first love is always God," Sebastian said, if only to remind himself again about the truth in the verse. "If I delight myself in God, He will give me the desires of my heart. You are the desire of my heart, Emmeline Eleanor O'Hanlon."

Emmeline's lips quivered.

Sebastian was alarmed when he saw tears shimmer in Emmeline's eyes.

Before he got cold feet, Sebastian reached into his blazer pocket, and retrieved what looked like a tiny music box. "I brought you an anniversary gift."

Emmeline stared at it. "It's so pretty. What tune does it play?"

"The wedding march," Sebastian said softly as he dropped slowly to his knees.

Emmeline's fingers flew to her periwinkle necklace.

There was a hush in the rotunda of the old church. The crowd surrounding the two of them quietened.

Sebastian lifted the box toward Emmeline and opened it. Inside was a brilliant diamond.

"It's not lavender or purple or whatever color your necklace is," Sebastian said. "But it's pure white to remind us of the purity of God's love. I want to love you with God's holy love, Emmeline. Will you let me do that every day for the rest of my life?"

Emmeline seemed to be unable to speak.

"Will you marry me?" Sebastian asked. "Right away, if possible—but I'll wait a day or two if we have to..."

Emmeline laughed.

"I want to listen to your laughter all day long, my dear Em. Say yes?"

"Yes," she whispered. "I mean, not right away, you know. A proper wedding requires proper planning. There's new music to be composed... Rehearsals to be scheduled..."

"Food to be catered... Menus to be printed..." Sebastian reached for her ring finger.

Emmeline did not protest.

The flawless diamond ring glittered on her finger, under the chandeliers high above them.

When Sebastian rose to his feet, everyone applauded as he wrapped Emmeline in his arms—his favorite thing to do.

Emmeline lifted her chin, but Sebastian didn't need any prompting.

He kissed her slowly, on her chin and near her lips at first, because he didn't want to look desperate.

And because he had learned patience over the span of the year as he waited for this day when he would see Emmeline again.

So what's another second—or minute?

Sebastian felt Emmeline's hands on his waist. She didn't make any sound, didn't say any word. She simply waited.

Let's not wait any longer.

Sebastian savored their sweet and public kiss that lingered into the July evening, as if the moment was reserved for them alone, but it wasn't a moment of their own making.

It was a moment given to them by God.

Sebastian was confident that, in Emmeline's heart, she also remembered what she had told him over a year ago now.

He was sure that it would be the theme for the rest of their lives together.

Don't forget God.

CHAPTER FIFTY-NINE

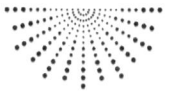

*O*ne month later in late August, Sebastian took a week off to spend time with Emmeline in Athens. The fall semester had begun, and Emmeline was in her last year of her master's program, though she was mulling over the idea of staying on for a Doctor of Musical Arts degree in harp performance.

Friday felt different to Sebastian when he woke up in the hotel sandwiched between the University of Georgia and downtown Athens. It was past ten o'clock in the morning and Emmeline was in class.

He spent the next half an hour reading his Bible and thanking God that Emmeline had accepted his proposal back in July. He wasn't sure how he would have felt had she said no.

"Please don't let Em change her mind," Sebastian prayed aloud in his hotel room.

After he prayed, he planned his day. It was the easiest plan he'd ever had: wait for Emmeline to finish class.

He had invited Emmeline to lunch with him, but she'd said she had a rehearsal at lunchtime and must eat on the go. However, she said he could stop by the music room to watch the small ensemble rehearse for an upcoming string performance.

Sebastian changed his invitation to dinner instead, and was glad that Emmeline agreed.

So. He decided to drink a cup of coffee with cream for his mid-morning breakfast and go downtown to scope out a good restaurant for dinner. He hadn't been back here in years, but he recalled cooking events in the past.

After a quick shower, he walked out into the bright sunshine. It was the last Friday in August, and the heat index had peaked. The baseball cap he had on didn't help his neck from roasting in the sun.

Walking around the iconic Arch erected in the late nineteenth century, Sebastian followed a crowd of students crossing Broad Street. He went down College Avenue, and decided to stroll around town until he saw a place he could stop for lunch.

After the crossed Clayton Street, he wandered in and out of shops, stopping to check out the menus pinned outside quaint bistros. His stomach growled when the aroma from an Indian restaurant played tricks on his nostrils even as a "Closed" sign hung on its door.

"What? It's not twelve yet?" Sebastian talked to his watch. "That's what I get for skipping breakfast."

He walked further along the street, telling himself to return to the Indian restaurant at noon.

And there it was.

A corner antiquarian bookstore. A small cart of hardcover books outside looked dusty, as though no one was interested in dollar books anymore. The wooden door, between two tall windows, looked antique.

"Maybe they have old cookbooks," Sebastian whispered to no one.

And into the bookstore he went.

"Good morning," the clerk behind the checkout counter said. Her hair was all white, but her smile was very bright. "May I help you find something?"

"Yes." Sebastian closed the door behind himself. "I'm looking for old cookbooks. I want to say Julia Child, but she's twentieth century. I'm looking for old recipes from the renaissance world."

"Renaissance? Hmm..." She shuffled slowly around the counter. "We might have some medieval cookbooks, but renaissance is a bit later."

"I know, but medieval is fine too." Sebastian followed her to the back of the bookstore.

Books piled up to the left and right of him. Books were on the bookshelves that stretched to the ceiling. Books were everywhere.

But nary a customer except for Sebastian.

The lady stopped at a bookcase. She put on her glasses. "They're around here somewhere."

Dusty leather-bound books—that looked like they hadn't been touched in decades—stood tall and regal on the bookshelf, taunting the ravages of time and seasons. Spines showed gold lettering. They had the look and feel of being law books or law-related books.

The lady stepped to another bookcase. "Or maybe here. I remember my father putting them on one of these shelves in this room."

"No worries. I've got time." Sebastian waited for the lady to get out of his way.

"Speaking of time, if you had come two weeks from now, this bookstore would have been closed."

"Why?" Not that Sebastian needed to ask. After all, he was the only customer in the store. If he walked out empty-handed, the bookstore would not have a sale from him.

"My husband passed away six months ago." Her eyes were far away. "He helped me manage this bookstore for the last seventy years since the day after we got married. I can't do it alone. My granddaughter wants me to move to North Carolina to live with her."

"What will happen to the bookstore?" Sebastian looked around. It was a corner shop. Tall windows with plenty of light coming in.

Outside, people walked back and forth around the corner. Watching them cross the intersection, Sebastian couldn't help but think that this bookstore was in a prime location in downtown Athens.

And yet, nobody else came inside.

If they cleared all the tables and books, there would be plenty of space for tables and booths—

What am I talking about?

"I'll sell it," the clerk said. "I'll give the money to my great-grandchildren. What good will this bookstore do me if Armand is dead?"

Sebastian assumed Armand was her husband's name.

"How far back does this space go?" Sebastian asked.

The clerk pointed. "It's pretty long. Plus upstairs."

"Upstairs?" Sebastian's eyes widened.

"This way. Let me show you the stairs." She took her time.

When they reached the harlequin hallway, the wrought-iron staircase stared back at Sebastian, daring him to climb it.

"Do you have more books upstairs?" Sebastian asked.

"Yes, but it's more of a reading room for the young ones, although they don't come here much anymore, since UGA built more study halls that open around the clock."

Sebastian nodded. "May I go upstairs?"

"Yes, but I can't go with you. My knees." She pointed.

"No worries. I'll just take a peek. Is there an elevator?"

"No elevator."

Sebastian wondered how much it would cost him to install an elevator connecting the two floors for...

He stopped midway up the stairs.

What am I thinking?

Emmeline only had two years to go at UGA. After that, she would move home to Atlanta. That would be a better place for him to open another Sage Café.

And yet.

He had sold his catering business, and had some money to spare. He could still open a restaurant in Atlanta after he and Emmeline moved there. However, he did not think he would be stretched too thin if he opened one here.

At the top of the stairs, the wood floor stretched all the way to a bank of windows facing the street. He stood there at the window, watching the crowded intersection below.

If he priced his entrées right and made many menu items affordable for college students—while at the same time offered higher-end fare for those who could afford it...

Elevators.

He needed two elevators, one for the customers and one for his servers.

Perhaps Athens could be a testing site for his expansion into metro Atlanta. Although the college town was not technically a part of the sprawling suburbs of Atlanta, it was no more than an hour's drive from the top end of the metro.

Even after Emmeline graduated and they left town, Sebastian could hire a chef de cuisine for this place. Surely culinary students would want to intern there.

What about his original Sage Café on St. Simon's Island? Well, it would still be there. He'd interview chefs to run that place, while Sebastian himself would live in Athens with his new bride.

Sebastian went downstairs.

"I found two medieval cookbooks," the clerk said. "One is a facsimile, so you would need to be able to read medieval English to read it. The other is in modern English."

"Wonderful." Sebastian followed her to an empty table by a window.

On the table were the two books. They looked like hefty volumes.

"I could have carried them here myself." Sebastian sat down.

She pointed to a nearby cart. "Wheels. Greatest invention ever—after the Gutenberg Press."

Sebastian smiled.

Sitting at the table, his eyes wandered outside the windows as the noonday sun shone in through the trees lining the street. There was plenty of sunshine, but none of the July heat.

Either the windows were insulated, or this location was simply...

Perfect.

Sebastian knew exactly what he wanted to do, but first, he must pray for God's wisdom. After all, he believed that God had led him here.

CHAPTER SIXTY

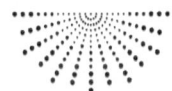

*E*mmeline wasn't sure what Sebastian was so excited about, but he insisted that they must get there before six o'clock. He had undoubtedly crisscrossed North Campus and South Campus to reach her off-campus apartment. In fact, he was fifteen minutes early and Emmeline had still been in the shower when he texted her.

She hurriedly changed into a floral blouse and a pair of denim shorts, and tied up her still-damp hair in a chignon. She figured it would dry in the August heat, although it was late afternoon.

After locking her apartment, she made a beeline for the elevator.

Outside the building, Sebastian was revving up his engine at the front entrance.

What's going on?

She climbed in the SUV and buckled in. "Thank you for picking me up."

"No problem. Is it more economical to stay off-campus?" Sebastian backed out of the parking lot.

"Not really. I'm doing this so that my parents can come visit me without having to pay for a hotel room."

"Good idea."

Emmeline smiled. "What do you want to talk about?"

"I want to show you a bookstore." Sebastian drove on Lumpkin Street toward Broad. "I hope we can find parking."

"I don't know. It's Friday." Which was why Emmeline wore a pair of hiking boots. She expected to walk to the restaurant and back—wherever Sebastian had picked for their dinner.

She let him choose because she had been in class all afternoon, and Sebastian was the chef and should know where to take her, right?

As expected, they circled the blocks multiple times, and ended up parking at least three or four blocks away from where Sebastian wanted to take her, and it was 5:45 p.m.

"Okay. I hope we have enough time." Sebastian shut his door, came around to the passenger side, helped Emmeline out of the SUV, locked the vehicle, and held her hand as he led her down the sidewalk.

They went one block without talking. Then Emmeline stopped. "Wait."

Sebastian turned toward her. "What?"

"One minute."

"I don't know if we have one minute."

"Yes, we do." Emmeline stepped toward Sebastian. She placed a palm on his chest.

He still looked like he was about to miss a train or a flight or something.

Emmeline reached up and cupped his clean-shaven jaw in the palms of her hands. She smiled as her lips met his. She deepened the kiss, deliberately taking her time.

He wrapped his arms around her and relaxed.

The noise of the small city ebbed away—vehicles ceased to honk, people stopped talking. The world was still around them.

They hugged for a while.

"If we keep doing this, I'd never make it anywhere on time." Sebastian chuckled.

"Are you calming down now?"

"You took my breath away."

"Take a deep breath." Emmeline waited.

Sebastian couldn't stop smiling.

"Sometimes I get nervous before I go onstage. I pray and ask God for His peace," Emmeline said.

"I already prayed." Sebastian produced a phone from his pocket. "I'll call her and tell her we have to walk four blocks."

"Good idea. Ask her if she would keep the door open for us."

"I hope so."

"If not, how about tomorrow?"

"She doesn't open on weekends, and I'm going home on Sunday."

"That's a loss of business to close on weekends," Emmeline said.

"I know."

While Sebastian talked on the phone, Emmeline prayed. Sebastian hadn't disclosed to her what he was excited about. Whatever it was, he wanted to share it with her.

That warmed her heart.

When he hung up the phone, he reached for Emmeline. "She's going to wait for us."

Emmeline nodded. "Let's go."

They walked quietly for a while until they reached a traffic light. They were not alone waiting for the crosswalk sign to change. In the crowd, Sebastian wrapped his arm around Emmeline's shoulders and kissed the top of her head.

"You're amazing," he whispered in her ear. "You know how to calm me down."

Emmeline smiled. "Don't forget God."

He kissed her again through the "Walk" sign and then some.

When they reached the antiquarian bookstore, the sun was still in the sky and the temperature was humid.

They were the only people in the bookstore. Emmeline wondered how it would stay afloat.

Sebastian introduced the owner to Emmeline. "Lucy is selling this bookstore and moving out of town."

"To retire and see my great-grandchildren," Lucy said.

"That sounds wonderful," Emmeline said. "How many great-grandchildren do you have?"

"Five, and two more on the way."

"Wow."

Lucy beamed. "All my grandchildren are in the Carolinas."

"How did you end up here in Athens?"

"My husband used to teach here. My grandfather owned this bookstore, and Armand would come in and sit in that corner over there." Lucy pointed to a table by the window, with nostalgia in her eyes.

Emmeline stepped toward the table. "And you met."

"Yes, we met." Lucy smiled shyly. "Within a month, he asked my father for my hand in marriage."

"A month." Emmeline glanced at Sebastian.

"Took me seven months to pray about proposing to you." Sebastian smiled.

"I heard."

Sebastian's eyes widened. "You did?"

Emmeline nodded. "You've been praying since January."

"Skye! She told you." Sebastian shook his head.

"Armand prayed too." Lucy shuffled back to her seat. "Feel free to look around."

Sebastian held Emmeline's hand. "Let's go upstairs. I want you to see the windows."

Emmeline followed Sebastian up the wrought-iron stairs. When she felt they were far enough away from Lucy, she asked him what this was about.

"Going bookish?" Emmeline teased.

"What do you think about Sage Café Athens?" Sebastian blurted out. He stretched his arms. "We could have live music on both floors every Friday night. Just like Saffron."

Emmeline didn't respond. She prayed for God to give Sebastian clarity. "It's a big space."

"Look out the windows." Sebastian ushered her there.

She looked at the intersection below. "If this is such a perfect location, why hasn't anyone snapped it up?"

Sebastian nodded. "Good question. I'll call my real estate agent, and have her send an inspector and an appraiser."

"This building looks very old. I wonder if you'll need to do plenty of restoration work."

"I've thought of that too."

"You might call Brinley. Brooks Reno does this kind of stuff. She might know of a trustworthy company out of Atlanta who could come out here."

"Good idea."

"It's probably a historic building, so you might have all sorts of rules," Emmeline said. "Might be why no one has taken up the project."

"Or Lucy wouldn't sell."

"Memories. Nostalgia. It's hard to let go."

"But she's up there in age. Do you know she's turning eighty at the end of the year?" Sebastian asked. "She lost her husband six months ago. Sixty years of marriage."

"That's a lifetime." Emmeline felt sorry for Lucy. "So sad."

Sebastian brushed a strand of hair away from Emmeline's cheek. "I don't know what I would do if we were married for sixty years and then you died."

"Or you." Emmeline touched his arm. "I don't think I'd remarry at eighty."

Sebastian laughed. He wanted to kiss her again, but she walked past him. "We're talking business. What are your plans for this place?"

"Well, I'll need to install a commercial kitchen. Plus elevators."

"Sounds costly."

Sebastian nodded. "It will be worth it."

"Why are you doing this?"

"Because I want to be with you after we marry." Sebastian stood by the window. "I don't want to be on St. Simon's Island while you're here in Athens. I'm going to move here."

"When are we getting married?" Emmeline asked.

"As soon as possible."

"We could wait until I graduate."

"That's almost two years from now." Sebastian looked away. "I can't wait that long."

Emmeline stood to his left as they looked out of the window. She held his left hand with her right hand. It was warm. He gently squeezed her hand.

"When do you think is God's timing for us to get married?" Sebastian asked.

Emmeline lifted her left hand to display her engagement ring. "We're absolutely certain about each other, right?"

"Yes." Sebastian waited.

"I would like us to be married at Seaside Chapel," Emmeline said.

"At the wedding chapel?" His eyes lit up.

Emmeline nodded.

"It's a beautiful place."

"With great acoustics," Emmeline added. "But it's booked most of the time."

"We just need a couple of hours."

"Plus the reception."

"We can do the reception at Saffron on Jekyll," Sebastian suggested.

"Maybe your sister can cater."

"I'm sure she can."

"I want to ask her to be my maid of honor," Emmeline said.

"She'll be thrilled. I'm thinking that Matt could be my best man. Matt, Ivan, and Benicio. Groomsmen all."

"Sounds good. The only question left is when."

Sebastian nuzzled her hair. "As soon as you get a break from school."

"That's after Thanksgiving."

"Let's get married in December then." Sebastian pulled her gently toward his chest.

"Which December?"

"The one coming up."

"In five months?" Emmeline wrapped her arms around Sebastian's waist.

Sebastian nodded. "Why not?"

"If the wedding chapel is available."

"If God wants us to marry then, it will be."

Emmeline smiled. "I like your attitude."

CHAPTER SIXTY-ONE

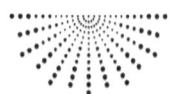

*E*ven though her home church was Midtown Chapel in Atlanta, Emmeline chose to have her wedding at Seaside Chapel on St. Simon's Island, where she had happy memories of spending time with Sebastian.

Sebastian told her that marrying on the barrier island was a great idea because they both wanted Skye to cater the wedding reception to be held at Saffron on Jekyll. It would be easier for Skye from an operational and logistical standpoint.

However, their December plan fell through because Seaside Chapel was fully booked through the first week of the year. Providentially, an event moved out of the main sanctuary into a bigger location in town, leaving the sanctuary available just for one day in the first week of January.

Emmeline felt as strongly as Sebastian did that God

truly wanted them to marry because of that change in schedule. Sure, it was on a Tuesday morning, but they were still getting married in any case. Pastor Gonzalez was available.

Their January wedding came before classes began for the spring semester at the University of Georgia. That way, Sebastian and Emmeline could go to Athens as a married couple and live together. The last thing either of them wanted was to spend the first six months of their married life apart.

The church had repainted the sanctuary back in October in preparation for the Thanksgiving and Christmas holiday celebrations. The fresh coat of paint made the sanctuary look light and airy, a reminder that they were on the Georgia coast.

Flowers were everywhere in the sanctuary, as though the outdoor garden on the church grounds had overflowed into the sanctuary—as if it were springtime. However, in January, the grounds outside were cold and dry, the grass withered into stubbles on the ground.

This evening, their rehearsal dinner had gone well, even though Emmeline was too stressed out to eat. After dinner, bridesmaid Skye drove her to the church because Emmeline had left her purse in the sanctuary after the rehearsal. Emmeline wasn't usually this care-less, but the big event had made her all nervous. She only planned to marry once in her life.

Emmeline took one last look at the sanctuary, checked to be sure her purse was still hanging off her shoulder, and then told Skye that she could close the old wooden door.

Emmeline drew a deep breath and thanked God for everything. She prayed that the wedding day would go well, and that there wouldn't be a sudden snowstorm in the morning. A snowstorm? She was surprised at her own thought.

"What?" Skye locked the door.

Emmeline zipped up her goose-down coat. "Nothing."

Skye fished for her car key. "Ready?"

"I have to be, in more ways than one." Emmeline followed her friend down the hallway.

"Let's go home and get some rest. Tomorrow is your big day." Skye led her out of the church building to the parking lot.

Emmeline glanced to her left, where the parking lot extended toward the boardwalk and the pavilion in the distant darkness. She could hear the strong waves, louder in the night when there was no other noise. The wind from the ocean felt cold against her face.

Under the outdoor lights, the parking lot was empty, but she remembered where Sebastian had first proposed the silly idea of faking a relationship, which eventually turned serious for both of them.

Emmeline recalled how Sebastian jump-started her old van. Right here in the parking lot.

Skye unlocked her car door. "I'm sorry I was against the fake girlfriend project—initially, anyway."

"You were practical." Emmeline got into the car. She rubbed her palms together. This might be the southern USA, but winter was still cold to her.

"If I had thought it through, I would have still disagreed with it." Skye drove out of the parking lot.

"Well, if I had thought it through, I probably wouldn't have done it."

"And missed Prince Charming, a.k.a. my big brother?" Skye laughed.

"If God wanted us to get together, we would have— one way or another."

"I'm glad it worked out," Skye said.

Silently, Emmeline prayed that God would bring a special someone into Skye's life too. Emmeline wanted Skye to be as happy or happier than she was.

"Thank you for letting my parents and me stay with you all week," Emmeline said. "That's super nice of you, considering we're taking up space in your condo."

"You're my friend. Besides, I work all week anyway and I'm rarely there." Skye turned down the street leading to the river. "Hope the condo is not too small for y'all."

"Not at all. My parents walked outdoors a lot this week—they love the river—and that gave me a lot of space."

Not only that, Skye had given them a fifty percent discount on the wedding reception catering downstairs in the fellowship hall. Originally, they had planned on having the reception at Saffron on Jekyll. However, the weather forecast said that Tuesday morning was going to be cold. Emmeline and Sebastian decided to bring food to their guests instead so that they didn't have to leave the church building until after lunch was over.

This wedding that could have cost Emmeline's retired parents a bundle ended up being manageable, and they were able to pay cash for everything.

Thank God.

Claude had stayed back in Atlanta for most of the week, but he arrived that morning. Tonight, he was sleeping over at Sebastian's rental house overlooking the ocean.

That house was something else.

Emmeline didn't want to tell Sebastian what to do, but she loved the view. With the new restaurant in Athens, Sebastian could not afford to buy the house at this time. Emmeline didn't complain about it. God would provide them another beach house later—if they still wanted one.

As long as she was together with Sebastian, Emmeline didn't care where they lived.

Emmeline's phone played a tune that she had composed, played on the harp, and recorded. It was Mom, texting to find out where she was.

EMMELINE

On our way back from the church.
See you in a few minutes.

MOM

Do you want me to heat up some leftovers for you?

EMMELINE

No need. Go to bed. Get some rest.

MOM

I'm trying, but my only daughter is getting married tomorrow. I'm all nervous.

EMMELINE

I'm nervous too.

MOM

I'll pray for us.

EMMELINE

Thank you. And if you really want to do something after you pray, feel free to heat up some food for me.

MOM

I will.

"Once a mom, always a mom," Emmeline said after she put away her phone.

"Must be nice to have parents who love the Lord, each other, and their kids," Skye said quietly.

"Yes, praise the Lord for that." Emmeline realized that both of them had one brother each, but that was where the similarities ended.

Skye's parents had passed away a long time ago, when Skye was still in high school. The two siblings ended up living with their uncle and aunt, who were Christians. Otherwise, Sebastian had been all Skye had.

"I'm still amazed that you bought Seb's share of Saffron," Emmeline said. "You must love your brother very much. It was such a sacrifice. I know you had to sell your home."

"Houses come and go, but brothers... I only have one."

"Me too. Thank God, we have Claude back."

Skye nodded. "Speaking of him, how's he doing?"

"Fine as far as I know. He still lives with Mom and Dad—or as they like to say, he's taking care of them by being handy around the house and doing the yard work." Emmeline knew that wasn't what Skye was asking. "He's been in counseling at Midtown Chapel."

"Sorry I don't have enough room in my condo for him," Skye said.

"Nothing to be sorry about. He's fine staying with Seb. In fact, I suspect that he'd rather hang out with his future brother-in-law," Emmeline said. "Besides, Seb's house is closer to SISO. Claude could drive there in five minutes to rehearse with the ensemble."

"I'm glad SISO lets him use their harp. I can't imagine driving a harp all the way from Atlanta to here."

"Well, we do it all the time on tour. Just need to get a big van."

"Didn't you say it's the conductor's harp?"

Emmeline nodded. "Mr. Petrocelli's, yes. He and Dad go way back, and Claude told me he has been asked to compose a few string pieces for SISO."

"While Claude stays in Atlanta?" Skye parked the car in front of her condo building.

"Not sure. He's considering moving to St. Simon's. Mr. Petrocelli says he wants Claude to fill in for him when he's out of town."

"Conducting?" Skye asked.

Emmeline nodded. "He's thinking of reviving his career."

"Sounds like a plan to move forward," Skye said. "In any case, thank God he's home now."

"Yes." Emmeline smiled. By the mercy of God, they had found Claude again—because Sebastian paid a high-priced private investigator firm to help. Since the investigators themselves found Claude, Sebastian donated the reward money to the soup kitchen. "God is so good to us. He answers our prayers."

So many answered prayers.

Emmeline's heart was full.

Very full indeed.

CHAPTER SIXTY-TWO

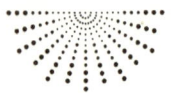

he moment Emmeline heard "Danzas Españolas" emanating from the Seaside Chapel main sanctuary through the closed door, she couldn't believe her ears that her brother, Claude, was back from the dead. Once lost, now found, Claude had been making his return in the music world. There was no one else in the whole wide world—besides her dad—that she'd rather see play the harp at her wedding.

Standing outside the closed door between her and the wedding aisle, Emmeline squeezed Dad's arm. They were waiting their turn.

Emmeline's bridesmaid, Skye, and Sebastian's best man and confidant, Matt, had gone ahead of them.

A medley of hymns followed. More arrangements from Claude, which he had worked on for the last several months.

"I'm nervous," she whispered to Dad. Her palm felt sweaty.

"Just imagine you're at a performance," Dad said. "You're never nervous onstage."

"I hide behind my harp, Dad."

Dad patted her hand. "Don't forget God. 'He who dwells in the secret place of the Most High shall abide under the shadow of the Almighty.' Psalm 91:1."

Emmeline drew a deep breath. "I shall hide in the shadow of God."

"Let's pray." Dad bowed his head and prayed quickly for Emmeline's nerves.

The music ended.

Silence.

The ushers opened the door, and Richard Wagner's "Bridal Chorus" burst onto the scene, a chorus of violin, cello, and harp. Emmeline had lost count of the number of times she had played this processional classic at weddings over the years. From time to time it had crossed her mind that she would like for the 1850 music to be included in her own wedding, and now it was.

Emmeline's eyes watered, and she couldn't see too far ahead of herself except for the red carpet beneath her feet.

She put on a smile, but in her heart, she was praying and praying.

Before she knew it, the music ended as she reached the podium, and there he was.

She had seen men cry in her lifetime—Dad and Claude were emotional creatures underneath their tough shells—but to see Sebastian's eyes and nose red moved her. She wanted to hug him and kiss away the tears.

But those were tears of joy, not sorrow.

As he stepped forward to receive her from Dad, Sebastian mouthed, "I love you."

And Emmeline nearly fell off the podium.

"I love you," she mouthed back as he took her hand.

"Dearly beloved..." Pastor Gonzalez began the wedding ceremony that included several prayers that Emmeline and Sebastian had written themselves.

Emmeline glanced over to find Sebastian grinning endlessly as they said their marriage vows to hold each other close through life's ups and downs.

He was still grinning when he placed the wedding ring on her finger, and when he wrapped his arms around her and planted a sweet kiss on her lips.

How does one kiss and grin at the same time?

"Friends and family, ladies and gentlemen, I introduce to you Mr. and Mrs. Sebastian and Emmeline Langston," Pastor Gonzalez said.

Emmeline Langston.

Her new name still sounded foreign to her. It would take some getting used to not having to put an apostrophe in her name henceforth. She had opted not to go with Emmeline O'Hanlon-Langston because that would be a mouthful to pronounce.

When the string trio started playing "Wedding March in C Major," a classic composition from Felix Mendelssohn, Emmeline and Sebastian held hands as they walked toward the open doors behind the sanctuary to the cheers and applause of their wedding guests.

Emmeline knew every note of this 1842 recessional piece, common as it might be, and found herself humming as Sebastian led her through the doors to the rotunda outside. When they reached the elevator, Sebastian made sure that they were the only people in the elevator.

The door closed.

"A moment with my wife," Sebastian whispered.

Wife.

That was another word Emmeline had to get used to. "Yes, husband?"

Husband.

Another word for the new chapter of their lives together.

Sebastian nuzzled her ear. Emmeline didn't wear any earrings—neither clip-on nor pierced—and she felt his gentle kiss on her earlobe.

Sebastian's lips brushed her cheek and then met her lips. Without hesitation, they claimed each other in a long kiss as a newly married couple—until Emmeline pulled away.

"Did you press *one* for basement?" She eyed the elevator control panel.

"I will in a minute. I thank God every day for you, Emmeline Langston. When I thought I had my love life all planned out, God had a better idea—the best plan ever. I can't imagine being with anyone else for as long as I live."

"Likewise." Emmeline cupped his clean-shaven jaw in one hand. "I just know you'll make a wonderful father."

"We can get started right away if you want." Sebastian's forehead was on hers.

"In God's timing," Emmeline said softly.

"Yes, in God's perfect timing."

CHAPTER SIXTY-THREE

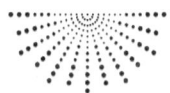

Sebastian could have afforded a more expensive honeymoon, but they had no time, with school and all. Emmeline suggested they go somewhere close. Jekyll Island was too close, so they agreed on a few nights on St. Mary's and Cumberland Island. After that, they had to pack up and drive back to UGA before Emmeline's spring semester and more renovations of Sebastian's new corner restaurant.

They both agreed that come May, just before summer began, they would take a weeklong trip to Europe to taste the cuisine there and to attend some harp concerts. They'd have more time then to relax and enjoy themselves. It would be a real honeymoon—not a harried one.

He was particularly delighted that Emmeline was easy to please. He promised her that next summer, they would take a second honeymoon if she could skip summer school. He knew about her fear of flying, but he figured they'd have five months to work on it. Maybe she wouldn't be so fearful with him around. If that didn't work out, he'd take her on a cruise instead.

After their short honeymoon, they scoped out the best route to get from St. Simon's Island to Athens. Three days before school started for the spring semester, they made their way across Georgia to get Emmeline back to their rental apartment off campus. There was cheaper married housing on campus, but Sebastian needed a bigger kitchen.

All was quiet in the SUV. They had been listening to some harp music, and had taken turns driving. They could have gotten there sooner, but they stopped to have lunch along the highway between the Georgia coast and the college town.

Sebastian was driving on the last leg of their journey, all the time wondering how he could ever leave Emmeline. He thanked God that he had made the right decision to open Sage Café Athens. The renovation work was tremendous and had cost him a fortune. However, with several award-winning chefs in that little college town, Sebastian felt quite at home.

However, after dropping off Emmeline, he had to return to St. Simon's Island to train a new chef de cuisine at his flagship Sage Café. His sister, Skye, had no time to keep an eye on the restaurant for him since she was busy managing Saffron on Jekyll plus her own personal chef business.

"We'll figure it out," Emmeline had told him before they left the Georgia coast. "God has a plan for us. Besides, it's only for a month or so. If you get this done right, you don't have to drive back and forth between Athens and St. Simon's."

"We'll be separated." Sebastian didn't want that. The four months he had been away from Emmeline after she had accepted his proposal had been nothing but agony.

Now that they were married, he didn't want to be separated from her at all.

Sebastian glanced over at his pretty bride, who had dozed off in the passenger seat. She looked lovely even when she napped. She was all he ever wanted for the rest of his life.

He was sure he had made the right move to open a brand-new Sage Café Athens so that he could live with his wife in their first year of marriage. After all, he could have his test kitchen in Athens.

His mind kept returning to the next couple of months, when he would have to drive back and forth between Athens and the coast. Was there another way?

Sebastian was mulling over those thoughts as he followed traffic onto Baxter Street in downtown Athens.

Emmeline was still asleep—

Sirens.

He glanced at his rearview mirror. "Seriously?"

Yep. Sure enough.

Flashing blue lights tailed their SUV.

Sebastian pulled over to the emergency lane, and put the vehicle in Park. He placed both hands on the steering wheel.

On the passenger side, Emmeline stirred.

～

*T*he Athens-Clarke County police officer took his time. Emmeline watched him walk slowly to the driver's side. She heard the crunch of gravel on the emergency lane through the open windows.

"License and registration, please," the officer said to Sebastian.

Sebastian handed them over.

"Where are y'all heading?"

"Home. We just got married last week, and we're returning to campus from our honeymoon on the coast." Sebastian flashed his gold wedding band.

"Ah, newlyweds. Can't wait, huh?"

"No, sir." When Sebastian said that, Emmeline felt blood rush into her face.

"Y'all going eighty in a forty-five-mile-per-hour zone." The officer lowered his head to see Emmeline in the passenger seat.

"We were?" Sebastian's voice was calm.

"Yup. I'm standing here wondering whether to give y'all a warning on account of your wedding or to give you a ticket to teach other newlyweds not to speed to their bedrooms. Y'all have a lifetime yet, right?"

"I'm sorry, sir, for not paying attention."

"City limits, young man. College town. Kids everywhere. Gotta be more careful. There's a whole world outside your marriage, hear?"

"Yes, sir. Sorry, sir."

"I'll make it quick." The officer wrote them a ticket.

Emmeline felt bad that she, too, hadn't been looking at the speed limit signs. Well, she had been napping. She reached for the muscle strain in her neck.

"Have a good marriage!" The officer grinned.

Sebastian took the ticket from him. "With God's help, we will."

Emmeline smiled when Sebastian said that.

The officer was soon gone.

Sebastian pulled out of the emergency lane. He was mumbling something.

Emmeline reached for his arm across the center panel behind the gearshift. "Let's pray that the rest of our lives will be steadier."

"I'm not going back to St. Simon's without you," Sebastian said.

"How did you figure that was going to work? Who's going to train your new chef?"

"I'm going to pray about promoting someone who already works for me. No training required."

"That's an idea. When did you think of that?"

"Just now."

Emmeline nodded. "It's always good to listen to the wisdom of God."

"So you think it's wise?"

"Yes, I do."

"I'm confident that God would approve this." Sebastian's voice seemed determined. "After all, I'm meant to be with my wife."

Emmeline thought about it some more. "You know, it might be a good plan. You'll need to oversee the final renovations at Sage Café Athens anyway."

Sebastian nodded. "I'll cook for you. Test new dishes on you. I'll work on a cookbook."

"A cookbook?" Emmeline raised her eyebrows. "When did these ideas pop up?"

"In the last twenty or thirty minutes."

"While you were speeding?" Emmeline chuckled.

"I forgot my foot was on the accelerator." At a red light, Sebastian smiled. "What do you think? Yes? No?"

"Have you prayed about this?"

"I've been praying, so I would say the ideas could be part of the solution."

Emmeline nodded tentatively. "Let's pray more, get a confirmation from God, and see where we go from here."

As they were quietly coasting along in the SUV, Emmeline started to warm up to the idea of having Sebastian nearby every day.

"God sure knows how to bring people together," Sebastian said.

"If we delight in Him, He does give us the *real* desires of our hearts."

Delight yourself also in the Lord, and He shall give you the desires of your heart.

"Amen, my love." Sebastian reached for Emmeline's hand, holding it gently.

Emmeline smiled all the way on their cruise through downtown Athens, toward their apartment on the other side of campus, toward the blessings that God surely had prepared for them as Mr. and Mrs. Sebastian Langston.

DEAR READER:

Thank you for reading *His Wake-Up Call*. Did you enjoy the story of Sebastian and Emmeline? If so, you might also like my next novel, *His Morning Kiss*, the story of Sebastian's sister, Skye, a busy personal chef. We revisit the Brooks family when Brinley's older brother, Diehl, returns home to St. Simon's Island to spend the summer in his sister's beach house, where

Skye cooks his meals for him. There is a spread of family drama, a side dish of suspense, and a whole lot of love.

His Morning Kiss (Seaside Chapel Book 3)
JanThompson.com/morning

BRINLEY BROOKS-MCMILLAN IS IN HIS LONGING HEART

Diehl's younger sister, Brinley, kicks off the Seaside Chapel series when she returns to Seaside Island to spend the Christmas holidays with her wealthy family. There's her great-aunt Ella, whom Brinley is left to babysit. There's her trust-fund-baby sister, Zoe, who is in love with an erstwhile hairstylist, who happens to be the brother of Brinley's acquaintance, Ivan, first violin in the Sea Islands Symphony Orchestra. One thing leads to another, and Brinley ends up spending time with Ivan and his grandmother, Yun, both devout Christians who live in a rundown cottage.

His Longing Heart (Seaside Chapel Book 1)
JanThompson.com/longing

HELEN HU IS IN ONCE A THIEF

In *His Wake-Up Call*, Sebastian hires Helen Hu to help Emmeline find her brother, Claude. Helen has her own story in *Once a Thief* (Protector Sweethearts Book 1), where she goes to Greece and Italy to find her missing mother, an erstwhile thief with a belated conscience. Fifteen years ago, Mama Hu stole some bejeweled eggs, and now she tries to return them to the wrong owners. Unfortunately, she gets abducted. How does Helen get her mother out alive? She sets a thief to catch a thief, but does reformed criminal Reuben Costa have other plans?

Once a Thief (Protector Sweethearts Book 1)
JanThompson.com/thief

JOIN JAN THOMPSON'S MAILING LIST

Sign up for my mailing list to keep up with my publication news. In addition to beach romances, I also write romantic suspense and near-future romantic thrillers.

Subscribe to Jan's book news:
JanThompson.com/newsletter

A FREE EBOOK FOR YOU!

A Christian beach romance novel, *Ask You Later* is the story of artist Leon Watts, who returns to Tybee Island and Savannah to jump-start his fledgling career. This novel is a part of the Savannah Sweethearts collection, and happens one year before the Seaside Chapel series begins.

Download this FREE novel now:
JanThompson.com/ask-seaside

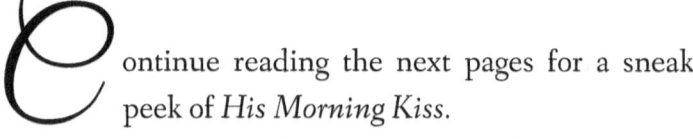 ontinue reading the next pages for a sneak peek of *His Morning Kiss.*

THE NEXT NOVEL IS HIS MORNING KISS

SEASIDE CHAPEL BOOK 3

A father of two, widowed billionaire Diehl Brooks returns home to St. Simon's Island and falls in love with his sister's personal chef. Will complications from his unfulfilled first marriage threaten his chance for love a second time around?

A SELFLESS PERSONAL CHEF...

Chef Skye Langston cooks for local residents and visitors to the Golden Isles. When her friend and client,

Brinley Brooks, asks her to cook for her older brother, who will be in town for the summer, Skye is wary. Although they move in different social circles, she has heard a lot about Diehl Brooks, once the most eligible bachelor on the island. Now their worlds intersect in his sister's beach house. Seeing him almost every day changes Skye's opinion of him, but she tells herself that she is only being kind to the widower, as the Bible asks Christians to be kind to others.

A SINGLE-AGAIN BILLIONAIRE...

Having drifted away from God, almost-forty-year-old Diehl doesn't know how to come home. After being tragically widowed, he works himself aground, leaving his two school-aged children with their nanny and grandparents. Diehl burns out at work, and is forced to take a sabbatical before he destroys the multi-billion-dollar family business. On St. Simon's Island and the neighboring Seaside Island, his casual friendship with his sister's personal chef quickly turns into something romantic, but his past shows up to collect yet another pound of flesh.

A SPLINTERED FAMILY...

Diehl might be newly single again, but his first marriage has long tentacles. When secrets from his marriage-of-convenience threaten his present-day happiness, Diehl is convinced he is not good enough for Skye. Why would God bless him with love a second time around when he failed the first time?

In the middle of his emotional angst, Diehl's children throw his life into a tailspin. Even as Skye's presence soothes his soul, Diehl has a hard time believing in happy endings. How can God give him sweet promises of a better tomorrow when his life is so bitter right now?

His Morning Kiss is the third novel in *USA Today* bestselling author Jan Thompson's **Seaside Chapel** Christian small-town beach romance series. This book was previously published as *Sing with Me*.

Continue reading for a sneak peek of the first two chapters of this novel...

HIS MORNING KISS CHAPTER 1 SNEAK PEEK

SEASIDE CHAPEL BOOK 3

Diehl Brooks woke up to the flapping of wings where the sun shone into his bedroom through the open French doors. Thin white curtains fluttered on both doors leading to the balcony, beyond which he could see clear blue skies above St. Simon's Island, and hear the constant waves of the Atlantic Ocean. It had been music to his ears since his childhood summer days with his three siblings, back when Parker had been alive and their youngest sister, Zoe, had been a scrawny thing.

And as for his middle sister, Brinley, she was always Brinley.

To this day, Brinley cared for the rest of the family more than they cared for themselves. Diehl hadn't planned on taking a sabbatical until Brinley had stepped in. Being the level-headed sister that she was, Brinley saw Diehl's soul and knew he needed a time-out. Dad agreed, and they made Diehl stay home. Only Diehl couldn't stay home. He had to work. So Dad decided to come out of his semi-retirement and run Brooks Investments for the entire summer—right out of Diehl's Atlanta office.

Dad said he had to save the company.

From his own son?

Diehl closed his eyes to hear the ocean again, a balm of Gilead for the pain in his soul. If he could just hear the ocean, it would smooth out the wrinkles from the one year of woes he had undergone, for which he could blame no one but himself.

And Isobel.

He could always blame his dead wife.

The crashing of the waves on the sands of the Georgia coast always put him at ease, beckoning sleep to come again. Sleep, sweet sleep.

To sleep away his sorrow...

Flap! Flap!

What on earth?

Diehl's eyes popped open again.

There, circling the fan above him was a lone sparrow. A little brown bird with nowhere to go.

"That way, little one!" Diehl pointed to the French doors beyond his Californian king-sized bed and the oak floor. "Go back to your family."

And for good measure, he added, "Out there."

Not in here, where there were wounds in his heart at the perpetual roil of crisis after crisis in his life, as though God was trying to get his attention.

God, whom Diehl had ignored for years.

What had God done for him? Could anyone tell him? Where was God when Isobel drove her car over the cliff on the Amalfi Coast between Sorrento and Positano? Why hadn't God prevented Isobel's 800-horsepower Pagani Huayra BC Roadster from hitting the rails and going airborne?

Better yet, why hadn't God stopped her from speeding on the winding road on a rainy day?

God could have done all that and more.

Sometimes Diehl wondered why he had married the same woman twice when they hadn't gotten along since day one. Their first marriage had somehow lasted nine years. Their four-year divorce lasted longer than their second marriage to each other.

Six months after their second wedding, Isobel was dead.

Could God have prevented them from being divorced from each other in the first place? He could have kept the family together from the beginning for the sake of their two children, Elisa and Ethan. After all, wasn't God pro-family?

Well, to be honest, Diehl knew that Isobel always had a wandering heart. Diehl couldn't keep her in the house, even though it had been her own decision to give up a high-paying corporate job to stay at home with the kids so she wouldn't miss Elisa's first words and Ethan's first walk.

She had made the decision herself to stop working.

Low maintenance, she was not, although Diehl hadn't cared that she had spent millions renovating their twelve-bedroom family home near the Chatta-hoochee River in the ritzy Buckhead part of Atlanta just so they could have grand Christmas parties with friends Diehl didn't know they had.

As long as it had made Isobel happy.

He had to make her happy. He had no choice. After all, she had threatened to take the kids to Italy and never return.

Perhaps he should have let her.

So many years and two kids later, they were done with each other. They went through a bitter divorce and custody battle. Isobel's lawyer dragged their family dirt all over court. She had recorded everything he had ever said about Brooks Investments and the transactions and mergers, and threatened to make them public.

Diehl had told her what he did because he wanted her to see how hard he worked to provide for the family, his billions in inheritance from Grandpa Brooks notwithstanding. He still put in the effort to keep the money in the family.

It was all for the future of their children, he had told her.

She hadn't cared, had she?

All Isobel had wanted was to be free. And Diehl alone knew that. To the rest of the Brooks family, Isobel had painted herself as a victim, especially when she talked to Diehl's sister. Consequently, to Brinley, Diehl was to blame for the failed marriage. It took a few years for Diehl to explain his side of the story to her.

Their prenuptial agreement had all sorts of clauses in it, and at the end of the day, Isobel won. Diehl bought her a cliff house in Positano and another in Sorrento, as if one wasn't enough.

And he bought her an Aston Martin Valkyrie.

And she bought herself a Huayra.

Yep, Isobel liked her fast cars. And one took her over the cliff.

Flap! Flap!

"Go!" Diehl yelled at the sparrow. "Go already! I told you to fly out on your own, stupid bird!"

He watched the sparrow. Maybe it was afraid of something.

Somewhere at the back of his mind, a Bible verse wanted to pop up. But he had been away from the church for so long that he couldn't remember much. Still, surely there was a verse about sparrows.

He felt an urge to google the verse, but he didn't.

He had left his Bible in Atlanta, but truth be told, he hadn't opened that Bible in years. He had kept it only because Grandpa Brooks had gifted it to him when he graduated from high school years ago. It was one of the precious things that reminded him of Grandpa.

Like this entire island. Whenever he was here, he felt an urge to change his life, be a better person, improve his perspective, and seek a higher learning.

And return to God?

Perhaps.

Brinley expected him to go to church with her family. Maybe he would. Maybe not.

Diehl had rarely been back to the small hundred-year-old church by the sea since Grandpa Brooks passed away. He could recall the few times he went to Seaside Chapel in the last twenty years. Once was for the wedding of his now-deceased older brother, Parker. The second time, it was for Parker's funeral. Brinley's wedding was the last time he stepped foot in that church. That ceremony brought back a lot of memories about Parker, who had told Brinley he wanted to dance with her at her wedding.

How ridiculous it was for Parker to drown in a boating accident at sea, leaving behind a loving wife and two kids.

Same as him.

Diehl made himself a mental note to call his sister-in-law. Maybe Riley had some tips for him on parenting two kids after losing a spouse. What was the probability of both of them being widowed within ten years of each other?

Diehl had always liked Riley. She still had shares of Brooks Investments—whatever Parker left for her. But Riley never went to the Brooks building in downtown Atlanta. In fact, she rarely left her house, as far as Diehl knew.

At least Diehl made himself carry on and work after...after...

Why had God allowed this to happen?

Why?

Flap! Flap!

Diehl sighed. "I'm sorry, little sparrow. You're not a stupid bird."

Diehl crawled out of bed. He could see now that the whitewashed room with a few mirrors here and there to make the space look bigger, the curtains that framed the French doors, and whatever else Brinley put in the room, had confused the poor bird.

"Come here!" He said softly to the sparrow as he padded to the French doors. "Showing you the exit."

The bird flew in circles and then out to freedom.

A realization hit Diehl. He had left the French doors open. "Really, Brin should put a screen here so that the mosquitoes don't fly in."

The open door meant he hadn't set the alarm in the middle of the night when he arrived. He had driven all the way from Atlanta instead of flying in their family jet because Mom wanted to use it to pick up the kids from Hawaii, where they had been staying with their maternal grandparents for the school year.

It was summer now, and the two sets of grandparents were negotiating how to share their grandchildren between Hawaii and Georgia.

Diehl opted to stay out of it.

Anyway, he drove to St. Simon's the night before in his Ram 1500—just in case Brooks Renovation had any work for him to do while he was in town—and fell asleep without showering or unpacking or setting the house alarm.

Nobody had broken in—he hoped. He had slept through it all, in any case.

Diehl climbed back into bed. It was a big bed, too big for one person, but in many ways, it was better to be alone than to have a bickering wife.

Bickering?

Diehl stared at the ceiling.

He could not recall many moments of bliss with Isobel. They always fought. They fought so much that his sister Brinley had to break up their quarrels. Mostly words, which Diehl could have won hands down.

To his credit, he had never lifted a fist at Isobel.

Or the children, who had to put up with their mom and dad arguing every time they were together. It was always the little things, like which restaurant to eat out at or whether Elisa should be allowed to wear short skirts and put on makeup before she reached puberty. Family stuff.

Isobel had always complained about everything. She hated their neighbors—who were almost never there. She hated Atlanta, with its humid summers. She hated the Georgia coast—too plain compared to Amalfi. She hated everything.

Diehl found peace at the office. He loved working. Work was life to him, and life was work.

Ironically, not for the rest of the summer this year.

Banished to the Georgia coast to rest his brain and heal his heart, Diehl had opted not to stay in the Brooks family home on Seaside Island. Not with Mom constantly nagging about how he was *not* raising his two children.

Wasn't having a full-time bilingual nanny with a bachelor's degree in sociology enough?

Maybe Dad should put Mom to work. Then she would stop harassing Diehl about the kids.

Then again, poor Mom. She hardly saw her grand-children.

Every Christmas for years, Isobel had taken the kids to Hawaii, where her parents lived, running that pineapple plantation of theirs. It was warm in Hawaii in December, and the kids loved it. However, it meant that Diehl's own parents hadn't been able to spend Christmas with the kids for years.

So he could see why Mom was all agitated with her sudden role as mother figure now that Isobel was...

Dead.

Gone.

Diehl found himself sobbing softly into the down pillows.

The mother of his children. The woman he had married in his twenties, divorced when Elisa was only seven years old, and remarried when their daughter was eleven and their son turned eight.

"Why did I remarry her?" Diehl couldn't pin down a reason.

Somewhere in the noise, he'd found out that Isobel's bank account was dry. All those millions she had gotten from the divorce proceedings were gone very quickly.

Did he feel sorry for her? Isobel needed him. He liked being needed.

So he had remarried her.

Several months into their second marriage, Isobel flew to her vacation home in Positano and bought that Huayra. She called from Italy, asking if she could stay for a few months there—alone. No husband, no kids. To catch her breath, she said. Their second time around had been a whirlwind to her.

A whirlwind? What on earth did that mean?

And she never returned to the States.

Within a month of their last conversation, she was gone.

Since then, Diehl had been at the bottom of an emotional well that affected everything in his life until now.

I have to get out of this funk.

"Where have I gone wrong, God? Help me. Help me."

~

His Morning Kiss (Seaside Chapel Book 3):
JanThompson.com/morning

Seaside Chapel:
JanThompson.com/seaside

Subscribe to Jan's mailing list for book news:
JanThompson.com/newsletter

HIS MORNING KISS CHAPTER 2 SNEAK PEEK

SEASIDE CHAPEL BOOK 3

It wasn't Skye Langston's job to fill the bird feeder in the side garden outside the kitchen window, but standing at the farmhouse-style kitchen sink, rinsing out the dishes for her assistant to put into the dishwasher, she could clearly see that the feeder was empty and that someone ought to feed the birds.

The birdbath next to the feeder under the shady live oak trees looked like it needed to be refilled as well. The water had all but evaporated from the tiled top on this hot June day.

Where did Brinley get that bath?

Seven months pregnant, Brinley Brooks-McMillan spent more of her time indoors at her other house. She hadn't been to this beach house in a while and had mentioned that someday she might sell it. The cleaning lady had aired out the place before Skye came the day before to fill the refrigerator and pantry.

However, no one had filled the bird feeder or birdbath. Probably in days.

Skye didn't recall if it had rained in a few days.

Her feet felt tired. She had been working non-stop for the last two weeks driving from house to house on St. Simon's and also Seaside Island, cooking for vacationers. They came in droves about now, and their summer life was easier if they didn't have to cook for themselves.

Most of the time they ate out in the local area restaurants, but Skye was glad to accommodate some of their special preferences and dietary requirements. Some people had food allergies, and if not them, their kids.

She often planned the menus after consultation with her clients, but not this one. Brinley simply told her that Diehl ate "anything" but was partial to peach cobblers. Brinley asked her to cook some mushroom risotto, which Skye had made for their Seaside Chapel women's Bible study group on some Tuesday nights.

Last night, Skye made a peach cobbler as a welcome present.

She and her assistant, Marlo, had been here since ten o'clock in the morning. Brinley had told her that Diehl liked to eat his lunch at noon, but that he might be late.

Well, his truck was parked outside. He was probably still upstairs somewhere. She hadn't heard anything.

When Skye and Marlo had arrived, the door was not only unlocked but the alarm wasn't set. In retrospect, she should have called Brinley and asked if Diehl was here, but Skye had so many containers to haul into the house to cook lunch and prepare for dinner that she had forgotten all about calling anyone.

Besides, it was relatively safe on the island, as everyone knew. And most importantly, Brinley had given Skye a key to the beach house so she could come and go any time. Apparently, Diehl had signed off on that too.

In fact, Brinley had said to walk right in. She said her brother wouldn't mind because Skye was like family.

Am I like family?

Skye wasn't sure she wanted to have much to do with Diehl. She had heard things about him that unsettled her.

Skye and Marlo made quick work of the prepared ingredients—Skye liked to get everything ready before she arrived at the client's house—and the mushroom risotto was soon in the oven. Then it was out of the oven.

And still no sign of Diehl.

Skye glanced at the clock on the wall. It was past noon. She had to leave soon because she had a final rehearsal that afternoon with Brinley and their friend from church, Avery Chung. Avery usually played the trumpet, but she was singing a duet with Skye this time, while Brinley played the piano accompaniment.

Skye dried her hands, and messaged Brinley and Avery in their group chat, while Marlo finished loading the dishwasher.

Other than mushroom risotto, they had made cucumber sandwiches for the afternoon. Skye had no idea whether Diehl liked that or not, but since he hadn't returned her calls when she tried to find out what he wanted to eat, she decided that he was going to have cucumber sandwiches with his tea this afternoon.

Skye chuckled. He probably wasn't the tea and finger sandwich sort of guy—considering the giant gas-guzzling charcoal-colored Ford pickup truck in the driveway—but it was his fault for not returning her call or replying to her email. She even attached a link to the menu software she had paid a lot of money for to simplify her life as a personal chef.

If the client wouldn't discuss with her what he wanted to eat, then every day would be full of surprises.

Of course, now that Diehl had arrived in town, she'd

finally get a chance to speak with him in person and ask for a meeting to make sure the next three months would go smoothly for both Diehl and her chefs.

After all, she was too busy to chase after clients. She had a personal chef business to run and a restaurant to manage. If she wasn't cooking at clients' homes, she'd be at Saffron on Jekyll Island, looking after her forty-nine percent share of the award-winning restaurant, which had been her brother's.

Sebastian and his ex-girlfriend Talia had co-owned the place once upon a time. To help her brother out in his messy relationship back then, Skye bought his minority share of the company. Unfortunately, majority partner Talia lived in London and didn't care much about the day-to-day operations. Skye ran the restaurant and did all the work, but only received the profit as a minority partner.

Skye had sold her million-dollar oceanfront house on St. Simon's Island to buy out Sebastian's share, and now she lived in a rental condo by the river where she could see the sunset from her screened-in porch, although she didn't have much time to enjoy the scenery.

Skye didn't want to sell her land on Seaside Island to buy Talia's shares. Nor did she want to downsize Skye's the Limit and fire any of her twelve personal chefs. And she did not want to dip into her savings and stocks any more than she needed to.

It would be unwise to cash out everything Uncle

Miller and Aunt Irma had left her, which had formed the seed of her businesses now and kept her out of financial debt. In fact, she had multiplied her fortune by wisely investing in her business.

She might consider investing in her brother's future ventures in Atlanta, but there was still time to think about that. Sebastian now lived in Athens, Georgia, where his wife, Emmeline, was finishing up her master's degree in harp performance at the University of Georgia. His goal was to start a new flagship restaurant in Atlanta after Emmeline was done with graduate school.

"What did she say?" Marlo asked, wiping down the countertop and island.

Marlo had been a godsend to Skye. He worked hard, had no family obligations, and was available at any time. He was attending Brunswick College to get a degree in culinary science. He was such a good cook that Skye almost suggested he aim for a chef's hat. But then again, who was she to tell him what to do?

"I'm waiting for her to text me." Skye put her phone back into her apron pocket. "I kid you not, Brinley told me to come right in."

"What if her brother walks around in his underwear?" Marlo laughed.

"I know, right. My brother wore boxers at home all the time—and probably still does even though he's married."

"No comments about myself."

Skye washed her hands. "We don't know where he wants to eat. Dining room or kitchen table."

Marlo shook his head.

"Let's set the dining table. We can always move either way."

"Right."

"Thank you for working with me today and adjusting to our client's schedule." Skye looked for silverware to set the table. "I would normally tell you to leave if you want, since we've been here half an hour past our time, but I'd rather not be alone, so thank you for staying."

"No problem."

Obviously, Skye didn't want to be alone with Brinley's older brother, who was all by himself in this beautiful house, although he was single again.

Not only did she have a professional reputation to keep, she was also concerned that the guys at church she might be interested in would change their view of her if she were found alone with a backsliding Christian—possibly even an unsaved person—such as Diehl, who had once cussed out Pastor Gonzalez when the latter asked him if he had ever accepted Jesus as his personal Lord and Savior.

Diehl had insisted that he was a believer.

Who had fallen away from the faith?

Was it because he was a gazillionaire? The verse from 1 Timothy 6:9 came to Skye's mind.

But they that will be rich fall into temptation and a snare, and into many foolish and hurtful lusts, which drown men in destruction and perdition.

What did the verse mean? Skye had been pondering it for a while. She and her brother had worked their way up from nothing. Now they were successful business people. Would they someday fall into "temptation and a snare" or would they be able to stay on the straight and narrow path of serving God with their successes?

What about Diehl? Diehl was successful too. But he had received a shoo-in job at his father's company. Not that he wasn't working as hard as everyone else. However, he probably had it easier.

Maybe?

Skye felt bad for being judgmental—

Or jealous of his immense wealth?

She shook it off.

The women at church who had grown up with Diehl in their childhood summer days—some of whom he had dated in years past—all warned Skye to stay away from him. He had a reputation for being a trap—although he had only been married twice, to the same woman.

A trap?

And here I am in this house, cooking for the next three months.

"I'm yours if you want me to stay all day," Marlo said.

"I have a rehearsal at two and then we'll be over at Mrs. Morton's at three, and then back here at five." Skye read off her schedule for the day as she walked toward the refrigerator with her phone.

There was little for Marlo to do, really. However, Skye liked having someone to talk to. She touched the side of the baking dish on the counter. It was still warm.

She found a thick mitten and used that to line the refrigerator shelf. She put the mushroom risotto on the mitten, closed the door—

And shrieked.

Diehl Brooks stood there, grinning at her. "Do I look that bad?"

He seemed to have just stepped out of the shower. His hair was damp. His five o'clock shadow was untrimmed. His T-shirt had designer holes in it, yesteryear's style where five-hundred-dollar shirts came ripped here and there.

A rag. Skye wouldn't use it to wipe the kitchen floor.

"You must be Chef Langston," Diehl said.

"Skye."

"Pretty name. I believe I've seen you before—at various dinners at my parents' cottage, for example." Diehl extended his hand.

Ah. He remembers me.

Skye hesitated. She had just done the dishes. Her

palms were rough. She was going to apply some lotion to her fingers. She did not want his first impression of her to be that she didn't have soft hands.

Why would it matter?

"Would you like your lunch now?" Skye asked instead.

"You can call me Diehl." His voice was cold. He retracted his hand.

"I'm sorry. We're not answering each other's questions." Skye drew a deep breath. "Let me start over. I can't shake your hands right now because my hands are rough. I've been doing dishes, and I left my hand cream at home."

"I have the best lotion ever. Let me get it." And he dashed upstairs.

"That was unexpected." Skye glanced at Marlo, who shrugged.

Skye opened the cabinets until she found dinner plates. She put a plate on the island counter and waited. She had no idea if Diehl wanted to eat or not.

She glanced at her phone. Text message from Brinley.

"Yes, I know he's here," Skye said to no one.

Diehl was back, not even huffing. He looked athletic and fit. Muscles everywhere, even on his thighs and calves. Maybe he worked out a lot. Cycled some, maybe.

But why did she care?

Skye stared at the bottle and laughed. "Coconut oil."

"The best. Put your palms out," Diehl said. He poured a couple of drops on them.

Skye rubbed her palms together. "My coconut oil is in a jar. How do you get yours out of that bottle in the winter when it solidifies?"

"I just put it in a warm tub of water." He placed the bottle on the island counter. "Now can you shake my hand?"

"Is it important?" Skye asked.

"I don't suppose it is. But I went to a lot of trouble to get you the lotion."

"You ran up and down the stairs and got some exercise. You're welcome." Skye opened the refrigerator again. "Mushroom risotto for lunch?"

Diehl made a face. "Could you cook me some breakfast?"

"Breakfast wasn't on the menu today. Your sister said that you'd be here for lunch."

"I arrived last night—two in the morning, in fact."

"We did see your truck outside when we got here at ten."

"Ten? I didn't hear you come in."

"You left the front door unlocked and the alarm off."

"Did I? I must've been tired after a long day at work. I had to drive five hours to get here."

Skye nodded. She pointed to the labels on the glass

containers in the refrigerator. "We labeled everything. Reheat according to the instructions."

"Could you add breakfast for today, please?"

"Chef Joseph will be in tomorrow morning at eight for breakfast—unless you want to adjust that time."

"Adjust it to now."

"Well, if you had answered the emails I sent you, we might have known you'd want breakfast today at lunchtime."

"Sorry. I was busy."

"Starting tomorrow, we'll prepare three meals a day for you—except on days when you eat out. However, before we can go forward, we do need to meet and figure out what you want us to cook for you all summer. I have some sample menus we can look at. We usually do that *before* we show up to cook."

Diehl nodded. "Any time. I have all day."

Skye pointed to a pretty clock on the wall. "I have to go to a prescheduled activity. For today, we will be back at five to cook you dinner—unless you want to eat the risotto for dinner as well."

"I don't like risotto."

"Your sister said..."

Diehl made a face. "I used to like it. Not anymore."

"Peach cobbler?" Skye asked.

"I love peach cobbler."

Skye pointed to the pie on the table. "I'll put that in the fridge in a minute."

"I still want breakfast."

Are you a kid? "We don't have time to cook you breakfast now at such a late notice."

"He can cook." Diehl pointed to Marlo.

"Marlo's my assistant. He's not a chef. At Skye's the Limit, only chefs cook."

"Skye's the Limit?" Diehl grinned. "But no breakfast."

"If we'd had that meeting, you could have told me, right?"

"Are you rubbing it in?"

Well, yes. "No, sir."

"Don't *sir* me. It's Diehl."

"Well, Diehl, for today, your lunch and dinner are on me. I didn't want you to pay for what you won't eat, although your sister said you'd eat anything."

"Including breakfast." Diehl stood his ground.

Marlo made a sound.

Skye glanced at the clock again.

Under her breath, she prayed for mercy as she was thinking about walking out and never return to this client.

A verse popped into her head, stopping her from doing anything really bad, like opening the refrigerator again, taking out the risotto, and throwing it in his face. Well, she had never done that before, but there was always a first time—although she'd have to clean up the floor afterward.

Also, she might ruin her reputation and that of

Skye's the Limit personal chef service, not to mention taint her testimony as a Christian.

Okay. Let's not throw food at new clients.

She tried to remember a verse.

But love your enemies, do good, and lend, hoping for nothing in return; and your reward will be great, and you will be sons of the Most High. For He is kind to the unthankful and evil.

Luke 6:35. The words of the Lord Jesus Himself.

Is Diehl my enemy?

Maybe the verse meant that if she had to be kind to her enemies, how much more to someone in between friend and enemy—say, a friend's older brother she hardly knew.

Skye drew a deep breath. She leaned against the kitchen island and checked the schedule on her phone. "I mentioned that Chef Joseph will be here at eight tomorrow morning. Do you prefer another time?"

"Wait. I'm connecting the dots. You're not cooking for me tomorrow?"

"Didn't I tell say that Chef Joseph will be here?"

"I wasn't paying attention."

"I don't work on weekends or on Wednesday nights," Skye explained. "Saturday is my day off and Sunday is church day."

"My sister says you're the best. I'm not sure I want anyone else cooking for me."

Skye began to realize that Diehl was looking for familiarity, for things that were not constantly or unexpectedly changing. She had tried to prepare him for how she managed her business, but he had apparently not read that email either.

"The details of the contract were in the email," Skye said. "One of many emails I sent you."

"Frankly, I just assumed Brin took care of everything. She knows what I like to eat, but I can see that a few things fell through the holes. Breakfast, for example."

"And risotto?"

"Yeah."

"She signed the contract on your behalf since this is her house, but it looks like we need to clarify something here. She hired a personal chef who rotates among clients, and not a private chef who works exclusively for you," Skye said. "I have twelve personal chefs working for me, and a bevy of assistants who shop and help us prepare the meals for our clients."

"I thought Brin hired me a private chef. After all, she gave you the key to the house and the security code to come in and cook for me, so I don't have to get up and unlock the door for you."

"She did that because she trusts me. We're friends."

"Are we friends?" Diehl asked.

"Well..."

"Friends don't let friends skip breakfast."

"Is that right?"

"Uh-huh."

Skye didn't know whether to laugh or cry. She had to do what the client wanted—within reason, of course —because he was paying the bills. If he wanted breakfast for lunch, who was she to deny him the special meal?

"Also, can you be my private chef? I don't want to share." He looked serious.

Skye tried not to read too much into that, but she didn't know what he meant. For now, she would take it literally.

"Frankly, I don't know if you need a dedicated chef who works in this kitchen only. You're on vacation and you'll be more flexible if you can eat at The Priory or at your sister's home or out in restaurants."

"If I hadn't let my private chef go, he'd be with me today. He traveled with my family to our vacation homes, and he also handled all my dinner parties, which Isobel..."

His voice trailed off.

Skye knew exactly who Isobel was. Her heart sank.

He cleared his throat. "No worries. I'll eat the risotto."

Skye did everything she could not to give the poor widower a hug. She felt sorry for him, although he was going to make her late for her rehearsal at church. She couldn't miss that, could she? After all, the whole point of the rehearsal was so that she could better minister to others—

Ah, especially the unchurched.

From all that she knew about Diehl through his sister, this man needed to be ministered to. How could Skye not see that? He had gone through so much after getting his wife back and losing her again. Skye remembered how everyone had cheered in Sunday school that Brinley's older brother had finally reconciled with his wife.

Within months, she was tragically killed in a car wreck, leaving behind a husband and two elementary-school-aged school children.

Skye's heart melted.

She turned to Marlo. "Let's cook some breakfast."

His Morning Kiss (Seaside Chapel Book 3):
JanThompson.com/morning

Seaside Chapel:
JanThompson.com/seaside

Subscribe to Jan's mailing list for book news:
JanThompson.com/newsletter

READ A FREE NOVEL

ACKNOWLEDGMENTS

Many thanks to my Georgia Press publishing team for keeping up with my writing schedule.

The first edition of this novel was copyedited by Dori Harrell and proofread by Lenda Selph. The second edition of this novel was copyedited by Lenda Selph, and proofread by Lesley Ann McDaniel and Judy DeVries. Thank you very much, ladies!

A special thank you to my loyal readers who have been with me from the beginning. Your enthusiasm for every book I write is encouraging and inspiring. May God bless you!

I am grateful to God for my husband and son for their support and encouragement. I also thank God for my parents and my three brothers for my happy and memorable childhood. I'll always remember my beloved mother and my late father for having instilled in me the love of reading and writing from a very early age. I miss my father here on earth, but I will see him again in heaven someday.

Most of all, I am eternally thankful to my Lord and Savior, Jesus Christ, who died on the cross to save me from my sins and rose again from the grave to give me eternal life. Without Him, I can write nothing (John 15:5).

Joyfully in Jesus,
Jan Thompson
John 3:16

BOOKS BY JAN THOMPSON

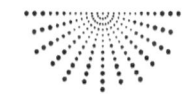

CONTEMPORARY CHRISTIAN CITY, COASTAL, AND BEACH ROMANCE

Seaside Chapel (7 Books)
JanThompson.com/seaside
Savannah Sweethearts (12 Books)
JanThompson.com/savannah
Vacation Sweethearts (8 Books)
JanThompson.com/vacation

CHRISTIAN ROMANTIC SUSPENSE AND NEAR-FUTURE TECHNOTHRILLERS

Protector Sweethearts (6 Books)

JanThompson.com/protector

Defender Sweethearts (6 Books)

JanThompson.com/defender

Binary Hackers (4 Books)

JanThompson.com/binary

Subscribe to Jan Thompson's mailing list:

JanThompson.com/newsletter

SEASIDE CHAPEL

Welcome to *USA Today* bestselling author Jan Thompson's Seaside Chapel Christian beach romance series. These novels are set on real-life St. Simon's Island, Georgia—a beach town where history is all around and the future is a moment away—and the neighboring fictitious Seaside Island, where the rich and famous live.

Savor the small-town atmosphere and the warm southern beaches of St. Simon's Island and the idyllic Golden Isles along the Atlantic Ocean. Enjoy the music of the orchestra and hymns of the church, and hang out with our Christian friends who attend Seaside Chapel, a little church by the sea known for its beach weddings and fair share of love and life.

As these Christians grow in their knowledge and understanding of God, they are tested in their spiritual maturity, their love lives, and their relationships with others. Share their heartaches and healing, and cheer them on as they celebrate faith, family, and friends.

∽

JanThompson.com/seaside

- Book 0 (Prequel): *His Surprise Proposal*
- Book 1: *His Longing Heart*
- Book 2: *His Wake-Up Call*
- Book 3: *His Morning Kiss*
- Book 4: *His Quiet Serenade*
- Book 5: *His Waiting Love*
- Book 6: *His Beach Retreat*

SAVANNAH SWEETHEARTS

Welcome to the new south! From *USA Today* bestselling author Jan Thompson come these clean and wholesome, sweet and inspirational Christian romances set on the romantic beaches of Tybee Island and in the coastal town of Savannah, Georgia. Meet a group of multiracial and multiethnic churchgoing Christians who love the Lord, work hard in their careers, and seek God's will for their love lives. Against a backdrop of ocean, sand, and sun, these inspirational romances showcase aspects of the human need for God and for one another. Have some tea, settle in a comfortable reading chair, and enjoy these sweet celebrations of faith, hope, and love in Jesus Christ.

JanThompson.com/savannah

- Book 1: *Ask You Later* (Artist Romance)

- Book 2: *Know You More* (Multiracial Romance)
- Book 3: *Tell You Soon* (Asian-American Romance with Suspense)
- Book 4: *Draw You Near* (International Romance)
- Book 5: *Cherish You So* (Wheelchair Billionaire Romance)
- Book 6: *Walk You There* (Old-Meets-New Tour Guide Romance)
- Book 7: *Love You Always* (Romance with Suspense)
- Book 8: *Kiss You Now* (Multiracial Romance)
- Book 9: *Find You Again* (Multiracial Romance)
- Book 10: *Wish You Joy* (Christmas-Themed Romance)
- Book 11: *Call You Home* (Deaf Chef Romance)
- Book 12: *Let You Go* (Asian-American Romance with Suspense)

Read *Ask You Later* (Book 1) for free: JanThompson.com/ask-free

VACATION SWEETHEARTS

Travel with our friends from Savannah, Georgia, to the coast and to the mountains. Cheer them on as they celebrate the immeasurable grace and undeserved mercy of God through Jesus Christ.

The Vacation Sweethearts novels are a spin-off of Jan's Savannah Sweethearts series, and fans will recognize familiar faces from Riverside Chapel, a church in the coastal city of Savannah, Georgia. In fact, we might even visit the beach town of Tybee Island from time to time to visit old friends and beloved families...

JanThompson.com/vacation

- Book 0 (Prequel): *Time for Me*

- Book 1: *Smile for Me* (International Romance)
- Book 2: *Reach for Me* (Romance with Suspense)
- Book 3: *Wait for Me* (Romance with Suspense)
- Book 4: *Look for Me* (Romance with Suspense)
- Book 5: *Pray for Me* (International Romance)
- Book 6: *Care for Me* (Small Mountain Town Romance)
- Book 7: *Cheer for Me* (International Romance)

Read *Time for Me* (Prequel) for free: JanThompson.com/time-free

PROTECTOR SWEETHEARTS

Private investigator Helen Hu and her associates specialize in searching for missing persons and hunting for lost treasures. Join them in their adventure suspense around the world in *USA Today* bestselling author Jan Thompson's Protector Sweethearts, a series of Christian Romantic Suspense with a side of mystery.

Protector Sweethearts is a spin-off of Savannah Sweethearts and Vacation Sweethearts.

JanThompson.com/protector

- Book 1: *Once a Thief*
- Book 2: *Once a Hero*
- Book 3: *Once a Spy*

- Book 4: *Twice a Fighter*
- Book 5: *Twice a Convict*
- Book 6: *Twice a Soldier*

DEFENDER SWEETHEARTS

Defender Sweethearts is a sister series to the Protector Sweethearts Christian romantic suspense collection. While the heroes in Protector Sweethearts search for lost treasures and lost people, the Defender Sweethearts novels focus on protecting the helpless and hopeless. The main characters in Defender Sweethearts come from the supporting cast in Protector Sweethearts.

JanThompson.com/defender

- Book 1: *Never a Traitor*
- Book 2: *Never a Hostage*
- Book 3: *Never a Fugitive*

- Book 4: *Always a Maverick*
- Book 5: *Always a Champion*
- Book 6: *Always a Guardian*

BINARY HACKERS

Like more suspense with your Christian romance? Like to read suspense thrillers? If you're looking for clean near-future romantic suspense without compromising the Christian faith, these books are for you.

From *USA Today* bestselling author Jan Thompson come these inspirational near-future cyberthrillers combining technothriller and romance, starting with Binary Hackers that feature computer specialists living at the edge of cyberspace, where they have to juggle being law-abiding truth-telling Christians while carrying out their assignments by any and all means possible.

The Binary Hackers series is set in the same story world as Jan's other books, and characters from the other series may make cameo appearances in this series and vice versa.

JanThompson.com/binary

- Book 1: *Zero Sum*
- Book 2: *Zero Day*
- Book 3: *Zero Base*
- Book 4: *Zero Trust*

ABOUT JAN THOMPSON

USA Today bestselling author Jan Thompson writes clean and wholesome contemporary Christian romance with elements of women's fiction, Christian romantic suspense with an air of mystery, and inspirational international thrillers with threads of sweet Christian romance. Jan's books are for readers who love inspiring stories of faith, hope, and love in Jesus Christ.

Raised on a tropical island in the eastern hemisphere, Jan now lives and writes in the western hemisphere. Her international background gives her a unique multicultural and multiracial perspective to her novels and books. The island has never left her, and she reminisces about beach life in her beach romance novels.

When Jan is not busy writing small-town stories, she writes big-city romantic suspense and international technothrillers, a nod to her previous career in computer science. She weaves technology with human interests, reflecting the current and future digital world. And romance. There's always romance.

Beyond the printed page, Jan is a wife, mother, avid

reader, former quilter, erstwhile pianist, occasional artist, and chief of staff to the family cat.

Find out more about Jan Thompson:
JanThompson.com

Subscribe to Jan's book news mailing list:
JanThompson.com/newsletter

For God so loved the world
that He gave His only begotten Son,
that whoever believes in Him
should not perish
but have everlasting life.
—John 3:16